Love is

C S Adams

Love Is In The Air

♥

Second Chances

Three years after tragically losing her husband, forty-three-year-old Cecilia Bancroft is whisked off to Barbados by her best friend, Jasmine in the hope of giving her a new lust for life and maybe even a second chance at finding love.

Opposites Attract

A timid librarian in the Cotswolds has been in love with her best friend's outgoing brother, Bertie, since forever but she's not even a blip on his radar. An invitation to their mother's wedding in Barbados could change that. Do opposites attract?

Pink Café

Down trodden forty-five year old housewife Mary dreams of escaping her controlling husband. As one door closes another one opens... right at the Pink Café. There is a chance of freedom and a chance of finding love. Does Mary have the courage to take the steps to change her life?

Pasture Prime

After a photo shoot twenty-two year old super model Kat finds herself stranded in the snow, in the middle of nowhere and the only person to come to her rescue is one angry farmer. For reasons beyond her control Kat has to stay for a few days on his farm. And to her utter disbelief, sparks fly between them. But does the city loving girl take a chance or does she moo-ve on?

Spoilt For Choice

All twenty-three year old Bella wants after a hard term teaching is to put her feet up, relax and spend time with her sister and enjoy the Christmas festivities. Instead, thanks to her annoyingly good nature, she finds herself setting up a fudge stall in a quaint Cotswolds village. Having no idea of the intricacies of running a small business, naturally, problems arise. But what she hadn't planned on was not one but two knights coming to her rescue. Is she lucky in love or do they get the heave-ho?

Contents

Second Chances

♥

Chapter One

♥

Wednesday 3rd December 2014

Cecilia wandered down the stairs, making no effort to hurry. It was still the early hours of the morning and not even the birds had woken up yet. Not that she would have hurried even if she had been up at her usual time anyway. Her life had changed down a gear or two since her offspring had flown the nest. She didn't need to put on so much of a 'I'm doing fine' façade now. Although at this moment in time, she wasn't fine, she thought, not at all as she felt the beginning tell-tale signs of a faint coming on. A wave of nausea came over her and a weird buzzing noise sounded in her ears. Quickly, she reached out and, whilst fumbling for the bannisters, she glanced down momentarily. Dust. There was dust in between the spindles of her beautifully carved wooden staircase. She was horrified. It wasn't just a little bit of dust either, it was at least an inch thick of grey fluff. It was awful. What would Doug think?

'Oh,' she cried out with a strangled gasp. 'Oh no!' Cecilia clutched her stomach and gingerly sat down on the stairs.

Tears began to stream down her face until she was sobbing uncontrollably and animal-like noises were escaping from her.

Grief was so hard. She had thought that after all this time she would be ok now. She'd ridden the worst of it, that was for sure. Earlier on, she had barely even made it out of bed. The grief was too raw then you see. However, time had helped, and the children, most importantly the children. But it could still take hold of you at any time. You couldn't see it coming, not really and you certainly couldn't control it, well, she couldn't anyway.

Though today was going to be the hardest day she'd had in a while. Because today, it was not only her birthday when she was going to be lucky forty-three, down on your knees, as a bingo caller would say but it was also the third anniversary of her husband's death. She breathed in deeply for four seconds and exhaled for seven. This exercise had helped her in many moments of anxiety and even now, she could feel herself getting steadier.

Eventually Cecilia rose from the hard wooden stairs. She was now quite cold despite the fluffy pink dressing gown and matching fluffy bunny slippers she wore, a present from her darling daughter who thought it would make her smile. She pulled the cord tight and made her way towards the kitchen. She needed a coffee. There was no way she was going back to bed now.

As she sat down at the counter sipping her coffee, her thoughts strayed to three years ago.

She could remember the lead up to it ever so clearly. It was a Saturday morning so Clarissa was making her way back home from boarding school having had an away hockey match, and Bertie was caught up in some kind of meeting at work that he couldn't get out of and would get home late afternoon. Doug had told her to get her glad rags on as he'd booked her favourite restaurant, a sweet little Italian bistro in town that served the best dough balls imaginable. They were going to have a family meal to celebrate her big Four-O. She'd walked her neighbour's dogs that morning, then gone to the hair salon for a quick blow dry. She'd just got back and was choosing what dress to wear.

It was like the movies, that's how it had played out in her head practically every day since then. You see the happy birthday girl getting ready for her night out and the doorbell goes, she doesn't know who is at the door but is hoping that her friends have come to surprise her or someone has managed to get home sooner than expected. The wife goes to the door, opens it slowly and peers round the door to see who it is. Standing there are two people, looking apologetic for disturbing her, they explain who they are and explain why they are standing in front of her. That was her, that was her opening the door that day to those two policemen. Was Douglas Bancroft her husband? Yes. Indeed, he was.

'I'm sorry to say but your husband was involved in a car accident,' said the kind looking man. 'Unfortunately he died at the scene. His car went off the road.'

Cecilia lay her head on her hands and sighed.

Suddenly, she came out of her reverie as she heard a loud and frantic thumping on the front door and then the doorbell rang.

'Cecilia! Cissy! Open up, it's Jasmine! I've tried your phone but you're not answering, please open the door!'

Cecilia got up and walked over to the front door in a daze. Her phone was on silent. No-one usually rang her at this time. I mean it wasn't even five o'clock, she thought.

What was Jasmine doing here at this ungodly hour? She hoped nothing bad had happened. Her feet gathered pace as she grabbed her keys off the hall table and opened up the door. Jasmine stood there looking beautiful as always with her big brown eyes shining, her black hair braided neatly around her head and a big smile on her face. But what really stood out was the fact that her friend looked as though she was about to go to some Caribbean fancy dress party in the darkest depths of winter. She was wearing these gorgeous glamorous silver sandals, a floaty green and orange floral dress with a green cashmere wrap draped around her shoulders. Cecilia looked at her not quite believing what she was seeing.

'Jasmine,' she finally stammered, probably looking quite flummoxed. And it also wasn't often that her friend or anyone for that matter had seen her with bedhead and no makeup. She let out another sigh, 'What is going on and why are you dressed like that?'

'Happy birthday!' she cried. 'We are going to Barbados today, on your birthday! I've booked it and you can't say no. I've planned it especially for you, the kids are dealt with. Bertie is happy to be engaged elsewhere doing whatever he does and Clarissa is off to France after Uni has finished skiing with the twins. You are coming to stay with me, and Richard of course, for a month. From now until early next year,' she announced with a flourish.

Clarissa still looked rather puzzled. 'But Jas, you can't be serious...the kids...Christmas...' she faltered.

'The kids are absolutely fine, and are excited for you and think you need a change of scenery. You've haven't been out there in ages. And this time you stay with us,' Jasmine commanded, clearly not wanting Cecilia to find a way of backing out. 'Anyway,' she continued, 'the flight is leaving in four hours so we'd better get a wiggle on. Come on, let's go!'

What must have been barely twenty minutes later, Clarissa had managed to shower, change and shove random clothes and shoes into a suitcase, all under the watchful eyes of a now very crazed friend. She had basically given in to Jasmine. It seemed that everything had been organised and she supposed that deep down, it was actually really what she needed. Barbados, here we come!

Chapter Two

♥

Cecilia was sat in a sun lounger half in and half out of the sun. In one hand was a rum punch and in the other she held her phone waiting for her messages to be replied. It was still her birthday, that hadn't changed but the scenery had and thank goodness for extraordinary friends, she thought with a smile. Her friend had bustled her into a waiting taxi, dragged her around the airport and then literally pushed her onto the plane. There had been no time for second thoughts.

The moment the doors of the airplane had opened and she'd stepped out into the Barbados sunshine, instant humid heat had enveloped her. It was like stepping into a sauna. Nothing had changed in the ten years or so since she'd last been here. There was still a group of musicians dressed in floral outfits playing the steel drums greeting locals and visitors alike as they entered the airport. It had made her smile the first time she had seen this and it had made her smile again. Although, the first time she had been nervous with anticipation as Doug had gone on ahead without her to get things sorted and start his job where-as this time it felt familiar and somehow comforting.

But now just being here, in this beautiful garden with the bright red, orange and pink Hibiscus flowers and the little white Frangipani giving off such an intoxicating aroma made her feel relaxed. The lush palm trees with their fronds bending down over a view of a glistening turquoise blue sea, that she was yet to step into, set the tropical scene. Also her huge brown sunglasses that she had bought on a whim at the airport now adorned her face keeping out the glare of that hot sun.

Cecilia had been invited here a few times by Jasmine's parents for a dinner party or a lunchtime barbeque when Doug had been posted here as a naval officer, and she never tired of being here. Jasmine's family home was a single storey villa that had a sweeping semi-circular drive lined with poplar trees. As you entered the house, it opened into an alfresco sitting and dining area. From there a footpath went through the centre of a beautiful landscaped garden which then led to a patio which was where she was now sunbathing. A low stone sea wall surrounded the patio for privacy and a little gate opened onto a stunning white sandy beach. Few people swam in this stretch of the sea or walked along the beach as it was a little known cove. It was like your own slice of paradise.

A beep on her phone made her glance down and see who had replied first, Bertie or Clarissa. It was of course Bertie, her twenty-three-year-old son. It read: :-) bday mum! Glad U R ther. hav :). I M. spk s%n. lots of luv. Cecilia read it through a few times and still only managed to translate a few words. She'd spoken to him and Clarissa countless times about how they texted her. She wasn't one of their friends and she hadn't managed to get the hang of this new fandangled text speak.

'Have you heard from the children yet?' spoke a voice from behind her.

'Yes, I have,' Cecilia said. 'It's from Bertie but he's writing in shorthand again, you're better at this than me, can you help me please?'

Jasmine laughed. 'Come on, give me your phone. Ok, it says, Happy birthday mum! Glad you are there. Have fun. I am. Speak soon. lots of love.'

Cecilia's face still showed some uncertainty, 'Well at least he's absolutely fine about me being here.'

The phone beeped again. It was from Clarissa this time, her daughter who was younger than Bertie by three years. :-) bday. hOp U R k. uni iz goin weL. spk s%n luv U.

'Ok so I can read that text,' she said turning towards Jasmine who had now plonked herself on the adjacent sun lounger. 'The kids are fine. Thank you Jas, for doing this for me.'

'I did it for me too, you know Cissy,' she replied smiling. 'For totally selfish reasons too, mind you, I can now sit back and relax for the holidays now knowing that you are in good hands. Mine.' She looked up at Cecilia with concern, 'You can heal out here, in the waters, in the sun, you really can. You'll see.'

Cecilia quietly contemplated on what Jasmine had said. It was time to properly heal and let Doug go, not to forget him, no never, but just let him go for her sake and the children's sake. Doug would never have wanted to see her like she had been, a shadow of her former self.

'Right,' she said, 'I'm going for a dip in the sea, it looks gorgeous and I'm not used to this heat yet. Are you coming?'

'No, not yet, you go on ahead, I'll join you for a swim later. Richard said he'd arranged for a gardener to come for an interview at four today. Our gardener let us know a few days ago that it was time he retired. He's seen our family through a couple of generations and he said it was time to hang up his tools. He waited until now so that we could be out here for the winter hols to find someone suitable to replace him, but I just don't think he's replaceable,' Jasmine sighed then glanced down at her watch, 'Gosh, he's coming in ten minutes. I must go and change. Enjoy your dip. See you in a bit.' And with that she rushed off.

Cecilia heaved herself out of the sun lounger and slipped her feet into a pair of silver Birkenstocks. Not the most beautiful of sandals to look at but they were ever so comfortable. She made her way over to the gate and looked left and right down the beach. It was completely empty, so she decided to leave her towel and flip flops on the wall. She had to walk to the left a little bit before she could go into the sea because directly in front of the house was a coral reef.

The soft white sand felt lush beneath her feet and the water felt even better when she launched herself in.

'Oh, no, not my new sunglasses!' she cried out, trying to stop them from drifting away on the current. She had forgotten to take them off, but with them off, she then realised that everything was so much brighter and unforgiving beneath the glare of the sun. She gave another stifled scream as she looked at her pasty white body. She'd been looking at herself through her sunglasses and had completely forgotten that she had not had that most important preliminary fake tan spray before the sunny beach holiday. A big no no in her books.

She glanced around frantically hoping that no-one had suddenly appeared on the beach to see this awful ghostly apparition. Cecilia let out a small moan for there, not ten feet away, was the most gorgeous handsome man she had seen in a long time. He was wearing a blue t-shirt that showed off his lovely broad shoulders and a pair of khaki three quarter length shorts. His reddish brown hair was worn to his collar and parted to one side. She couldn't see his eyes but they seemed to be looking over in her direction. Mortified and thinking no more about the cool and refreshing swim she had been yearning for, she shot out of the sea and fled as fast as she could back towards the villa. She had to get some fake tan and quick, even if it came out of a bottle.

It was about nine o'clock at night and Cecilia was getting ready for bed. Jasmine and Cecilia's jet lag had kicked in and so had decided to have an early night, well early night for Barbados. It was actually two in the morning in England and so she'd done pretty well. After her dip in the sea earlier on, Jasmine had once again come to the rescue and managed to unearth an already opened bottle of fake tan. Jasmine had warned her that she didn't know how long it had been opened, it might not have necessarily been owned by a recent house guest. But surely, Cecilia thought, it would be ok. Anything was better than being an illuminous beacon attracting needless attention.

So having stripped down to her bikini, Cecilia slapped on copious amounts of cream trying to cover every inch of her body. Cecilia glanced at herself in the mirror as she was doing it. She looked better already, even though she was tired, the heavy drawn-out look was disappearing. She'd spent so long just trying to get through the weeks, even the days at times that she had begun to neglect herself.

Shock and trauma could do that to you. She had done the basics at the beginning, after Doug's death, because Clarissa had only been seventeen years old and needed to see that her mother was alright. Cecilia was sure that Clarissa would never have managed to do her A-Levels had she not. Unfortunately, Bertie had seen her at some very low points for he would turn up unannounced to check up on her. He would see her curled up in a ball on the kitchen floor sobbing or find her in her pyjamas having not washed for a few days. He was her rock then and still was

Although something had definitely changed in her for sure because she had in fact been thinking about the man on the beach. A few months ago, she wouldn't have even thought about another man other than Doug. Doug was still there but it was as if some of the grief was fading and she was starting to see life again and other people around her more clearly. Cecilia now felt with certainty that this holiday was going to recharge her batteries and she could begin to hope that one day she'd have a second chance at finding love again.

Chapter Three

♥

Thursday 4th December 2014

Cecilia woke up to bright sunlight streaming through the curtains. Rolling over she glanced at the owl clock perched on the side table. It was six o'clock. Perfect. Surprisingly she'd had a really good night's sleep and she couldn't remember when that had happened last. Jasmine had promised her that they wouldn't make a big deal of her birthday yesterday but that they would invite a few friends round for a dinner party on Saturday night. Coming from Jasmine though, a few friends would end up being quite a big party as things tended to snowball with her, she couldn't say no to people very easily. Cecilia said of course that was fine, it was Jasmine and Richard's house, of course people could come round. But now she was feeling rather nervous as she had become rather antisocial since Doug's death. She'd seen a few of her best friends but she found that she couldn't cope with dinner parties anymore, as normally she would have been with Doug. Cecilia had accepted a few invites however inevitably the host would invite another single man to balance everything out. She had felt so uncomfortable and would miss Doug all the more so in the end she had stayed away and made excuses, then eventually the invites stopped coming.

It seemed the time had come for her to come out of her shell. She could do this. There would only be a few people.

Cecilia grabbed the nearest shirt, shoved it over her head and made her way to the kitchen. She used to love the mornings in Barbados when it wasn't too hot and everything seemed to be at its slowest.

With her coffee, she wandered down the path to the bottom of the garden and sat down on the wall and looked out over the sea. The waves lapped gently against the shore and a fisherman was casting his fishing net further out. A hummingbird whipped by her and she shut her eyes momentarily feeling the warmth of the sun on her face. But then she felt a pressure around her and a tingling sensation was going down her spine and she shivered. Some people said that if you felt that, it was someone walking over your grave but then she heard a deep cough.

Cecilia opened her eyes quickly to see where it came from, and walking past her with a bemused expression on his face was the gorgeous man she had seen the day before. He gave a little salute with his right hand, as if to say hello however couldn't actually voice it because he was trying to stifle his laughter. She quickly looked up and down the beach to see what could have made him laugh then she realised it must have been her for no-one else was there. How rude, she thought angrily and immediately she sent a scowl in his direction then got off the wall and marched up the path without so much as a goodbye.

Cecilia ran into her room and sat down at her dressing table, face in her hands, feeling quite annoyed with herself. Normally, well before Doug's death that is, she would have said something to him but instead she had run off like a rabbit that had been caught in headlights. And why did she do that, she asked herself? The answer was that he unsettled her. When she'd looked at him, butterflies had appeared in her tummy and she just couldn't control them. She'd had them with Doug and she never thought or even expected to feel them again but here she was like a little school girl with a big crush on a random and rather good-looking man on the beach. She growled at herself in frustration then raised her head to take a look at herself in the mirror.

Cecilia let out a scream so loud that it made her jump out of her chair. She touched her face and started rubbing at it ferociously. At that moment, the bedroom door opened as Jasmine's concerned face peered around it.

'Cissy, are you alright? What's happened?' she asked, then Jasmine clapped eyes on Cecilia's shocked face and she started howling with laughter. 'Oh, Cissy, you didn't half scare me but...what exactly has happened to your face?'

Cecilia looked at her dejectedly, 'It was the fake tan I put on last night. I don't know what happened, the bottle might have been opened for too long and gone off, or I went to bed too soon and rubbed some of it off.' For Cecilia's face was a sight to behold, it was covered in brown, orange and white streaks. She would have made a great tiger right now. She daren't tell Jasmine that somebody had seen her in this state because Cecilia was embarrassed enough as it was. He had obviously been trying not to laugh at her predicament and right now she hoped she never saw him again, butterflies or no butterflies.

'Don't worry Cissy it will have calmed down in a couple of days' time and at least you can cover it up with make-up,' said Jasmine trying to cheer Cecilia up. Cecilia wasn't so sure; she was just going to carry on laying low for a few days. To be honest, she still didn't feel like going out and about yet. Maybe next week she would take some trips out around the island. Anyway the sun would also hopefully help with the colour of the whiter patches. At least her children weren't here to see this fiasco. Clarissa would have had a field day.

Chapter Four

♥

Saturday 6th December 2014

Once again she was sitting in front of her dressing table but this time Cecilia couldn't believe her eyes for the difference in her was quite remarkable. She almost looked as good as the time before children. The sun and total relaxation had done wonders to her even after only a few days. Her skin was now a nice golden tan, with no hint of any streaks in sight (thank goodness), her mousey hair had been bleached blonde with the help of some lemon juice (recommended by Jasmine) and her hip bones were no longer jutting out like a skeleton.

She had been laying low but it was now time to come out of the tunnel in which she had been hiding in for some time. Cecilia was feeling a tad nervous about chatting to people she didn't know but a rum punch would hopefully sort that out. She did a twirl in the mirror, checking herself out for one last time. The black sleeveless Audrey Hepburn style dress that she had brought out with her at the last minute, fit her perfectly.

Her strappy one-inch diamante sandals click clacked along the stone floor as she made her way out to the end of the garden. The garden looked magical with hundreds of fairy lights twinkling in the trees and candles and torches had been lit to light the way down the path. She could hear Richard's deep laugh sounding out throughout the night and the echoes of laughter around him. Everyone had made an effort and looked very glamorous. The men were dressed in tuxedos and most of the women were wearing flamboyant dresses.

'Cissy, darling,' called out Jasmine as she walked towards Cecilia holding out two rum punches. She offered one to Cecilia and whispered, 'You look wonderful.' But Jasmine was the one who looked amazing. She had left her hair natural and huge gold hooped earrings hung from her lobes. An off the shoulder silver and gold sequined floor length dress clung to her willowy body like a glove which offset her dark skin. 'Come on,' she said as she put an arm around her waist and guided Cecilia down the path towards what Cecilia could only think of was pure hell. Jasmine deposited her next to Richard and asked if he could introduce her to everyone as she had to pop off to the kitchen as chef wanted a word. Richard returned her anxious look with a cheshire cat grin then five pairs of eyes landed on her with expectancy. Breathe, she thought, smile, she thought, she could do this.

Five minutes later, Cecilia found herself off to one side away from the groups, needing a few minutes' breather. Richard had done brilliantly and had truly tried to make her feel comfortable. His friends were lovely and seemed to say the right things to her upon introduction however she would need to ask Richard and Jasmine quietly what some of the names were again because she couldn't remember them all. The main person who stood out was a tiny, slip of a woman who made up for her stature with the biggest of bubbly personalities, her house was next door. Her name was Bea, short for Beatrice, she was unbelievably wealthy having married well then continued to do well in her divorce settlement too. Unfortunately, her husband had been caught in flagrante with the secretary, very cliché and not alright, thought Cecilia feeling lucky that Doug would never have done that to her. Bea seemed to have got over it though and had been having fun dating numerous men. They'd met once before at some yacht gala and had got on really well, their conversation was effortless so she would probably gravitate over towards her later on.

'Erm...excuse me....' said a deep voice coming out of the darkness from the beach, 'Please could you help me by unlatching the gate from your side? It would be much easier than...'

'It's you,' rudely interrupted Cecilia having peered into the night to see who it was. 'I'm afraid it's a private party. It's not for any old riff raff coming off the beach looking for some free drinks, you know,' she replied rather primly. For some reason this man had really got underneath her skin and she was being uncharacteristically impolite.

'No, I'm sure it's not and you're very lucky your tan has evened out as you might have been lumped with me.' He laughed then. A beautiful laugh that turned into the sexiest smile. This man was impossible. Who did he think he was?

Her question was partly answered as he pointed towards Bea with a smirk of amusement, 'I'm staying with that lady and I have been invited. Now where is that invite?' he said patting himself down as if looking for it.

Cecilia knew full well that no invites had been sent out as such and that he was getting his own back on her. Oh, she thought, feeling rather downhearted, he was one of Bea's boyfriends. Not that that mattered. She wasn't exactly interested in him, was she? She wasn't looking for anyone. Only a few days ago she'd been sobbing on the stairs. The breakdowns had become less and less but this... What she was feeling now was new to her, it was like a little school girl crush that was getting out of control. She had built it up in her head over the last few days since she'd first seen him on the beach. With Doug it was a slow burn, they had been friends, then one thing had led to another and it just seemed right to get married and have children. But this... she thought again, she had to control herself. Flustered, Cecilia bent down to lift the latch but was having difficulty pulling back the secondary latch that went on at night time. A woody and yet subtle intoxicating citrus aroma emanated from him as he leaned towards her to help. She looked up then, at the most inviting, warm and exceedingly sexy hazel eyes. Suddenly, a quiver shot through her as if she had been electrocuted for his hand had come in contact with hers as they both jiggled the lock. She stepped back in shock and nearly went careering into Bea who'd caught sight of them and was coming over in their direction.

'Ah Foxy, there you are,' she smiled as Mr Fox, a perfect nickname for him, kissed Bea on the cheek. 'I see you've met Cissy, Jasmine's dear friend who's come out for a month on holiday from England,' Bea paused, looking thoughtful and turned towards Cecilia. 'Actually, she lives in the same neck of the woods as you do in Gloucestershire, have I got that right?'

A lump had formed in Cecilia's throat as she looked from the beautiful Bea to the handsome Mr Fox. She took a sip of her drink which immediately gave her the courage she needed as it was pretty potent stuff.

'Well, I I...I...I...live a few m...m...miles from Cheltenham,' she stuttered. Fortunately, out of the corner of her eye she saw Richard was trying to get her attention and was beckoning her over. 'Mmm...well, I'm sure we'll have a chance to chat later. It seems I'm wanted, I mean, in demand.' Cecilia walked briskly across the patio towards her knight in shining armour, glad for an excuse to get away.

'Right, birthday girl, Jasmine has informed us that food is ready.' And with that, he took her hand and put it through his arm and led her down the footpath. His silver mop of hair tickled her ear as he whispered, 'How are you doing?' He looked at her expectantly with his kind blue eyes. 'It's not too much for you and too soon, is it? Jasmine means well but sometimes she pushes too hard, she wants what's best for you and she wants you to be ok again.'

'I'm fine, thank you Richard, I really am. This is actually the best I've felt in months, even years. What you said to me all those years ago about time being healer, you were right. I love Jasmine and what she's done for me, what you've both done for me. Thank you.' Her eyes began to well up but then she saw Jasmine, smiling at her. While everyone had been having pre-dinner drinks on the patio, she had been decorating the dining area. Pink, green and yellow streamers hung from corner to corner, similar coloured balloons floated from the chairs, one of which said birthday girl on it, and tiny little fairy lights covered the ceiling. With the lights dimmed, it looked like the night sky had been brought inside. It was beautiful.

'I hope you like it,' Jasmine said taking her hand and squeezing it quickly, 'You used to like this before…well…you know…you just used to like having fun. Is it ok?' Jasmine asked now unsure of herself.

'I love it,' replied Cecilia. 'And please stop worrying about me now,' and then she lowered her voice to make sure no-one else could hear as everyone had caught up with them now. 'I think I've got myself in a pickle.'

'What's that supposed to mean?' replied Jasmine out of the corner of her mouth. 'What pickle?'

Cecilia was about to answer Jasmine when, the source of her being in such a pickle, came towards them. He was circulating the table looking at the name place settings to see where he was to be sat. Jasmine's eyes roamed over him, looked briefly at Cecilia and saw how a deep red blush was creeping up her neck and she started to fidget next to her. Jasmine knew who he was as Bea had mentioned him to her and had rang her a few days earlier to ask if the invite could possibly be extended to a plus one. Bea had filled her in on her guest and Jasmine was delighted as her motto, and it used to be Cecilia's too, was the more the merrier. It would actually even up numbers.

'Anthony,' Jasmine said, 'how lovely to meet you.'

'Nice to meet you too, and might I say, your home is out of this world,' he said, his eyes darting around in all directions. 'To be honest, I've never seen so many stunning houses in such a short space of time.'

Jasmine laughed and agreed with him, 'I know, this house has been in my family for quite a few generations and has been updated over time but we have kept most of the original layout as it's suited us. We come out here for as many holidays as Richard, the girls and I can take. But, it's lovely to see you here tonight to join in with celebrating my best friend's birthday. Have you had a chance to meet her yet?'

'Actually, I have had the pleasure of meeting her, but it wasn't a proper introduction,' he said smiling and looking over at Cecilia, who was becoming more and more like a tomato. He turned his full attention then on Cecilia who didn't want to be in his spotlight as she was feeling terribly embarrassed and angry at herself for having been so rude to him earlier.

'Hello,' she said graciously, 'I'm Cecilia Bancroft, widow, mother of two and fortunate to have some great friends,' and she gestured to Jasmine who had slowly disengaged herself from the conversation and was making her way towards her husband. Cecilia gulped. Great, she thought, I am now alone with him. His mere presence made her heart pound. She could barely hear herself think. Flustered, she asked, 'And you are?'

'I'm not riff raff,' he paused laughing. 'At least, I hope I'm not.'

Cecilia grimaced. 'Yes, well, that wasn't one of my finer moments, I'm sorry.'

'I thought it was quite funny actually, especially as I've noticed you a few times on the beach over the last few days. I was looking forward to meeting you properly.'

Cecilia tried not to show any surprise but inside she was in turmoil. Why did he want to meet me? Did he feel the same way that I felt about him? What am I thinking? He's with Bea, she thought, so snap out of it.

'I'm Anthony Fox, Foxy for short as you probably heard Bea earlier. Never married. Father to none, that I know of,' he added, 'and equally lucky, like you to have great friends.' Cecilia noticed then that the twinkle in his eyes left briefly when he mentioned having great friends and she wondered what that meant. However as quickly as she had seen it go, then, she saw it back again. Cecilia started feeling uncomfortable as there were so many questions she felt like asking but would probably sound rather rude.

Suddenly a loud gong sounded, signalling that it was time everyone sat down. He smiled then pulled Cecilia's chair out so that she could sit down. Cecilia could have sworn that she was going to be sat next to someone called Matthew, but no, obviously not. Then he took his place right next to her. Cecilia began to panic and looked over at Bea who was sat next to Matthew. They were laughing at something and she was being quite touchy feely with him. Although, who wouldn't, Matthew was another good looking man. He reminded her of the man who played Thor in the Avenger's film. Clarissa had persuaded her to watch it as it was the only one they had agreed on at the time. She racked her brains, what was his name? Hamsworth...

'Penny for them,' asked Anthony. He had been looking at her while she had been deep in thought. 'And who or what is Hamsworth?'

'Oh, did I say that out loud?'

'Yes, you did,' he chuckled.

'I was just looking at the man next to Bea and thought he looked like...have you seen the Avenger's films?'

'Yes I have. They're fun to watch. Why?'

'The guy who plays Thor, what's his name?'

'Chris Hemsworth.'

'That's it!' shouted Cecilia, startling a few people around the table, including Thor himself. Why did she keep on doing that at the moment? She didn't mean to tell Anthony what she had been thinking, but it was like she'd been injected with truth serum when he was around and there was absolutely no filter on her mouth whatsoever.

Anthony noticed her discomfort and quickly distracted her. 'So, your children...boy? Girl? What ages are they?'

And so throughout a wonderful starter of huge char-grilled shrimp and then a delicious main course of seasoned flying fish and fried plantains, Cecilia talked about her children. She explained how she'd met Jasmine out here and that coincidentally their girls went to the same boarding school in Cheltenham. Then she talked about Bertie's start-up business and somehow followed it by talking about Doug, their life together and what happened the day of the accident.

'And so that's why I'm here really, for a change of scenery.' Cecilia felt so comfortable with Anthony. He was a very attentive listener and made comments and asked questions in all the right places so she had carried on and on telling him about herself but now the coffee was being served and she knew very little about him.

'I'm sorry. I'm so rude,' she slurred, the alcohol taking effect. 'I've done nothing but talk non-stop about myself. I really would like to know more about you, as long as Bea doesn't mind?' she added as she didn't want to come in between them, whatever they had going on at the moment. Anyway, it was all about wanting to know him on a friend level. Wasn't it?

'Why would she mind?' he asked with a quizzical look on his face. 'She's not my keeper.'

'Oh well...mmm...that's alright then, so have you seen much of the island yet? I could show you some of the sights and Bea could come too.'

'No, I've just been relaxing these last few days. And no, I'm sure Bea will be fine if I go off, she has plenty of things she wants to do without me hanging around all the time like a bad smell. So yes, that would be lovely. However, Bea and I are off sailing for a week with some friends of hers but I will be back on Sunday the fourteenth.'

'Brilliant,' smiled Cecilia. 'I will pick you up in the morning on Monday fifteenth. That's a date!' She then realised what she had said in her drunken stupor. 'Well not a date, but I mean that's a good date, if it's good for you,' she burbled.

His face beamed and he still managed to have that quirky smile plastered to his face as if he was trying to stop himself from laughing at her again but he just replied, 'Yes, I would love to.'

No sooner had he uttered his last word than Jasmine had flung her arms around them both and was shouting, 'Come on, get up, it's time to dance.' She then proceeded to drag them up off their chairs and pointed them in the direction of the dance floor whilst she carried on around the table, trying to coerce some more ladies and gents to get up and have a boogie. Throughout the rest of the night, Cecilia drank, danced and laughed, then danced some more. She was twisted and whirled around the dance floor till she realised how tired she was and collapsed in the nearest comfortable looking chair. It was only going to be for a couple of minutes but somehow she managed to drift off to the various sounds of party go-oers around her dancing to the tunes the dj produced, way into the early hours of the morning.

Chapter Five

♥

Sunday 7th December 2014

'Cissy,' Richard said gently patting her arm. 'Cissy, wake up, everyone's gone.'

Cecilia opened her eyes and looked around her in a daze, momentarily forgetting where she was.

'Oh goodness,' she gasped. 'I don't know how I slept through the party. What time is it?'

'It's about five o'clock. Jasmine is out there on the sun lounger; we're going to watch the sun come up. Would you like to join us?'

'Oh, yes, that would be lovely, thank you.'

'I'm just going to make Jasmine a cup of tea, would you like one too?'

'Yes, please,' replied Cecilia shivering slightly.

'You go on down and I'll grab you both a wrap too, it can get a bit chilly at this time in the morning.'

Richard helped her up out of the chair then after making sure Cecilia was alright darted off. Cecilia couldn't quite believe she'd slept through so much of the party. She'd drunk quite a lot and remembered dancing.

'Oh no,' she wailed as she had also just remembered that she had suggested that she take Anthony out for the day and he'd agreed. She started to panic. She liked him, actually she liked him rather a lot but he was taken. And she couldn't even cancel because he was away for a week. Cecilia had now reached the end of the garden where Jasmine was lying down. She was looking up at the stars that were beginning to fade into the sky as dawn approached.

Jasmine smiled when she saw Cecilia and said, 'Hello Sleeping Beauty. Did you have a good night? I can't remember us dancing so much in a long time, my poor feet.'

'I had a lovely night, and thank you again for organising the party for me. I haven't had so much fun in a long time.'

'From across the table, I could see you were getting along really well with Anthony. Every time I looked over you were being very animated and he did look very attentive. Might I ask whether you being in a bit of pickle is to do with him? It was the way you looked when he came over towards us. You were rather flustered and I wondered whether there was a bit of a coup de foudre going on.'

Cecilia could feel her face burning up and her heart immediately began to speed up. Jasmine had always been very perceptive and she read people very well but love at first sight? No, definitely not, she told herself. There was no way, was there? And there it was, the doubt. Is that what why she'd been reacting the way she had towards him? He'd gotten under her skin for sure. Jasmine was still looking at her with a mischievous smile on her face.

'I...I....well...' stammered Cecilia. And then she thought she might as well tell Jasmine about all the run-ins with

Anthony.

'I'm all ears,' said Richard handing over the teas and wraps to the two women. 'What's been going on with you and Mr Fox?'

And so Cecilia launched into her embarrassing moments with Anthony much to the delight of both Jasmine and Richard who couldn't stop laughing. Richard laughed so much he had to hold his stomach. Cecilia then joined in finally seeing the funny side of the events.

'So Cissy, how do you feel about him? asked Jasmine.

'He's gorgeous,' Cecilia replied after a few minutes. 'He's handsome, he's funny, he's kind and he's great to chat to but, and this is a huge but, he is taken by an equally utterly beautiful kind woman.'

'By whom? What? That's not what I heard!' exclaimed Richard and Jasmine at the same moment.

Puzzled, Cecilia said, 'Well by Bea of course.'

'No,' cried out Jasmine. 'You're quite mistaken, he is totally single and available. Bea told me that he's just a friend who needed help and she offered him a place to stay and a holiday so that he could clear his head. A bit like you really,' she added.

Single? He's single. He did say that Bea wasn't his keeper earlier on. And he'd agreed very quickly to her idea of going out for the day. Cecilia moaned, she had told him it was a date, but then that it wasn't. She did like him and she did want to get to know him. But what if he didn't feel the same way about her and what if she got to know him and then realised she hadn't got over Doug, that wouldn't be fair. And what if...ok...stop with the what ifs.

'We made arrangements to go out for the day when he got back from sailing with Bea,' she announced. 'I said that

I'd show him a bit of Barbados in return for talking at him all night.'

'Oh, that's lovely,' said Jasmine clasping her hands together in delight. 'You obviously like him and from the little bit that I saw, he likes you. He certainly wasn't looking at you like a friend would. How exciting! I can't wait to see how it goes.'

'But I'm nervous,' Cecilia said, 'and I'm scared. I haven't been with anyone else in a long time. And I still miss Doug.'

Richard had been quiet and pensive, looking out over the sea until he said, 'Cecilia, you're going to be nervous. Change can be scary, the unknown can be scary, as you know well. But if you don't try something new when an opportunity arises you don't know whether something or someone fabulous is going to come into your life. You gave a chance on Doug. You had many wonderful years with him and you had two lovely children. You have also grieved him and you will always remember and miss him but do you want to carry on the rest of your life on your own? Would he want you to?'

'No, he wouldn't, he'd want to see me be happy and live life fully,' she said with tears in her eyes.

Jasmine got out of her chair then and squeezed in next to Cecilia and wrapped her arms around her into a hug. 'Sweetie, it's time to start living again.'

Cecilia, Jasmine and Richard then sat in silence, each in their own thoughts as the sky began to change into beautiful hues of orange, yellow, pink and red.

Chapter Six

♥

Monday 15th December 2014

It's D day, it's D day today. It's arrived, thought Cecilia as she was scrabbling around in the garage for some flippers and snorkels. Not date day though. No... Yes, it could be. She had been on tenterhooks all week. Jasmine had done her utmost to distract her but prepare her for the occasion at the same time and Cecilia had actually enjoyed it. They'd had lots of girly lunches at various beach restaurants and cafés, sometimes Richard joined them if it fitted in with his golf. The beauty salon had done very well out of them too. Cecilia felt like a very pampered poodle. Jasmine had also dragged Cecilia to some gorgeous local boutiques where they both came out very much poorer than when they had entered them.

Whilst that was all going on, they discussed where Cecilia could take Anthony for the day. Cecilia wanted to make sure that the activities were fun and light, not romantic, as she was still uncertain as to her own feelings, let alone his in spite of what Richard had said. It was more about getting to know each other, well mainly Cecilia getting to know Anthony as that was of course the whole reason why she'd suggested seeing him for the day. Or was she fooling herself, she'd had some alcohol and the buried feelings had risen to the surface, it hadn't been the whole reason at all, she really had wanted to spend more time with Anthony Fox.

'Finally...got them!' she cheered. Jasmine had given her vague directions as to where they could be but other people had put rather a lot of other paraphernalia on top. Almost to the point where she'd got distracted and nearly changed parts of the day's itinerary. There were polo sticks, (but she'd need to find the ponies), and a leaflet advertising the drive-in cinema (what a fab idea, but way too romantic), a free ticket to the local Mount Gay rum factory (that was when she faltered, but alcohol and a handsome man might not be the best combination for a first...well...she didn't know what) and an old cart wheel, (which reminded her of a lovely day she'd had many moons ago at a plantation house). So, after much procrastination, she chucked the snorkels and flippers into the back of her hired jeep, along with towels, and a spare change of clothes.

Jasmine had rung up Bea for Cecilia earlier just to let Anthony know what he needed for the day and time of pick up. Cecilia looked at her watch, five to ten. And with that she jumped into the driver's seat and zoomed down the driveway, trying not to think too much, and just looking forward to the day ahead, just as Richard and Jasmine had told her to do, however the butterflies in her stomach would just not go away. And it got worse when she turned right out of the drive and then right into the next drive for there he was looking as sexy as ever. Focus, Cecilia thought, focus. Anthony was casually leaning against one of the white stone pillars of the porch wearing a khaki polo shirt, and some three quarter length chinos. She didn't quite get to his feet, as she was drawn to his face that had somehow got more handsome in the past week. There was some stubble on his face along with a healthy glow. Sailing and lots of fresh air had taken away his worry lines on his forehead, she noticed, as she edged closer to him.

'Nice ride,' he said as he got in beside her. 'I've seen people driving these and they look like a lot of fun.'

'It's more of a tourist thing. I've never been in one before, even when I used to live here, so now I'm a tourist this time round, and I thought, why not?'

'Excellent,' he said smiling at her. 'Right, now having spent most of my time wearing a life jacket this week, I have become kind of attached to them so when I got the message to bring my swimming stuff, I hope that it involves a life jacket.'

Cecilia laughed, 'You will have to wait and see.'

Cecilia concentrated on the road even though all she wanted to do was look at him. Her heart was racing and there was nothing she could do about it. It felt as if they were in a bubble that was being squeezed around them, not even the freedom of having no doors on the car helped.

'So,' she said trying to bring a certain amount of normality back to her, to him and to her surroundings. 'How was your trip?'

'Luckily it was uneventful. We actually flew to St. Lucia, which is such a different island compared to Barbados even though they are close to each other. I had no idea. Have you been?'

'Yes, I went once,' then she remembered she had gone there on a babymoon with Doug before Bertie was born. They had been celebrating the end of Doug's job posting in Barbados prior to returning to England. Memories started flooding back but miraculously there was no pain, a dull ache maybe, but no nausea or gut wrenching misery. 'Yes, the difference is amazing, the coral island of Barbados with white sands versus the volcanic island of St. Lucia with its brown sands and mountains.'

'Did you not go sailing then?' she asked.

'Yes we did, we sailed from St. Lucia to Martinique. It was an amazing experience as I've never been sailing before but the crew were all friends of Bea and they'd had some space on board so invited us, well Bea, I just tagged along for the ride. As soon as we left Rodney Bay I was no help whatsoever so I kept up front, out of the way. Fortunately, I wasn't sick, somehow I have sea legs.' Cecilia took a peek at his legs. She couldn't help it. They were gorgeously tanned. And then her eyes looked at his thigh that she had a sudden urge to squeeze. No. No. What was she thinking? Must focus on the driving. Not on his anatomy. Just drive and then his voice entered her mind. 'Martinique was also a stunning place. I just wish we'd had more time in St Lucia though, it was more of a pit stop. In Martinique, the others swam a lot and did some snorkelling but I chose to go ashore. I wanted to visit the little cafés and see the more cultural side of St. Anne.'

'So you didn't go snorkelling then?' inquired Cecilia, hoping she hadn't missed anything when she had got momentarily distracted by his physique. She nearly took another peek. What was she doing?

'No,' he said. 'But the walks on the beaches were lovely, and the little wooden houses were beautiful.'

That was close, thought Cecilia, she didn't have to change their plans. Snorkelling might have been a bit boring if he had already done it a lot recently.

'Oh wow,' she replied. 'It sounds like you had an amazing week.' But there was no time for further conversation since they had arrived at their destination and she continued with a flourish, 'We're here!'

Cecilia and Jasmine had chosen one of their favourite beaches which was off the tourist trail and relatively local to Jasmine's house.

'It's called Freshwater Bay,' Cecilia said. 'It's quite a bit quieter than the other beaches on the island but there is some good snorkelling too.' And with that, she pulled out a flipper from the back of the jeep and waved it around. 'But first, we are going jet skiing.' She pointed to a jet ski which was waiting for them on the beach. A young man with dreadlocks tied back in a ponytail and wearing only a very vibrant pair of swimming shorts stood by and waved at them. He was a friend of one of Jasmine's daughters and had been quite happy to help out by lending his jet ski out for an hour. Cecilia started walking towards him not noticing the unhappy look on Anthony's face. 'Have you done any jet skiing before?' she asked. She heard a muffled 'no', and thought that maybe Anthony was so busy looking at the beautiful scenery in front of them, he could barely utter a word. Because it was stunning, she couldn't get enough of the white sandy beaches stretching from one point to the next and the clear turquoise blue sea.

'Cecilia,' called Anthony in a strained voice. 'I'd be quite happy to just walk along the beach looking for seashells. You go off and enjoy yourself.'

Cecilia looked at Anthony and saw that he was quite uncomfortable. Did he not want to go on with her or Jason, the guy who'd brought the jet ski? What was wrong with him? Maybe he was bored with her already and was having second thoughts?

'You can drive,' he said suddenly.

Cecilia had begun to second guess what she was doing with him and realised how disappointed she had felt at the thought that he didn't really want to be here with her. 'Ok,' she said not wanting him to change his mind.

Five minutes later, they were on the jet ski with their safety jackets and had been given strict instructions on what to do and what not to do. In the end, Jason had persuaded Anthony to drive and in his words, 'let the fine lady sit behind him.' Anthony went quite slowly at first and Cecilia had her hands on her legs not wanting to touch him as her stomach was doing huge flips already. His confidence grew and he hit a wave head on, the jet ski jerked up and Cecilia grabbed him putting both hands around his waist. He let out a whoop and the tension she had noticed earlier disappeared. His face softened and Cecilia could see what he would have been like as a child as the serious part of him also faded away. She was now up against him holding on as he bounced over the waves. She smelled his cologne, the same one from the other evening, mixed in with his natural odour made her heady. His effect on her was unreal, it was totally freaky and rather unnerving. Cecilia really couldn't believe that she was having these feelings of such unadulterated attraction.

They went up and down the little stretch of coast until they saw Jason waving them in. Somehow they had managed to drift near a coral reef where it was more shallow but it also meant that there were more waves.

Cecilia held on to Anthony tightly as the jet ski rocked to and fro and up and down and then she saw sheer terror on Anthony's face.

'We'll be alright,' she cried out to him not expecting this type of reaction to a few waves, albeit bigger waves than normal. But just at that moment, the heavens decided to open. Large drops of water fell around them producing a splash effect on the ocean. She had been having such fun that she hadn't noticed the big black clouds coming steadily towards them.

'I can't do it,' he shouted nervously.

Cecilia who really hadn't planned on this abrupt change of weather or Anthony's reaction to a bit of a stormy sea felt rather upset that it could have all gone so wrong so quickly. That was another reason she hated dating, not that this was a date, but by not knowing the other person very well you could do or say something that could tip the balance out of your favour. Whatever Anthony was going through, she had to help him somehow.

'Yes, you can,' she shouted in his ear against the onslaught of water from both the sea and the sky. 'We'll be fine. Just take it easy and look at where Jason is on the beach and focus on him'.

'Ok,' he muttered through gritted teeth. The jet ski lurched forward as the waves pushed them along. It really wasn't that bad, thought Cecilia. He must have had worse on his sailing trip. What was going on?

A few minutes later she and Anthony landed ashore with no more mishaps. Jason looked up at the sky as if to say typical, then smiled and patted Anthony on the back.

'Right, I'm going to head off. See you around,' he said and jumped up on to the jet ski and headed off out of the cove.

'Come on,' Cecilia said. 'Let's get out of this rain and dry off, there's a little beach bar up there.' Anthony nodded, still looking visibly shaken from the ride. Cecilia quickly grabbed her bag with the dry towels from out of the car and darted over the sand towards the pretty blue and white painted shack that stood a couple of hundred metres away. An awning with a red hibiscus protruded out protecting the bar's clientele underneath from the variable weather conditions. Unfortunately, it was rain today.

Once they had dried off and some interesting fruit cocktails with little plastic reindeer sticking out of them were in their hands, they both looked out at the pelting rain in a semi-comfortable silence. Cecilia looked across at Antony's face every now and again wondering whether he was going to tell her what had happened out on the jet ski or whether she should just take the plunge and ask. He was frowning and looking rather downcast, totally different from the jokey guy she had first met. Not knowing what to say or do next, she excused herself and mumbled that she needed to go to the ladies. She wound her way between the tall wooden tables and stools that were largely occupied by some local octogenarians playing cards. One of the group, a large rotund woman with a weathered face gave Cecilia a knowing friendly toothless smile as she sidled past.

'What am I doing?' Cecilia muttered as she sat down on the toilet. She could only think that as the date, or whatever it was, had gone so drastically wrong so quickly that it must be an omen, warning her that she was currently on the wrong track. She had obviously made a huge mistake by agreeing to take this man out for the day that she barely knew. And if it was meant to be then it would have gone a lot smoother. The only thing for her to do now was find a way to back out graciously and forget him. But that was going to be difficult because she had actually rather liked the feel of him and the idea of having someone in her life again, to love and to hold and to share experiences with. No, really, she thought, what was she doing sat in this toilet cubicle, contemplating her life, whilst facing a door that had paint peeling off it with various engravings of declarations of love and... She stopped and looked closer at a lopsided drawing that suddenly drew her attention, 'Ew...' she shuddered in disgust, she really had to get out of here now. The little bar obviously catered for the younger generation too, at least, she hoped it did, and the special artwork was not from one of the folks that were currently inhabiting the seating area outside.

As Cecilia walked back to the table, Anthony turned round as if sensing her, and smiled sending unbidden sensations throughout her body. She sighed inwardly. Maybe more contemplation was needed because her thoughts were all over the place and backing out now was not an option. At least he seemed to have composed himself, she thought, and she was now glad that she had scarpered to give them that much needed breathing space.

'Sorry about earlier,' he said before she'd barely taken her seat. 'There's actually something I want to talk to you about that I don't usually go around telling people.'

Cecilia was about to go on the negative merry go round in her head of all the worst possible things that she was about to be told but was saved as he blurted out, 'I can't swim.'

Cecilia looked at him, her mouth opened and shut like one of those electronic garage doors that had got stuck.

She was stuck for words. The first thought was why on earth hadn't he told her right from the start that he couldn't swim. The second thought, which actually sent more unwanted butterflies go totally berserk in her stomach, was that he meant he'd liked her enough to do something crazy like going on a jet ski with her.

'Why didn't you tell me? We could have done something else. There are a lot of other things in Barbados to do other than being in or on the sea?' she asked.

He took another sip of his drink and said softly, 'No, you don't quite understand. I haven't told anyone before that I can't swim.'

'What?' exclaimed Cecilia and the bar went instantly quiet as about eight pairs of eyes gravitated in their direction. 'What do you mean you haven't told anyone before now? she asked in a hushed voice. 'I mean,' she continued, 'it's not exactly a big deal is it? Quite a few people don't know how to swim.'

'I've never learnt because either I haven't had the time or money. I've managed to avoid most situations. And I've felt rather embarrassed that I couldn't do something that everybody else has achieved as part of their childhood. You see, my parents had me later on in their lives. I was their miracle baby,' Anthony smiled then. 'But my mum's health was never that great. So,' he paused, 'I ended up helping my mum or my dad in between school. And then I just never had the inclination to learn and the years passed by. Plus, knowing how to swim didn't really matter until recently when I've been invited onto yachts by clients or like this past week, sailing.

'But didn't you even tell Bea? She's your friend isn't she?' asked Cecilia.

'She is a friend, but I met her through business first and I've also got into the habit of just not talking about it and avoiding the issue.'

'Oh right,' said Cecilia looking out to sea wondering what to say next. A tinny song of Queen's 'Fat Bottomed Girls' suddenly broke the heavy silence between them. 'Oh, won't you take me home tonight? Oh, down beside your red firelight, oh and you give it all you got Fat bottomed girls, you make the rockin' world go 'round.' Cecilia grimaced in embarrassment as not just eight pairs but ten pairs of eyes were now looking inquisitively in her direction. Cecilia sunk inwardly as she realised she'd forgotten to change her ringtone after Clarissa had mucked around with it, and who had obviously found it funny to put that particular song on. At least Anthony was finding it amusing and that smile of his had returned. She pointed at her phone and mouthed 'sorry, my daughter,' when she saw who was ringing. Anthony gestured at her to say take the call.

'Mum! cried an anguished voice over the phone.

'Darling, what's happened, are you alright?' asked Cecilia frantic with worry. Cecilia heard a moan and then a frustrated yelp. 'Clarissa, what on earth is going on?

'I'm stuck.'

'What do you mean you're stuck?'

'The zip is caught and I can't get it undone and I can barely breathe,' whined Clarissa with an additional sound of exaggerated heavy breathing tagged on for extra theatrics. Now Cecilia realised it was her daughter being overly dramatic, she calmed down. 'I was trying on my old ski suit hoping it still fit me. I managed to wriggle a bit to get it on and breathed in a bit to do the zip up but then I breathed normally and I couldn't move,' Clarissa sighed.

'And now the zip is stuck and I've been trying for ages to get it unstuck but it's not budging. Also there is no-one around to help at the moment.'

'So you thought you'd ring your mother, even though she is not even in the same country as you,' asked Cecilia, 'rather than go down the hallway to ask someone for help?'

'I am not walking down the corridor like this,' replied Clarissa. 'I can't believe you even suggested that? No, what I would like to ask is, if I cut myself out of it, could you possibly transfer some money over so I can buy another one? It doesn't fit me anyway.' Cecilia was silent at the end of the phone momentarily letting her daughter squirm as payback for the awful ringtone she had put on her phone. 'Mum?' asked a little voice. 'Are you still there? Please?'

'Yes, sweetheart,' replied Cecilia. 'I will send you over the money, now is there anything else you need for the trip?'

'Mmm...I'm not sure, actually, yes there is, can you ask Jasmine if they have spare skis and boots for me at the lodge or do I need to hire some. Because if I need to hire some, I don't have enough money in my account for those extras. I forgot to ask Kat or Bella but as you're there with...'

'I'm not with her right now,' Cecilia said, 'so I'll ask her later and will get back to you.'

'Oh sorry, I hope I didn't catch you at a bad moment,' Clarissa paused then asked, 'Er, where are you by the way, out of interest?' Cecilia felt herself going bright red as she glanced over at Anthony who was trying to look as though he wasn't overhearing the conversation. He was staring at a slightly odd nativity scene in the corner of the bar that bore no resemblance to the usual Bethlehem theme. Three wise men were on surf boards aiming for a little island with a tropical beach hut on, inside which was Mary and Joseph in their swimsuits drinking soda looking down at a baby. She thought she saw a shark lurking nearby in the crinkly blue paper making up the sea but...Oh yes. Clarissa.

Vaguely Cecilia found herself stuttering, 'W...w...well, I'm...um...I'm...' She really didn't want to divulge to her over imaginative daughter that she was sitting in a bar with a single and very attractive man. Clarissa would make a big deal out of it, which it was, and Cecilia also wasn't sure as to how much Anthony could hear. It was still raining so going outside was not an option and heading back to the toilets was another no no.

'Mum! Are you ok?' Clarissa's voice suddenly changed to concern.

'Oh sweetheart, I'm good. I'm in a bar with a friend, of a friend of Jasmine's and I'm showing him around...'

Cecilia's eyes gravitated over towards Anthony again only to find him lifting an imaginary glass to his mouth then pointing towards the bar. Cecilia nodded at him hoping that he would bring something back to the table a little stronger than the fruit cocktail she was currently drinking. She then brought her focus back to the current phone call and realised she'd missed what her daughter had just said.

'Mum! Mum! Are you there? Did you hear me?' cried out Clarissa.

Cecilia sighed, 'I'm here darling, sorry what did you say? The music is a bit loud in here.' And as if to back up her lie, the music turned up a notch and what sounded like Shaggy's version of 'Little Drummer Boy' came blasting out of the speakers above her head.

'Him?' cut in Clarissa. 'How old is he? Is he single? Is he good looking? Is this the first time you've been out with him?' Clarissa clattered off a barrage of questions and Cecilia felt very much as if she was under fire.

'Yes. Not sure. Yes. Maybe and NO!!' Cecilia gave as good as she got but then she heard her daughter sigh at the other end of the phone.

'Does that mean none of your business? I mean, mum, it's about time. I know you loved dad, still do, but Bertie and I want you to be happy and you really haven't been. If there is an opportunity, please take it, promise me?'

Cecilia smiled at Clarissa's sweet nature. 'We are just friends,' she replied starting to blush as feelings were rising which totally contradicted what she was telling Clarissa. 'Yes, just friends. Right, I've got to go, our food has just arrived,' she said telling yet another lie but it was actually Anthony returning with two chilled bottles of Barbados' own Banks Beer. 'I'll send you over the money and I'll speak to you soon. Hope you get out of that ski suit without hurting yourself. Text me, won't you, to let me know that you're ok? And write proper words please, it takes me forever to work out your texts otherwise.'

'Ok,' said Clarissa. 'Love you, bye.'

'Love you too sweetheart.'

Anthony gestured towards the beers as Cecilia put her phone down on the table. 'I hope you like beer. I wasn't sure, but, I can get you something else if you like?'

'Oh no, that's perfect, thank you,' Cecilia replied and took a huge gulp feeling the cool nectar slip down her throat. It was actually just what she needed, the sweetness of the cocktail was getting a bit sickly. A bowel of chips would be nice right now too, she thought wistfully, then laughed out loud as a little hand-weaved basket full of chunky chips landed in between them.

'What?' asked Anthony looking puzzled at her random laugh.

'You must be reading my mind,' smiled Cecilia. 'Beer and chips was just what I wanted!'

Anthony smiled then noticeably relaxed. The conversation flew then, both of them laughing at Clarissa's predicament and Anthony regaled Cecilia with the awkward moments that he'd been in, not being able to swim over the years. Now that Anthony had admitted his secret, everything that he had kept bottled in came tumbling out. And with the laughter, the music got louder in the beach café, more people crowded into the little wooden shack, and the drinks flowed. Cecilia then realised as she became more and more tipsy that she was actually enjoying herself with Anthony. And it wasn't just the beer goggles that she now had on that made her think he was gorgeous, he was truly.... Whoa... Suddenly her head spun a little and she grabbed the table to steady herself.

'Are you alright?' asked Anthony leaning towards Cecilia.

'Oh yes,' she giggled, 'My head's swimming!' Then Cecilia gasped as she realised what she'd said and quickly apologised. 'Sorry, I mean...I didn't mean to say that.'

Fortunately, Anthony had taken the unintentional pun with good grace and was laughing with her. Thank goodness, she thought. She hadn't meant to upset him, he was so nice, so kind, so...so...sexy. Slowly she felt herself leaning towards him, he was like a magnet and he seemed to be drawing closer to her. His nose was so strong, his eyes were so...so...deep and his lips...mmm...tasted delicious. Oh my gosh, we're kissing, she thought, her head spinning a bit more now that she'd closed her eyes as well... I wish this could go on forever.... Wow, he was a good kisser too. Exceptional, in fact. A bit different to Doug but...Oh no, Doug! Doug! This isn't Doug, she thought. Quickly she pulled away, not sure of what she was feeling anymore. This is wrong. It felt wrong. It felt like she was cheating on Doug! Oh no!

With those thoughts running through her head, she leapt back and in her drunken state, she blearily looked at a stunned Anthony, and mumbled a 'Sorry I can't do this' and ran.

Chapter Seven

♥

Tuesday 16th December 2014

Cecilia felt as if she was having a déja-vu and everything that had happened in the last several days had been a dream. It was such a cliché even thinking it. A dream. But it hadn't been though, had it? She was sitting at the kitchen counter with a steaming hot coffee and nursing a very sore head. The last few hours had been a bit of a blur and the ones before that had been even more blurry, much to her dismay.

As soon as she'd ran out on Anthony, she'd headed straight towards Jasmine's home, leaving the hire car at the beach. All she wanted to do was get her things and get out of the country and back home to where everything was familiar and where she felt the closest to Doug. Jasmine had initially been worried at her state when she'd burst into the house but Jasmine, being Jasmine had sorted out a standby flight for her to get home that evening and helped pack her bags whilst she took a very cold shower. She'd cried then. Cried a lot. She felt so bad and she couldn't shake off the feeling that she'd been unfaithful to Doug. It just wouldn't go away. She knew he wasn't around anymore and she knew that he would want her to meet someone else so why couldn't she just move on?

It came to her then. It was fear. Fear that she would fall in love and then lose them. She didn't want to go through the feeling of being abandoned again. Doug obviously didn't mean to abandon her but she felt abandoned all the same. With Anthony, she had felt herself falling deeply for him, they seemed to fit like a jigsaw puzzle. Literally all the pieces had fallen into place. They had the same interests, the same humour and after that kiss, they definitely felt the same way about each other. Oh, that kiss. Then she clasped her head in hands as she realised she'd just left him without an explanation. How awful had that been for him? But what could she have said? Because any reason that she'd hoped to have given him would have looked lame and pathetic.

During the midst of her reflections, the drone of the doorbell rang. Definitely déja-vu. Well it certainly wasn't going to be Jasmine. Cecilia peered through the keyhole to see her next door neighbour, Hester, dressed in her garden clothes looking excited. Cecilia was relieved, she liked Hester. Hester was a kind woman who had no children but helped anyone and everyone out. On the odd occasion when Hester was not feeling too great, she was in her eighties and had a few ailments, Cecilia would walk her two gorgeous golden retrievers, Marigold and Poppy. When Doug died, she and her husband, Frank, had asked her to walk their dogs quite a lot. She was sure it was more of a way to get her out of the house.

'Hester,' Cecilia said smiling, 'I've only just got back and was going to pop round to see how you were doing.'

'Well, I didn't expect to see you back so soon. I got the note you posted to say that you'd be away for a month but then I saw some lights on and was just checking to see if everything was alright?'

'Oh that's kind Hester, thank you. Yes, my plans changed.'

'Have you got a moment, dear?' asked Hester.

'Yes, why?'

'You didn't have time to see Marigold's pups before you left and they are absolutely gorgeous. You must come and see them before they go to their forever homes next week.'

'I'd love to,' said Cecilia as she grabbed her keys. 'Did you find out who the dad is?'

Hester smiled with a knowing look. 'Come on, come see them and maybe you can work it out yourself.'

Cecilia looked down at the writhing golden fur balls clambering over each other, trying to get the closest to mum. To the right a movement caught her attention as a little black body uncurled itself and on unsteady legs attempted to join the stampede. The puppy fell, whimpered then got up and suddenly launched itself on top of the others. Cecilia laughed.

'They're gorgeous aren't they?' said Hester. 'I couldn't have imagined this outcome even if we tried. You know Marigold slipped out at the bottom of the garden? Well she actually made it to the other end of the village...'

Cecilia gasped. 'No way! It's not old Bill's big black poodle who's the father, is it?'

'Yes, the very one. We looked up the cross and they are actually supposed to be quite popular these days...a Goldendoodle.'

'Have you managed to sell any yet?' asked Cecilia wistfully.

'Yes. There were five girls and two boys. There's just one girl and one boy left.'

'Can I pick one up?'

'Of course you can.'

Cecilia kneeled down and picked up the one that she was most drawn to and soon held him in her arms. His little black face looked up at her with such adoring eyes that she knew she needed him as much as he need her.

'Is this one still available?' she asked.

Chapter Eight

♥

Wednesday 24th December 2014

'Oh...shit!' echoed a deep voice around the house.

And that is what Cecilia heard as she came in from the garden with Moriarty. What was Bertie doing home and why was he swearing, she thought, as she and her new little sidekick rushed into the hallway. There she found her somewhat tipsy son lifting his foot up in dismay and inspecting the dog poo which had now been smeared all over his nice expensive Italian leather shoes. Next to him was also a rather tipsy, actually after looking closer, a decidedly drunk willowy blond female with bright red lipstick smudged over half of her chin. Half of which was also over Bertie and had somehow managed to reach down his chest. Act cool, she thought, laughing inside at Bertie's idea of bringing a girl home while the mum's away.

'Hello darling,' she said crossing over to him, stepping over the poo and giving him a kiss on the cheek. 'How lovely to see you, I didn't expect to see you for Christmas. And you've brought a friend, how nice.'

The blond girl went bright red and tried to re-arrange herself and seemed to be sobering up very quickly.

Bertie, whose mouth had finally decided to catch up with his foggy brain looked at his mother in utter astonishment and blurted out. 'But Mum! You're supposed to be in Barbados. What happened? Why are you home?'

'I had a change of plan and decided to come home.'

'Oh...' he said, then looked down at his shoes then looked at the culprit who was now trying to sniff and clamber up the legs of... What was her name? Oh God, this was so embarrassing. He'd only just met her in Cheltenham, in a bar, having just got off the train from London. It was the prerequisite Christmas Eve drinks with his old mates from school and she'd been there too and one thing had led to another and... What was her name? Think Bertie, think!

'Right, well this is...um...'

'Fiona,' said the blond girl next to him who looked as though she wanted to take her leave as soon as possible and was inching her way back out through the front door.

Cecilia trying to put her at ease, took her arm and gently lead her around the large wooden table in the entrance hall steering her to the right, towards the sitting room whilst Bertie was still trying to compose himself.

Cecilia looked around the room regarding where to best place the somewhat drunken young lady. No to her expensive four seater cream sofa she'd just bought. And definitely a no to her antique two seater that had belonged to her grandmother. She grimaced. It was going to have to be the threadbare and very grubby chair that the dog had taken to because the thought of vomit anywhere else filled her with dread.

'Would you like a drink, tea, coffee or perhaps some water?' asked Cecilia.

'Er...water... please,' said Fiona who now looked like she wanted to jump out of the window.

'Bertie,' hissed Cecilia with a fake smile plastered across her face. 'Kitchen...now!'

Bertie floundered briefly then squared his shoulders and tried to walk to the kitchen with dignity despite having one shoe off, his tie draped loosely around his neck and his shirt hanging out.

'Wait there,' she ordered as she hastily scurried off to clean up Moriarty's little accident.

As she left she took a swift glance back to see Bertie looking rather dejectedly at the floor. What was he doing? Jasmine said he had made plans for Christmas. This girl obviously wasn't his girlfriend. For one thing, he couldn't remember her name and also she'd never known him to bring a girl home to meet her. She knew he left a string of girls heartbroken in his wake. She'd tried to talk to him about it but he always brought everything back to her to avoid discussing it. She sighed, on a positive note, at least he was home for Christmas.

'Bertie?' He looked up as she walked in.

'Mum, I'm so sorry. I was having drinks with the lads in town and I've been working so hard I was happy to chill out at home on my own over Christmas.' At that, Cecilia's eyebrows went up and motioned towards the sitting room. 'Yes well, that wasn't planned, I had a few drinks and she wasn't going to stay...just keep me company for a few hours.' Again Cecilia's eyebrows raised. 'Mum! She lives in the next village along. I remember that much! Also I think she mentioned she was one of Clarissa's friends from school. I didn't tell you about my Christmas plans because

I didn't want you to worry and from what Clarissa told me it sounded like you were having a good time out there with Jasmine. I mean, when was the last time you had a good time. You look amazing! Not that you didn't before but...' Again, Cecilia thought, Bertie had managed to turn it around back to her. He really did mean well.

'Ok, but let's give Fiona some tea before she goes back home to her parents. I wouldn't want them to think we didn't look after her. Do you?'

'No. I'm sorry.'

Cecilia brought out some fried egg sandwiches to Fiona and Bertie only to find Moriarty had made himself quite at home and was now sat in the lap of Fiona getting lots of attention.

'He's lovely,' Fiona said taking her plate. 'And thank you, you needn't.'

'Oh, I just thought it might help soak up a bit of the alcohol.' Fiona nodded as she happily took a big bite.

'Mum, when did you get him and what is he?' asked Bertie ruffling the curly mop on the puppy.

'He's a Goldendoodle.'

Bertie grunted, 'There's nothing golden about him!'

Cecilia then proceeded to tell them about Moriarty's parentage while they ate and Cecilia also kept on looking at Fiona thinking she'd definitely met her before but couldn't place her.

'So,' Cecilia said finally. 'You're an old friend of Clarissa's Bertie tells me.'

'Yes, Fiona Ryes from...'

'Fiona Foureyes!' blurted out Bertie.

'Bertie!' admonished Cecilia wondering what had got into Bertie. He wasn't normally this rude.

'Sorry, it was...I just meant...I mean that was your nickname at school?' asked Bertie.

Fiona glanced down sadly at her feet 'Yes it was.'

'But...I didn't recognise you, you look so different,' said Bertie.

'I lost some weight,' she said quickly.

'Yes...but...' carried on Bertie but then saw his mother's stern glance and he went silent.

'Well, it's lovely to see you again,' Cecilia said looking down at her watch. 'Right, I'll drive you home and then I can get an early night. I seem to still have some jet lag. Flying never did agree with me.'

Chapter Nine

♥

Thursday 25th December 2014

Cecilia took a deep breath in then as she breathed out a white cloud billowed and floated away to nothing. She felt like that right now. In Barbados she had been going with the flow and felt bold but now she was back to her England life, she felt non-existent. Not to the children but to the world in general. She had begun to feel alive and then her guilt had sent her running. And now she was home, here, with Doug's presence, she realised it felt different from before. He was slowly slipping away from her and it scared her. Raising her head to the sky, she whispered, 'Happy Christmas Doug. I love you.'

It was a beautiful start to a Christmas day. The sun was beginning to rise over the fields at the end of her garden. Frost sparkled and there was so much it looked like a scatter of snow. Moriarty was loving the crunch of the grass and he was now scampering around the rose bushes nose to the ground after some interesting scent then his head perked up and he gave a squeal of delight and shot past her like a dynamo on a mission.

'Morning, young chap,' said Bertie squatting down to give him a stroke. 'Morning mum, Happy Christmas.'

'Happy Christmas to you too, sweetheart. I didn't expect you to be up so early. Did you sleep ok?'

'Yeah, I'm feeling a little bit rough though,' he said sheepishly.

Cecilia chose not to reply as he already felt bad enough about the day before.

'Are you alright?' Bertie asked.

Cecilia looked at him weighing up whether to spill the beans. Moriarty barked as if on cue which saved her from having to answer straight away.

'Come on then. Let's go and get us some breakfast,' she said quickly.

As they sat down to a sumptuous breakfast of...a bowel of cornflakes. Well no, it wasn't great and not that sumptuous at all because Cecilia had indeed forgotten to get much in the way of food for the festive season. However, Moriarty, as Bertie pointed out, had everything from balls, chewies, dog bed and matching blanket and some very nice looking dog bowels which had water elaborately written on one and food on the other. Not that Moriarty could read in the slightest but evidently this practice was normal in households with pets. Bertie shook his head in disbelief. When he'd eventually got his head around his mum being at home, he then thought, brilliant, now I'll get a decent roast turkey Christmas dinner with all the trimmings. But no. It was not to be. Luckily, at the last minute, he had shoved into his bag some nice tinned foie gras and other little delicacies from a Fortnum and Mason hamper a client had given him to keep him going over the next few days and there should be enough to go round.

'Well, that was delicious,' Bertie said patting his stomach with a mischievous grin.

'Oh Bertie,' chided Cecilia with a smile. 'You're fortunate there was enough milk for the two of us.'

'It's alright. We won't starve, we can always eat some of Moriarty's dog biscuits. Look,' he said waving his hand to the packet on the side, 'it's healthy and nutritious.'

'It's the first time I've had a dog on my own and I wanted to make sure he's got everything he needs,' said Cecilia.

'What about your needs, mum?' asked Bertie. 'Are you making sure you've got what you need?'

Cecilia stared out of the window, not wanting to reply and not wanting to admit to Bertie that she wasn't at all sure what she needed anymore and that that had changed quite recently. Bertie sat there in silence. He was used to her mulling things over in head. He had nowhere to go and he wanted to get to the bottom of why his mother had come back early. According to Clarissa, she'd been in a bar with a man and seemed to be having fun. Now that was unheard of. Before Barbados, she had barely left the house and she'd let herself go, although he wouldn't have dared say it to her face but she'd actually shaved her legs and her nails had been done, both sets, as in not just her fingers! It hadn't been just a shock of seeing her home but her whole demeanour and appearance had changed.

'I met someone Bertie,' said Cecilia. 'I didn't expect to. But I did. I had quite strong feelings for him then the guilt kicked in and I felt as though I was betraying your father. And it wasn't the same as being with your father either. It was strange, it felt nice and it felt wrong.'

Bertie looked at her as if to say go on, I'm listening.

'Then I just wanted to feel near Doug again, and it's home where I feel the closest to him but since I've got home, it's not the same. And so I got...a dog.'

'So that's it, a dog fills up your life now and you're happy.'

'No. I'm not but a dog definitely helps,' said Cecilia giving Moriarty a stroke. 'He's therapeutic, when he's being good. Plus, he's still only a puppy.'

'Ok,' said Bertie getting rather exasperated. 'But you liked this guy a lot and you had fun and had some nice chats?'

'Yes,' said Cecilia wistfully also thinking of the dreamy kiss.

'Mum, time heals. It's been three years since dad died and as Clarissa and I have said many times, we would love for you to meet someone else. And it seems that it might be now. What was this guy called?'

'Anthony. But I don't how to get hold of him and even if I did, I was so rude. No, I've missed that boat.'

Bertie ran his fingers through his hair, ran out of the kitchen, then came back with his laptop.

'Well, why don't you try dating some men, test the waters so to speak then if it truly isn't the right time then you can leave it for a while?'

'I suppose I could ask some of my friends and get the word out that I'm looking. But that just sounds so...so...as if I'm for sale or rent even. Come and look at me, do you like what you see...I don't know Bertie. In the past I was usually friends with my boyfriends first, having met them at school or at Uni.'

'Right mum, you're going to have to have an open mind for what I'm going to suggest and lots of people do it to find love these days. Ok?'

'Ta da!' he said with a flourish whilst pushing the computer screen Cecilia's way. Cecilia squinted with her eyes as she took in all the details.

Slowly she started to read, 'snap.com find your love match and you've made it...SNAP! A pair.'

'Oh Bertie, no, I couldn't possibly,' said Cecilia.

'Mum, seriously, read on.'

'Cecilia, 43, widower, 2 grown up children. Loves dogs, walking, eating out and seeks a man 30-50, with a GSOH, kind and likes similar hobbies,' Cecilia looked at Bertie with an amazed look. 'Are you really thinking this is going to find me a nice man? There's probably all kinds of weirdos on here. No! Absolutely no! Take me off here immediately Bertie.'

An incoming message flashed on the screen and Bertie whooped.

'You've got a message already. Come on, give it a go. Look, you always meet in a public place and you just go for one drink. Easy.'

'But normally if you meet someone who's a friend of a friend then you know roughly they're not going to be some axe murderer. Anyone of these men could be... could be...a...'

'Mum, try it. I've done it a few times and one of my mates is about to get married to a girl he met through this website.'

'Fine,' said Cecilia feeling far from fine. She couldn't believe she'd given in so easily. But this was obviously the new way of meeting people these days and she'd become out of touch.

Chapter Ten

♥

Wednesday 31st December 2014

'Happy New Year!' cried the chorus of people around the dining room table clinking their glasses together.

'Happy New Year, Mum!' shouted Clarissa as she pulled Cecilia into a warm embrace and planted a very alcoholic imbued kiss on her cheek.

'Yeah, Happy New Year Mum!' joined in Bertie as he put his arms around her shoulders. 'Let's see what this New Year may bring you,' he said with a very mischievous grin.

'Happy New Year!' Cecilia said beaming at her two children as well as Jasmine, Richard and their girls, and a few other faces who'd appeared as the day had worn on. Cecilia couldn't believe how happy she was feeling right now and it had all started with...do you know what, she didn't know exactly when, but what did matter was that her life was looking rosier now and she was actually looking forward to the year 2015.

Bertie had been brilliant the last week and had really bolstered her up. He'd ended up staying at home longer than planned and been skyping his work colleagues from time to time if anything had come up. Moriarty was settling in very nicely too.

The morning had started in the way it usually did these days; waking up early, letting Moriarty out to do his business, having a few cups of coffee before Bertie sleepily joined her, going for a walk, reading some of her latest novel she'd picked up on Amazon and so on. However, around five o'clock the doorbell had rung and there standing before her was her daughter, a younger version of her but looking out through panda eyes. She was also laden down with various sized bags and grinning from ear to ear.

'Hi mum!' she said and then continued to drop her bags at her feet, narrowly missing Moriarty and launched herself at Cecilia.

'Darling, what a wonderful surprise! I didn't expect you home for another few days. Where's Bella and Kat?' she asked looking over Clarissa's shoulder for Jasmine's twin girls.

'It's fine, they've gone home, they'll be around in a mo.'

'Are you going out later?' asked Cecilia wondering why they were home in the first place. Perhaps there was a better New Year's Eve party for them to go to with their friends at home here. Oh well, she thought, I'm sure Clarissa will fill me in on her plans. She was never one to keep quiet about her activities, which she was glad about, mind, but not everything. Sometimes it was hard not to step in and be the overprotective mother, but she'd learnt some time ago that rather than lecture, it was best to just be there to pick up the pieces afterwards. Lesson learnt, mistake never to happen again!

'Clarissa,' said Bertie interrupting their conversation. 'Nice tan marks!'

'Thanks,' smiled Clarissa punching Bertie playfully on his arm. 'I know I can always count on you to point out the obvious with no regard for diplomacy.'

'Why would I?' he said, 'You're my little sister, it's part of my role as big brother to annoy you as much as possible.'

Cecilia looked at the two of them as they battled it out. They'd come such a long way and Doug's death had brought them closer together. Because they did used to have the most awful arguments before...

'Oh you've got to be kidding me?' shouted Clarissa looking down at her bags in disbelief. Moriarty was clearly marking his territory and had decided to cock his leg over Clarissa's faithful suitcase that she'd had for years. He'd only just started doing this and liked to practice it as much as possible.

'Sorry darling,' said Cecilia removing the bag and quickly taking it away to be cleaned. 'He gets excited at seeing new people.'

'So?' whispered Clarissa out of the corner of her mouth at Bertie. 'Is she as good as she looks at the moment? Because...wow...'

'She's fine,' said Bertie quickly as he saw his mother coming back with Clarissa's bag.

'I was just saying how great you looked to Bertie,' she said smiling. 'Barbados seemed to agree with you, and dare I say it, could it have been to do with a certain single man you were showing around?'

Bertie blanched at his sister's foot in the mouth remark and dug his elbow into her ribs to make her shut up.

'Ow!' Clarissa squealed. 'You big oaf! What did you do that for?'

'Bertie, it's ok there's no need to beat up your sister. Clarissa, the sun and the change of scenery was great however,' she said more slowly, 'there are some details of the holiday I wish to remain firmly in the past.'

'Oh,' cried Clarissa forlornly sounding more like an eight-year-old than her twenty-year-old self. 'That's not fair. I bet you've told Bertie. You always tell him more stuff than me.'

Cecilia didn't reply to her daughter's last comment because Clarissa was right and it wasn't fair but she just didn't want to go through the mortification again of repeating the scene out loud. It somehow seemed worse than the constant replay in her head. She was trying to get Anthony out of her head but she was on a losing streak. She was thinking of what to reply to Clarissa when after looking past the panda eyes, Cecilia noticed a few blisters on her lips which looked quite ferocious.

'Clarissa, what happened to your lips?'

'Oh,' said Clarissa now looking rather sheepish, 'they're just cold sores from the sun.'

'You're not going to get any snogs in anytime soon then,' said Bertie teasing her. At that point, the doorbell rang again. Clarissa then took this as an opportunity to make a quick dash up to her bedroom with her bags away from the prying eyes of her mother whilst Bertie went in search of Moriarty in the hope of stopping him from relieving himself on anything other than the grass outside.

'Hello,' said Cecilia seconds later as she looked at five faces she thought she vaguely recognised.

'Hi,' drawled one dark haired girl who had thick black eye makeup on, a dozen piercings up her left ear and one in her lip. 'We're here for the party!'

Cecilia barely registered what the girl had said as she was too busy staring at the girl. She had never seen someone with so many piercings up close and was right at that moment wondering how difficult it would be to eat with that huge ring through her lip but then the word 'party' rang out an alarm in her brain.

'Party?' she shrilled, her voice going an octave higher than it normally did. 'And you are friends of...'

'Cecilia!'

Cecilia looked behind the five expectant faces to where the voice came from as a friendly pixie like face pushed through precariously balancing plates of food.

'Hi Cecilia,' Bella said going on tiptoe to give her a peck on the cheek. 'Happy Christmas!' And with that she went on past heading straight towards the kitchen. The dark haired girl who'd spoken first then took this as a sign to enter with her two bottles of Malibu and Coca Cola in one arm and four pots of what looked like potato salad in the other. Behind her came a guy with long hair who was desperately trying to blow some wayward strands from out of his mouth whilst carrying a box of red wine and a cooked ham.

'Happy Christmas Mrs Bancroft. Thanks for having us. This is a great idea.'

Great idea indeed, Cecilia thought, she was going to have to words with Bertie and Clarissa. No wonder she scuttled away out of sight so quickly. Cecilia should have known then that her daughter was up to something. Hang on a second, wasn't that Eddie who'd been carrying that ham? He was one of Bella's and Clarissa's old school friends. She knew she'd recognised him.

'Happy Christmas Mrs Bancroft,' said the remaining girls and boy as they filed past. Cecilia did know them but how they'd changed since she'd last seen them. It was amazing what a few years of life after school could do to a person and she smiled fondly as memories of her children and their friends had filled up their house with laughter and there had been quite a few shenanigans. Talking of shenanigans.

'Bertie! Clarissa! Come here, now!' she screamed at the top of her lungs. It had been sometime since she'd used them but they seemed to be working, like riding a bike really. They weren't naughty teenagers anymore but they were certainly acting it now. Party indeed, and without telling her. They knew she liked to plan at least some details of an event.

On cue, Clarissa entered from stage left and Bertie entered from stage right both ready for the showdown.

'I'm sorry!' they said in unison.

'It was supposed to be a nice surprise for you. A new year, a new way of doing things and a new start? Jasmine and Richard are even coming along later,' said Bertie.

'What?' said Cecilia almost speechless. It wasn't a party for the kids, it was a party for her. Oh, she felt so guilty in the way she had reacted. She should have known better and had more faith in her children. And Jasmine and Richard had cut their holiday short and so had Clarissa and the girls for that matter. Oh no, she felt really bad now.

'I'm the one that should be sorry for coming to the wrong conclusion,' said Cecilia. 'So what's the plan?'

Clarissa looked her mother up and down. 'Get changed?'

Cecilia descended the stairs a good couple of hours later. She hadn't meant to take quite so long getting ready however after the shower, she had laid down on the bed for just a couple of minutes to rest her eyes only to find herself opening her eyes much later. She had lazily looked around her room to suddenly sit up in bed and remember there were quite a few people downstairs, some of whom she didn't know very well, making themselves at home and preparing for a party. Luckily she was nice and tanned so didn't need much makeup. She slapped on some bright red lipstick which matched her short glittery sleeveless dress and heels whilst humming a Chris de Burgh song. 'Lady in red, is dancing with me...cheek to cheek....' She sighed then. If only things hadn't ended up the way they had with Anthony, he could have been here tonight...with her...dancing cheek to cheek. Oh stop it, she thought, I've got to stop thinking about him. But the image of him kept popping into her mind. She'd made such a mess of things and now she'd agreed to this online dating malarkey. As long as no-one finds out. Just her and Bertie.

Uptown Funk was blaring out of the speakers throughout the house. It was Clarissa's most recent fixation and had played it so many times over one weekend that even Cecilia began to sing along to it 'Too hot...hot damn. Say my name you know who I am...'

'Nice moves,' said Bertie as he caught his mum looking radiant and happy coming down the stairs then he grabbed hold of Cecilia and began dancing with her.

'Well,' said Jasmine as she entered through the front door on Richard's arm. 'I do believe we have arrived just in time.

Cecilia rushed up to Jasmine and gave her a ginormous hug but Cecilia could barely feel her underneath the huge black faux fur coat. 'I can't believe you're here and that you've cut your holiday short.'

'Oh it just wasn't the same after you left,' winked Richard. 'It was a bit quiet and this party was not to be missed.'

Jasmine smiled. 'According to Kat...ah here you are darling...' A gorgeous tall and willowy girl came in from the cold. She was Bella's twin sister and was a model. Although her face was beautiful, she seemed to have a permanent scowl upon her face which only seemed to disappear when either Bella or Clarissa were around.

'According to me what?' she said.

Jasmine paid no attention to her manner and carried on airily, 'According to you, once Bertie had rung up and suggested a party might cheer Cecilia up, Clarissa roped in you and Bella to make it happen. There was no stopping her.'

Cecilia smiled at her children's thoughtfulness. They were good children, she thought, at times, as she remembered the way Bertie had behaved to Fiona only recently. But then she glanced over at Bertie only to find him chatting amiably to her. He must have felt bad and invited her. That's a good thing. She seemed nice enough although a little bit lost.

'I've got some lovely bubbly here and I brought some rum punch in case you were getting withdrawals. Which shall it be?'

'Definitely the rum punch,' said Cecilia her taste buds starting to tingle.

At some point in the evening, they all clamoured into the long dining room which was decorated in black and silver balloons, lots of fairy lights, (Cecilia did love fairy lights) and sparkly streamers which hung from the two chandeliers that topped each end of the mahogany table. The table was laid up for fourteen, a bit of a squeeze but manageable. The carver sideboard was set up as a buffet with all the food everybody had brought with them. Clarissa had even organised one of Cecilia's favourite dishes, baked salmon in foil with garlic, lemon and herbs.

'I made that,' whispered Clarissa in Cecilia's ear as she passed. Cecilia mouthed a silent 'how?' and 'when?' but

Clarissa just smiled and touched her nose knowingly. Cecilia shook her head in disbelief. A lot of the time, Clarissa was a drama queen and it felt like she couldn't manage a thing and then she would do something like this and pull it off with seeming ease. Contradictory was the only word for her. Contradictory with a heart of gold.

Once they had all sat down with plates piled high, Cecilia turned her attentions to the young man on her right.

'I can't believe how much you've changed, Eddie. What have you been up to since you left school?' asked Cecilia.

'I'm in IT, I do stuff with computers,' he said.

'And that's not all the stuff you do, is it Eddie?' piped up Kat who was sat opposite Cecilia and had been looking like a wet blanket for most of the evening. At this Eddie turned a deep shade of red. What was that supposed to mean thought Cecilia? I ask a simple question and...

'I didn't intend to...it just happened,' he said then plumped his chest out. 'Anyway I'm good at it and it gets me extra money.'

Cecilia looked at Eddie waiting for a reply when Kat said, 'He's a butler in the buff.'

'A what?' asked Jasmine.

'A butler in the buff,' replied Bella coming to her mum's rescue. 'It's basically a naked waiter.'

Cecilia looked in disbelief at Eddie. Not because she thought he couldn't do it but that there was actually something like that. God. She needed to get out more. She'd never heard of that type of thing but then again neither had Jasmine.

'So you serve people, what food? Drink? With no clothes on? But what happens if you spill something hot on you down...' And as she said it her eyes followed down too.

'Mum,' interrupted Bertie quickly as he saw where Cecilia's mind was taking her. She had had a few to drink and god knows what she would say next.

'S'alright Mrs Bancroft. We wear an apron so we're not exactly bearing all,' said Eddie with a grin.

'You must have so many girls wanting your number,' said Cecilia not realising she had actually spoke out loud.

'Mum!' whispered Bertie through gritted teeth.

Eddie just laughed. 'I haven't actually, women tend to gravitate towards the other waiters. They must see right through me as I'm a just geek at heart.'

Clarissa, who'd always had a slight crush on Eddie at school thought it was a bit mean of Kat to spill the beans. She had been in a bad mood for a few days now, something was eating at her but she doubted she'd spoken to anyone about it.

'Now now Kat if you're letting on about other people's secrets, what were you doing with the ski instructor? I saw those furtive glances between the two of you at the bar,' said Clarissa smiling.

'Oh what?' shouted out Bella in disbelief. 'You get all the good looking ones. He was hot...like really hot. Okay, now I'm so jealous.'

Kat suddenly laughed and her whole face lit up. 'Nothing happened! Anyway how would you know missy Clarissa Bancroft, you were too busy trying to not let your face catch fire.'

'Oh crap,' said Clarissa feeling like she wanted to disappear. Why couldn't girls' holidays be like stag dos? What happens on holiday stays on holiday!

'What do you mean?' gasped Cecilia in horror. She couldn't fathom how fire had been anywhere near her daughter's face. 'You haven't started smoking have you?'

'No!' said all three girls in unison.

Jasmine looked much like Cecilia did but Richard's eyes were twinkling mischievously. He obviously knew what happened then or had some thoughts on the matter. Before he met Jasmine, he had been quite the man about town, and known for his rather silly but adventurous antics. He had toned down somewhat, particularly when the twins were born.

'We all had a go but Clarissa went one step further and it backfired,' said Bella.

'It's called a flaming Sambuca,' said Clarissa.

'Well I know what that is,' said Cecilia rather indignantly. She wasn't that far over the hill that she didn't know what that was. 'You have a shot of Sambuca and set fire to it, wait till it goes out then knock it back.'

'Yup. Correct,' said Kat. 'However Clarissa wondered what would happen if you put the shot of Sambuca straight in your mouth then light it.'

'It would have been alright if I hadn't have dribbled a bit. Hence the lips,' she said pointing at some ferocious looking blisters.

Bertie looked at his sister and felt a bit sorry for her. Mum would be furious with her but wasn't going to show it in front of her friends. 'Mum's going on a date in three days' time,' he blurted out before he could think about what he was saying. Oops, he'd definitely consumed way too much alcohol. He was going to be in trouble now with his mum too.

'Mum!' cried out Clarissa. 'That's brilliant. Where did you meet him? Is he the man on holiday?'

'Oh did she tell you about him?' said Jasmine, not realising that Cecilia hadn't told her daughter what had happened. 'He was gorgeous and kind and they got on brilliantly.' Jasmine looked at a bewildered and shocked Cecilia. 'How nice, you decided to get in contact with him. Bea said he was very into you and wasn't the same after you left.'

Cecilia felt herself sinking into her chair, getting smaller and smaller. She was going to kill Bertie. Cheeky so and so. She knew he'd been trying to take the heat off Clarissa but to tell everyone about the date. And now Clarissa, thanks to Jasmine, will want a full explanation of what happened. Oh God, how was she going to get out of this one.

'Er no, um, I didn't get back into contact with him, rather Bertie has decided to um...'

'I signed her up to snap.com and she's actually got not one but three dates lined up over the next few weeks. She's been very much in demand,' Bertie said proudly.

Cecilia could feel herself going even more bright red. Get me out of here, she thought. She didn't want to look at anyone. She didn't want their judgement.

'Oh,' said Eddie, next to her. 'That website's quite good. I know a few people who've found love through that site. I haven't mind, but not through lack of trying. But it doesn't mean you won't Mrs Bancroft,' he added quickly.

Thank goodness for Eddie, Cecilia thought.

'That sounds fun,' said Jasmine. 'You make sure you give us all the goss.'

Chapter Eleven

♥

Saturday 3rd January 2015

Oh my god, this really is D day, date day, thought Cecilia as she sped through the narrow country lanes, grinding the gears as she went. She'd had to borrow Clarissa's little Rover Metro at the last minute as her normally faithful Range Rover had some funny glitch and she couldn't even get the door open. She'd wanted to postpone, she had cold feet anyway about going on this date but Clarissa had pooh poohed the idea and shoved her car keys in her hands and said, 'Go for it, mum. No excuses.' It had been ages since she'd driven a manual hence why she was making such a pig's ear of it. Cecilia heard a scrape along the side of the car as she went straight into a pothole and lurched into a bramble hedge. She grimaced as it sounded just like nails being raked down a blackboard. Clarissa had also neglected to tell her that the heating was broken so she was sure that her slightly damp hair which she'd hoped to dry before she reached her date now fell heavily due to the new formation of ice patches.

Clarissa screeched to a stop as she overshot the entrance to the pub and saw a sign that vaguely looked like the place she was looking for. Paul, her date, had suggested a 'quaint' pub in the countryside reasonably close to where she said she lived, (obviously she hadn't really told him where she lived) called The Lucky Duck and had she been there. There being quite a jaunt from home and not wanting to be caught out, she just replied saying that it sounded delightful. Delightful was now the last thought she had in mind though regarding the place. A battered sign dangled from a pole and where there was a faded D, somebody had taken it upon themselves to add an F. She hoped this wasn't also a sign of what the potential clientele would be like when she entered the establishment.

Upon arriving into the car park, a burnt out car was the first thing to catch her attention. A bright orange highway cone also adorned what would have been a nice looking rose garden. Cecilia grimaced. Right this was too much, she was backing out right now she thought, but then to her dismay a five foot eight nervous looking man with a short army hair cut came out of the pub clutching a huge bunch of flowers. It was Paul, her date. Too late now. She was there and he had seen her for he was waving to her and grinning from ear to ear motioning her to stop at the space in front of him. Why she had agreed to go through with this, she never knew. Her hands felt warm and clammy despite the cold and her tummy was doing somersaults and not in a nice way either. Not like the lovely butterfly feeling she had with Anthony but more like some wet trainers being spun around in a washing machine.

Cecilia plastered a fake smile to her face and gritted her teeth. She could do this.

'Paul?' asked Cecilia, making sure that this was indeed her date whilst clinging on to a small glimmer of hope that she could still escape her situation.

'Yes. Cecilia?' asked Paul looking very pleased with himself as he looked her up and down.

'Umm...n...n...nice to meet you,' she said wishing she'd had the guts to say no instead but unfortunately her conscience was hedging towards the halo end right now.

'It's great to finally see you after the messaging, you look much better in the flesh,' he said still appraising her.

Cecilia didn't know whether this was a compliment or not. Did people really say that these days and to a person. Flesh, she repeated to herself in her head, 'flesh', the word, it just sounded so...oh never mind, it was probably her being too literal.

'Here,' he gestured holding out the flowers. 'These are for you, I thought you'd like them.'

'Ah yes, thank you,' said Cecilia politely then winced as they were practically thrust towards her and her thumb caught on a thorn. Well, that was nice of him, the flowers. I mean, he didn't have to get them. He did seem nice. She must give him a chance.

'Come on in,' he said beckoning her towards the pub. 'They've got a fire going inside, it'll warm you up, you look half frozen. Wine? Beer?'

'Umm...' said Cecilia thinking it was the weekend but drinking at eleven in the morning? 'Maybe a coffee?'

The pub was actually rather nice and cosy once inside. A different assortment of sofas and chairs were grouped around square wooden tables and old jugs hung from the beams. There was indeed a roaring fire that warmed the whole place. Behind the bar an unshaven man with the most beautiful green eyes and black hair that curled around his ears was meticulously polishing the glasses. She wouldn't have minded him being her date. There was just something about Paul that she didn't like immediately and she normally trusted her gut.

'What can I do for you?' the barman asked.

'Can I have a cappuccino?' said Cecilia wondering what Paul was going to have. He was busy studying what Ales were on offer and muttering to himself.

'I'll have the same but I might try one of those ales with lunch though,' he eventually said looking at Cecilia expectantly. 'In case we get hungry?'

Cecilia cringed, she was going to struggle having a coffee with this guy let alone being subjected to a meal too. She felt so uncomfortable right now that she sincerely hoped their conversation would alleviate the dread churning in her stomach.

'So,' he said as he plonked himself down right next to her on the sofa. Bit close, thought Cecilia, thinking he would take the seat opposite her. Not comfortable. Really not comfortable with this. Has he no idea of personal space? She shifted away from him as subtly as possible inching her bum centimetre by centimetre in the opposite direction.

'...as you know I'm thirty-six years old, younger than you, buy hey I love a cougar.'

Cecilia's mouth opened into a big O. Was he serious? That was his leading sentence into a conversation. She was still in shock as he carried on.

'I've just come out of the army, I've saved up and bought myself a two bed house on a nice estate, so you won't have to work. I'll look after you. Maybe get you a better car, that one does seem to be a bit of a rust bucket. I'll give you a make-up and clothes allowance...' he continued, not realising that he had lost Cecilia completely by this stage. Oh God, he's a control freak. This date is over. He hasn't even asked me if I want to be looked after. And he's being rude about my car, which isn't even my car. We've only just met and he's planning our life together. Someone out there might like that but it certainly wasn't for her. I wonder what he'd say if she told him that she already had a mortgage free four bed house and a Range Rover and practically unlimited spending money due to her last husband's savviness. She didn't want to put him down and make any comments to this effect so maybe this was her time to dash to the loo and evaluate the situation.

'Oh, where are you off to?' he asked sadly, suddenly noticing his date was getting up from the table. 'Are you leaving?

Wish I was, thought Cecilia but she just returned another fake smile and said, 'Need to pop to the Ladies.' But while she was saying that she was also wondering if there was in fact a back door where she could make her escape.

Once more she found herself sat on the loo in a little cubicle contemplating her choices. The first one being, just leg it out the front door. The second being, try to find a back door and leg it. The third being...oh great...there was no third choice. Oh yes there was. Get Clarissa to ring her at the table and say there was an emergency at home. That would do it.

'Mum! How's it going? What's he like?'

Cecilia proceeded to recount the details of her little adventure so far.

'Oh mum, you've got to get out of there, he dissed my car for starters. He sounds like a right materialistic knob.'

'Clarissa, language!'

'Sorry but just leave, walk through the pub, out the door and come home.'

'I can't be that mean and walk right past him without a word.'

'But what are you going to say to him? Is there a window in there that you could climb out of?'

Cecilia sighed down the phone to her daughter, 'I am not going to climb out of a window.'

'Go on,' jeered a deep husky voice that came unexpectedly from above her. Cecilia quickly looked up in a fright thinking a man was peering over her stall but it seemed to be coming from the open window above her head. 'Climb out the window, I'll help you down.'

Cecilia stood upon the loo seat and peered outside to see what looked like the resident chef leaning against the wall having a cigarette smiling up at her.

'Having trouble, love?' he asked.

Clarissa's voice was getting more and more exasperated as she could hear what was going on but her mother had gone silent.

'Darling,' said Cecilia to her daughter moments later as she clambered down from the toilet. 'I'll be home soon.' And with that she marched towards Paul in a hurry, and walked past him towards the front door shouting out in a rush, 'I'm terribly sorry but I've got an emergency at home. Must dash. Lovely to meet you. Bye.'

Chapter Twelve

♥

Wednesday 7th January 2015

Another sodding date that she felt as though she couldn't get out of. Her kind, loving and thoughtful albeit obstinate children had cajoled her (or rather worn her down) into a second date despite the disastrous outcome of the last one. And what was worse they even quoted to her what she used to say to them 'If at first you don't succeed, try, try again!'

So here she was sat in a corner booth at ten o'clock on a cold chilly Wednesday morning in a nondescript café of her date's choosing. The man, supposedly a popular artist, was her next date. The photo he'd sent her looked like it had been taken a few decades ago. He had longish dark hair then which fell like curtains on either side of his face. His face looked Italian and was very animated as he flung paint onto a canvas. So why on earth had he chosen here of all places. This place had no soul. Grey and faint blue covered nearly every wall, table, chair and crockery, even the art which looked mass produced had grey and blue paint splashed over it as if someone had knocked over the paint tin by accident. The only decent thing going for the café in her eyes was that there were two front doors opposite each other so at least she could do a runner easily this time.

'Hi Cecilia, is it?' gasped a man as he leant down proffering his hand in her direction. She nodded and then received rather a limp handshake. If she'd squeezed any harder, she was sure his bones would have snapped beneath her grip, he was so fragile.

'I'll just grab my usual, do you want anything else?' he asked breathlessly.

'No thank you,' she uttered while trying to stop herself from getting up and leaving him when his back was turned. The photo was indeed taken a few decades earlier and he must have told her a few white lies with regard to his age too unless he was just extremely unlucky in his genetics or lifestyle. More like forty going on sixty. Okay so he'd lied to get himself a date but maybe his personality would now shine through and they'd have a nice time, she thought hopefully.

When he came back though he didn't sit down. 'Look, I don't mean to be a pain but I usually sit over there,' and pointed to a table in the corner that had a full view of the whole café. Without waiting for her reply he bustled over to his spot and gave daggers to a couple that were nearing it. She heard him say, 'Sorry seat's taken.' Then he proceeded to settle himself on the soft cushioned banquette leaving her the wooden rather uncomfortable looking seat. So, he's chivalrous, not. And he's adaptable, not. Great. This was the time she could have walked out but no her legs betrayed her and she walked in the direction of her date.

'Thank you,' he said as Cecilia finally sat down. 'I'm looking out for my ex.'

'Oh, why are you looking out for your ex?' asked Cecilia.

His eyes kept on darting around the room behind her as he drank his espresso. Cecilia thought that a coffee was probably the last thing he needed right now and it was very disconcerting that he was continuously looking over her shoulder rather than concentrating on her, seeing as though they were on a date.

He gasped suddenly. 'There she is. She's there. Quick, laugh and look as though you're having fun with me,' he said desperately. He let out a loud strangled laugh that quite frankly sounded as if he was having a coronary. It didn't help that he was clutching his arm and going bright red. Was he actually having a heart attack? She literally leapt over the table to come to his aid knocking over her hot coffee everywhere. His strangled shriek then turned into 'Ow, ow what are you doing?' He grabbed some napkins and started mopping up all the while looking over her shoulder. 'All I asked you to do was laugh and smile, not make a move on me!' he said in exasperation.

Cecilia looked at him in bewilderment not believing what she was hearing.

'Well that's not very gracious of you, I come over to help you as it looked like you were having a heart attack, knock over my coffee by accident and you have the cheek to tell ME off!

'She's gone,' replied her date. 'I never had the chance to make her jealous. You,' he said looking at her with wild eyes. 'You ruined it for me.'

'You deceitful, weak minded, manipulative lowlife!' Cecilia couldn't say the exact words that would dignify what she was feeling right now as next to her table two pairs of eyes belonging to what must have been a two and three year old were staring at them. He was just a weak pathetic man who would use another woman unbeknown to them to get at another woman. He was spineless and this was most definitely the last date from snap dot bloody com that she was going on. Her children were going to have to back off or else, she thought determinedly, as she picked up her bag and left the vicinity without another word.

Chapter Thirteen

❤

Thursday 12th February 2015

This is lovely, thought Cecilia as she leant back in her chaise longue in the orangery basking in the heat of the sun that was gracing the Cotswolds. Cecilia loved the sun and the orangery was one of the best investments she had made in the last few years. It was so much better than a conservatory as they stayed warm all year round. Moriarty lay sprawled across the floor tired from a very long walk across the hills that morning while she sat with a cup of tea and the latest book from her favourite author Trisha Ashley...Ah...Heaven.

After the two catastrophic dates, Cecilia put her foot down and informed her children that she was by no means going on any other date ever again. Bertie was now back in London and Clarissa had returned to University leaving Cecilia, for the moment, drama free. It had taken Cecilia some time to get over those experiences and only regretted the fact that she had made such a monumental mistake with Anthony by leaving him there the way she did. She couldn't recall how many times that she had wanted to ask Jasmine to find out his phone number for her from Bea. But what would she say? Jasmine had tried to talk to her about him but she was still mortified.

'Jasmine?' asked Cecilia as she got out of her chair and Moriarty leapt up and started weeing over the floor in excitement. 'Oh for goodness sake, Mori!' Cecilia opened the orangery door to let her dog out into the garden and Jasmine in from out of the cold. 'Have I forgotten lunch together or something?' asked Cecilia blearily coming out of her sunny cocoon.

'No darling. I'm sorry but you didn't hear me at the front door so I popped round the back. There was something I wanted to chat to you about but didn't want to do it over the phone.'

'Oh ok, well, would you like a cup of tea?' asked Cecilia wondering what on earth Jasmine wanted to talk to her about as normally they chatted about anything and everything over the phone. What was so important that she had to do this face to face? She hoped Jasmine wasn't ill, or Richard, or anyone else that she knew because that would involve a face to face.

Jasmine saw Cecilia's face drop and reached out to her quickly. 'It's nothing bad Cissy, come on, sit down, forget the tea.'

Cecilia saw Jasmine draw in a deep breath and there was a moments silence as Jasmine looked as though she was considering how to broach her.

'Jasmine?' asked Cecilia tentatively.

'Right well, you know it's Valentine's day this Saturday?'

'Yeees,' replied Cecilia slowly, thinking oh my god what has Jasmine got up her sleeve.

'I would like you to do one thing for me. Do you remember when I helped you out a while back and you said you owed me one? Well I'm calling in my favour now.'

Cecilia was speechless. What? When did she owe Jasmine one? She couldn't remember. Oh no. What did this mean? It had to be to do with a date otherwise why would she have mentioned Valentine's Day? The problem was that Jasmine had done so much for her, the trip to Barbados alone, so Cecilia was stuck.

'Er...Ok. What do you want me to do?' asked Cecilia.

Jasmine looked really pleased that it looked like she was getting her own way and quickly said, 'There's a speed dating event at The Royal Oak over in Little Brisington on Saturday that I want you to go to.'

Once more, Cecilia was bereft of speech. She had plenty of words going around in her head at twenty knots (some of them too rude to say to Jasmine) but was unable to let any of them loose.

'If you go, I won't utter the word date to you ever again. But I really would like you to do this, for me, please. I have a good feeling about it.'

Cecilia sighed. 'What do I have to do? I've heard the children mention something like it before but....'

'It's ok, just get there for eight pm and they'll explain everything when you get there.'

With that Jasmine got up, 'Right well, I must go.' Jasmine looked at her watch. 'I've got to pick up Richard from a boozy lunch with his golfing pals.'

Cecilia was still pretty much lost for words that she uttered a goodbye and kissed Jasmine on the cheek as she waltzed out the door. 'Oh and don't forget to tell me how it goes. And umm...dress code is black tie! Have fun!'

Chapter Fourteen

♥

Saturday 14th February 2015

'Sorry, lovely,' said a woman with a straight blond bob and deep crimson lipstick as she sidled past Cecilia trying to get to the bar.

Cecilia felt as though she was at a witches' convention. This was supposed to be a speed dating night and there was not one man in sight, well, except for the pair of young strapping lads behind the bar who had very tight t shirts on that showed off their well-defined muscles. Unless, oh dear, she'd got the wrong pub.

Jasmine had given her directions via text and there had been a big sign outside announcing that it was time to find love on Valentine's. Cecilia groaned through a smile on her face as once more, she was totally out of her comfort zone. Cecilia was jostled again as two women, around her age, screamed in delight at finding each other. Although it wasn't exactly hard as the bar space was only a few metres wide and the rest of the room was taken up with two rows of square tables, a chair on either side of them.

'Here have this,' said the woman with the blond bob as she came back from the bar. 'Red wine alright? You look as though you need it? First time? I'm Annie by the way.'

Thank god, someone has saved me, a nice kind face too, Cecilia thought as she gladly accepted the glass. 'Thank you. I'm Cecilia. And yes it's my first time. How about you?'

'Nah, I've done this loads but don't seem to be able to find the right man and keep them too,' she laughed. 'This is my first time here, though, but Sammy, my mate found love here so she suggested I give this one a go. It's smaller than the ones I normally go to. There's just twenty women tonight.'

'Just twenty women?' asked Cecilia counting ten tables. Where were the men?

'Yeah, it's not a long evening.'

'Right, ladies!' shouted one of the lads from behind the bar. 'It's time for the event to start, you will all have been given your number on arrival so please take your seats now. Numbers one to ten find the correct table in this room and numbers eleven to twenty please follow me through into this other room.'

Cecilia looked down at the piece of paper that was crumpled in her hand and that she had barely registered.

'Oh you're eleven, I'm two so I'll see you later. Hope you find your valentine tonight,' said Annie.

'You too,' smiled Cecilia nervously as she began to follow the other women tottering on their high heels along a corridor. She could see that the women had made a big effort in their appearance and were definitely dressed to impress. She just hoped that the men that were there were worth impressing.

Cecilia's table was the first one on the right as you came into the room. On the outside the pub had looked quite small but she realised it was a tardis as off the corridor there was also a skittle alley from behind which she was sure she heard some men laughing. Maybe that's where they were keeping them, out of the way until it was time. A little bit like cattle really. This was a cattle market. Okay, she thought, I can do this. I really can. Fortunately, there was a bottle of red and white wine on the table, so she helped herself. Dutch courage was definitely needed.

She looked around the room whilst she waited and saw some of the women nervously rearranging their dresses or putting some extra lipstick on. Cecilia looked down at her dress then to make sure it hadn't ridden up when she sat down. It was one of her favourite dresses, an off the shoulder black Bardot dress which showed off her curves but not too much flesh. Cecilia cringed inwardly as she remembered her first date. She would never think of the word flesh in quite the same way again. She shuddered and hoped tonight's men would be different but if not, well three minutes was all she had to put up with from each person. She didn't have to run if it wasn't working out. They would just leave under their own steam and move on and she wouldn't have to see them again. Yes, Cecilia thought, maybe this speed dating malarkey wasn't a bad idea after all. Maybe Jasmine was doing her a favour, instead.

'Hi,' said a gentle voice bringing her out of her thoughts. 'Is it ok if I take a pew?'

'Er are you supposed to?' asked Cecilia wondering if he was the first date or just a random person looking to sit down.

'Um, well yes, I'm number eleven like yourself,' he said timidly tucking his mousey brown hair out of his deep blue eyes. His eyes were lovely, thought Cecilia.

'Oh right, nice to meet you. Is this your first time speed dating, it's my first time so am I allowed to ask you your name or do I keep on calling you number eleven?' Cecilia looked down at the sheet that she'd picked up from the table. On it was a grid with numbers one to twenty and beside each number was a comment's box and a mark for her to make out of ten.

'It's up to you, but no, this isn't my first time, I just like to get out to meet women. I love women. They are beautiful and nice to look at,' he said with a huge grin. Cecilia observed he was looking genuine and not remotely sleazy but still felt rather uncomfortable.

'What do you like to do?' he asked.

'Do?' asked Cecilia. 'As in what like?' This was becoming rather hard and not at all easy.

'What do you do in your day, in your life?' he asked with sincerity.

'Umm, well as this is my first time here, why don't you answer your question first?'

'I get up in the morning and I make my mum a cup of tea in bed then I make her breakfast, then I clean the house before work. I work in an electrical shop in town in the fridge department. I help lots of women choose their fridge. And...'

Cecilia switched off after that, she knew it was rude, but this wasn't her ideal man and in one minute's time, yes she did glance at the timer on the wall, he would be gone and she really didn't want to see him ever again. She would just quickly ask him which shop he worked at in case she happened upon him.

'Number eleven?' the man said waving his hand in front of her face.

'Yes?'

'I said what do you do?'

At that moment a bell clanged and his face fell. 'Oh that's a shame, I never got to hear about you, maybe after...?'

'Er no...,' said Cecilia feeling utterly mean at being so abrupt. 'Oh look, here's my next date.' And Cecilia couldn't have been more happy to see a very tall and athletically built man enter the room and look for her table. His white shirt was straining against the muscles and she could see veins pulsing through his arms. He wasn't her normal type but she was happy for number eleven to get up and leave the table.

'Are you alright?' he asked looking at the man who'd just vacated the seat.

'Yes, I'm fine,' she uttered although felt far from fine and took a large gulp of wine.

'Good,' he said. 'Right, I don't want to waste my time or yours so all I want to know is do you eat healthily? The odd glass of red wine can have its benefits but not too much, obviously,' he said eyeing her up.

'Um...well... yes I eat healthy food.'

'Do you eat red meat?' he demanded.

'Yes, yes I do. I do a lovely spaghetti bolognaise and a beef casserole,' replied Cecilia wondering if he couldn't cook or something.

'Oh,' he said and quickly wrote something down on his paper.

'Do you work out?'

'Do I work out what...the weight?' Cecilia was thinking this was another peculiar conversation.

Number twelve relaxed visibly then, 'Oh great you do weights, you'd be able to spot me then.'

'Spot what? You don't have to spot anything when you weigh out ingredients unless you want to spot the bay leaves at the end when you need to take them out,' said Cecilia.

'What are you talking about? I asked you if you work out as in exercise at all?'

'Oh,' said Cecilia. 'Yes I take my dog for a walk every day.'

The man looked at her in disbelief and looked slightly miffed, 'You call that exercise?'

'Well yes I do actually, you can get quite puffed out walking up and down the hills on the walks I go on,' Cecilia replied indignantly having had quite enough of this man belittling her.

The bell rang and not a moment too soon. He leapt up out of the chair as if he'd burnt his bottom. Gone, she thought, she didn't even have to do the running. Excellent. But then she realised that she was only two down and there were another eighteen men to go. God help her. She was going to kill Jasmine for this. Favour or no favour.

'Cecilia? Cecilia, is that you?'

Cecilia's heart almost stopped in shock as she recognised the voice and looked up slowly at her next date number thirteen. And there he was, the man that she hadn't been able to get out of her head the last few months. He was wearing a tuxedo and his reddish brown hair flopped over his mesmerising eyes as they looked out at her. He was smiling. Yes, thought Cecilia, he was smiling at seeing her which meant he was possibly not angry at her.

'Anthony?' Cecilia said softly. Don't muck this up, Cecilia. Don't muck this up, this time.

Anthony sat down and grabbed her hand in his, not giving her a chance to escape.

'I've thought about you non-stop since you left me at that bar. I've wanted to phone you, see you,' said Anthony quickly.

Cecilia gasped not properly hearing everything Anthony was saying as she felt so bad. 'I'm so sorry I left you there. I'm really sorry, I didn't mean to. It's just that once I left, I felt I couldn't see you again. I couldn't find the words to explain. Wait! You wanted to phone me and see me despite what I did to you? Why?'

'Because that time I spent with you was the most fun time I've had with any woman I've ever met. You're easy to talk to and you are the most beautiful woman I've ever met too.'

Cecilia looked at him in disbelief at his words and it took a few moments to register she was the woman he was talking about.

'You're not angry?'

'No. We'd had a few to drink and most relationships can be a bit rocky at the beginning when you don't know each other properly and you don't quite know what to say to each other. It's practically a mine field. But isn't it about not letting things blow out of proportion and trying to get to the other side in one piece and working together, so to speak?'

'Relationship?' asked Cecilia quietly. She was ready now to try a relationship with him, if that's what he was getting at.

'Yes. With me. Do you want to give it a go?' and as he said it he leant closer and kissed her across the table. Oh that kiss, thought Cecilia, yes, she really did want to.

Anthony broke away from her, 'So? Is that a yes?'

'Yes,' said Cecilia grinning from ear to ear as the bell rang for her next date.

Anthony then grabbed her and gave her another kiss.

'Oh great,' said a voice from behind them. 'I've got to sit out now for three minutes. Number thirteen,' he sighed. 'Unlucky for some, lucky for others.'

The End

Opposites Attract

♥

Chapter One

♥

Tuesday 29th December 2015

Millie looked away from the computer screen and rubbed her eyes. She'd been looking at a spreadsheet for so long that the numbers had begun to move around as if doing a funny little jig. While she'd been working away, the light winter drizzle outside had steadily got worse and people were scurrying about going in and out of the shops with their bags and some were dragging their reluctant children with them. The rain now lashed against the windowpanes and where a bit of the gutter had come away a few weeks ago with some snow, water now gushed down making a horrendous noise. The building which housed the local library was an old building and the council was struggling to keep up with the ongoing repairs. So god knows when that was going to be fixed.

The automatic doors opened and a young woman with two excited children entered. Millie smiled at them as they came in dripping wet despite their umbrellas. The children rushed to different parts of the library whilst the mother was left juggling her shopping and the wet coats which her offspring had also shrugged off.

'Here, give me those coats, you're the first ones in this morning. I'll just put them here and I've already put a bucket out for wet umbrellas to go in,' said Millie.

'Oh, thank you Millie,' said the lady. 'Did you have a good Christmas?'

Millie thought back to her rather stark and dull Christmas with her parents. She had no brothers or sisters. Her father liked things in a certain way, at a certain time and, well, even she and her mother had to be a certain way and do things the way he liked it. Her mother did as she was told and so did Millie, as Millie had learnt the hard way that to do otherwise would mean the wrath of her father and that it just wasn't worth the trouble to go against him. She couldn't wait to move out. She was saving up to put down a deposit on a house. Thankfully, it was also her father's wish that she saved up for a deposit too so nearly every penny that she earned was accounted for. She was only allowed to spend a certain amount on presents and on clothes. (Yes, that word 'certain' cropped up a lot when it came to her father). Millie was such a regular customer in the charity shop next door, they knew her so well that quite often they would keep a skirt or jumper aside in her size that they thought she might like.

'Yes, it was lovely. And you?' replied Millie with a smile.

'Oh yes, it was very busy. The children loved it of course. I had my brother down with his children too so it was quite chaotic but they left yesterday so I thought I'd come in and change the books.'

'Right, well I'll let you get on and I'm here if you need me,' said Millie as she went back to looking at the figures on the screen, leaving the mother dithering as she wondered which ends of the library to go to depending on which child was up to more mischief.

The door opened again and in came Mr. and Mrs. Nelson, a lovely elderly couple who had to be in their nineties. They shuffled in out of the rain, supporting each other. Mr. Nelson collapsed an umbrella big enough to shield at least four people from the elements. Neither of them were wet and whilst he deposited the umbrella into the bucket, Mrs. Nelson slowly walked towards Millie.

'Hello dear, are there any computers free at the moment or do we need to book?'

'No, it's ok Mrs. Nelson, you can go right on ahead and take your pick. Not one booking yet today and you're one of the first to come in.'

'Oh, that's wonderful,' said Mrs. Nelson with a beaming smile.

'Good,' said Mr. Nelson as he joined his wife. 'Our son promised to send some photos over of their Christmas in Australia. We do miss them so much since they all left. We don't half miss seeing our grandchildren grow up. Oh well. He keeps on at us about some face thing but we're lucky we can just about send emails. Anyway come on then,' he motioned to his wife, 'let's go.'

And with that Mrs. Nelson put her arm through his and they walked off. Millie sighed. They were such a lovely, kind couple. She would love to meet someone who loved her and cared for her like they obviously did. Her parents weren't the best role models of how a loving relationship should work. Her father controlling, her mother doing his bidding. There was no mutual respect, trust, friendship to speak of. She'd tried to talk to her mother to get her to leave her father and try to find someone nice but all she said was 'where would I go?' and 'who'd have me?' and then she'd look down at her dowdy shapeless clothes that she'd gotten used to hiding behind. Millie however was biding her time. Her clothes showed off a bit more of her curves but anymore and her father would say something so, for the time being, until she could leave, she looked nearly as drab as her mother.

As a teenager, when she'd managed to escape and go to the odd party, her best friend Clarissa, who was luckily the same size as her, lent her some clothes that were more in keeping with a young girl of that time. Millie was sure that if it was allowed her father would have put a chastity belt on her as well. Luckily those went out with the Middle Ages.

Speaking of which, not the chastity belt but her best friend, she was the very next person that came flying, literally into the library as the wind had whipped up Clarissa's umbrella and one of her arms was flailing in the wind trying to grab the end of the umbrella to prevent it from turning inside out. Finally, as the door closed shut, Clarissa harrumphed in disgust as black rivulets of water ran down her face. She hadn't put on a waterproof mascara then.

'Hi Mills, Happy Christmas! Can I nip to the loo? I'm desperate,' asked Clarissa and Millie tossed her the toilet key. 'I'll fill you in after, I've got so much to tell you,' Clarissa said quickly as she disappeared through the nearest door to her right.

Millie laughed inwardly. Clarissa was such a breath of fresh air and they had kept each other sane throughout their childhood. Millie had first clapped eyes on Clarissa aged eleven. They had both started secondary school together and because their surnames were close alphabetically they would usually end up sitting at the same desk in class. Hers being Brown and Clarissa's being Bancroft. Over the years, Clarissa had kept Millie from being dragged down by her father and Millie had grounded Clarissa and given her stability when her father had died in a car crash.

'So,' said Clarissa when she came back now looking more like she'd been dragged through a hedge backwards. She'd obviously, somehow, dried her hair using the hand dryer in the toilet which was no mean feat. Her black mascara was still rather smudged too but she still looked stunning with her sparkly blue eyes and blond hair sticking up everywhere. 'Mum's got engaged!'

'What? Seriously? Oh that's fantastic news. When? How?' asked Millie thinking that it was indeed wonderful that Cecilia, Clarissa's mother had found love once more.

'Anthony was sooooo romantic,' gushed Clarissa. 'You know those Russian dolls where you take the top off one doll and then there's another smaller one inside and then...'

'Yes, the Matryoshka dolls,' interrupted Millie.

'Oh right yes,' laughed Clarissa. 'Trust you to know the proper name for them. Anyway, he gave those dolls as a Christmas present to mum and as she opened up the very last miniature doll, he had put a ring in it. And he got down on one knee and said how much he loved and admired mum and that he wanted to spend the rest of his life with her.'

'What a lovely idea. Anthony's so nice and such a kind man. You're lucky you're going to have such a nice step father too.'

'Well that's not the last of it, they're also going to get married in Easter, in Barbados next year, only four months away! Whoop whoop!' said Clarissa jumping up and down.

'As they met there, they wanted to get married out there and Jasmine and Richard are all on board and even planned it with Anthony before he proposed. Can you believe it?'

'Oh my god, that's so soon and in Barbados, you're so lucky. I would love to go to Barbados and be there with you all. The furthest I've been from England is to northern France when we went to Normandy for our D Day school trip.' When their school friends, twin sisters Kat and Bella used to talk about their holidays at their grandparent's home in Barbados, she was just ever so slightly jealous. And now she was feeling it again. It wasn't about her three friends going to the wedding without her, it was that they were off on an adventure and she was still stuck in her dead end, no fun life.

'Let me ask mum, I'm sure she'll say it's fine. If you pay for your ticket I'm sure we can find a place for you to sleep.'

Millie gasped. 'Oh no I couldn't possibly! I just meant that it would be nice, I wasn't inviting myself.'

'Mills, it's fine,' said Clarissa.

'No really Clarissa, I can't. I wouldn't be able to get the airfare. Can you imagine me going up to my father and saying that I wanted to use up my house deposit to go on holiday? No way,' Millie laughed almost hysterically. 'He'd say I was squandering it needlessly. He'd say, oh I don't want to think what else he'd say.' Millie looked up to see her best friend's sad eyes staring back at her.

'Have you not got any put aside for a rainy day, so to speak?' and gestured outside. 'Millie, you know I've supported you as much as possible but I really do think at your age, you must start to stand up against him. You're twenty-one. You can even drink in America now. You're legal for everything. Not that you need to be twenty-one to drink in Barbados though. But...you just can't let him control your life forever Mills.'

'I know, but I was just waiting till at least I wasn't living with him anymore because if I move out, I can barely afford a bedsit on my wages and then I wouldn't be able to save up either. He's got me by the short and curlies.'

Clarissa laughed loudly and snorted at the same time. 'Amelia Brown, I do believe that is the first time I've heard you say something rude in such a long time.'

'Rude? I wasn't rude.'

'The short and curlies?' whispered Clarissa looking down towards her zipper. 'Pubes?'

'Clarissa. No,' replied Millie feeling a blush coming on and rather glad no-one else was in hearing distance. 'I meant that my dad has me by the scruff of my neck. Short and curlies at the back of the neck?'

'Well, I rather like my interpretation of what you said,' smiled Clarissa. 'But have you got any money that he doesn't know about?'

'Maybe,' said Millie, not really going into it any further because if she revealed how much she had squirreled away, Clarissa wouldn't leave her be and demand she go. Millie just didn't know whether going would be worth the consequences.

'Anyway,' said Clarissa realising she wasn't going to be able to persuade her friend any further on the subject today, she would leave it while the matter was at least still a possibility and then try again another time. 'I really popped in to...'

'...use the toilet,' said Millie smiling.

'No, well yes that too. But no, I wanted to ask you how your Christmas was?'

'Same as usual. But thanks for asking.'

'I told you, you should have come to ours.'

'What and leave my mother with him? It's fine. It's over now. Same old.'

Clarissa looked down at her watch and made a face. 'Right, I've really got to go. I volunteered to run an errand for mum to go to the shops. I probably shouldn't be too long as she was in the middle of cooking. Bertie basically ate some stuff he shouldn't have done so now we haven't got enough of it. With the amount I've got to buy, I think his stomach's a bottomless pit. He's doing some fitness thing to get more muscle or bulk up or something or other. I don't see the point. He gets the girls anyway and he does plenty of exercise.'

Millie had a vision then of Clarissa's brother which she would definitely not be telling her best friend about. Millie was in love with Bertie and had been since forever but he'd never noticed her. And why would he? She was certainly not his type, for one she had brown eyes, brown hair, was medium height and was curvy. He went for the exact opposite in every way. So, Millie just looked from afar. She was the embodiment of unrequited love.

'Mils, I said I've got to go,' said Clarissa waving her hands about to get Millie's attention. 'I'll ring you later.'

'Oh ok,' said Millie as she leant towards her friend for a hug. 'Speak soon.'

Chapter Two

♥

Thursday 31ˢᵗ December 2015

Millie had feigned a headache earlier on in the evening so she didn't have to spend New Year's Eve sitting with her parents, watching something her dad had put on. As usual he would never ask either Millie or her mother whether they wanted to watch it too, he just did as he wanted. Sometimes it was interesting, sometimes it wasn't and tonight all Millie wanted to do was wallow in her thoughts without her dad's disapproving looks. He'd already told her off for wearing her cosy holey tracksuit bottoms that had bleach stains running the length of them and her favourite baggy ripped t-shirt not to mention that she'd tied her hair up with a pencil and half of it was escaping and looking 'ever so scruffy'. What did he expect? He wanted her to save money and not spend too much of it on clothes but then wanted her to be smart and respectable at all times, even at home. Millie thought back to what Clarissa had said to her a couple of days ago and was struggling to let it go. Millie had had enough of him controlling her. It was time to do what she wanted. But what...

Here she was, at home, again (no thanks to the weather which had interfered with her plans, being snowed in would do that and even Clarissa's suggestion of getting Hamish, one of her farmer neighbours to come out in his tractor to get her for the party didn't work as the roads were too treacherous even for a tractor). So, yes, here she was on New Year's Eve trying to come up with some new year's resolutions on how to be a new Millie. A new gutsy Millie who didn't wither when it came to confronting her dad, who didn't resign herself to her pathetic boring life. Ok, so first she needed sustenance.

Minutes earlier, Millie had looked around her drab room with its discoloured wallpaper that was slowly uncurling from the walls, the grey wardrobe that matched the grey chest of drawers that also matched the striped dark and lightish grey curtains that hung like wet lettuce from the poles. Just like her life, it was all very grey save for the multi-coloured blanket that was now wrapped around her, the one her mother had knitted her years ago. The only bit of colour, the bit of rebelliousness? But Millie didn't even really have that any more, the rebelliousness of her teenage years. I need alcohol, she thought. Sustenance. Just a little bit to embolden me, to make plans. Alcohol was also forbidden in the house and yet a medicinal brandy was allowed by her father, but obviously, only he was allowed it. Well not tonight. Millie knew exactly where he kept it so before she could change her mind she crept downstairs to retrieve it from its hiding place.

Millie tiptoed back up the stairs being careful where she trod. The floorboard creaked. Millie winced. Seriously? In all the years that she'd gone up and down these stairs without being noticed, the one time it creaks she's grasping her father's coveted bottle of brandy to her chest? Really?

Her father's booming voice enveloped around her. Millie felt sick. He made her feel sick. 'Amelia? Is that you? What are you doing?' Millie stayed silent hoping he'd go away. 'Amelia? Come here, now.'

'I can't right now, I've got an upset stomach. I just had to get some Pepto Bismol from the kitchen. I'll see you in the morning. Got to go,' squeaked Millie. And with that Millie rushed upstairs into the bathroom, sat down on the toilet, opened up her dad's bottle of brandy and took a huge swig. The alcohol burned her throat as it went down and she held back a choke. Oh how she needed that. So she took another. And another. And another.

'Amelia? Millie?' whispered her mother from the other side of the door some time later. 'Are you ok? It's just that your father sent me up here to see if you were alright? You've been in there an awfully long time.'

Millie quickly hid the bottle behind the shower curtain in the bath and got up, staggering slightly, to open the door to her mother. She couldn't hide from her mum; her mum didn't deserve it. They were a team, the two of them against her dad.

Millie opened the door and pulled her mum into the bathroom shutting the door behind them and turned the water on in the sink till the noise could drown out their whispering.

Millie's mum, Mary, looked in concern at her daughter's weird behaviour. 'What are you doing?'

Millie put her head into her hands then looked up, tears now running down her cheeks. 'I can't do this anymore, mum.'

'What? What can't you do?'

'This, this way of life. Father. You.'

'Me?' said Mary.

'Not you you. Just you and father, being the way you are together and the way he is with me. I would rather sacrifice having my own house and rent than stay here any longer. Come with me, we can do it together.'

'I can't Millie, I'm scared of what your father would do. I couldn't cope on my own either.'

'You wouldn't be on your own. You've got me.'

'Millie we've discussed this. You know it's not just that. I've don't have a job. I haven't worked in years and I don't have any money. And I'd be on my own. Who'd want me? Anyway, I've only ever known being with your father.'

'Alright, mum... Alright. It's ok,' Millie got up and grabbed the bottle from the bath and downed a lot more of the brandy upset that she just wasn't able to change her mother's mind.

'Amelia Brown,' said her mother looking stern but ashen at the same time. 'Please tell me that is not what I think it is?'

'Yes,' said Millie dejectedly. 'Yes, it is. I needed it. I really needed it.'

'How much have you had already?' her mother said trying to look at the bottle just as Millie was struggling to hide it behind her back realising that she might be in a bit of trouble now. 'Half the bottle! Half the bottle? You're drunk and you've drunk your dad's brandy. Really Amelia!'

Millie's mum paced around the bathroom, a thing she did when she was stressed but was finding it hard going as the bathroom was on the small side. There was also the added disadvantage of there being now not only one but two adults in the space and one of which was now swaying precariously on the side of the bath.

'Right. Give me that bottle NOW.'

Millie almost flung the bottle at her mum. She didn't want it any more. It hadn't been a good idea in the first place. One slug of alcohol settled the nerves. Any more and she knew it was downhill from there. You didn't feel any better. You just did things you wouldn't normally do and most of the time regretted it afterwards. This occasion was going to be no different than the others but did she learn? No, obviously not. What had she done?

'I'll put it back before your father finds out. Here, we'll add some water to it so he won't notice it's gone down.' Millie's mum then scurried out the door without looking back.

Moments later, Millie went back to her grey room which had turned into a spinning thingamajig from the fairs and face planted on to her bed just in time to hear Bridget Jones' voice belting out from her little TV in the corner of her room 'All by myself, Don't want to be, all by myself anymore...'. That sounds about right, thought Millie. And I really don't want to be but what am I going to do?

Chapter Three

♥

Friday 1st January 2016

And how did Millie's few minutes start on the first day of the new year? Was she jumping up out of bed and putting on her exercise leggings, her trainers and going for a nice jog around the streets? Was she bounding down the stairs with new found resolve and telling her father what she thought of him? Was she saying yes to the trip to Barbados and going bikini shopping online so that she could finally get Bertie to notice her? Well, that had been the list that she'd scribbled down on the now scrunched up piece of paper that had been collecting her sleep dribble throughout the last couple of hours since. A bleary eyed Millie scrutinised the paper willing it to come into focus so that she could begin those new year's resolutions but to the corner of her eye all she saw was a snail with flashing lights coming out of its backside then more flashing lights as it streamed across her vision.

'What the...?' She'd only had a little bit to drink last night. She'd been a bit tipsy mind or maybe more than tipsy. Things did seem a bit hazy. But still.... She blinked again then scrabbled for her phone as its bleeping noise was coming from somewhere beneath her bed. She lunged, fell off the bed in the process but managed to grab it before the caller rang off.

'..el...o?' she mumbled into the phone.

'Millie? Mils? Are you there?'

Millie lay where she fell not bothering to move, one of her legs half off the bed and still with one eye on the super charged snail that seemed to be zooming around erratically.

'Hi.'

Clarissa then proceeded to rattle off everything Millie had missed the previous night. Millie tried to make the right sounds but for some reason her ears, her mind and her voice couldn't keep up with Clarissa. Millie grunted and said some ohs and oos at what she thought were the appropriate times. Then she heard something about Barbados. Ooo yes, Millie thought. 'Yes. Yes,' Millie muttered out loud imagining herself there right now. Palm trees. White sandy beaches. No parents. A rum punch. Best friend. Oooo best friend's delectably gorgeous hot brother. 'Yes.'

'Brilliant,' Millie heard Clarissa say at the end of the line.

'Rissa?' mumbled Millie again. 'There's some snail streaking around, I can't think. Too much noise...too much movement.'

'Oh you're watching Turbo. Love that film. Is it on tv now? Oh fab. I'll go watch it. Speak to you later. You keep cutting out. I can't hear you very well. I'll call you later with the details. Can't wait. Love you. I'm proud of you. Bye.'

Millie picked herself up off the floor and looked towards the snail.

Chapter Four

♥

Friday 15th January 2016

Many days later after trying to avoid Clarissa from persuading her to go to Barbados, well, two weeks to the day, Millie had finally used up all her excuses. It was time to face her formidable but most caring friend. Millie had had a stomach upset for quite a few days after over indulging on the alcohol but had got no sympathy from her mother this time, which she supposed she understood. Her mum did have to cover up for her. Fortunately, her father had left her alone after hearing her vomit a few times the morning after. Millie had actually felt better after that but wanted to avoid everyone till she had done some more thinking. She had overheard her father muttering at some point about the brandy tasting different than normal but her mum had smoothed the matter over quickly and he soon piped down.

So, the bravado that she had felt before the drinking of the brandy and during the drinking of the brandy soon rapidly deteriorated into nothingness. Not even a whimper of something to build up again. Life would continue as normal until she had enough money saved up to buy her own house, however many years that was away. She had worked it out but it was so depressing selective amnesia had kicked in and all she knew was that at least it was the one thing she and her father agreed upon.

Millie shivered in her barely warm winter coat that had seen the best of its years already but was all she could dare to afford right now. She'd eventually decided upon plan A of saving up to buy her house. All she had to do now was save up as much as possible to bring forward the forgotten date and have the courage to face Clarissa and the inevitable disappointment which was why Millie was now standing outside her friend's house freezing to death. She was about to ring the doorbell again when Cecilia opened the door.

'Millie, Happy New Year!' Cecilia brought her into a hug and ushered her into the warmth of her home. 'Clarissa's popped out I'm afraid but do come in. She should be back soon.'

'And congratulations to you on your engagement. It's...' replied Millie, only to be nearly pushed down as a huge black curly dog leapt up at her trying to lick her face.

'Moriarty, would you get down,' chided Cecilia and pulled him down gently.

'It's fine,' said Millie bending down to give him some attention.

'It's so lovely you decided to be there for our wedding. I wanted you there as you've been a big part of my family for such a long time but didn't think you could make it. Thanks to one of Jasmine's friends in Barbados, all you girls are able to stay in one apartment together.'

Millie kept her face down and carried on cuddling Moriarty, thankful that he was there. When had she agreed to go there? And who was paying for it? How was she going to reply? For once she was stuck for words.

'Mum, wait. I'm back,' shouted out Bertie's voice as Cecilia was closing the front door.

Millie's heart started to pound. Bertie always had this effect on her. His deep voice seemed to reverberate throughout her body setting it on fire. The blushes came then as the fire crept up and up. It didn't help the fact that when she looked up her eyes came level with a pair of muscled and very well sculpted thighs the size of tree trunks. Her eyes wandered up. Look at the face, look at the face, look at the face. Bertie's face glistened with sweat and his breath was coming out fast and heavy. Well looking at his face didn't help in the slightest as she'd already clapped eyes on every inch of him.

'Millie!' Bertie exclaimed. 'Happy New Year! I'd give you a hug but I'm dripping.' Millie gulped and couldn't have cared less what state he was in.

'I was just saying to Millie how wonderful it is that she's coming to my wedding.'

Oh yes, that, thought Millie trying to gather her thoughts together.

'It's going to be brilliant. You girls are luckier than me. I've got a room in a house on my own with a woman who's supposed to be a bit miserable,' said Bertie.

'Bertie, if she's kind enough to let you have a room in her house for free then she can't be that miserable.'

'Maybe I'm supposed to cheer her up.'

'Bertie I hope you're not being obscene,' muttered Cecilia.

'Of course not, I just meant tell a joke or two.'

Millie had managed to shut her goldfish mouth while they were chatting but hadn't managed to tear her eyes away from Bertie and was unfortunately too busy thinking about what Bertie would look like on a beach in Barbados. Or in the sea. Right, be brave, be bold. She knew what she was going to do. Millie stood up with a big smile plastered to her face.

'I can't wait. I'm really looking forward to it. Thank you so much for letting me come. It's going to be amazing.'

Chapter Five

♥

Monday 21st March 2016

Millie had begun her morning the way she normally did, had the same boring conversation at breakfast with her parents (yes, she wasn't allowed to skip breakfast and yes, she had to sit at the table properly, her father's rules) however this morning was totally different from any other morning she'd ever had. She had tried to sit there indifferently even though deep inside she was a bag of emotions and was struggling not to fidget or burst out in hysterical laughter at how her parents were going to react when they found out what she was doing.

Clarissa, meanwhile, had taken great delight in what Millie was doing and had done nothing but support her when she'd wanted to back out or tell her parents what she was up to. In the last couple of months, they'd prepared for the holiday and had fun doing it too. The one thing that had taken most of the time planning was 'Operation get on The Plane' without Millie's parents finding out. They'd ended up agreeing that simplicity was the best as every time they came up with a more adventurous idea, there were just too many holes in it and more things to go wrong.

So here Millie was, sat at the breakfast table being dutiful Millie, obedient Millie almost sweetly sick Millie so as to keep her father at bay and her mother for that matter as their relationship still wasn't great after the brandy episode. She'd already lied about going to work for the day. Task 2 accomplished. Task 1 of get suitcase packed had already been achieved as over the previous weeks, Millie had taken her summer clothes to Clarissa's house on the sly and this morning she had chucked the few remaining things, including makeup and passport into a bag.

Millie glanced at her watch and got up from the table taking her bowl with her to the kitchen. Her legs felt like jelly. Fortunately, her parents made no effort to get up. Her father carried on reading the newspaper and her mother continued to stare out of the window deep in thought. I can do this, Millie thought, I really can. Everyone else goes on holiday, maybe not as extravagant as this one but she'd had years of lost holidays to catch up on. She was so excited about going but it was dampened down by her acute fear of how her father was going to react to her disobeying him. She just had no idea. She had never actually pushed him very far as he was so controlling and had a dreadful temper on him that it genuinely scared her, even at this age. She felt so pathetic to be like this.

A few minutes later, carrying one extra bag than usual Millie walked down the stairs. Her heart was pounding so hard now. Clarissa had just texted her to say she was waiting outside the house. Millie was hoping her mother was no longer staring out the window as this deviated from Millie's normal routine and would undoubtedly raise some suspicion.

'Alright, then,' said Millie loudly as she crossed the hallway. Nearly at the door, just two more steps. 'See you later.'

She opened the door and quickly shut it behind her. Clarissa waved madly at Millie with the biggest grin on her face and beckoned her to get in the car. Millie needed no invitation. She flung her bag in the backseat and just as she was getting into the car, Clarissa couldn't contain herself and shouted out. 'You did, it Millie. We're going to Barbados. We're actually going to Barbados and we're going together. Whoop whoop.'

Millie cringed inwardly and started to panic as just at that moment she saw her father wheeling the bins down the drive. He was looking straight at them, at the car, at Clarissa and at her. Oh no. After all their planning, they'd forgotten about recycling day.

'Amelia, what's going on? Where are you going?' he shouted his face going a beetroot. Steam was almost coming out of his ears he was that enraged. 'Did I hear Barbados? Are you going to Barbados? What is this nonsense! You are going nowhere. You get out of this car now.'

He went up to the passenger side where Millie was sat looking terrified and tapped on the window motioning for her to wind the window down. Millie looked at Clarissa beseechingly not knowing what to do as she was literally rooted to the spot. Much to Millie's dismay, Clarissa had also turned a shade whiter.

'I said get out of the car, NOW, Amelia Brown.'

Be brave, be bold. Be brave, be bold. Millie's mantra kept going around in her mind.

'Clarissa, floor it!' shouted Millie.

'What?'

'Put your foot down, let's go, before I change my mind.'

'But..'

'It's too late, let's just go now, quickly, please.'

With that, Clarissa put the car into gear and sped down the short drive. Millie looked back as they pulled out onto the road to see her father shouting and shaking his fist towards her and her mother, having heard the commotion, was patting him on the shoulder trying to calm him down.

The two girls remained in shocked silence for but a minute as Clarissa drove through the little streets.

'Oh my God!' Millie exclaimed her hand covering her mouth. 'I mean, I did it, we did it. Did you see his face? He properly scared me, I thought he was going to smash your car window in.'

'I know you've told me about him Millie but I seriously didn't know he was that bad. Honestly Millie, it was time you stood up to him. He can't treat you that way.'

Millie's phone rang. It was her father. Well she wasn't going to pick it up yet. He needed some time to calm down a bit and she needed to create some distance between them. She just hoped that he didn't jump in the car and try and follow them. Actually, could he? Would he, more to the point? Millie muted the phone.

'Clarissa, you don't think he would come after us do you?'

'What? And make a scene in front of other people? He can't stop you from going on holiday. You're not a child anymore, Mills.'

'No, you're right. It's just when I'm like this, I don't think straight. What would I do without you?'

'Well, you'll never have to know. Come on, let's put some music on, we don't want him to ruin our adventure together. Back then, when you said, 'floor it,' it felt like we were Thelma and Louise.'

'Who?'

'It's an old film, 1990's I think, with Brad Pitt in. It's about two besties on a road trip who get into a bit of trouble along the way. Bit like us back there with your dad. Right what do you think of this song to start the proceedings?'

Clarissa turned up the volume as Madonna's voice belted out of the car's speakers.

'Holiday Celebrate Holiday Celebrate. If we took a holiday...'

Clarissa then shouted out 'Yeah, we are.'

'I love Madonna,' shouted out Millie, rocking to and fro while her phone continued to vibrate in her lap. Four missed calls so far from her father. She'd ring him later... maybe. 'It's time for the good times, forget about the bad times, oh yeah...'

Many songs later and after a mere fifteen missed calls from her father, the girls were entering the airport car park and that was also when her mother's number flashed up on her mobile. Millie wanted to let her mum know how long she was going to be away and to say sorry but what if it was actually her father at the other end pretending to be her mum. Before she could procrastinate any further she swiped the screen and said a short hello ready to cut the phone call off immediately.

'Amelia?'

Millie breathed a sigh of relief. 'Mum, I'm sorry I didn't tell you. I got invited to Clarissa's mum's wedding and I knew dad would make a scene then I wouldn't end up going.'

'Your father mentioned he thought he heard Clarissa say Barbados. He's beside himself. That's where the wedding is then? Anyway I had to get out and go for a walk to get away from him. There's no going back now Millie. He's so angry.'

'I know, scarily so. Is he being ok with you?'

Silence.

'Mum, are you still there?'

'Yes. How long are you going to be away for?'

'Ten days.'

'Ten days? Alright.'

Millie looked down at her phone as her mother cut her off. No 'have fun'. No 'I love you' or 'stay safe'. Nothing.

'Well?' asked Clarissa looking over at her as she turned off the engine.

'It's fine,' replied Millie brightly. She didn't want her stuff to spoil Clarissa's time. All this was supposed to be a happy occasion. I mean Barbados, of all places.

Millie screamed then, a really high pitched scream and she lurched back into Clarissa as there was a loud tap on the window and the door was wrenched open.

'Whoa whoa whoa. What the...?' cried out Bertie. 'Millie? I didn't mean to scare you? Are you alright?'

'It's ok, she'll be fine. Give her a minute or two. We've had a bit of a showdown with her dad and it wasn't particularly nice. It's just made her bit jumpy that's all. Millie's scared he might show up here so thought it was him then.'

'Oh. Why? What happened? Does he not want you going with us on holiday?'

Seeing Bertie standing there instead of her dad made Millie recover pretty quickly.

'There's a whole host of reasons why he doesn't want me to be on holiday. But I'm here now. And I don't think he will turn up. So come on, let's go. I'm nervous as it is about going in a plane for the first time.'

'I'm sure I can distract you,' said Bertie.

Millie gulped as Clarissa rolled her eyes at her brother in exasperation. I wouldn't mind him holding my hand, she thought, for a long...very long period of time.

As luck would have it, Millie ended up sat in the window seat of the airplane with Clarissa next to her and Bertie sat in the aisle seat. It was so that she could get the views, the girls could chat but more to the point Bertie wanted to be able to stretch his legs out. So no holding hands then. But the views more than made up for it and she actually hadn't been afraid when the plane took off. For one thing, her father was way down below and more so as the houses gradually became smaller and smaller. No more thinking about him. She'd been brave, now it was time to have some fun with her friends and enjoy sun, sea and sand.

Millie then passed out. The tensions of the past weeks had crept up on her and so she slept. She slept throughout the drinks being served, then the food and watched none of the films on offer. Clarissa eventually nudged Millie awake as they were about to make their descent. Barbados was beautiful anyway but the bird's-eye view was breathtaking. Millie was going to capture every moment.

'I forgot to check, there aren't any sharks near the beach are there?' Millie said as she looked down at the coastline.

'Yes, no,' said Bertie and Clarissa in unison.

'Bertie!' warned Clarissa, knowing Millie would probably take Bertie at his word as she seemed to hang on to his every word anyway. 'No, there aren't any sharks and if there are, they are way out at sea.' At Millie's still unbelieving face, she added, 'Ok, fine. I checked, alright? I was worried too. Satisfied?'

'Yes.'

'And I was going to book us all on the party boat called the Wicked Folly when we arrive. I thought you'd love it. They go way out to sea, sailing down the coast and then for fun you can walk the plank,' said Bertie watching the girls for a reaction particularly Clarissa who had unsteady sea legs.

'The what? There's no way I'm going on a boat, let alone walking the plank. Bertie, you're an ass. Stop winding us up. Millie and I are going to be topping up our fake tan on sun loungers and drinking cocktails for the next few days with Kat and Bella. You're the one mum's got to run errands around the island. Ha.'

Bertie's face fell as he'd momentarily forgotten the multiple jobs his mother had loaded upon him.

'Oh wow,' cried out Millie as she stepped down off the airplane. From being in England, then getting used to the air conditioning on the plane, to this, the heat and humidity literally took her breath away. She almost forgot to breathe it was so heavy, it didn't help that there was heat coming off the engines near her and that the tarmac had been soaking up the rays of the sun throughout the day. As it seeped into her bones, she could feel her body begin to relax. A light breeze blew across as she let out a deep breath herself.

'Come on Millie, you're holding everyone up,' said Clarissa.

Millie looked behind her feeling rather embarrassed and mumbled a sorry before she walked down the rest of the steps keeping her eyes glued to the floor in case she got distracted again. As the passengers marched across the runaway, in a hurry to get to passport control, music from a live steel band drifted across welcoming them to the island. Millie had read about steel bands and listened to recordings but to hear them live, was just magical.

'Come on Millie, you'll get to hear them again at some point while we're here. We've got to get going. It'll take us hours to get to our luggage at this rate. We'll be the last in the queue.'

Millie sighed and rushed after Clarissa, Bertie having already gone ahead without them. There was just so many new sights and sounds, and senses.

Millie and Clarissa finally walked out of the terminal lugging their suitcases behind them, to find Bertie parked up in a soft top jeep.

'You took your time,' he laughed. 'And before you saying anything Clarissa, as I'm doing all the errands I've got the car. Mum said that Kat and Bella have also got a car between them so you'll be covered for lifts.'

'Fine, then I'll ride shotgun. Millie are you alright in the back?'

Millie nodded.

'The house I'm staying in is a couple of houses down from Jasmine's on the beach. Your apartment is only about ten minutes' walk from me so you'll be fine even if you find yourselves without a car.'

'Trust you to get yourself accommodation on the beach,' moaned Clarissa.

'You're with your best friends! I'll swop then, go on, but I don't think Millie would want me sharing a room with her, do you?'

I wouldn't mind, thought Millie dreamily.

'Oh I'm sure she wouldn't mind,' said Clarissa, who knew full well that Millie had had a crush on her brother for years but never actually talked about it with her. Millie would be mortified and Clarissa also knew that her brother was afraid of commitment so didn't want to encourage anything that would cause heartbreak for those closest to her. Bertie had never mentioned Millie in any other way than being her friend. Bertie just wasn't interested in her.

Millie looked at Clarissa quickly wondering if she had said it out loud but the siblings had already started squabbling about something else now. She switched her mind away from them and began to take in the views as the jeep made its way onto the main road.

As soon as Millie clapped eyes on the sea, she wanted to go for a swim. It was a gorgeous turquoise and glistened at her invitingly in the foreground of the setting sun.

'Can we go for a quick swim?' asked Millie.

'No,' said Bertie and Clarissa at the same time, at last agreeing on something but it didn't look good for her.

'We've got a full schedule for our first night. Supper first at Jasmine's house with mum and Anthony, then drinks at the twins' favourite bar, then we're going to dance the night away. There's a popular DJ who's in Barbados only for a few days. Kat knows him so she's managed to get us all on the list,' said Bertie swerving as he narrowly missed a goat or two.

Clarissa looked at her anxiously. 'It doesn't give us long to get ready. Tomorrow we'll go for a swim. We can have a day at the beach nursing our hangovers.'

'Ok, tomorrow.'

Forty-five minutes later, Bertie pointed out Jasmine's house and where he was staying. He then turned off to the right and a few roads down turned into a cul de sac.

'This is where I leave you. Madison Heights. I'll see you later. Don't be late.'

In front of Millie stood two white buildings. On each level there was a little veranda from which cascaded beautiful exotic looking plants with huge leaves interspersed with tiny pink flowers.

'Millie, am I going to have to do everything for you. Stop looking and start moving,' said Clarissa dragging the bags out of the boot before Bertie drove off with them.

'Clarissa! Millie!' shouted out a voice from the veranda above them. Bella waved madly at them then disappeared from view shouting out, 'Kat, they're here. I'll come down and let you in.'

Bella flew out of the door and pulled each of them into a huge hug.

'I'm so glad you're both here. Just to warn you, Kat's a bit grouchy at the moment. Her agency found out she was out here for a bit so gave her some work to do, modelling some local's new swim wear range. On the plus side, we got given some fancy bikinis for free. They're lush. Anyway how was the flight? How's things with you Millie?'

'We'll fill you in while we get ready,' said Clarissa. 'Have you started on the cocktails yet?'

'No we thought we'd wait for you, this holiday is going to be such fun,' smiled Bella grabbing Millie's suitcase.

What seemed like hours later to Millie, the four girls emerged from the flat. Millie had got changed in a matter of seconds and slapped on some mascara then proceeded to watch the girls get ready until Bella, who'd finished first, laid her eyes on Millie and gasped. Immediately, she felt rather shy and awkward. She hadn't been out out, like dancing out for ages. It had been pubs mainly. Kat, not having any subtle bone in her body, spoke first.

'Mils, you can't go out wearing that. That's for day time wear. Plus you need Barbados wear.'

Millie was utterly speechless. What was she going on about? She looked down at her pretty, well what she thought was, a pretty, pink polka dot t-shirt dress.

'Kat!' retorted Bella. 'Millie, the thing is, it's kind of a special night tonight so the dress code is Black Tie. You need to wear something a bit more, well...' Bella tried to find the right words without making Millie feel bad.

Millie paled and realised she was out of her depth. Oh, I don't own anything like that, she thought. Clarissa had then finally come out of the bathroom and saved Bella and Millie from any further awkwardness.

'It's ok, I brought some things you can wear Millie. I packed extra just in case. Come on, I've already planned what you're wearing. Sorry, I forgot to tell you. You don't need to worry,' said Clarissa dragging Millie into the bathroom.

So Millie now barely recognised herself. Admittedly, Clarissa had done an amazing job on her. Her brown hair looked elegant and hung in glossy waves about her shoulders framing smokey eyes and bright red lipstick. Gone was the pink t-shirt dress and instead she wore a fitted black dress that showed every curve. Millie felt naked but at the same time she felt free, womanly and fabulous. She was going to rock this look. Kat looked effortlessly gorgeous in a green sequined dress that skimmed her hips down to the floor. Bella was in a similar dress to her but it was red and Clarissa shone in a black sequined string top and a turquoise puff ball skirt, that matched her eyes. Kat, who was wearing flat shoes, and needed no extra height got into the driver's seat of a white mini moke.

Millie looked at the car with no doors to speak of and was wondering how she was going to get in with her dress being so tight.

'Bum in first, then legs follow,' said Clarissa as she smoothly sat down in the back. Millie tottered to the car in the high heeled shoes she'd been encouraged to wear and bent her body and attempted to aim her bottom for the seat only to find herself missing and falling hard on to the metal frame of the car. God, that hurt, thought Millie as she shuffled back onto a soft padded cushion.

'You'll get used to it,' said Kat. 'Right, are we all in? Let's go!'

They'd driven up a sweeping semi-circular drive that was lined with poplar trees from which sparkling lights twinkled. The lawn was neat and the borders bulged with beautiful flowers of pinks and purples. Millie looked in wonder at the grand white single storey villa in front of her. Kat opened the door and an old man with a very straight back walked slowly to greet them carrying a round silver tray of various drinks.

'Miss Katherine, how wonderful to see you again.'

'Bobby!' screeched Bella and hurtled towards him stopping in time to give him a warm embrace before the drinks he was carrying took a tumble.

Bobby smiled. 'Well hello Bella. I'm so glad to see you both, it's been awhile.' His rheumy eyes glanced in the direction of Millie. '

'I'm Amelia. Millie.'

'I'm Bobby. If you need anything while you're here, please ask.'

Millie didn't know whether to curtsey or hug this most kind and humble looking man.

'Bobby first started working for my great grandfather,' explained Bella.

'Yes and he shouldn't be working now. You're here as family tonight,' said Richard, the twin's father who'd appeared from out of the kitchen carrying a plate of cocktail sausages. 'Put those drinks down, there's younger legs here that can carry those.' And he gently took the tray from Bobby and handed it to Kat then handed the hot food to Bella. 'Hi darlings,' he said giving them both a peck. 'You look lovely. Your mother needs a bit of help tonight. And no Bobby, it's not for you to do.' Kat and Bella hurried off into the throng of people out on the terrace.

'Clarissa, Millie, did you have a good flight?'

'Yes thank you Mr Fletcher-Jones,' Millie said feeling quite overwhelmed by the whole situation.

'After all these years, Millie, please, call me Richard, I've told you that before. Come on you look as though you need a drink. I should have let you have one of those drinks before I sent Kat off with them. Rum punch?'

A rum punch was immediately placed in the girls' hands. 'I've already done the honours,' smiled Bobby.

'Bobby makes the best rum punch on the island. Thank you Bobby.' Richard then put his arms around Clarissa and Millie's shoulders and guided them through the alfresco seating area and down the path that was lit up by lots of little tea lights. Clarissa then ran ahead as she'd spotted her mother among the guests. Millie not knowing where else to go followed after Clarissa but at a much slower pace, she was clumsy as it was and didn't want to make a scene by falling.

'Clarissa,' said her mother giving her hug. 'You look beautiful. Bertie mentioned that Millie's dad made a bit of a hoo ha over her coming out here. Is she alright?'

'Don't worry, she'll be fine. But he even gave me a fright. I don't know how she's put up with him. Anyway...shhhh...' said Clarissa as she noticed Millie slowly making her way over towards them. 'Don't say anything about it, we'll just concentrate on having a nice time and looking forward to your wedding. She would be embarrassed if she knew you knew, ok? And you, Bertie. Don't say anything to anyone else. Bertie, are you listening to me?'

Both Cecilia and Clarissa then noticed that Bertie was indeed not listening to a word his sister had been saying as his whole attention was fixed on an ever approaching Millie tottering up the path. Clarissa couldn't believe it, he had not once paid any attention to Millie in all the years they'd been friends and now he was looking at her as if she were the only woman in the universe. She just hoped he didn't act on his impulses then drop her like a ton of bricks as per his past record with women. Clarissa had tried to ask him why he couldn't commit and have a longer relationship than a couple of months. It definitely wasn't his lack of finding a woman as he was like a magnet to the opposite sex. He went for the same type though, every time and they tended to have the same interests or pretend to but they never lasted long. Clarissa didn't know whether to warn him off Millie or encourage him. She should probably stay out of it...but that wasn't in her disposition.

'Close your mouth dear,' spoke Cecilia first out of the corner of her mouth into his ear. 'She is beautiful though isn't she?'

'Mmm....yes, she is....mmm....I...well....she....I've never seen her like....' muttered Bertie going a bright shade of red.

'Hi Cecilia,' said Millie looping her arm through Clarissa's to steady herself. 'This place is so magical. The house, the garden, everything. Thank you again for inviting me here. It really means a lot to me.'

'Oh Millie, I'm so glad you came and you look beautiful tonight, doesn't she, Bertie?' said Cecilia with a rather mischievous grin.

'Yes...er...very...right, well I'd best go and help Richard.' And with that he darted off.

Well, that was weird thought Millie. Bertie was usually really friendly and chatty and he would have made some comment not just stutter. He didn't even look at her.

'Come on, Millie,' said Clarissa. 'I'll show you around. Just over there is a little gate that leads right down onto the beach. We'll probably spend our day there tomorrow with hangovers. Speaking of which, do you want another rum punch or should we try a different cocktail?'

Millie was thinking that perhaps she should have a glass of water as the rum punch had gone straight to her head but after Bertie going off like that, she felt like she needed another drink. He just left, he couldn't even look at her when his mum said she looked beautiful. Millie felt like a fool for holding such a torch for him for so long. He would never think of her the way she wanted him to and he obviously hated the sight of her so much. So enough was enough. No more pining after him. Tonight she would have fun.

'What cocktails are there?' asked Millie.

Clarissa met her question with a grin and then led her back towards the bar.

Millie perched on a bar stool with yet another cocktail of some sort in her hand. She was buzzing and her body felt alive with the music thumping, the crowd dancing, people shouting to each other above the noise all the while various lights either twinkled or flashed depending on where you were looking.

Dinner and drinks at the house had been lovely, and it was a nice start to Cecilia and Anthony's wedding celebrations. She couldn't wait to see what it all looked like in the light of day. Solange, the cook, had promised flying fish sandwiches, which Millie was also excited to try and Bobby had said he would make up a Bloody Mary, his take on it though, whatever that meant but it sounded dangerous. The bar that they went to after had been interesting. It was run by two friends of Kat's who were funny, quirky and a lot of fun so much so that their energy seemed to flow into their bar. It was a simple bar and not much to look at, pretty much a wooden shack on the beach with limited décor but what was there worked. And now they were at an open air nightclub set in a cove down on the beach.

Again when they'd been dropped off by the taxi, the outside hadn't been much to look at, but when you entered you had to wend your way down paths and steps to reach the bottom. The bar and wooden seating area surrounded a dance floor and above which a criss cross of lights hung above them. Wooden bridges and waterfalls among the palm trees and sand made it seem like a scene from Never Never Land. All that was missing were the pirates but instead there were hot steaming bodies gyrating to the fast tempo of the music. Millie loved the freedom in which they all moved. There was no judgement from anyone. Everyone was just enjoying themselves and getting wrapped up in the dance.

Dancing was actually one of Millie's secrets, apart from her infatuation with Bertie, that she had never told anyone about, not even Clarissa. When she'd been little, she'd been sent to ballet class but she was more interested in other types of dancing and of course her father had forbid her to learn those. Through dancing she was able to express herself when she couldn't elsewhere so she had spent many hours in her bedroom on the internet looking at videos and learning different moves then adapting them to suit her mood. She had nothing to lose now, she didn't care what Bertie thought, her father wasn't here and everyone looked so carefree, so buoyed up by drink she made her way to the dance floor without saying a word as to where she was going.

Millie found herself a suitable corner away from the prying eyes of her friends and began to sway and move her body. She lost herself in the music and she soon moved her way into the mass of bodies and Millie danced with both men, women and in groups until a hand lifted her up onto a platform where she danced and danced oblivious to anything but the music.

Bertie had waited ages for the drinks, it was three rows deep at the bar and unfortunately his suave and charm did nothing to get himself to the front any sooner. But while he waited he'd thought of nothing else but the transformation of Millie. She'd literally turned from a caterpillar in a cocoon, hiding from the world, at her parents' house and at work to a butterfly. Bertie's whole body had gone into shock; his heart had pounded so hard through his ribs. He'd literally felt as though he'd been electrified when she'd walked down that path. How had he not properly seen her before? She was indeed beautiful as her mother had pointed out to him but this was Millie that had sent him into this weird never before felt sensation.

Millie had been there hanging around with Clarissa, his little sister. Intelligent, sometimes shy, sometimes outspoken Millie who he'd wanted to protect, he thought, like a big brother. He hadn't really acknowledged her changing into a woman, a beautiful woman at that. Bertie quickly side stepped a man walking on unsteady feet going past him towards the bar.

'Sorry mate,' he laughed and slapped Bertie on the back.

'S'alright,' Bertie answered thankful he hadn't dropped the drinks. He wasn't going back there again in a hurry. He'd even ordered double the drinks to make sure. The girls owed him one.

As Bertie looked around to get his bearings, once again his body seemed to convulse and everything around him went in slow motion for there up on the podium was Millie, a very sexy Millie whirling and twirling around to the music. Bertie hadn't even known Millie could dance. Her curvaceous body moved in a way which made him stir and he couldn't help but look at the neckline of her dress where sweat dripped down to her breasts. How in god's name had he not noticed her? Why had it taken him so long? But most importantly what was he going to do about this new found realisation?

At the table there was only Bella and Clarissa engrossed in a conversation, Kat was nowhere to be seen and Millie was still up there dancing. Once he'd spotted her, it was no good, he was transfixed.

'Bertie! Bertie!' said Clarissa impatiently beside him trying to get his attention. She followed her eyes to what held his gaze then screamed. 'Whoa, Millie! You go girl!

Whoo hoo! Bella, look Millie's up there. Wow, she's amazing. I never knew. Come on Bella, let's go join her.'

The two girls scrambled out of their seats.

'Bertie, stay there and look after the table will you, we'll be back in a bit,' said Clarissa as Bella dragged her through the crowd.

Bertie didn't utter word. His hand searched for a shot and he knocked it back. What was he going to do? Maybe it was just a tonight thing. First day of holidays. Barbados and its magic. The alcohol. Maybe tomorrow in the light of day, Millie wouldn't have this effect on him. But what if it didn't? It was just lust anyway. Lust never lasted. He knew that. Love. Now love was what his parents had. He never wanted to fall in love. And luckily he hadn't...so far. Because to love someone then lose them, he'd seen it, he'd seen it happen to his mum. The devastation and chaos it left behind. He didn't think he was strong enough to go through what his mum had gone through so the easiest thing was to just not feel it. That had actually worked for him until now.

'Oh that was so cool. Millie you are so good at dancing. Can you teach me that step where...?' overheard Bertie as the girls gradually made their way back for refreshments. Millie was grinning and had a lovely glow about her. She looked at him then, rather shyly and her face seemed to redden slightly. Had she seen him stare at her? How embarrassing.

'Bertie, whose are whose?' Clarissa asked pointing to the drinks and wondering again why her brother was being so weird. Was it Millie? Twice now in one night he'd seemed enraptured by her as if she were the only one in the room. Even the girlfriends he'd brought home before, he'd never been so attentive to them and focus solely on them.

Bertie handed a drink to each of them. He avoided each of their gaze and tried to think of something to say but he was still stuck for words so he gave up. He was going to call it a night. He felt a bit sick and it didn't help that the object of his affection was standing so close to him that he could feel the magnetism of her drawing him in. If he didn't leave now, he would do something he would regret.

Chapter Six

Tuesday 22nd March 2016

'It's too bright,' moaned Clarissa lying flat on her back, face directed right towards the source from which her discomfort came from.

'Put your sunglasses on then,' said Kat, who was sitting comfortably under a palm tree in the shade doing a crossword.

'Ughh, I don't want panda eyes again. It took endless amounts of make up to hide them and they took ages to disappear. You're fine, you've already got lovely brown skin. I don't want to be pasty white on the wedding photos. Mum and Anthony will put a framed picture, pride of place, on the mantelpiece and I'll look and see it all the time.'

'I was born with it,' said Kat.

'Well, I wish I had been too.'

Bella ever trying to be the piece maker cut in. 'Clarissa you've got fake tan on...'

'Yes, but with streaks. Somehow I always end up with streaks.'

'And,' said Millie, 'you normally look like a gorgeous English rose.'

'What pink?' said Clarissa with a disgusted look on her face.

'No! When you talk about someone being like an English Rose, it means that they are an attractive girl with a delicate, fair-skinned complexion regarded as typically English,' said Millie.

'There's nothing delicate about Clarissa,' snorted Kat.

'Ha, ha,' said Clarissa as she leant over to Kat and gently punched her arm. 'Millie, how can you manage to speak so eloquently today. The day after drinking you usually can't string two sentences together.'

'I think it was all the dancing and I drank water for the latter part of the night.'

'Did you? I did think you were knocking back the gin and tonics rather quickly. Huh, Bella and I were trying to keep up with you.'

'Yeah, I stopped too,' said Kat glugging some ice cold water from a bottle. 'I've got to appear at an event tonight and tomorrow during the day so didn't want to look puffy.'

Bella groaned in commiseration. 'Yes, and you railroaded me into helping you.'

'Well, you've got the chat Bells. You can schmooze and talk the talk whereas I can't and don't even bother,' replied Kat. 'The least I speak the better quite frankly. You know how I tend to put my foot in it.'

'Yeah, don't we all.'

'Oh right,' said Clarissa sitting up. 'Does that mean you've got the car tomorrow?'

'Yes,' said Kat. 'You and Millie can do what you want.'

'We can't do that much without a car,' moaned Clarissa.

'Take the bus. Work out where you want to go and Bella and I'll help you. We know the routes pretty well.'

'They're fun too. And you get to listen to all sorts of music that the drivers put on,' said Bella.

'I am not taking a bus. I want to be free to come and go where and when I choose. We're only here for a short time. Oh look, perfect timing, there's Bertie. I'll ask him if we can have the car tomorrow or at least for some of it.'

Millie's heart lurched at the mention of Bertie. Trying not to look too obvious, luckily she had some very large dark sunglasses on, Millie glanced to where Clarissa was looking. Then, somehow there came, from the inner recesses of her mind, the Baywatch theme tune thumping out loud and clear while she gazed at an ever approaching Bertie. All he was wearing were some navy blue swimming shorts, his torso muscles rippled as he moved. His biceps bulged and his thighs were firm and tight as his feet pounded into the wet sand at the water's edge. Millie couldn't take in enough of him. He'd obviously been for a swim too because his blond floppy hair was slicked back and glistened in the sun going blonder by the minute. Ok, so pining for Bertie had indeed begun again, and in earnest.

'Bertie!' shouted out Clarissa getting up out of her sun lounger. 'Ow...ow...hot sand, hot sand! Where are my flip flops? Ah, there they are. Bertie!'

Oh great, thought Bertie. Just what he needed as he heard his sister shouting at him and beckoning him over. During his morning exercise, he'd only just managed to convince himself that the changes he felt for Millie was definitely jet lag and alcohol. Well, at least now he could put it to the test. Bertie reduced his pace and jogged over to where the girls were but instead of his heart rate slowing down, it sped up. Millie was wearing a floral bikini top that moulded her breasts perfectly and the matching bottoms showed off her wide curvy hips and thighs. Concentrate on Clarissa. Concentrate on Clarissa he muttered as his nether regions throbbed. This could be embarrassing.

'What's up?' he said.

'Is there any chance Millie and I can have the car tomorrow? Kat and Bella need theirs and we want to go see some sights.'

Bertie looked at Millie without thinking and then regretted it. Millie had got up now and was walking over to him. She was breathtaking. Why had he never noticed her before in that way?

'Hi,' she said smiling at him.

'Hi,' he said shyly. He looked down at the sand then back up to her. Both of them looking awkward in each other's presence for the first time.

'Mmmm...' said Clarissa noticing Bertie and Millie's body language. 'So? Can we?'

'What?'

'Have the car. Tomorrow.'

'Er...' Bertie scratched his head trying to get his thoughts together and remember what things he had left to do for his mum and Jasmine. 'Yes. You can have it for the morning but bring it back by about three.'

'Thanks,' said Clarissa.

'Yes thank you,' said Millie.

'Er...no problem,' replied Bertie still looking unsettled. 'Right well, have a good rest of the day and I'll see you later for dinner with mum and Anthony.'

Millie watched him as he set off again down the beach, her tummy fluttering. He'd looked at her then. He didn't say as much as he normally did but at least he'd paid her some attention.

'What's up with him?' asked Kat. 'Anyone would think, the way he's behaving, that he's got the hots for Millie.'

'Don't know,' muttered Clarissa and plonked herself back down on the sun lounger thinking this wasn't the right time to talk to Millie about Bertie. 'C'mon Millie, let's work out what we want to do tomorrow. Anything you've read up on?'

The hots, thought Millie. Is that what his change in behaviour meant? Really? Me? The hots? Her head began to reel with the thoughts of what this could mean. He fancies me? But I'm nothing like what he goes for. Is Kat sure? Clarissa wasn't sure. So, I'm not sure. Forget it, Kat must be mistaken. She must be.

'I've actually made a list, so pick something that we'd both like. I don't want you to be bored,' said Millie knowing Clarissa's tastes.

Chapter Seven

♥

Wednesday 23rd March 2016

'Wow!' said Millie in awe as they drove in to where Bertie was currently staying. The lawns were neatly manicured and water flowed over a rockery that protruded from a small island on the driveway.

'Not too shabby, is it? I can't believe he was moaning about staying here. Crazy lady or not, he's got it sorted. I mean our apartment is nice, don't get me wrong. But look at this outdoor space and it's right on the beach.'

The front door opened and out came Bertie looking not so happy.

'We're on time,' said Clarissa.

'Yeah, thanks for that.'

'Are you ok?' asked Clarissa.

'Yes. I just want to get out of here before Geraldine comes back, or Gerry as she wants me to call her. She's just a bit full on. She won't leave me alone.'

'Oh,' said Millie. 'Is there anything we can do?'

Bertie looked at Millie as if seeing her for the first time and flushed. 'Umm...no, it's alright. How was your day?

What did you finally decide to do?'

'Well, I decided that I wanted to go and visit this cool cave that Bella had mentioned that we shouldn't miss then I chose to see a botanical garden which was on Millie's huge to do list. I don't do history and she had way too much on there. Sorry Mills. I mean you had at least three plantation houses. Isn't one enough?'

'I just like that kind of thing. I told you it was fine.'

'Quick, give me the keys,' whispered Bertie as the sound of a car was heard slowing down and getting closer. 'She's back.'

'Bertie, is she seriously that bad?' asked Clarissa looking to where a slim woman wearing elegant shoes stepped out of a top of the range BMW convertible. Clarissa didn't know about cars but she knew this one was expensive. Geraldine must have been in her fifties but was trying to look much younger and was as neatly presented as her lawn.

'Bertie!' she cried out with a sickly tone. 'I'm so glad I caught you, I didn't manage to get a few things and thought you wouldn't mind helping me out, you wouldn't would you? It's for my soiree tomorrow night,' she said now putting her arm through Bertie's and looking at him with such adoration that it bordered possessive. She then made a flamboyant gesture of eyeing both Clarissa and Millie up and down and said, 'And who do we have here?'

Bertie took the opportunity to disengage from her clutches and sidled up to sandwich himself between Millie and Clarissa.

'This is Clarissa, my sister.'

Geraldine's features changed to look a little friendlier. 'Nice to meet you, I can see the resemblance now. Ah yes, you're all coming tomorrow night to partake in my wonderful hosting.'

'And this,' said Bertie putting his arm around Millie's shoulder's and pulling her into him, 'is…my girlfriend, Millie.'

'Oh…Right,' Geraldine said through gritted teeth. 'You never told me you had a girlfriend Bertie.'

'It hasn't come up in conversation,' said Bertie giving Millie a squeeze hoping she'd go along with him. Millie was just standing there like a statue with a fixed grin on her face. 'Right, are you two off over to see Kat and Bella? They've come back and are already on the beach, I've just seen them.' Bertie then gave Millie a quick peck on the lips and went towards the car. 'I'll see you later.'

The three women remained there looking at him as he drove off. Geraldine looked affronted and was trying to conceal it. Clarissa's eyebrows were furrowed as she wondered what her brother could have been thinking by using Millie to get out of the situation he was in and Millie stood there, literally looking love struck, with doe eyes and a rather smitten face.

Geraldine pulled herself together and politely offered them a drink.

'No, we're fine but thank you, we'll grab something with Kat and Bella. Come on Mills,' Clarissa said pulling Millie along.

Once they'd covered as much distance as possible so as not to be overheard Clarissa swore.

'What was Bertie thinking? Or maybe he was wasn't,' fumed Clarissa. 'I mean what do you think?' she said turning to Millie. 'Are you alright with my donut of a brother?'

'Umm...' said Millie shyly. 'I...ummm...it's just to get Geraldine off his back. I mean it doesn't mean anything, does it? I don't mind.' Millie didn't quite know what to think. It had happened so quickly. Bertie obviously expected her to be his girlfriend for the rest of the holidays. But he could have just told Geraldine he had a girlfriend back in England, why get her involved? He had been acting weirdly around her recently.

Clarissa meanwhile was wondering whether this was the time to let Millie know that she knew how Millie felt towards Bertie but she hated interfering. She didn't want to ruin her relationship with Millie in case she took it the wrong way. Millie just admitted it was a show but how hard would it be for her to put on a show when her feelings were real. Oh god, this was going to get messy. She just hoped it wouldn't impact on her mum's wedding. If her mum found out the truth of how Bertie had used Millie a whole load of crap was going to hit that fan.

'Ok, well if you're sure. We'll have to have a word with Bertie to see how he wants to play it.'

Chapter Eight

♥

Thursday 24th March 2016

'Mum, where's Bertie?' asked Clarissa as she caught up with her just before she and Anthony went inside Geraldine's house.

'Inside I expect, Geraldine's probably got him doing something or other. I do feel a bit bad. We really should've found him somewhere different to stay, Jasmine's even admitted that Geraldine is more of a mare than we thought. Poor Bertie. And he's so been good with helping us out too. At least most of the wedding preparations have been done now so he can properly relax and enjoy his holiday.'

Millie hopped from one foot to the other nervously beside Clarissa stretching the dress out behind her. She was sure people could see her knickers. Bella had promised her otherwise but she was still uncertain. Again she was dressed in one of Clarissa's numbers, at least this time it covered up more of her flesh. The only problem was it seemed to show more of her shape as the material clung to every inch of her and it had a slit up to the thigh on one side which she was actually grateful for as it made walking so much easier.

Millie was hoping that she'd have had a chance to talk to Bertie before now but he'd obviously been too busy. She wasn't sure exactly how to behave when she saw him. She had had trouble concentrating on her book today at the beach, which was unheard of. Fortunately, Kat's friends had turned up with a couple of jet skis and a speedboat so they'd spent the day falling off an inflatable banana, skis and a woogie board or was it boogie? Millie had lost track of all the activities and the names associated with them after a while but soon declined them when she'd felt she'd drunk her fill of the sea and was starting to feel rather sick. Now her body ached in places that she never knew could and being here was the last thing she felt like doing.

'Are you staying here all night?' said Kat carrying a bottle of champagne in each hand as she passed Clarissa and Millie still hovering in the entrance foyer. 'Bella's on the beach already and bagsied some seats. There are a couple of fire pits down there.'

'Alright, we'll come along with you now. I was keeping an eye out for Bertie as I need a quick chat. But I'll catch him later,' said Clarissa hurrying after Kat. 'You'll be out of Geraldine's way then too and everyone else's for that matter,' she whispered to Millie.

Millie tried not to look like a gold fish as she walked through the house. It was set up in a similar way to Jasmine and Richard's but the décor was eclectic to say the least. It was so busy and over the top with there being a large amount of bold and flashy pieces of art standing literally in your face. It was almost overwhelming. It was like an art museum that hadn't been displayed very well. She wasn't usually this judgemental but having met the owner of the house who was quite rude and arrogant, it was hard not to be. She looked at the hundred or so guests standing in little groups around the garden, drinks in one hand, canapé in the other. Not one sign of Bertie.

At the end of the garden, a wooden gate opened to some steps leading down onto the beach much like at Jasmine's house. A couple of the houses along this stretch were built at the same time a good few years ago by the same builder. They had two bedrooms and came with a large alfresco dining area and garden that stood right on the beach which meant great parties. And that was what was happening right now. Fortunately, some people had brought their own instruments and were doing a fantastic job of drowning out the rather staid music that wafted down from Geraldine's party.

'Ahh, the holiday has begun,' said Kat collapsing on one of the comfy beach chairs. 'I can finally put my feet up and chill. Who's wants some champers?'

'How did you manage to get two bottles?' asked Bella holding out a glass.

'I know some of the guys they've hired in the kitchen. Anyway I'm saving their legs. They don't have to come out here now to top us up.'

'Fair enough,' muttered Bella who didn't want to have a run in with Geraldine. Geraldine was not one to get on the wrong side of. God knows why her parents had asked if Bertie could stay here. Everything must have been booked up or been way too expensive. Well, Cecilia and Anthony hadn't left much time to book everything for a wedding out here and Easter was one of the busiest tourist times in Barbados.

'Mmm...that's good,' said Millie. The alcohol slipped down nicely and took the edge off the evening.

'Yes, not bad,' added Clarissa swaying to the music. 'Thanks Geraldine,' she muttered sarcastically. She hadn't appreciated the way Geraldine had spoken to her yesterday either. God knows how Geraldine had behaved to make Bertie act so desperately. 'Where are you going?' Clarissa asked Millie as she noticed her getting up.

'I need to go to the loo,' said Millie.

'But you're supposed to be keeping out of everyone's way.'

'Why's that?' asked Kat.

'Well, um, she...oh...it doesn't matter,' said Clarissa thinking why should she worry about what everyone was up to. Bertie had got himself into this mess. And Millie didn't seem to care. So, fine. She was staying out it.

'Hey, if you pop into the kitchen and say you're a friend of mine, they might give you another bottle,' said Kat.

'Okay,' replied Millie quickly who was desperate to go to the loo. Luckily it was the same layout as Jasmine's house so at least she knew where she was going.

Millie gingerly walked up the steps, trying not to fall. She was so clumsy, particularly in high heels. Even though she wanted to look around at the guests and the garden, she kept her head down, she didn't want to attract any attention. Millie felt uncomfortable at situations like this when she was out of her element. If the location changed and all these people were in her library, she would be fine but this was so different. There was an elegance, finery and grandeur to the party where the exotic plants added to the ambience. It was another world. Even the bathroom was striking with its gold taps and in place of a normal spout, water cascaded down gently from a wide opening like a miniature waterfall.

She sat down on the loo with relief. A few minutes to herself. Her holiday had been fun so far, the restaurants, the dancing, the sightseeing, the beach, spending time with her friends and she'd barely thought of her parents. Millie had made the decision to come on holiday so she was making sure that they wouldn't ruin it for her.

Bertie had been out of character though. He wasn't his normal self around her. She really needed to talk to him and for once without Clarissa being there. Kat thought he'd got the hots for her, so she was hanging on to that miniscule chance that he might. Her heart fluttered at the thought. Millie had gone along with Bertie, yes she was probably mad, but if they acted as girlfriend and boyfriend it might shift something in them to make them closer. Well, that's what she was hoping. If it didn't work, she had no regrets. She would have tried and then at least she could move on.

'Millie!' cried out Bertie as he hurried towards her.

'Hi,' Millie said almost stuck for words now that it was just the two of them, albeit with a room full of people, but still.

Bertie gently grabbed her arm and guided her towards the corner behind a large wooden totem pole to get some privacy.

'I'm so sorry,' he said. 'I had no idea I was going to say that the other day but she just wouldn't leave me alone. I tried to tell her but she won't take no for an answer. I didn't want to spoil it for mum and Anthony. And she's been family friends of Jasmine's for years, I didn't want to make a scene. A girlfriend in England just wouldn't have been enough to deter her.'

'Um...so...um...' Millie gazed into his beautiful blue eyes. She didn't think she'd been up so close to his face before now. She even noticed a tiny scar cutting down through his eyebrow making him look more rugged. 'You want me to be your girlfriend for the holiday.'

'Yes, if that's okay with you. You don't have to you know. I'd quite understand if you didn't want to. I know I'm asking a lot.'

'So...would that mean deceiving your mum and everyone else too?'

'Oh god, I hadn't thought that far. I just wanted to get her off my back. She's so persistent.'

Millie laughed then, breaking the tension. 'Don't worry, I'll be your knight in shining armour.'

Bertie smiled then in relief, properly looking at her in detail for the first time that evening. She was stunning. There was nothing else to say. She was just stunning. Her eyes, her hair, her face, the little freckles that showered her nose and cheeks, her body. Oh her body. That dress which left little to the imagination. His body answered his thoughts and he had no idea what to do about his body or his thoughts.

Bertie felt someone staring at them. Sixth sense, whatever you call it, but he knew it was Geraldine. Without thinking, he embraced Millie and put his lips to hers. To his amazement, he felt her lean into him and their kiss deepened simultaneously. He couldn't get enough of her soft delicate lips. Their tongues met and if felt so cheesy to think of but it was as if electricity flew between them. He didn't want to stop. They fitted perfectly together. It was the best kiss he'd ever had and he couldn't believe it was with Millie, his sister's best friend who'd he'd known for years. A mousey nerd, well that's how he'd unfairly thought of her. All those women who'd come through his life. Unless the girl was blond and modelesque wafer thin, they didn't figure on his radar. Yet it was Millie now who was turning him inside out and back to front. Kind, safe, lovely, beautiful brown haired voluptuous Millie. With a jolt, he realised how much she actually meant to him, and that he'd been slowly falling in love with her. He couldn't do that. He couldn't bear to go through what his mum had. To love someone so much and then lose them. He wasn't as strong emotionally as his mum. He just wasn't.

Meanwhile Millie, when Bertie grabbed her, had thought be bold, be brave. Give him a kiss as if it could be the last one she would ever get from him. The one and only kiss. She was going to make the most of it and oh my, it was...just...amazing. Her legs went like jelly so she had to lean into him. He didn't seem to mind as he was as reciprocal in their passionate kiss. But then she felt him tense.

Bertie broke away first. Bertie looked flustered and scared. Scared? Why was he feeling that, thought Millie? She looked around, albeit rather dazed. No-one was looking in their direction.

'Don't worry Millie, about being my girlfriend. I mean pretending to be... um... my... err...'

'Girlfriend? Oh ok, if you're sure. I would have done it, if it helped.' Millie was trying not to show any disappointment but she was still feeling the after effects of the kiss throughout her body and quite frankly she wanted more. Maybe he hadn't liked it and felt it was too strange. Whatever the reason, he was still acting strange and she couldn't understand why he looked scared.

'Thanks anyway, um, I'll sort it. I'll see you later.' And with that he darted off. Millie slowly made her way back to the beach.

'Oh,' said Kat as she saw her approaching, 'Didn't you manage to grab another bottle?'

'Um, sorry I forgot to go,' Millie replied still a bit out of it.

'Did you manage to catch up with Bertie?' said Clarissa as Kat and Bella sauntered off in search of more alcohol.

'Mmm...yes, I did.'

'Well, what's happening?'

'Um...oh...well...Bertie said not to worry about being his girlfriend.'

'Oh good, he's come to his senses at last,' muttered Clarissa. 'It was a ridiculous idea in the first place.'

'Mmm...' said Millie dreamily.

Clarissa stared at her wondering if perhaps Millie had drunk too much already. 'C'mon, let's go for a paddle. It will sober you up a bit.'

.

Chapter Nine

♥

Monday 28th March 2016

'Arghhh, I can't believe you've got us here this early,' moaned Clarissa, as she glugged some coffee and shovelled some eggs Benedict into her mouth.

'It's not exactly early, and you're the one that begged to be my bridesmaid. You, Kat and Bella,' said Cecilia.

'I did, I do, it's just...well...'

'You've had a week of doing what you want. So today, I need you for the rehearsals. The wedding is tomorrow and it's the reason we're all here.'

'I know. Sorry.'

Cecilia gently ruffled Clarissa's hair.

'Millie, you're welcome to stay or have you got plans?' asked Cecilia.

'I'm going to visit a plantation house on the other side of the island. Kat has given me the bus routes but if I'm not back by dark, could you send out a search party?' Millie laughed uncertainly. Kat had said it was fine, but she still felt uneasy. What if she got on the wrong bus? Or she forgot to get off at the right place?'

'You don't need to get the bus. I know which plantation house you want to see and it's near where Bertie is going surfing today. He could take you. I'm sure he won't mind. Ah darling, perfect timing...' said Cecilia as Bertie was seen coming in through the front door.

'Oh great, what do you want me to do now?' said Bertie bending down to kiss his mother on the cheek and nodding a quick hello to everybody else sat around the table.

'As you know, the girls are busy with me today and Millie's on her own.'

Bertie felt himself go red at the mention of her name and tried not to look at Millie then. He had avoided her as much as possible since the kiss. He didn't like how she was making him feel.

'She wants to see the plantation house, right by where you're going today, and she was going to take the bus. You wouldn't mind taking her would you? You'd probably find the plantation house interesting and she could have a swim at the beach.'

'The beach is a bit rough for a swim, that's why I'm going surfing,' said Bertie trying to wiggle his way out of spending a day with Millie. That's the last thing he needed.

'Oh right,' said Cecilia in a puzzled voice.

'It's ok,' said Millie quickly. 'I'll be fine.'

Bertie sighed feeling bad that he was making Millie take the bus, and he knew it wouldn't be just one bus she'd have to take but a couple of different ones. He looked petty and his mum knew it. It was unlike him. He'd have to manage his feelings towards Millie and try and push them away.

'No. I'll take you,' said Bertie.

'Thank you,' said Millie who also tried to avoid Bertie's gaze as she didn't want to look at that mouth of his which had given her so much pleasure.

Clarissa meanwhile had been watching Bertie and Millie and wondered what was going on between the two of them. They were both acting strangely and were tip toeing around each other much like walking on hot coals. It was rather uncomfortable to watch and unsettling. Even her mother was looking at them with some degree of interest. Clarissa wondered whether she knew about Millie's feelings too. Well they'd be home soon and everything would go back to normal.

'Are you ready to go now?' asked Bertie, 'Or do you need to get some things from the flat?'

Millie, still a bit lost for words that she was now going to spend a day with Bertie on her own, didn't answer straight away.

'No, she's good to go now,' answered Clarissa for her.

'Ok then, let's go,' said Bertie. Bertie headed out the door, Millie traipsing after him.

They both got in the car in silence.

'Sorry about the other night,' said Bertie at the same time that Millie asked how he'd been.

'Sorry, you go...' they both said, again in unison.

Millie laughed nervously and Bertie laughed with her.

'I hope you really don't mind taking me today, I don't want to put you out,' said Millie quickly before Bertie could say anything. She really didn't want to talk about the other night or the kiss. She wanted to kiss him again so much it hurt but she knew it wouldn't happen. It had obviously been a mistake to him and she didn't want to dwell on it, particularly with him. She had to move on now.

'No, not at all. It's just the beach where I go surfing, the sea is quite rough and I know you're not a strong swimmer. You're not a strong enough swimmer for the swells is what I meant. But you'll probably be fine.'

'I hadn't planned on going swimming today. I've got my book to read. I'll probably do that while you surf.' Millie thought that that was probably going to be the last thing she was going to do when they hit the beach. Watching Bertie surf was going to be one of the top highlights of her holiday.

'Ok,' said Bertie with relief. 'So we'll go see this plantation house, have a bit to eat then go to the beach.'

'You don't have to come in. I'll have a quick look around, grab some leaflets then I'll be out.'

'A quick look around?' asked Bertie. 'You really just said that you wouldn't take long in a history museum? Millie, I think I know you far too well to know that you will want to know about everything in every single detail.'

'Well...maybe not a quick look but just not as long as I'd normally take,' said Millie laughing when she took in Bertie's sceptical face.

They drove through fields and fields of sugar cane until they found the sign pointing them to their destination. Bertie parked the car then started to get out.

'Oh, are you coming in then?' asked Millie.

'Well I might as well, it beats sitting here for goodness knows how long on my own.'

'I'll pay for you then,' said Millie, 'seeing as I'm the one dragging you out here.'

'I'll buy lunch,' said Bertie.

'Deal.'

Two hours later, the two emerged from the basement of the plantation house squinting into the afternoon sun.

Bertie was surprised. What he thought was going to be a very dull morning had been fun. Millie's thirst for knowledge and her excitement was contagious that at times he asked questions before she did. Bertie wasn't usually interested in going to see museums and learning about history, he'd found the trips quite boring at school and the monotone voice of his history teacher hadn't helped. He'd also enjoyed Millie's company, once they'd gotten over the uncomfortable bit at the beginning. Not only did he find her stunning but he found her easy to talk to. He hadn't noticed this before as Clarissa was always around somehow taking the attention away from Millie. But this holiday Millie seemed to have come out of her shell. Bertie groaned as he remembered her kiss and how his body had reacted and how he couldn't seem to stop thinking about it.

'Are you hungry?' asked Millie.

'Yes, I am. Have you had a Bajan roti yet?' asked Bertie.

'A what?'

'Roti. They're delicious. We'll grab a couple and take them to the beach.'

The wind swept Millie's hair into her eyes as she tried to focus on the words in front of her but the scenery was just amazing. It wasn't just the picturesque little cove where the palm trees swayed and the waves crashed and rolled back and forth against the shore, it was the man walking into the sea with his surfboard that was taking her attention. Drips of water ran down his sculpted body which made it glisten in the sunlight. Bertie set her whole body on fire. She'd never spent the whole day with him on her own before and it had set her on edge. Butterflies fluttered in her tummy, her hands were ultra clammy and not just from the heat either. She had enjoyed visiting the plantation house, learning about the history and how sugar was produced but all the time she'd been aware of his presence beside her. And now that he'd stripped down to his shorts, she was feeling exceedingly hot, in both senses of the word, and very bothered. The sea looked very inviting at this moment in time, dangerous or not. Bertie had warned her about this stretch of the sea but a little paddle wouldn't hurt surely, just to cool down a little, and maybe get a closer look. She knew that he wanted nothing to do with her but this was the last time she would get a glimpse of that magnificent naked torso.

The water was a lot colder on this side of the island and it took her breath away at first. However, it wasn't until she was in the water that she realised she needed a pee. Millie looked around, there was not a loo in sight, nor a hut, nor a potential rock to hide behind. As the wave came in, she quickly lay down but as she was concentrating on the task at hand, she failed to notice a second much larger wave coming in right behind it. It crashed over her head, Millie spluttered and tried to stand up but then she felt her body being pushed and shoved and then a force was pulling her out to sea, deeper and deeper till she could no longer stand. Another wave came crashing down on her and she went under. Sand and stones were thrown against her as she tumbled around not knowing which way was up. She was running out of breath now and she was panicking. The waves were relentless and she just couldn't quite push up past them. She took in a mouthful of water as she ran out of air.

Millie rolled to her side and coughed, water splurting out. She felt hands over her, gentle, patting her on the back, the other cradling her head. A pair of worried eyes looked down at her.

'Millie? Millie? I'm here. It's Bertie.'

'Oh my god, I couldn't breathe.'

'What happened? One minute you're reading on the beach and the next minute I just about see your head bobbing up and down and then it was gone. You nearly gave me a heart attack. Seriously, what were you doing? I did warn you.'

'I...um...I went for a paddle and um...' said Millie struggling to talk as her throat felt as though it was lined with shards of glass. 'Water?' she rasped.

Bertie leant over for a bottle of water not wanting to let Millie go. He thought she'd gone. For a moment he'd lost sight of where she was and it seemed like ages until he managed to get to the spot where Millie had gone under. She'd even drifted off a few feet but luckily with the waters being so clear he had spotted her figure way below. Adrenalin had taken over but now he held Millie in his arms tired and shaken. The one thing that he was most scared of happening, of losing the girl he loved, nearly happened. Oh my God. He loved her. He looked at Millie only to find her gazing lovingly right back at him. Bertie knew that Millie had had a school girl crush on him but this was a grown up, very adult and beautiful Millie. The way she was looking at him, he knew she loved him too. His heart pounded with fear and his chest began to tighten. He pushed Millie up into a sitting position then quickly got to his feet.

'Are you feeling alright enough to walk?' he asked looking flustered.

Millie still a bit dazed but wanting to get back mumbled that she was and gingerly began to pack her bag.

Chapter Ten

♥

Tuesday 29th March 2016

'Kat! Bella! Have any of you seen my shoe? I've lost my blasted shoe! Where the hell has it gone? Are you sure you haven't seen it? I swore I put it with the bridesmaid dress. Bella, they did give us two shoes at the store didn't they? They didn't forget to put the other one in?'

Millie sighed and pulled the sheet over her head trying to block out Clarissa's deafening monologue then she felt a rough shake to her shoulder.

'Millie! Millie! Have you seen my shoe?'

'No,' returned Millie not wanting to get up right now. Her body still ached from yesterday and she'd pretty much been in bed since Bertie had dropped her off at the door.

'Millie? Are you ok?' asked Clarissa momentarily forgetting about her lost shoe.

Millie hadn't told the girls what had transpired. When she'd got back she just told them that she thought she'd got a bit too much sun and needed some rest and wouldn't be going out with them that night. They'd had a good moan and then were concerned and eventually left her to it. She still felt in shock. If it wasn't for Bertie, she didn't think she'd still be here now. And on the way back in the car, Bertie did not utter one single word. It was her fault that she hadn't listened to him and her fault that he'd been scared. He was very angry at her. She was really stupid at times, for all the books that she'd read, her basic survival instinct was dreadful.

'I'm fine,' said Millie pushing the bed sheet away from her. 'C'mon, I'll help you find it. Where did you find the other shoe because the other one must be reasonably close by?'

'Ah well, now I come to think of it, I might have tried them on last night. I think I wanted to wear them in a little so I wouldn't get blisters today. Oh…I've just remembered. Well done Millie, you're the best.' Clarissa darted towards the balcony and began looking behind the plant pots. 'Yes, I've found it! Thank god I didn't actually chuck it over the wall.' Clarissa put the shoe on and grimaced. 'These are so uncomfortable. I thought they were only a little bit small when I tried them on in the shop but these are way too small. I'm sure my feet have grown. My feet couldn't possibly have grown.'

'They might have done. Your feet might have swelled in the heat,' said Millie heading for the bathroom.

'Oh great.' Millie heard as she shut the door. Millie sat down on the toilet and put her head in her hands. Thinking of her parents had also brought up the fact that she was going home in two days. It was Cecilia's wedding today then one last day of sun, sea and sand and then the next day she would be returning to her controlling father.

A car horn beeped outside and moments later the four girls breathed a sigh of relief as they sat in a rather comfortable air conditioned limousine.

'Oh, this is lovely. I could stay in here all day. Hopefully, the cold will help make my feet go down before we arrive,' said Clarissa.

'I've found a bottle of champers,' said Kat rooting around in the mini bar.

'We'd better not,' said Bella. 'We should at least arrive sober.'

'I think I'm still drunk from last night,' said Clarissa. 'I think a hair of the dog is in order. One little drink won't hurt. Anyway why do people call it hair of the dog? Millie you must know, you know everything.'

'Not everything but yes I know this one. Hair of the dog is shortened from 'hair of the dog that bit you'.

'What?' asked Kat.

'Way back when, if you were bitten by a rabid dog, they said that the best cure would be placing some of the rabid dog's hair onto the infected area. So it literally means the best cure is to have a bit of what troubles you. If you're hungover from alcohol, then you have a bit more.'

'I don't know whether it's worked for me in the past,' said Bella.

'Nor me,' said Kat. 'But I think it will at least take the stress out of today. I love a wedding but being a bridesmaid is more work than I thought, yesterday was worse than a photoshoot and that's saying something. I didn't realise your mum was so particular about stuff.'

'She is and she isn't. I think she's just nervous about marrying again and it's Anthony's first time so she wants to make it special for him,' said Clarissa.

'It's brilliant that mum managed to book the venue before it became too popular. I love the idea of the large beach hut set just back from the edge of the cliffs. The views are amazing. You haven't seen it yet Millie have you? asked Bella.

'No, I can't wait,' said Millie looking out the window as they drove the same way she and Bertie had gone the day before. The same sugar fields went past, then the car took the left fork instead of the right and the tarmac road soon changed to a much bumpier road where the limo swerved to try and miss the larger potholes.

'Ow!' said Kat. 'I think they might need to mend the road before it gets too popular. We should have brought the jeep.'

'Yes, but then we would have had the hassle of picking it up tomorrow. At least this way, my feet have cooled down enough to bear these shoes and the limo will take us home whenever we want,' said Clarissa draining the remnants of her glass. 'Right, we're here.'

Millie stepped out of the car and looked in awe. The venue was basically a large field that had been recently landscaped. The beach hut seemed to hold the cloakrooms and a put up kitchen. A foot path then led to a round patio which currently had some tables and chairs upon it, these were beautifully decorated with crisp white table cloths and vases full of orange, red and white Lilies. A huge gazebo, from which hung hundreds of fairy lights, covered the patio giving much needed shade. Then from the patio area, another path led towards the cliffs where Millie could see some chairs had been set up in front of an arch laden with Bougainvillea, the same flowers outside the apartment.

'Oh Christ, thank God you're here,' said Bertie rushing out of the hut towards them. 'The wrong ice sculpture has turned up and it's too late to change it.'

'What's come instead?' asked Clarissa.

'Come and see for yourself.'

Kat was the first one to laugh, seeing the funny side of it. 'Well it's not that bad, at least they got the Greek part right. Your mum wanted an ice sculpture of Cupid, didn't she?'

Millie looked in disbelief not daring to put her foot in it. She was already in Bertie's bad books and this was one of the jobs his mother had asked him to do. There, in all its glory was a gladiator, and it was showing off a little too much of his glory to be classed as decent for a wedding.

'Eddie told me about one of these, but I've never seen one. It's called a vodka luge,' said Bella.

'A what?' asked Millie.

'He was doing one of his naked butler events when he first saw it, it's become quite popular. You basically pour the shot into the top, the liquid runs down through the middle of the sculpture and you drink it when it comes out of the...'

'Yes, thanks Bella,' said Bertie. 'I'm sure we've all got the idea.'

'Well we don't actually have to use it like a luge, and we could hide the inappropriate appendage,' suggested Millie thinking that perhaps coming up with a solution would be better than saying nothing at all.

'So not just an ice sculpture then. Cool. Bertie, I think you've outdone yourself. It's brilliant. We'll do what Millie has said and then later on, after a few drinks, we could put it to good use. Mum might think it's fun and Anthony will probably see the funny side of it,' said Clarissa and she found a spare table cloth and tried wrapping it around the bottom. 'Mmm...' she muttered looking at it from all angles. 'It is rather big though.'

While Clarissa and Bella discussed the best way to drape the cloth, Millie's eyes were drawn to the beautiful arch where the ceremony was going to take place. The set up was magical. She never imagined you could get married in such a place. In her head, it was a church wedding, not that that wasn't nice, because it was but it just wasn't her. She wasn't particularly religious like her parents as it had kind of been forced down her at times. Her father was the loving family man in public and a controlling monster behind closed doors. He was a sham. And unfortunately no amount of going to church seemed to have had any effect on his behaviour over the years. If ever she was lucky enough to get married, she wanted it to be outdoors too.

Millie gasped. As she walked up the path in between the rows of chairs she imagined what it would be like until she arrived at the archway. The view was spectacular. The cliffs, beach and palm trees made a magnificent backdrop for the wedding. All thoughts of her parents got pushed aside. The sea breeze pushed her hair out of her face and she shut her eyes and let the sun wash over her. The light cleansing her.

Bertie was tying the last covers on to the chairs, in this wind they would fly right off the side of the cliffs. One of the last jobs on his list, then he could just relax and enjoy the wedding. He couldn't believe he'd mucked up the sculpture. Hopefully nothing else would go wrong. He got up and stretched his back and in doing so he caught sight of Millie under the arch. Her luscious brown hair was coiled up at the back with some strands left loose. Her skin had gone a golden brown in the sun which set off the pale satin dress that draped seductively over her curves to the floor. She looked like a goddess. But then the image came to his mind of her drowning. That was a sign. It was warning him to stay away from someone that could break your heart. And anyway they had nothing in common with each other apart from Clarissa. It just wouldn't work he thought with determination although his heart was telling him otherwise. No, he needed to stay away from her and it will be easy once they go back to England. She was easy to avoid then. Bertie took one more look at Millie then turned and walked away.

The sound of cars drawing up and doors slamming brought Millie out of her reverie. That and also a high shrieked holler of her name being shouted out.

'Millie! Everyone's starting to arrive. Anthony and mum are on their way, separately obviously, but the registrar isn't.'

'What do you mean the registrar isn't? Isn't coming at all or coming late?'

'Don't know at this moment in time. I've just had a phone call, there's been an accident and I can't find Bertie to tell him. The problem is the registrar has another appointment after mum's wedding so if he doesn't make it in time to do this wedding then well I don't know what will happen,' said Clarissa. 'Jasmine and Richard aren't here yet so they can't help and Kat and Bella have gone AWOL. You wouldn't think there were too many places to hide out here, but there you go.'

'What sort of accident is it? What did they say exactly?' asked Millie impatiently.

'Oh I can't remember exactly, but there was a mention of goats and the car going off the road into a ditch. They're trying to get someone to pull the car out, but it could take some time.'

'Clarissa, send the limo to go get him.'

'It's gone.'

'I thought it was supposed to stay here to be used at our convenience?'

'Oh, maybe Kat and Bella took it.'

'Okay well let's get hold of the chauffeur company to ring the chauffeur and find out where he is and whether he can go and pick up the registrar,' said Millie putting an arm around Clarissa. 'It's going to be fine. I'll sort it out while you go and entertain the guests and make sure they've got drinks. If they've got a drink in their hand, they're less likely to watch the time. I'm sure the ceremony will only be a little late.'

Millie found a single chair to the left side of the arch, right at the end and sat down in relief. The wedding ceremony was going ahead only an hour later than planned. She'd found out when tracking the chauffeur down that Kat and Bella had had to disappear off in the limo to do an emergency mission to get champagne. Bertie had been in a flap as something else had gone wrong. Everything had arrived for the cocktail mixture that guests were to have after the wedding had taken place and the wine was cooling in the fridges in the hut ready for the meal but the suppliers had forgotten the champagne to do the toast. In the meantime, Clarissa had taken what Millie had said a little too literally about the guests having a drink beforehand and thought 'a drink' translated to an alcoholic one so the orange juice that was supposed to be offered on arrival had turned into one of Clarissa's favourite drinks, a screwdriver. With Clarissa mixing the drinks, it also meant that quite a few people were already tipsy and unsteady on their feet. She was known to be rather heavy handed.

The first few notes of Ellie Goulding's song 'Love me Like You Do,' drifted across and everyone got up to welcome the bride. Some people needed more help than others to get up. Bella came first down the aisle, then Kat, followed by Clarissa. Their fiery red dresses seemed to come alive in the sunlight and lit up the way for Cecilia. She'd chosen a simple cream halter neck dress for her day but what stood out was the way her eyes sparkled with happiness. Cecilia looked stunning. Millie looked for Bertie then to see how he was faring after the stress but he wasn't looking at his mother, he was looking at her. Millie's stomach seemed to drop. He was gorgeous. Her heart began to hurt at her predicament. They got on with each other, well she thought they did and they had chemistry. The kiss had been amazing. But he kept his distance and yet he didn't, like now, his eyes seemed to bore into the very depths of her soul. Millie could hear the words 'Only you can set my heart on fire on fire...' while she stared back at him then Bertie seemed to snap out of whatever trance he was in and he looked away, embarrassed. Could he like me, thought Millie? Was there still a chance something could happen?

As soon as the formalities were over, the canapés were brought out in earnest but also so were more cocktails.

'Ah bliss,' said Clarissa refilling Millie's cocktail. 'Photos done, we can now relax and enjoy the party.'

'Cheers to that,' said Kat.

'And cheers to your mum and step dad,' said Bella.

'It was a beautiful wedding,' said Millie dreamily.

'Is,' said Kat. 'It's not over yet. Oh wow, that smells delicious. Garlic mushrooms, yum. I hope we're sitting together, I forgot to look. One of my friend's weddings I went to last year, I got put next to the most boring person

I think I've ever come across. He didn't say a word and if he did, it didn't amount to much.'

'Are you sure it wasn't because you might have intimidated him? You do have a habit of doing that. Or maybe he was lost for words cause of your beauty,' teased Bella.

'Yes, we're on the same table,' said Clarissa quickly. 'I'm looking forward to the blackened red snapper. I managed to nab some in the kitchen earlier. Mmm.'

'Clarissa, have you seriously taken off your shoes already?' asked Millie.

'They hurt. Look. Look at my feet. See that,' she said pointing at a bulbous blister right on her heel. 'They'll be hidden when we sit and she won't care once the dancing begins.'

Once some food had been eaten and a few glasses of wine later, Bella, who was sat next to Millie asked, 'Millie, you never told us about your day yesterday, how was it?'

Millie reddened slightly however the girls still noticed despite her golden tan.

'What happened, then? Something did,' said Kat.

Millie looked at Clarissa as she felt bad that she'd put her brother in the situation that she had. It seemed that the girls weren't going to let it go so she proceeded to fill them in with the details.

'God, Millie!' exclaimed Bella with her hand to her mouth. 'Are you alright now? If it hadn't been for Bertie.'

'That must have been such a shock for both of you. I wonder why Bertie never said anything to us. I suppose he hasn't had a chance. Why didn't you tell us, when you got in? We would have stayed with you?'

'I was so tired, I didn't want to spoil your evening,' muttered Millie.

Kat laughed then much to the horror of the girls. 'Sorry, I didn't mean to laugh. I'm sure it was really bad. I'm glad you're alright, but you were in the shallow bit, Millie. No-one gets swept away going for a little paddle. Even you would have been safe, I'm sure.'

'Well, it wasn't just a paddle,' admitted Millie. 'I needed to pee and there was nowhere else to go so I had to go in a bit and well a wave came and...'

'You nearly drowned! You nearly gave me a heart attack because you needed to pee?' shouted Bertie who'd appeared seemingly from nowhere behind Millie.

It was time for Millie to not say a word now.

'Shh, keep it down,' said Clarissa.

'I don't think you know exactly what I went through, otherwise you wouldn't be telling me to keep it down,' whispered Bertie through gritted teeth and turning rather puce. 'She nearly drowned.'

And with those final words he stormed off.

'He'll be alright soon,' said Clarissa. 'Let him calm down and he'll come round. I'll go and see him in a bit and have a word.'

'I'm sorry,' said Millie.

'Don't be sorry, you weren't to know. I've never seen him like this before, well not since...' said Clarissa, '...since dad. I might just go and find him now. I'll be back in a bit.'

Millie watched sadly as Clarissa made her way across the patio to the arch to where Bertie now stood looking out to sea.

'Bertie?' Clarissa tentatively asked. When she noticed a big tear roll down the side of his face, she put an arm around him and laid her head on his shoulder and waited for him to talk.

'It was awful,' said Bertie finally. 'I couldn't control dad dying and that's hurt enough over the years but can you imagine if Millie had died because of me, because I hadn't tried enough? One more person that I would have loved and lost. I couldn't bear it. Seeing mum losing dad, it broke her heart. I don't think I could bear to either.' More tears rolled down his face.

Clarissa was momentarily stuck for words. This was the most Bertie had spoken to her about their Dad's death and his feelings. He was the one who'd been there mainly for their mum as she was still at school. It had all been a bit of a blur. All she'd known was that her mum was functioning to a small amount of normalcy when she came home for weekends and that Bertie had been there holding everything together. What she hadn't realised was what the ramifications had been for Bertie, the reason why he never committed to anyone of his girlfriends, the reason why he chose the wrong ones for him, to avoid losing someone he loved. And it seemed that he'd managed to fall in love in spite of his best intentions to avoid it and he'd nearly lost her.

'You've fallen in love with Millie, haven't you? And you got scared you might lose her?

'Yes.'

'Bertie, what happened to dad was tragic and painful but look at mum now? She's got her second chance at love. She's happy. What's the saying, it's better to have loved and lost than never to have loved at all.'

'I know, I get that but it's so hard. And what if I lost her a different way? She'd get to know me and then wouldn't like me and then she'd dump me?'

'What like you've done with all of your girlfriends? You made them feel the way you're scared of feeling. Anyway

Casanova, I know a couple of them have found love elsewhere and are married with children no thanks to your treatment of them.'

'I'm crap, aren't I?' said Bertie turning to face Clarissa.

'You've just been rather mixed up, rightly so after what we've been through. I certainly can't talk but you need to face your fear. You do know that Millie loves you back, don't you? She has done since we were at school. You could be good together.'

Bertie sighed. 'But we're nothing alike.'

'Opposites attract,' said Clarissa smiling.

'When did you grow up and get to be so wise?'

'I'm going to get back to the table. I'm parched,' said Clarissa and turned to walk down the path then suddenly called out. 'Bertie? I want you to be happy, but don't muck around with Millie's heart, she's got a lot going on too.'

Chapter Eleven

♥

Thursday 31st March 2016

Millie looked out of the airplane window trying to memorise every detail, knowing that this would be the last time she would visit Barbados. It was probably going to be the last holiday ever if her dad had anything to do with it. It had been the best time of her life, apart from the near drowning incident. Millie was glad that she'd been brave and gone through with the holiday. When she'd said goodbye to Cecilia, and they'd hugged, she'd nearly cried. Cecilia looked so radiant and happy with Anthony by her side. In a few days, they were off to St Lucia for their honeymoon, another place Millie would have loved to have seen. Unlike Barbados which was a coral island, St Lucia was a volcanic island with very different landscapes.

'I wish I could have taken more time off. Kat and Bella had the right idea,' moaned Clarissa interrupting Millie's thoughts. 'I've got work tomorrow. Back to London. Why did I choose to work in a restaurant?'

'Because you love food,' said Millie.

'But they have such unsociable hours.'

'Mmm...' said Millie thinking that she didn't mind the thought of going back to work. She loved her job as a librarian. What she was most worried about was the type of reception she was going to receive from her parents. She'd not heard from them since she'd last texted stating the return date. Maybe, just maybe there was an ever so slight chance that they'd had a change of heart, that it wasn't a big deal going on a little holiday and not telling them. Well it wouldn't be long until she found out.

Millie glanced past Clarissa where Bertie sat reading the inflight magazine. Since his outbreak at the wedding, he'd barely spoken to her. He was polite but that easiness that they'd had together was gone. All she had left was a ghost of a kiss that still lingered on her lips when she looked at him. Millie sighed then grabbed some headphones, tuned in to some classical music, shut her eyes and let the music drift over her.

'Alright, then take care both of you,' said Bertie as he was about to get into his car.

'Oi, give us a hug,' said Clarissa and whispered into his ear. Bertie looked briefly over at Millie and nodded.

'Bye,' said Millie brightly trying to cover up the fact that what she needed right now was a hug too. She was wanting this glorious holiday bubble to keep on going. With Bertie gone, and being back in the car, it would truly be the end.

On their return journey, there was no music and not much of any conversation to speak of. Clarissa, who hadn't slept on the plane, was feeling tired and Millie just didn't know what to say. Her stomach was doing somersaults and a sense of dread filled her.

As the car approached Millie's parents' drive, Clarissa checked with Millie for the third time if she was ok, but then Clarissa's face fell and she mouthed an oh my god. Millie looked to see what had made her react that way and stared in disbelief. Millie's clothes were strewn across the entrance. All of Millie's clothes from what she could see. Some of her knickers had even been scattered across the pavement coming to a stop near the public red post box. Millie choked back a sob. Clarissa ramped up on the side of the road, narrowly missing a pair of Millie's work trousers. Millie got out and looked up the drive. The rest of her belongings were spilling out of various bags and boxes. Some of the covers of her treasured books were flapping in the wind.

'What the…?' exclaimed Clarissa. 'Millie?'

Millie ran up the drive, took her key out of her bag and tried the lock. It didn't fit. She looked at the key to see if was broken or bent in some way. Nope. She tried it again. Millie rang the doorbell. No-one came. She went to try and look in at the window but the curtains were closed. They were never closed at this time of day. What was going on? She went back to the door and banged with her fists in desperation till they hurt. She took her phone out to ring her mum's mobile when Clarissa shouted for her.

'Millie, I've found a letter. It's addressed to you. I saw it in one of the bags.'

Millie rushed back down the drive and grabbed the letter ripping it open quickly. Clarissa looked at Millie's face while she read it hoping that there was a good explanation for all this.

'They've chucked me out.'

'What? Why?'

'They no longer trust me and if they can't trust me then they don't want me living in their house.'

'Just like that?'

Millie sank to the floor. 'Yup.'

'This is ridiculous,' shrieked Clarissa. 'They're being ridiculous. Is there any way you can change their minds?'

'They've also said if I don't take my belongings off their drive by nightfall then they are going to dispose of it themselves.'

Clarissa began to pace up and down muttering to herself while a shocked Millie sat on the tarmac drive with her stuff around her. After a few minutes, Clarissa went to her car put the back seats down, pushed the suitcases to the back and began to pile the bags and boxes into the boot.

'Millie, c'mon help me! You can't stay here!'

Millie got to her feet and like a robot did as she was told. It wasn't long until Clarissa's car was packed to the roof. Clarissa guided Millie into the passenger seat, placed a bag in the foot well between her legs and put a box on her lap.

'At least we managed to fit it all in,' said Clarissa.

As they drove off Millie didn't look back, not that she'd have seen much anyway with all her stuff blocking the view. Her hands trembled. If felt like she was in a dream. Clarissa was taking charge for one thing.

'You're going to stay at mum's house for a while. I'll give her a ring and fill her in. She's away for a good few weeks and in the meantime you can look for a little place to rent. Millie, it's what you always wanted but have been too scared to do it. It's not great the way it's come about, but Millie, you're free. It will just take a little bit longer to save up for a house, but you'll get there and in time, I'm sure you and your parents will be fine. You'll see. This is a good thing. It is, it really is,' said Clarissa loudly.

Chapter Twelve

♥

Friday 1ˢᵗ April 2016

Once again Millie was sat staring out the library window watching the rain lash down. April showers in the Cotswolds were beautiful but today it felt depressing. She wasn't supposed to be here but it beat sitting alone and staring at four walls at Clarissa's mum's house. Millie would have gone crazy today if she hadn't come to work and she wasn't looking forward to spending the first night alone in the house either. It all still felt a bit surreal, she'd gone from one good dream into a nightmare from hell.

Millie was now in the spare room of Cecilia's house with all her worldly possessions crammed in. Cecilia had been brilliant and had said she could stay as long as she needed to but Millie wanted to find a little place the sooner the better. Also Millie couldn't have asked for a better friend in Clarissa who'd spent till the early hours of the morning plying her with cups of tea, they both had work the next day, and encouraging Millie in her next steps. Millie left first giving Clarissa a big hug and tried not to cry.

It had been lovely seeing her regulars in the library and they had all remarked on how well she looked and how they'd missed her. Millie was close to locking up and thought that maybe she should have taken up another friend's offer of going out for a drink, it wasn't as if she had to check in with anyone anymore but jet lag was creeping in and her energy was spent after the emotional roller coaster she'd been on. She hadn't bothered trying to get in touch with her parents since they'd made themselves clear so she wasn't going to waste any more time on them. Her mission, and she would have to succeed, was to find a place of her own.

Now that Millie wasn't in walking distance to home, she'd had to borrow Bertie's bike. Clarissa said her brother wouldn't mind but her face read otherwise, however there was no other solution as to Millie's predicament.

. 'He won't be home in ages so he won't know. Seriously, he'll be fine. I'm sure he will.'

But Millie hadn't ridden a bike in ages so her ride to work had been quite precarious. Drivers didn't bother slowing down or drove within an inch of her. Potholes were more like ditches and those hills that she'd previously thought were slight slopes were definitely mountains. How was that? Millie would never look at cyclists puffing along the road the same way ever again. Millie would also need to buy herself a little car, another expense that would dwindle her house savings but needs must. To top it all off it was now raining quite heavily and soon enough, she found out that her waterproof coat was not waterproof.

'Oi, oi,' shouted some lads out the window as they passed her and some wolf whistled out of another.

'C'mon love, don't take up the whole road.'

Millie had only moved slightly into the road to avoid a lake, well not a lake, but a large puddle. She was sweating profusely by now and tried to give them her best scowl but they just jeered one last time then sped off leaving a whole load of smoke in their wake. Millie coughed as pollution hit the back of her throat instead of some much needed oxygen causing her to wobble, the tyre caught in an unseen pothole and she went flying into the hedgerow, brambles and all. She wouldn't cry, she just wouldn't. Instead she screamed at the top of her lungs, 'For F**k's sake!' which was quite unlike her but felt so good at that moment in time.

'Are you alright dear?' said a kind voice, coming up the road behind her, from beneath a huge umbrella.

Millie turned to see who it was glad that they hadn't sounded like one of those yobs earlier but it was worse, far worse. It was her vicar and he'd just heard her swear. The one and only time an expletive had come out of her mouth in public and her vicar, her parent's vicar, to make it worse had witnessed it. Not wanting to get into any kind of conversation, she leapt back on the bike and with breakneck speed hurtled away, adrenalin kicking in. How embarrassing! Thank God she wasn't going to see him in church again.

What seemed like a marathon later, Millie arrived back at her temporary home. She leant the bike in the porch area against the wall. It looked a right mess, strands of grass or rather clumps of grass were stuck in the spokes of the wheels. Mud was splattered over every inch of it. She would deal with it tomorrow, first she needed a shower as she was soaked through and some parts of her body were stinging where the brambles had cut through and she was sure she'd also landed on a very big rock.

Nice, hot warm water pelted down on her, this shower was so much better than she was used to, a proper power shower with different modes of jets. Lush. She didn't want to get out ever. It pounded away her aches and pains over her back and neck. A huge bruise was beginning to appear on her thigh and another on her elbow and other than a few scratches, she wasn't in too bad a shape. She put her face upwards and let the water cascade down the front of her body washing away the rest of the mud off. Through the water gushing, Millie thought she heard a man and a woman's voice. Maybe it was the next door neighbour, she wasn't used to the sounds around the house yet. Oh, the man didn't seem happy and it seemed to be getting louder. Millie quickly jumped out of the shower, put a towel around her and opened the door.

'Ahhhhhh! screamed Millie as Bertie also stood there screaming. She didn't know who had scared who the most.

'What are you doing here?' bellowed Bertie with a very red face. 'I thought the house was being burgled. And my bike, what happened to my bike? And,' he sputtered, 'what are you doing here?'

A rather feminine voice cut in before Millie could say anything. 'Millie, it is you! Oh my god, I haven't seen you in ages? How are you doing? Did you go out to Barbados for the wedding? Bertie was just telling me about it.'

Millie looked at Fiona, but she wasn't the Fiona she remembered. Gone were the thick glasses that had given her her nickname Fiona 'Four eyes'. She looked gorgeous and could see why Bertie was with her. Millie's heart sank. This was definitely worse than spending the weekend alone, she was now stuck with Bertie and her old school friend who was looking very much like a model.

'I almost didn't recognise you, you've changed so much. Um...well, yes I did go...'

Bertie looked at Fiona in disbelief. 'What do you mean by how is she doing? This is my mum's house and she is in it when she's not supposed to be!'

Millie was now starting to shiver in her towel and felt decidedly uncomfortable having to explain herself in front of them. 'Look, I don't mean to be rude but please could you go downstairs and pop the kettle on whilst I go and get changed and then I'll fill you in.' She went to turn to walk down the corridor when she heard a gasp from Bertie.

His face changed from anger to worry within a second. 'Your bruises. Millie, seriously are you alright? Has someone done this to you?'

A mirror in the hallway showed Millie that she hadn't come away totally unscathed as she'd previously thought as there were indeed quite a few swathes of red over her body.

'Really, I'm fine. Well, no I'm not but go on downstairs. Please? I really need a drink and I'm getting cold.'

'I'll get you something stronger,' muttered Bertie as he plodded down the stairs. Fiona followed behind.

So was Fiona, Bertie's girlfriend? Clarissa hadn't mentioned anything, just that she'd seen her at her mum's New Year's Eve party a few years back and that Fiona had looked incredible. And she really did. Oh great. Millie pulled on some random clothes, it really didn't matter what she looked like. She had given up on competing for his affections.

When Millie walked into the kitchen, she only found Fiona standing there awkwardly.

'He's gone to ring Clarissa.'

'Oh right.'

'So, I made you a cup of tea but if you don't want it...'

'No,' said Millie quickly. 'That's lovely, thanks.'

'I've just rung Clarissa,' said Bertie walking through the doorway.

'Yes, Fiona told me.'

Bertie glanced at Fiona then looked embarrassed.

'Look, I'm sorry for shouting at you. It was just rather... well...I did think you were a burglar,' said Bertie not knowing where to place himself and looking rather embarrassed.

'A burglar stopping to take a shower while nicking stuff? asked Millie. 'I mean it is a nice shower but really?'

'Well, at first, at first I thought it was a burglar but then I didn't expect to see you. Anyway, I'm sorry. And umm... well...it's awful what your parent's have done. I couldn't believe it when I heard.'

'Bertie? Let's just cancel our plans. I'll go and see mum and dad, they wanted to have more of a catch up with me. Sorry,' Fiona quickly said to Millie. 'I don't know what's happened but I think I need to leave.

'No, you don't,' said Bertie.

'No, really it's fine,' said Millie. 'Stay, don't go on my behalf. To cut a long story short, my parents don't want me living at home anymore, it was rather a shock, still is with the way they went about it but I'm just staying here for a few weeks while Cecilia's away on her honeymoon. I kind of need to find a place to rent before they get back.'

'Clarissa told me that mum said you could stay as long as you needed to,' said Bertie.

'I really don't want to be hanging around a pair of newlyweds.'

'Fair point,' said Bertie.

'Are you looking for your own place or a house share?' asked Fiona.

'Well, I was thinking of my own place but I could do a house share, depending on who I would be living with.'

'With me?'

'I thought you worked up in London and abroad. When did you move back to this neck of the woods?' asked Bertie.

Not girlfriend then, thought Millie with relief. Maybe friends with benefits? Or just friends? Her gut was telling her to go for it and take up this much needed life line. At school, Fiona had been nice. She still seemed nice.

'My company have opened up an office in the area and I went for the job and got it. I got tired of London life and missed home but couldn't bear to actually live at home and this three bed house came up for rent. I was about to advertise for someone to rent one of the rooms but...'

'I'll take it,' said Millie. 'As long as you're sure.'

'Definitely. The other bedroom is a bit of a box room, and I'm using it as that at the moment until I can get unpacked properly.'

'Oh well, that worked out well,' said Bertie but his face didn't look entirely happy. The two girls didn't hear him as they were now working out details of when Millie could move in and how much the bills were. Bertie had wanted to come home this weekend to sort his head out after the holiday and work out his feelings and being away from friends and distractions was the best. Fiona, had been unexpected, they'd met at the train station again and one thing had led to another. She was easy to be with and didn't seem to expect anything from him, just what he'd needed or so he thought. Then, to be faced with Millie, fresh out of the shower, looking sexy and dishevelled totally threw him so when she started screaming so did he.

What was he going to do now? He hadn't wanted to be left alone with Millie, until he'd sorted his head out but he didn't exactly want to flaunt the fact that he was seeing Fiona on and off knowing how Millie felt towards him. He was such a twat.

'Do you want pizza tonight? Mum's always got some in the freezer,' said Bertie raising his voice to get the girls' attention.

'Yes, I'll stay for pizza but then I'll go back to the house so I can make an early start tomorrow morning. It's a bit of a mess as I've still been commuting up and down from London until the office was fully set up,' said Fiona. 'You can move in tomorrow, if you want, or whenever you're ready. I'll come back with my car and help you.'

'Oh wow,' said Millie thinking how quickly everything had been resolved. Not her relationship with her parents but her accommodation problem at least. Sharing with Fiona meant that her outgoings wouldn't be as much than if she'd had her own place and it would be nice to get reacquainted with Fiona again. 'Fiona, thank you so much. Tomorrow would be brilliant.'

'Please, call me Fee, and you're doing me a favour too.'

That was a close call, thought Bertie as he sifted through the contents of the freezer. He realised he much preferred to be alone in the house with Millie tonight than hurt her feelings by having Fiona share his bed. Fiona had also come to Millie's rescue so he'd inadvertently helped. Pizza, drinks, then bed, alone.

Bertie woke up in the night to Millie crying. He knocked on her door and heard some sniffling and then a 'come in'.

'I'm...I'm sss...sorry. I didn't mmm...mean to wake you,' she cried into a ball of tissue. 'Now I don't have to think about where to live, I sss...started thinking about my parents...well, my mum mainly. I miss her. She won't answer my calls or even text me back.'

Bertie crossed the room, sat down on the bed next to Millie and put his arms around her. He hated seeing Millie so upset and he had no idea how to help her. He felt utterly helpless. Millie turned and clung on to him crying into his shoulder. They held on to each other until her sniffing subsided. Bertie felt awful, all the while she was in misery in his arms, his body betrayed him. All he wanted to do was to kiss Millie and get lost in her again. He wanted all of her. He loved her smell, it was intoxicating. Not the time, Bertie, he thought, not the time. Also Clarissa's warning flitted through his mind. Don't hurt Millie. His body stiffened when she moved. It took all of his will to get up and walk out of her room. It will never be the time.

'Night' said Millie as she laid back down and from exhaustion fell into a deep sleep.

Bertie struggled to get back to sleep then, his thoughts tumbled around and went back and forth.

Light streamed into his room and he woke up with a start momentarily disorientated. It was nearly lunchtime. He hadn't slept that late in ages but he had been up half the night and it had been a busy and stressful couple of weeks. Millie, he thought and leapt out of bed, shoved on some clothes and went in search of her. The door to her room was open. All her stuff had gone. Already? And he hadn't heard a thing. By the kettle lay a note. It basically said thanks for everything and that she'd see him around. Was that it? He'd forgotten to get her new address so he also had no idea where she'd moved to. She was gone. It was what he wanted, wasn't it? Things could go back to normal. He wouldn't get hurt. Millie would go back to being Clarissa's and now Fiona's friend. He had the weekend to himself and he had nothing to mull over anymore. Sorted. Done and dusted said his head but his heart said otherwise.

Chapter Thirteen

♥

Monday 4th April 2016

'Don't forget to bring your book back next time,' said Millie smiling to a young boy who'd just had to pay a fine. It wasn't a lot but his mum had taken it out of his pocket money so he was looking quite disgruntled.

'If you'd tidied up your room, you wouldn't have lost it, would you?' chided the mum. 'Right, let's go and get something for tea. What do you feel like?'

The boy's face lit up immediately at the prospect of food. Millie heard him deliberating as they walked out the door. That was an easy day, thought Millie, and now home to my tea. Home. Home was now a lovely semi-detached house with a little garden in the nearby village to where she worked so she didn't have to get a car yet. No bike was needed either as the bus passed by regularly, speaking of which, maybe she could get the earlier one. Millie was about to do her last round of the library for the day and check to see that everybody had gone when she heard the door open. Oh great, she wasn't going to catch that early bus now.

Millie swung round to see who'd come in. 'Bertie?' she mumbled. He should be at work. Oh he wasn't well. His normally sparkly eyes were dull and he looked haggard. 'Are you alright?'

Bertie strode towards where she stood and stopped in front of her and looked down. Millie looked more beautiful than ever. He couldn't believe that he'd been so stupid, that he'd held back in case he got hurt. He wanted to say he loved her, he wanted to say how much he enjoyed being with her and that when she'd gone, he'd missed her so much so it scared him. Not being able to articulate his words properly, he leant down, took her in his arms and kissed her, hoping that she really did feel the same way that he did.

Millie was so shocked that at first she didn't reciprocate but then she hugged him back and deepened their kiss. There was nothing but him. He tightened his hold on her as if he never wanted to let her go.

'Ahhh, that's lovely,' said a female elderly voice to the right of them. 'Isn't that how you first kissed me when you declared your intentions?'

'Yes, it was,' said a male voice.

Millie quickly broke away from Bertie and tried to pull herself together. She really shouldn't have been doing this here.

'Oh, Mr. and Mrs. Nelson,' said Millie feeling a little relieved as at least they were her regulars. 'I'm sorry.'

'Don't be dear,' said Mrs. Nelson with a smile. 'You just brought back some lovely memories from when we first met.'

'And you do make a lovely couple,' said Mr. Nelson with a twinkle in his eye.

'Are we?' Millie asked a little uncertainly.

'Yes, we are, if that's alright with you?' said Bertie, pleased that he'd finally come to his senses.

'Not a pretend couple, but for real?'

'Yes, for real,' said Bertie then went in for another kiss.

The End

Pink Café

♥

Chapter One

♥

Thursday 31ˢᵗ March 2016

'The locksmith is coming at ten thirty this morning to change the locks. So make sure you're here. I don't want her being able to wheedle her way back in after the way she's treated us. Ungrateful child! She wants to go off and do what she likes without a care in the world? Then she can go off and do it away from us,' shouted Gerard going puce in the face.

Mary's heart was breaking at the thought of how her daughter was going to feel when she returned home later that day. She'd only gone on holiday with her friends. Millie was twenty-one, it was about time she had some freedom and some fun for that matter. But Gerard was being his usual unreasonable self. He didn't like the fact that Millie had spent so much money on the holiday when she was busy saving up for a house and secondly she hadn't told him that she was even going. Mary had been upset initially too at that because Millie hadn't confided in her either when they used to tell each other everything.

Mary had really missed Millie. The last ten days were the longest that she'd not seen her daughter and it had been awful. Gerard had been furious when he'd seen his daughter drive off with her best friend and he said they'd almost ran over his foot. Secretly Mary wished they had but fortunately they hadn't otherwise Mary would've had to wait on him hand and foot, more than she usually did.

At least at the moment, Gerard worked from nine till five in an office half an hour's drive away five days a week. That meant nine peaceful hours in which she didn't have to deal with him. He'd moan about money and how they didn't have enough to spend on extravagances but at the same time she wasn't allowed to bring in any money herself. She was forbidden to get a paid job. Mary knew it was to do with his controlling nature and she hated it but couldn't bring herself to fight him. She didn't want to think about the times when she'd been brave enough to. She hadn't been able to leave the house for a good week until the bruises had died down and she could hide the evidence with make-up. He hadn't done it for a while but he threatened her with it from time to time to keep her in her place.

'Where would you go?' he'd say. 'You're useless. No-one would hire you. You wouldn't cope out there without me. You're a wreck, no-one else would have you.'

And over the years she'd become to believe him. Millie had tried to encourage her to leave him. But where would she go? She was forty-five years old, been out of work for near enough all of them. She had no family to speak of. Both parents having passed on a good few years ago. Actually, speaking of which, it was her father's fault that she was in this predicament in the first place... well partly his.

Mary had been born to two older parents. Her mother had died when she was seven years old so her father, a vicar, had brought her up along with the helping hands of some of the members of his congregation. When Mary was nineteen, he was diagnosed with an aggressive form of pancreatic cancer and wanted to put things in place before he died. One of the things on his list was to get his one and only daughter married off to a financially stable man preferably from his church. It was one less thing for him to worry about. Mary had vehemently disagreed to his idea. There was no-one of a romantic nature in her life at that moment and she wanted to wait until there was. But he was having none of it and, most uncharacteristically, used emotional blackmail until she felt as though she had no choice. It was basically an arranged marriage which seemed barbaric to her considering the times they were in. Her school friend, Elise, had baulked at the idea and tried to dissuade her from going through with her father's plan. But Mary had succumbed to her dying father's wish. In hindsight knowing what she knew now, she'd wished she'd had more of a backbone and thought about herself and her life. Filial duty was a hard thing to step away from.

And so who could be better than currently single thirty-four-year-old Gerard Brown who was part of her father's congregation? He had a secure job and had already bought himself a two bed house. Perfect.

What her father didn't realise was that in front of people Gerard was charming and cuddly and always had a smile on his face but (and Mary would realise this after they'd got married) behind closed doors he was mean, controlling and emotionally and physically abusive. Mary had seen him for years, sitting there on Sundays, giving her sideways looks. He'd made her skin crawl although hadn't been able to put her finger on it. She'd felt physically sick around him and still did twenty-six years later. If only she'd had the strength to stand up to him before Amelia (Millie) had been born. Because after that it had got worse, he also used to threaten that if ever Mary left him, she would never see Millie again. And now it had happened. But this time, she wasn't allowed to see Millie otherwise he'd throw her out on the street too. Mary shuddered.

'Make sure you clear her room out properly. I don't want to see any of her things when I come back from work. I'm going out for dinner tonight with Fred, a work thing so I'll get home late.'

Mary nodded.

'And...' he said straightening up his tie in the mirror, 'you are not to speak to her. Not one word. Don't even show yourself to her when she comes otherwise...'

'I know,' said Mary picking at a hole in her skirt.

'And...'

Mary let out a sigh and her shoulders dropped that much more.

'...here's a letter that I've written to Amelia letting her know the state of affairs. I want you to put it with her belongings. Make sure she sees it. I don't want to see her still here by the time I come home tonight.'

Mary nodded trying to keep her tears in. Just go, she thought, just go to work.

He looked at her. 'Give me a kiss then.'

Mary inwardly grimaced as she went up on tiptoe and gave him barely a peck on his proferred cheek. Thank goodness those days were gone when he used to pucker his hard thin lips for her to kiss.

'Bye,' he said and shut the door.

The locksmith had been and gone, it hadn't taken him long to change the front and back doors, not that Millie even had the back door key but Gerard wasn't taking any chances. Gerard had rung up promptly at twelve, on his lunchtime break, checking it had been done.

'You'll have to let me in when I get home as I don't have the new keys. Make sure you stay up. I don't want to have to bang the door down to get your attention. What would the neighbours think?'

Mary was sorely tempted to not let him in but as he said, the Parkers from next door, who Mary called the nosey Parkers, a very apt name for them, would probably call the police for noise disturbance.

Unfortunately, she'd had to ring in to work to say she couldn't make it. Well, it wasn't work but she liked to think it was. It was the only thing that Gerard let her do. Every day of the week she volunteered from ten till four in a charity shop in a nearby town. It helped to get her out of bed in the mornings and was a light relief from her home life. The ladies were nice too. They didn't know about Gerard. A few of them were friends but not really close ones that she could confide in. Mary was only allowed to do volunteering because it looked good within their church group and Gerard thought it raised his status in their neighbourhood. Little did he know, no-one actually gave a damn. He didn't notice that people gave him a wide berth whenever he approached them after the church service. He was too busy preening to think otherwise.

Mary heard a shout from outside. She was standing in her daughter's now empty bedroom twitching the curtains to try and see what was happening. Mary felt sick to the stomach, she hated seeing Millie's face full of shock. Millie began to run up the drive looking around at all the bags and suitcases full of all her belongings. Mary was more sick at the thought of how weak and pathetic she was. What was she doing to her daughter? Why didn't she stand up to Gerard and stick up for Millie? She knew the answers because she'd thought of nothing less over the last ten days since Millie had left.

Mary held her breath. She could hear Millie ringing on the door bell and banging on the door. Then Mary heard Clarissa shout, she'd found the letter that Gerard had written. Mary breathed again as she heard Millie's voice move further away from the house. She sneaked a look through a miniscule gap in the curtains. Millie had collapsed on the floor. She looked distraught.

'For heaven's sake! Get a grip!' Mary said out loud as if talking to someone that would help her. She was disgusted with herself. She sat down on the floor tugged her knees in to her chest and sobbed. What had her life become? She was weak and didn't deserve to be Millie's mother. Millie would never forgive her for this. She was sure. But what could she do?

Mary stayed in that position until the girls had long gone and night had come. She didn't want to get up. She wasn't hungry, she just wanted to stay in her little girl's bedroom.

The doorbell rang. It was Gerard.

'Good, you're up,' he said as she opened the door. 'I see she's collected her things. That will save us having to take it to the tip. Why's the house in darkness? What have you been doing?'

'I've been upstairs tidying up. I didn't want to waste money on lights that I didn't need.'

Gerard smiled. 'Well, I'm off to bed. Are you coming up?'

'In a little while, I've got a few last jobs to do.'

He clomped up the stairs. Mary was going to wait until he'd fallen asleep and then venture up. She couldn't face him tonight.

Chapter Two

💜

Trinity Sunday 22nd May 2016

Mary looked up at the vicar reading his sermon from the lectern. She'd had enough of church, her faith having disappeared years ago. She'd had enough of the same passages from the bible being read out. She knew them word for word and back to front but none of them seemed to have helped her. Keep the faith. Pray to God, pray to Jesus, pray to the Holy Spirit. She had a lot, an awful lot. But no-one had answered, nothing had changed and no-one had come to help her.

Even this vicar who'd taken over from her dad when he'd died had said he'd be there if ever she needed it. But who was going to believe her? It was her dad who'd chosen Gerard. Gerard sat there now next to her looking as if butter wouldn't melt.

'Oh,' the vicar had said over the years, 'you're so fortunate to have this lovely man by your side.'

Gerard would promptly put his arm around her and give her a squeeze and say, 'No, I'm the lucky one!'

Millie used to laugh at that.

'How can you stand it mum? He's so fake.'

Mary never answered.

Gerard dug his elbows into Mary's ribs. She grimaced.

'Rosemary is trying to get your attention. Go and see what she wants.'

Anything was better than sitting here, she thought and sidled along the row and hurried to where Rosemary was standing looking rather stressed out. Rosemary whispered into her ear.

Mary looked up to the rafters. Thank you for answering my prayers, she thought sarcastically.

Two minutes later, Mary's hand was stuck down a toilet pulling out wads of paper towels that one of the children from Sunday school had had fun doing. She just hoped that there wasn't a present waiting underneath. Mary couldn't see why Rosemary, the current vicar's wife couldn't have stuck her own hand down there and sorted it out. She was sure their hands were no different.

'You know the system, don't you? You used to spend a large amount of time here,' Rosemary had said.

Mary washed her hands thoroughly having pulled the chain. The toilet was now working.

As Mary made her way out, Rosemary pulled her aside.

'I don't suppose you'd mind staying here with me and give me a hand, it's just that Florence usually helps me out and she didn't turn up.'

Helping out with a bunch of three to four year olds was still a better option than going back to Gerard.

'Ok,' Mary said.

She regretted it as soon as she walked into the familiar room. Nothing had changed. There was still the same wood panelling going round the room, the black slate tiled floor and the huge stained glass window depicting St.

Christopher. In the middle of the room, were two hexagon tables and where should have been sat eight children sitting beautifully, was absolute chaos.

'I can't seem to make them listen to me,' said Rosemary.

Mary had to shout so she could be heard above the noise. 'Stop!' she screamed. 'If you don't all sit down, with your mouths closed and your hands on the table where I can see them then I will talk to your parents to make sure you can't watch your favourite TV programs.'

The children looked at her in shock recognising who she was and darted for their chairs.

Once they were all looking at her. Mary gravely nodded at them.

'That's better.' Mary turned to Rosemary. 'What activities have you got for them to do?'

'Well,' said Rosemary staring at the children being so obedient. 'I... um... seeing as though it's Trinity Sunday I thought that maybe...' And she went to the closet and pulled out a small box. In it was some cotton wool, a ball, two metal spoons, a wand, a cardboard tube and an assortment of other random items.'

'I've already spoken to the children about there being three in one. The God, the son and the Spirit so they need to come up with ideas of three different ways of using these different items.'

'Ok,' said Mary, 'why don't you give them an example?'

Rosemary picked up the spoons. 'If you put them together like this, they make a musical instrument. And the second way is...'

'Oooo... I know... I know...' said a little boy with long blond hair putting his hand up in the air waving it about.

'Yes Noah?' said Rosemary.

'You just eat with it.'

'Fantastic,' said Rosemary.

Another little boy with a very short haircut, put his hand up. 'Let me try.'

'Please...' said Mary. The boy looked at her and pulled a face. Mary gave him one of her sternest looks.

'Please,' he said reluctantly.

'Very well, Jacob,' said Rosemary handing him the spoons but not really wanting to let them go.

Jacob made another funny face and two of the girls laughed. Egged on by their laughter, he grabbed both spoons and bashed them on top of their heads. The two girls screamed simultaneously, one of them just sat there with tears running down her face, while the other much taller one leapt up and punched Jacob in the face.

'Ow,' he cried, 'there was no need for that, I was only showing that you could use the spoons to crack eggs. My dad has 'em for breakfast.' He rubbed his cheek and sat down in a sulk. Meanwhile Rosemary managed to calm the two girls down.

'Right, I'll hand these round,' said Rosemary.

Really? Was that completely a wise decision, thought Mary, seeing what just happened?

For a few minutes, the children looked at them and then had a think, then they began to put their thoughts into action.

'Andrew, why are you putting cotton wool in your ears?' asked Rosemary.

'Well my mum puts them in her ears because my dad snores.'

'Oh, right, that's great. What else can you use cotton wool for? Oh no, Matthew, please don't stick that wand up your nose.'

'I've got stuck bogey!'

Rosemary put her head in hands.

'Here use this tissue,' said Mary giving him a tissue. 'Big blow.'

'It's mine,' said a girl with long blond hair.

'It's mine,' said a girl with dark hair.

Both of them were playing tug of war with the cardboard tube.

'I got it first.'

'No, you didn't I did.'

Rosemary rushed over to them. 'Please don't fight. I'll see if I can find another one.'

The girls didn't stop and by the time Rosemary had returned with another one, they'd broken that one and were now both reaching for the one in Rosemary's hand.

'Oh I can't do this!' screamed Rosemary and left the room, slamming the door as she went.

Mary had been enjoying herself watching things unfold but now she was left in charge.

'Right I'm going to count to ten,' she shouted, 'and I want you to put all those things back in the box or...'

The children didn't need to be told their punishment for disobeying.

'Ah how nice. Have you all had a good morning?' said the vicar as he walked into the room seeing the children sat down nicely. 'You may now go out and see your parents.'

The children ran from the room shouting.

'It's so nice to see the children here learning.'

Mary tried to smile but she was sure it looked fake.

'Might I have a word?' he said.

Mary wanted to say no but Gerard would have a go at her later if she didn't.

He extended his hands and clasped hers. 'Now, how are things with you? I haven't managed to talk with you in a while.'

'Everything's fine,' said Mary.

'And Amelia? I haven't seen her here for a few Sundays?'

'She's just busy.'

'Yes, she looked rather busy the last time I saw her as she didn't stop to chat. She was on a bike and fell off it, she seemed to hurt herself but then peddled madly away before I had a chance to see if she was alright.'

Mary's heart sank at the mention of her daughter and the fact that he'd seen her and she hadn't. 'Yes, she's fine,' said Mary wishing she could get away from him.

'Well, if ever you need to have a chat, about anything, my door is always open,' he said sincerely.

'Thank you, that's kind. I'll keep that in mind.'

Chapter Three

♥

Saturday 28th May 2016

'This isn't done enough,' said Gerard lounging in their bed holding out the toast Mary had just made for him. 'I might as well be eating bread.'

Well make it yourself then, thought Mary. She wasn't his blooming slave. He had legs but he chose to use them rather selectively. He was off to meet his friends in an hour to play eighteen holes of golf, so why he couldn't get off his backside and get his own toast?

'I've been working hard all week. And you give me this for breakfast?' he said lifting up a piece of perfectly cooked toast dripping with butter, just how he liked it.

Mary gritted her teeth, took the plate and went back downstairs. Since Millie had left, he'd been taking it out on her and she was near to breaking point. Quite a few times, she'd nearly gone to the doctors for some antidepressants but she'd seen how people had changed once on them and not necessarily better. They were like filtered versions of themselves and she didn't want that. It worked for some but it wasn't for her. She needed all her wits about her because there was still a small ball of hope that kept her going, that at some point things could still change for the better.

She chucked the toast in the bin and begun to make some more.

On the table her phone rung. Please let it be Millie. It wasn't. It was the place where she volunteered at. Maybe they needed her today. She wouldn't actually mind going in, it beat sitting around here for the day cleaning and waiting until his lordship returned with yet more demands on her.

'Hello?'

'Hi, Mary?'

'Yes.'

'It's Doris.'

'Oh hello Doris.'

'Um… I'm afraid I have some bad news. We're going to have to let you go as we no longer need your services.'

Mary's stomach dropped and a huge wave of despair came over her. The volunteer job got her out of the house, meeting people. She had no friends, Gerard had seen to that. And she no longer saw her daughter. Now she had no place to escape to.

'However, if you're willing to travel a bit further, our sister shop over in the nearby town of Over Marton needs someone as it's expanding.'

'Really? said Mary.

'Yes, I'm sorry to muck you around and obviously we'll miss seeing you but they're lovely over in that shop too and would be happy to have you.'

'Oh right, yes. Thank you. Could I pop over there today and have a look?'

'Absolutely. I'll let them know you're coming.'

'Thank you,' said Mary.

'Well we're just sorry that you can't continue here.'

'No it's fine. I haven't been to Over Marton in a long time. It's a bit out of my way but thank you for the thought.'

Well that was unexpected. She still had a volunteer job albeit in a different place.

'Where's my toast?' shouted Gerard from upstairs.

'It's coming,' said Mary. Putting down some more bread in the toaster, the other ones had gone cold while she was on the phone.

Mary parked the car and walked along the path by the river into the town centre. It was beautiful here. Swans swam past and ducks waddled around in the reeds. Children played in the park, some in the playground and some were kicking a ball around. She crossed over a bridge just as a young couple went by rowing a little boat.

The charity shop that she was heading for was situated off the main high street down one of the little side streets. Finding the right street, Mary veered off up a cobbled street, only pedestrians were allowed down this bit. A high wall rose up to the left and on her right were lots of little shops. There was a crystal shop with dream catchers in the window, a little book shop full of second hand books, she'd have a peruse in there later. She almost walked past the charity shop as a huge pink flamingo had caught her eye instead. Or rather two pink flamingos. They were both standing on either side of the front entrance to a café.

People were making the most of the alfresco dining and Mary couldn't help but notice the cake that one of the diners was devouring. The slices were huge and looked delicious. Mary's stomach rumbled. The tables were covered in pink and white checked table cloths and were finished off by a vase of pink carnations and a pink awning protruded from the building. She'd never seen anything quite so garish, but in its own way it seemed to work. She was tempted to go inside and have a look, maybe she'd grab some lunch there in a bit.

Mary opened the door to the charity shop. Above her a bell tinkled. It was dark inside in comparison to the summer sun beaming down outside and so she perched her sunglasses on top of her head.

'Did you see Fiona trying on that top? She looked awful and she still bought it. She could have left it for someone more suitable,' whispered a lady's voice from the back of the shop.

'I know,' said another lady with a more elegant voice. 'Well, I was in here yesterday and somebody brought in some handbags and I wouldn't be seen dead wearing them but 'She' insisted we put them out,' gesturing to the back door.

'Which ones are those then?'

'Here I'll show you.'

It was then that they came upon Mary who was actually standing in front of said handbags.

'Oh, hello,' said the elegant lady. 'We didn't realise anyone was here.'

Yes, thought Mary that's because you were too busy being mean cows. Mary didn't want to work with people who talked about others behind their back and who were so judgemental. She had enough nastiness at home, she didn't need it during the day too. Mary was going to have to find a different place to volunteer at. She'd have to make a list and have a ring round. Fingers crossed she'd find somewhere because this certainly wasn't the place for her. Mary ignored the ladies and walked out the door.

A man rushed out with two plates in one hand filled with quiche and salad and in the other he held a basket full of bread with some butter perched inside. He deposited the plates with a cheery smile, then went to the next table and got their order. He saw Mary standing there looking.

'Hi, we're full outside, but there's one little table inside if you're looking for a bite to eat.'

'Yes, that would be great,' said Mary returning his smile which was very infectious.

Mary followed him into the café and past the flamingos.

'It's over there,' he said pointing to a round table for two in the far back corner. 'Menus are on the table, and the dishes of the day are on the blackboard. I'll be with you shortly.'

He rushed off, supposedly into the kitchen, giving Mary time to look around. If she'd thought outside was garish, it was nothing compared to inside. It was similar to a French bistro she'd once been to with the round tables and checked pink and white table cloths but the décor was, well, pink. One wall was covered with a wall paper that had dark pink little flowers on it. Against one part of it was a pink and baby blue juke box which was now belting out a popular 80's U2 song. There were more pink flamingos stood on pink shelves beside an abundance of green trailing plants. A big looking palm tree stood next to her taking up the corner and looking up she noticed three big baby pink chandeliers decorated in pink crystals. The other large wall had been painted a very dark pink and a huge light pink neon sign had the coffee shop's logo of a cup with two flamingos on it.

The place was heaving and it looked like there was only the man running around madly. He finally came to her table still with a cheery smile. Mary looked up at him and her heart missed a beat. He must have been roughly her age. Hazel eyes looked down at her and he had an infectious grin that Mary couldn't help returning. She hadn't smiled in months and yet this man was having this effect on her.

'Right, what can I get you to drink?' he asked.

'Earl Grey tea please.'

'No problem.' He looked around and nodded in the direction of someone who was trying to get his attention.

'Need a hand?' she asked, not quite believing she was offering.

'For real?' he said. 'It's just I'm looking for someone to help me here. Just put the ad in my window yesterday.'

'I'm free now to give you hand, I'm not sure about all the time. I haven't worked in a café before but...'

'I'm sure you'll be fine. Thank you. If you can do a bit of washing up and take food out to the customers and take away their plates once they've finished that would be a huge help. I'll pay you,' he added quickly.

Mary gulped. Pay me? Gerard wouldn't have to know. It was just for today.

'Ok,' she said getting up.

'I'll get you an apron and show you the table numbers, I've put up a diagram in the kitchen that you can look at if you forget. Sorry, I completely forgot to ask, what's your name? I'm Jim.'

'I'm Mary.'

'Nice to meet you and thank you so much for helping me out.'

Mary had waited so much on Gerard, and he was difficult, that serving to the diners' proved to be no problem. The lunchtime madness flew by as she ran around picking up plates and glasses, wiping tables, delivering the delicious food served by Jim. Not one customer complained about his food. And the clientele that came in varied from young teenagers to families to elderly people. Some people, who must have been regulars, commented on her being new and smiled at her. It was much more fun than standing around in a shop and she was going to be paid.

At two o'clock, everything had died down a bit and Mary was able to catch her breath. It was still busy but not all the tables were occupied. Mary put some more plates into the dishwasher when Jim came into the kitchen.

'You were brilliant. I can't believe you've never worked in a café before. Look if you need a job, I pay eight pound an hour. The hours are Monday to Saturday ten till three.'

Mary quickly did the maths in her head. Wow, that money would mean a lot to her. And, the hours fit in around Gerard's job. No. What was she thinking? If ever he found out. But how would he? He never once had popped in to see her where she last worked. She could get away with it. Mary couldn't believe she was thinking about taking the job. But if she saved up... and she had a job... could she leave him? Mary's stomach churned at thought of what Gerard would do to her if ever he found out. She breathed in deeply and sighed.

'Think about it,' said Jim as he walked out again.

Think about it, that wasn't a good idea. Mary could see herself going around and around in circles listing all the pros and cons, there were more pros than cons but the one con was a huge factor. Gerard was sixty to her forty-five. And he was set to retire in five years' time then he'd be home a lot more keeping an eye on her. What if she could leave him and find a little place of her own to rent?

She'd found a paid job hadn't she when he'd said that no-one would give her one? So maybe he was wrong about everything else and that she would be better off without him.

Jim came back into the kitchen again with lots of dirty plates and cutlery.

'Alright, I'll come and work for you. But I don't have any references. I could possibly ask for one from the last place I volunteered at,' said Mary but she really didn't want the girls there knowing what she was doing. The less people that knew the better.

'I'm good. I'm going to go with my gut here, and a big one it is too,' Jim said patting his tummy. 'You've already done an on the job interview and you've passed. How about we give each other a month to see if you like it and see how we get on? I'm sure we'll be fine though.'

'That sounds great,' said Mary.

'You need to give me your bank details and...'

'I need cash,' said Mary.

'Ok, that's fine. Don't forget to give me your contact details before you leave and then we'll sort out the paperwork on Monday morning.'

Mary returned home in a daze. She'd managed to find a job with a nice man in a fun place. And it was paid. She was actually going to be earning some money for the first time in her life and it made her feel good. She'd have to hide it of course. The only place where Gerard never ventured was her car. Whenever they went anywhere together, they would go in his car and he would drive. Where could she put it? Because it was such an old car, the under part of the back seat had begun to fray. What if she made a hole and hid it there?

Mary pulled over into a layby, pulled down the back seat and saw that it was indeed the perfect place to keep the money. He'd never find it there. Putting the seat back down, she got in the car and drove off. Millie would have a field day if she found out. It was just a shame that they were no longer on speaking terms. Tears began to roll down Mary's face, she wanted to feel Millie in her arms again and hear her voice. She had to leave Gerard and this was going to be the first step to make it happen. Once she'd saved up enough and she knew she had the job permanently, she might be able to have a look around for a little rental place. Seeing her daughter again outweighed anything Gerard could do to her. But a fear crept in and pushed away her bravery, leaving niggling doubts.

'You're back late?' said Gerard looking at his watch. His feet were up on a foot stool and he was flicking between channels on the television. 'I hate adverts. Put the kettle on, will you? I'm thirsty. It was hot out there today. Some good golf though?' His attention drifted back to the television again and so Mary went into the kitchen and put the kettle on.

'Lazy oaf,' she muttered.

Mary took his cup of tea to him.

'What no biscuits?'

Mary traipsed back into the kitchen and put a few biscuits on to a plate. Choke on them, she thought, depositing them by his tea.

'So? How did it go?' he asked suddenly as if remembering why she'd been late.

'They said they'd have me,' she said. 'But I've got to do a Saturday too.'

'Oh right,' Gerard paused. 'I suppose I play golf on Saturdays. What time will you be home?'

Mary wasn't used to lying this much to Gerard. Her heart was racing and her hands began to get clammy from the stress. She just hoped she made a good liar.

'Four? With the traffic and everything, and it's further away.'

Gerard snorted in disgust. 'Four? And is that week days too?'

'Yes.'

'I suppose so. Just make sure my supper is ready on time.'

'As always,' said Mary and walked out of the room.

Chapter Four

♥

Monday 30th May 2016

Monday couldn't come soon enough. Mary was so excited at starting her first job, she only hoped she didn't muck it up.

'Oh fantastic, you came a bit earlier,' said Jim coming to open the door to let Mary in. 'A part of me was worried that you'd change your mind. So glad you didn't.'

'Oh no. I'm quite excited,' said Mary.

Jim turned the sign to open. It was then that Mary noticed that the café was open seven days a week.

'Do you have help on a Sunday? They must be busy too considering what it was like on Saturday.'

'Yes they are but my friend's daughter comes in to make a bit of pocket money. She's doing her A-levels at the moment so has a lot of studying to do. She gets money and she's here regularly on a Sunday, it's a perfect arrangement.'

'Oh,' said Mary relieved that he hadn't asked her, she wouldn't have got away with seven days a week. 'So when do you relax?'

'Good question,' Jim said and laughed. 'Ok... it's relatively quiet here on Monday mornings so I can show you the ropes.'

'So you've already seen the layout of the café with the tables' numbers.'

Mary nodded. Jim came to stand in front of a black screen. Mary had seen him use it but it looked way beyond her non-technical brain.

'This is your fob and...'

'A fob? Golly, the last place I worked you just put in the amount and then the till popped open with a ping.'

'You put it up to the screen, it's a touch screen and registers its you. You then bring up the menu and press in what food or drink the customers are having and assign it to the correct table. It's easy to get their bill then. Right let's make up a pretend order...'

The doorbell jangled. The first customer of the morning. In walked an old lady, at least eighty odd, with brown dyed hair and a splash of bright red lipstick which matched her red skirt. She looked amazing and totally put Mary to shame. Gerard had moaned about her wearing lipstick years ago, he said it would attract unwanted attention and said it would be best if she refrained from wearing it. But seeing this lady looking so confident and cheerful, it made Mary want to put some make up on again. Maybe she'd treat herself with some of her earnings.

'Morning, Mo,' said Jim going over to her. He pulled out a chair for her to sit down and made sure he was comfortable.

What a kind man, thought Mary. She'd forgotten that there were people out there who were well mannered and respectful.

He beckoned Mary over.

'Now Mo, this is Mary. She's our newest member at Pink Café.'

'Hello Mary,' said Mo looking her up and down.

Mary felt a bit self conscious. She knew she looked dowdy. In the charity shop, she'd kept herself hidden, sorting out all the items that came into the shop but here she was on show.

'She looks nicer than your last girlfriend. Yes, I think you make a nice couple.

'No Mo. She's not my girlfriend. Anyway Mary is married.'

Mo snorted. 'That's a shame. I'm not normally wrong when it comes to match making, am I Bill?' Mo said as the bell jangled again and an old gentleman came in, very smartly dressed in a blue suit, shirt and tie.

'Nope, you're not wrong there, Mo. You picked out that Evelyn was for me straight away and we were together for a good fifty years. And you made a good choice for yourself too. She was married to her husband, Fred, for longer than I was with Evelyn.'

'Yup,' Mo said. 'And I've made hundreds of other good matches in my life.'

Mary blushed not sure what to say.

'As I said, Mary's married,' said Jim, looking at Mary and mouthing a sorry.

Mary smiled.

'Are you happy in your marriage?' asked Mo.

'Mo, now I think...' interrupted Jim.

Mary's face contorted.

'See, not happy. Wrong choice,' said Mo.

'I didn't choose him,' said Mary quickly. 'My father did.'

'What?' said Jim, Mo and Bill all at once.

Mary shrunk back from them. She didn't know why she was suddenly confiding in two old age pensioners she'd just met and her new boss who she was trying to impress. This wasn't going to help.

'I just had no choice on the matter.'

'That's terribly old fashioned,' said Mo. 'I thought that had disappeared years ago. I mean...'

'Ok Mo, I don't mean to be rude but before anyone else comes in, I quickly need to show Mary around,' said Jim.

Mary sighed inwardly relieved that he'd noticed how uncomfortable she was becoming.

'Right Mary, first you ask them what they'd like to drink. If they know what they want to eat, then you can take both orders but if not then you just give them some time.'

Bill and Mo left her alone after that as they were content to get on with their usual gossip over tea and cake. Jim had enough time to show Mary how to work the coffee machine before a group of about ten mums with their babies and toddlers entered the shop. Jim immediately found some paper and crayons for the older children and the mums flopped down on their chairs.

'Go on,' said Jim. 'Go and take their order, I'll be nearby to help.'

Mary gulped. Gerard's voice entered her head just as she was walking over. You're useless. You'd never be able to hold down a proper job. No she could do this. This was no different than when she helped out at Sunday school the other week.

'Well done,' said Jim when she returned to the counter. 'You remained calm in face of adversity and they were a tough crowd.'

Mary laughed. They had been difficult, as both children and mums had been indecisive over what to have and some had allergies. Mary looked at Jim to find him looking at her thoughtfully. Mary ran her tongue over teeth. Oh god, she thought, please don't let me have anything stuck there. He was making her feel nervous. She looked up at him and her heart missed a bit. His eyes were so warm and kind and thinking about what Mo said about the two of them had begun to get her thinking. He was very good looking and he seemed to be her age. Mary get a hold of yourself, she thought. You're married.

Chapter Five

♥

Saturday 4th June 2016

'What are you wearing?' said Gerard as she put his breakfast of eggs and bacon down in front him. He was looking up at her with sheer disgust.

'A dress,' said Mary knowing full well that that was not what he was referring to.

'You have lipstick on.'

'Yes, I do.'

'Why have you got that nonsense on for? You don't need it. Rub it off,' he said then picked up his knife and fork seeming to think that the conversation was over and began to tuck into the eggs, the yolk breaking and running everywhere.

Mary sat down, stuck her head into the newspaper and ate her cereal.

When Gerard had finished eating, he put his knife and fork down and patted his stomach. 'Just what the doctor ordered.'

It wasn't what the doctor had ordered, what the doctor had actually said at Gerard's last check-up was that he needed to lay off the fatty foods as his cholesterol was too high. If Mary had been the dutiful loving wife, she might have encouraged him to eat healthier. He does what he wants so who was she to argue, not over that anyway. Now her lipstick, mind, that was something worth fighting for.

Gerard looked at her properly then. 'You've put some black stuff around your eyes too. What have you got all that on for? You're only in the back of the shop.'

'Because I want to,' said Mary trying to stay strong.

'What are you up to?'

'I'm wearing some make-up, as I said, because I want to. Now is that all?' she said picking up his plate and walking away from him before he could answer. If she won this round, she might be able to finally build up her confidence. He left then without uttering a single word, not even a goodbye. Mary wasn't bothered. At least then she didn't have to give him the obligatory peck on the cheek. She loathed getting anywhere near him. Thank goodness, he'd stopped asking for anything in the bed department. That had just been nauseating.

Driving to work, Mary felt stronger than she had been in such a long time. She'd managed a week at work and it had been fun. Mo and Bill hadn't said anything else about her marriage but instead had regaled her with lots of stories about their misspent youth. Mary wished she'd had some stories to tell. She dreamed of romance now and wondered how her life would have turned out if she'd gone against her father.

'You look nice,' said Jim. 'Not that you don't normally, but you know, your... um...' and he motioned towards her lipstick.

Mary smiled. 'Thank you. I decided to take a leaf out of Mo's book.'

'Well, it suits you,' said Jim. 'Right, well, the today's specials are…'

'Morning Mary. Morning Jim,' said Mo arriving first into the café. Mo did a double take as she glanced at Mary. 'Nice colour,' she said then sat down with a knowing look at Jim as he helped her into her seat.

Mary noticed Mo's mischievous look in her eye. Mo was probably still thinking about her and Jim but Jim didn't think that way about Mary, did he? Over the past week, Mary had noticed him spying on her and quickly turning away when he'd thought he'd been spotted however Mary had thought he was just checking up on her to see how she was doing, it was her first week after all. Yes, that's all there was to it. Mo was wrong about them. Gerard had always said she should have been called Jane then she'd been plain Jane. No-one was going to look twice at her. What was she thinking? It was Mo's fault. She was the one putting false thoughts in her head.

Mary had forgotten how hectic a Saturday could be and soon the café was packed. Once or twice she put in the wrong order but Jim had been fine about it. Mary had been expecting the worst, that he'd shout at her, say she was useless, tell her she was fired but it never came because Jim was not Gerard. Bill was not Gerard. Not all men were like Gerard, a fact that she'd forgotten over the years as Gerard had implied that they were.

'Could you possibly do three hot chocolates for table five and four cappuccinos for table three?' said Jim.

'Yes, once I've done this tea for table twelve outside.'

Back in the kitchen, Mary grabbed the squirty cream and pressed but nothing came out.

'Come on,' she whispered. Shaking it again, it finally came out in one gigantic whoosh.

'Mary, I need...' said Jim coming up behind her.

Mary turned to answer him but the button failed to work and cream spurted all over Jim.

'Oh no. Oh no,' Mary blanched bracing herself again for Jim's reaction. 'I'm so sorry. I really am. Oh no it's all over you.'

'That's not the way I normally take whipped cream,' he said licking some stray cream from the corner of his mouth.

Mary immediately reddened at what she thought he was insinuating. And all thoughts, that weren't exactly pure entered her head.

Jim frowned then at her reaction then a light bulb seemed to come on in his head as he realised what he'd said.

'No... I didn't mean... I didn't... um,' Jim said going just as red as Mary. 'Um... I'm just going to go and clean myself up.'

Mary stood there stunned. What just happened? Had they flirted? Had Jim flirted with her more to the point or had she made a right boo boo and totally misinterpreted everything. She let out a huge groan then carefully squirted the cream on the hot chocolates. Don't let your mind wander, she thought, not back to him. She glanced quickly towards the door. Her stomach gave a flutter at the tiniest of thoughts that someone, another man other than Gerard, could find her attractive. Something else that Gerard had said couldn't happen.

Chapter Six

♥

Saturday 11ᵗʰ June 2016

Another week, another Saturday and she was still gainfully employed and loving every minute of it, particularly the weekly cash that she stashed away in her car. Mary even felt as though she was making a few friends with some of the regulars who were genuinely interested in her. She still hadn't let Jim know about her situation at home and it had been hard not mentioning that she had a daughter. For some reason no-one had brought up the topic of children yet. Mary didn't know whether Mo or Bill or Jim for that matter had any but maybe soon she would take Jim into her confidence.

It was nearly time for Mary to go home and she dreaded this part of her Saturday because she knew what awaited her on Sunday. A whole day with Gerard. Mary put a slice of banana cake on one plate and was just getting the carrot and walnut cake out of the cabinet when she happened to glance up. Mary stood there rooted to the spot with shock because Millie and another girl, who she hadn't remembered seeing around before, had just walked into the café. Millie was so busy scouring the room for the best table to sit at and talking animatedly to the blond girl that she hadn't noticed her mother right in front of her. Mary's heart slammed into her chest. She didn't want a scene here. After the way Mary had treated Millie and just let her father throw her out, she wasn't sure how Millie was going to react.

Mary quickly crouched down, pretending to get some cups out of the cupboard beneath the coffee machine. Oh no, what was she going to do? She shut her eyes tight and hoped Millie would walk back out the door and go somewhere else.

'Fiona, how lovely to see you. How have you been?' said Jim coming out of the kitchen.

'Good thanks, Jim. I've brought my new house mate with me, Millie. I had to get her to try the best cake ever.'

Oh god now there was no escaping.

'Yeah, and don't you know it. Nice to meet you Millie.'

Mary tightened up further into a ball. She wished she'd had Harry Potter's invisible cloak on right now. Suddenly a foot went into her.

'Ow!' she whimpered.

'Oh God, Mary, I'm so sorry. I didn't see you down there. What are you doing?' said Jim. 'Are you alright?'

She grimaced. Oh bother. She gingerly straightened up and turned round.

'Mum? What...? Is dad here?' said Millie looking around the café with tension in her eyes. Realising he wasn't, her body relaxed then she turned her full attention on her mother.

'Mum?' said Jim looking between Mary and Millie.

'Er... yes... this is my daughter, Millie. Hi sweetheart,' Mary said wearily.

'What are you doing here? Did dad actually let you get a job?' Millie asked.

'Ah well, not exactly no.'

'Have you left him?' Millie asked with excitement in her eyes.

'Er... no.'

'Oh,' said Millie. 'But you're doing something he doesn't know about?'

'Umm... well... yes,' said Mary looking at the floor. Suddenly she was enveloped in one her daughter's hugs.

'Mum, I'm so proud of you. I've missed you so much. I'm sorry I haven't rung you,' said Millie not letting her mother go.

'I'm sorry,' whispered Mary into her daughter's ear, tears running down her face. 'I'm sorry about everything.'

'It's ok. It all turned out well,' said Millie stepping back. 'I'm sharing a house with Fiona here, who's actually an old school friend and I've got a gorgeous boyfriend called Bertie, Clarissa's brother. I just wish I'd had the courage to leave home earlier.'

'Oh I'm so glad,' said Mary her body visibly sagging. She wiped away her tears and smiled and then really saw just how her daughter had blossomed in the last few months.

'Mum, you've got make up on,' said Millie wiping away some of the mascara that had run. 'You look lovely.'

Mary blushed.

Jim went off to serve another table and Mary watched him as he crossed the room.

'Does he know about dad?' asked Millie.

'No. It's only my second week here. It's not permanent yet. I've got to work another two weeks then he's going to see if he'll take me on for good.

'Oh right,' said Millie. 'So where does dad think you're going every day?'

'I told him I volunteer in the shop next door. I got laid off at my normal one and they sent me there but I didn't like it, it just wasn't the same and Jim needed someone. I want to leave him... your father...' said Mary. 'I can't go on. He's been worse since you've left.'

'Well we've got a spare room in our house,' said Fiona. 'It's not big, it's just got my boxes in at the moment but if you need a place.'

'Oh no, I couldn't,' said Mary. 'And I don't know whether I'm ready yet to take that step. I've only just got this job and I'm not sure I can afford it right now.'

Fiona shrugged. 'Well you're welcome to it whenever you want.'

Millie smiled at her friend and mouthed a thank you.

'Right,' said Jim returning to the counter. 'What will you girls be having?'

While her daughter and her friend ate their cake, Mary rushed around finishing off the rest of her jobs. She kept glancing over at her daughter. She was so proud of her. Jim hadn't mentioned anything to her in passing and she didn't know how much he'd heard.

'Go on,' he said. 'You can finish now, it's only a few minutes early. Just remember to take your half of the tips.'

'Thank you,' Mary said.

Mary pulled up a chair to the table and immediately her daughter grabbed her hand and smiled at her.

'Were you going to ring me?' said Millie.

'I wanted to. And I would have done once I'd been here for a while. I just didn't know if... And you know your dad checks my phone.'

'Mum, it's ok. I'm out of there and I'm doing fine. More than fine.'

Mary stuck her key in the lock and slowly turned it. She'd had such a lovely catch up with her daughter and now they were back in contact things seemed to be so much better. Well nearly. She'd lost time talking to Millie and Fiona that she was now an hour late.

'About time,' said Gerard when Mary walked into the sitting room. 'I said if you did volunteering in this new shop that you had to be home in time for my tea. I'm hungry and there's no sign of anything.'

'There was an accident so I had to take a diversion,' said Mary thinking quickly.

Gerard grunted. 'Well, if you're late one more time. Accident or no accident, you won't be working another Saturday again, do you hear me?'

'Yes,' said Mary. 'I'll just go and get on with it then.'

Mary walked into the kitchen, grabbed the leftover casserole from the fridge but her nerves were so fried that she dropped the entire thing on the floor. Oh god no, what have I done? Brown goop was spread across the kitchen floor, a few pieces of chicken had been flung to the other side of the room and got wedged under the cabinet.

'What's going on in there?' shouted Gerard.

'Nothing! I dropped a pan by accident!' Mary waited making sure Gerard didn't bother to investigate. It seemed he was happy with the reply.

Quickly Mary got on all fours and began shovelling it all into the pan. Spooning up the chicken from wherever it had landed, she placed that into the pan as well. She didn't have time to make him anything else and with him being in the mood he was already in; she didn't want to make things worse.

'Achoo.' Mary sneezed but didn't manage to avert her face from the pan in her hand. She didn't want to drop it again. Unfortunately, some of her mucus headed straight for the casserole. There was no way she wanted to eat that now.

Half an hour later, Mary took a plate of steaming mashed potato, casserole and peas into Gerard. His eyes lit up.

'I didn't realise there was any of the casserole left?' he said, his tongue licking his lips in anticipation.

'There was just enough for you,' said Mary smiling but hoping desperately that God wasn't going to punish her for what she'd done. However, 'Hell hath no fury like a woman scorned.' And Mary sat down on the other sofa, feeling quite content with her plate of fish fingers, mashed potato and peas.

Chapter Seven

♥

Saturday 18th June 2016

Another week had flown by and Jim seemed to be happy with Mary's work. They got on well together and Mary felt as though she was coming out of her shell. She was beginning to laugh and smile more. It helped that she'd made things up with Millie and that they'd arranged to see each other for a coffee before her shift started. It was difficult juggling talking to her daughter without her husband finding out but she was determined to make it work.

Leaving the house early that morning had raised some suspicion. She'd had to miss her usual breakfast with Gerard and left him to it. His eyebrows had raised at her first in surprise then they'd furrowed and his lips had tightened and drew taut. Surprisingly, he didn't argue or shout at her but just watched Mary's retreating figure.

Millie was waiting for her when she arrived at the café and she was beaming. For next to her, Mary could only assume, was Bertie, her boyfriend. He was very good looking and from a distance he looked like he had kind eyes and Mary liked the way he was gently resting his hand on the small of her back, almost protective. They looked like a lovely couple and Mary was glad that Millie had found a nice man to be with who would treat her right. For a split second, she was almost jealous of her daughter, for getting away from her husband and having freedom and finding someone that loved her back.

'Mum!' said Millie breaking away from Bertie and rushing forward to give her another hug.

Mary smiled and brought her in smelling Millie's newly washed hair. Millie was the first to let her mum go.

'Mum, this is Bertie, my boyfriend,' said Millie grasping his hand.

'It's good to see you again,' said Bertie. 'I'll go and get the drinks.'

Bertie went inside and they found a table underneath the awning. The summer sun was already beating down; it was going to be a hot one.

'How's it...? What are you...?' they both said in unison.

'You first,' said Mary laughing.

Millie shook her head and smiled.

'What?' said Mary.

'You. You're laughing. Do you realise the last time I heard you do that?'

Mary put her head in her hands then looked up at her daughter's concerned face. 'Oh Millie, that sounds terrible. I did used to laugh.'

'Well if you did, it wasn't often. Mum, I know we've had this conversation before but can't you leave him?'

'I want to. But even with this job, I still can't afford a place to stay and the bills.'

'You wouldn't have to pay for the little room at Fiona's. She's already said it would be fine if you didn't pay anything till you get on your feet.'

Mary shook her head. That just wouldn't feel right.

'I knew you were up to something!' said a deafening voice coming up the street.

Both Mary and Millie instinctively jumped up from their chairs in fright.

'Mary what are you doing with her?' Gerard said pointing at Millie. 'I forbid you from seeing her. And this is how you repay me? You go behind my back, after all I've done for this family. Like mother, like daughter. Devious and untrustworthy. I cannot believe this is what you've been getting up to on a Saturday while I've been playing golf. I thought you were acting strange. Now,' he said towering over Mary whose newfound confidence had totally left her. 'You come with me now or you too will find your clothes on the drive and no roof over your head.'

Mary looked at Millie. 'Sorry. I've got to go.'

'No mum, don't,' Millie said grabbing hold of her.

Mary whispered into Millie's ear quickly, 'Explain to Jim what's happened...'

Gerard pushed Millie's hand away. 'That's enough,' he said and held onto Mary's elbow non too gently as he marched her away.

Mary drove home crying all the way. She averted her rear view mirror so she didn't have to see Gerard's face in it, who was following closely behind. He was going to be unbearable now. And when was she going to see Millie again?

'You lied to me!' said Gerard shouting at the top of his lungs once they were both inside the house and he'd locked the door.

Mary shrank back. Thank goodness he hadn't found out that she hadn't been going to the charity shop either, she dreaded to think what he would have been like.

'I missed her,' Mary said in a small voice. 'You can't stop me from seeing my own daughter.'

'Oh yes I can,' he said moving towards her. 'It's my house, my rules so while you're living here you do what I say.'

Mary inched away from him. Spittle flew out of his mouth as he shouted and she didn't like the way he was being so aggressive, the last time he was like this...

Gerard grabbed hold of Mary and flung her across the room. 'Get out of my sight, you disgust me.'

Mary screamed as she fell against the corner of the cupboard. She put her hand to her cheek and held it there and felt a trickle of blood seep between her fingers. Seeing that Gerard had turned her back on her, she heaved herself up off the floor wincing as she went.

Mary turned the lock on the bathroom door and looked in the mirror at the damage. A huge scrape ran down one side of her cheek where she'd come up against a hinge on the door. A plaster wasn't big enough so she cut up some gauze and covered it up. She looked absolutely horrific. Her eyes were puffy and red and dark circles surrounded them where the mascara had run. A big patch of red was coming up on her cheek bone and around her eye. That was going to be a nice bruise. Although she was hurt, it could have gone a lot worse, a lot lot worse.

Mary sat down on the floor and pulled her knees up to her chest and began to cry again. She couldn't seem to get out of this mess she was in and her pride had stopped her from accepting the room where her daughter was renting. Her stupid pride. She had no job anyway now so even if she did go and live with her daughter, she would have to rely on her for everything.

'Have you finished?' banged Gerard on the door. 'I need to come in.'

Mary sighed.

Opening the door, Gerard pushed past her with barely a glance then shut the door behind him.

Mary had no idea what to do next but what she didn't want was to be anywhere near him so she took herself off outside into the garden and lay down on the grass. She looked up and just watched little wisps of clouds float across the sky.

Chapter Eight

♥

Monday 20th June 2016

Gerard picked up his briefcase and bag to leave then pointed a finger at Mary. 'I've added a tracker to your phone so don't even think of going anywhere you don't normally go. You'll need to go food shopping. I finished off the last of the milk and bread this morning.'

Mary nodded.

'Right, I'll see you later. And no talking to Amelia. I don't want her getting any stupid ideas into your head. Do you hear me?'

Mary nodded.

The door shut behind him and Mary collapsed onto the nearest chair. The weekend had been hell. She'd managed to cook, watch some television and do a bit of reading but just being near Gerard made her feel sick.

The doorbell rang. Mary got up quickly to open the door forgetting what she looked like.

It was Millie, who upon seeing her went an unnatural shade of white, gasped then went to hug her.

'Mum? Did dad do this to you?'

'Ow,' said Mary as Millie squeezed a bit too hard.

'Sorry,' she said and ushered Mary inside the house.

'Did he do this to you?'

'I stumbled and tripped,' said Mary. 'Anyway, you can't be here! Your dad would have a fit if he knew you were here. You have to go!'

'I'm not leaving you,' said Millie. 'I came to get you, it's all been sorted.'

'What do you mean it's all been sorted? What has?' said Mary.

'Jim's decided he can't do without you and has offered you a permanent job.'

'Yes, but...'

'And he also has a little room with an ensuite above the café that's been left empty and you can pay a peanut rent. He's also asked me to ask you whether you could possibly extend your hours too as he's been planning something but was going to talk to you about it when you'd been at the café for longer.'

'So, he's offering me more hours and a place to stay?' said Mary not believing what she was hearing.

'Yes. So come on, let's get packing. I caught the bus here so we'll go in your car.'

Mary didn't move. She was actually leaving her husband. She'd been dreaming of this moment for years and now it had actually come yet she was paralysed.

'Mum!' said Millie running up the stairs. 'Are the suitcases still in the attic? I'll get them down.'

'Yes, they are,' said Mary. She looked around the room taking it all in. This was going to be the last time she was ever going to set foot in this house again. All the furniture was Gerard's. All the pictures were Gerard's. Everything was Gerard's and he could have it all. Mary chuckled at the thought of him trying to use the washing machine or work out how to iron his shirts, he was too tight to get someone in to help him. He would finally realise how much she did for him.

'Ok,' said Millie barely an hour later. 'Are you ready?'

Mary nodded.

'This feels like déjà vu,' said Millie looking at the car packed to the ceiling with bags full of clothes and books.

'Hold on,' said Mary before Millie shut the front door. Mary rummaged around in her handbag then took her phone out and placed it on the hallway table. 'I'm ready now.'

'Your phone?' said Millie.

'Your father put some tracker on it.'

'Are you serious?'

Mary nodded sadly.

'He's become even more deranged than I thought. Evil bast...'

'Language!' said Mary.

'Sorry,' said Millie.

Mary gave her daughter's hand a squeeze. 'Thank you for everything.'

Millie smiled back trying to hold back the tears.

Mo clapped eyes on Mary first as Millie and Mary wandered up the street.

'Her husband did that to her,' Mo said out of the corner of her mouth to Bill. 'I told you he wasn't the one. He is...' she said looking towards where Jim was cheerily serving a customer. 'Are you alright? You look like you've been in the wars.'

Mary smiled weakly but was bowled over by Jim.

'Thank goodness, you're here,' he said. 'So you're happy with the new arrangements?'

Mary nodded. 'Thank you. They sound good. Are you sure it's alright?'

'Oh perfectly. You're actually the one helping me out. I wanted to find someone to go in the bedroom upstairs but hadn't got round to it. So it's a win win.'

'Do you want to go up and show your mother around and get her settled?' said Jim not mentioning a word about the huge cut and bruise on Mary's face.

Mary went past the kitchen and followed Millie through a door and up a narrow wooden staircase. The pink décor continued its theme up the stairs with the dark pink paint and onto the landing. When Millie opened the door to her new bedroom, she was expecting it be pink but instead the room was painted in a lovely warm light earthy brown. A white washed wooden wardrobe and chest of drawers stood against one wall and a double bed was already made up with crisp white sheets. A few pillows with hedgehogs and squirrels on had been placed neatly on the bed to finish it off. It was a lovely room and it had been years since she'd been in one that felt so light and didn't have Gerard's presence all over it.

Tears began to roll down Mary's cheeks. Millie gave her a light nudge.

'A fresh start,' Millie said. 'Right let's go and get your things.

Jim said Mary could park round the back of the café and that one space was now hers so between Mary and Millie going back and forth, it didn't take long until Mary's car was finally unpacked.

'Mum? Mum? Ah there you are.'

'There's no bath and no shower. Jim said it was en-suite. I presumed that it had at least one of those to wash in.'

Millie began to laugh at the look of horror on her mum's face. 'It's a wet room.'

'A wet what?'

'Look. Here's the shower head and hose. You stand underneath it.'

'But... where's the water going to go?'

'Here,' said Millie pointing to a hole in the floor which had a little grate over it.'

'But everything's going to get wet?' Mary had a vision of her waking up in the night, going to the toilet, only to have a wet bottom from a wet toilet seat and wet feet. And what about the loo roll and her towel? Everything would get wet.

'Yes, that's the point. It's not ideal but if you didn't have it like this, there would be no bathroom at all. I know it's different from what you're used to but at least you're away from dad now. Okay?' said Millie giving her mum's arm a gentle reassuring squeeze. Millie looked at her watch. 'I'm sorry but I've got to leave you. I only managed to get a few hours off from work and if I don't go now, I'll miss the bus.'

'Oh I'm so sorry, I forgot you're supposed to be there today.'

'Get yourself settled, maybe have a nap, you look tired and I'll ring the café and get hold of you later to see how you're doing. Love you mum,' said Millie leaning forward to hug her mother.

'Wait,' said Mary. 'You have my car. I don't need it now. I live where I work. You need it more than me.'

'What? No. I couldn't.'

'Please take it. It's also my way of helping you out.'

'Alright. Thank you. It means that it'll be easier to come and see you in the evenings then. I'll ring you at the café later to see how you're getting on.'

Mary hugged Millie and slipped her keys into her hand. 'Oh, before you go, I need to get my money from the car.'

'Your handbag is there on the bed,' said Millie.

'Umm... no... I meant my earnings from the last two weeks, I hid it in the car so your dad wouldn't find it.'

'Mum!' said Millie laughing. 'I love it. Who would have thought? Sneaky!'

Mary began to laugh with her but also she was thinking about how she'd got away with it. Also Gerard had no idea where she was, so he wasn't going to turn up in a hurry. She would have to deal with him at some point but when she was stronger, much stronger.

Mary woke up to a light knocking on her door.

'Mary?' said Jim.

Mary shot up off the bed, remembered where she was, pushed her hair out of her eyes and opened the door.

'I've made some food. Would you like to join me? It's just a little omelette and salad. I wasn't too sure what you wanted.'

'What time is it?' she said yawning, still feeling a bit dazed.

'Six.'

'Gosh, really? I was going to come down and help you once I'd unpacked. I'm sorry.

'I didn't expect you to. Considering...'

Mary noticed he didn't look his usual confident cheery self then caught a glimpse of herself in the bathroom mirror. A big purple bruise had appeared around a puffy eye and the gash across her cheek was looking fierce.

'Can I still work tomorrow? I don't want to put off the customers so I'll cover it up with lots of makeup,' Mary said quickly hoping Jim wasn't having second thoughts.

Jim looked taken aback. 'Of course you can.'

Mary visibly relaxed.

'So? Food?' said Jim smiling.

'Yes please.'

Jim's omelette was delicious. It was the first time a man had ever cooked for her and it was far tastier than anything she'd ever made. He was a brilliant chef and he was also kind, thoughtful and very funny. Mary smiled as she lay in her bed looking up at the ceiling. Jim had made her laugh tonight despite the situation she was in.

It did feel strange being on her own again. But it was nice. The pressure was gone. The anxiety and sick feeling that normally accompanied it was no longer there. And she finally realised that she was going to be ok. She had a job, a place to live and she had her daughter back.

Chapter Nine

♥

Wednesday 22nd June 2016

'Work it ladies. Tighten those buttocks. Clench those inner muscles.'

'What muscles?' panted Mary out of the corner of her mouth to Millie who seemed to be enjoying herself far too much while she was in abject misery.

'Inner muscles. You know, up inside?' said Millie gazing pointedly to her groin area whilst waving her arms around in time to the music.

'Inside?' said Mary nearly tripping up over her own feet. 'I can't even follow what steps you're doing let alone trying to concentrate on muscles.' Mary was still not understanding what the instructor or her daughter, for that matter, were getting at. She had no muscles full stop inside or out. There wasn't going to be any tightening going on and as far as she was concerned, her muscles worked far harder when she was carrying a stack of plates to and fro from the kitchen than flapping her arms around like she was trying to take off. Why she'd agreed to this... New start mum, Millie had said. New things to try.

Stepping up and down on a box in front of her was not what Mary had envisaged when Millie had persuaded her to join this exercise class. What was wrong with some good old Jane Fonda workouts? And all you needed was a mat. Mary shook her head and looked around the room. It was like she'd been in a time warp for the last twenty-five years. She'd become fuddy duddy, naïve and ignorant while everything had changed around her. Even Millie, from the looks of things, had struggled to keep up while Gerard had dragged them down and kept them almost under lock and key. This was going to be a big learning curve. Thank goodness Millie was there to guide her.

'You were brilliant,' said Millie to her as they both collapsed at a table within the leisure centre.

'I'm not sure about that,' said Mary who was still looking like a beetroot.

'Do you want to try Pilates?' asked Millie.

Mary looked over to the big blackboard to see what was on offer.

'I'll get some lattes but there doesn't seem to be any pie,' said Mary getting up from her seat. 'Is there anything else you want instead?'

Millie began to laugh and pulled Mary back down on her chair.

'Pi...la...tes,' said Millie slowly. 'Not lattes.'

'Oh. What's Pilates?' Mary cringed as she spoke.

Millie and Mary walked in through the back kitchen door to find Jim elbow deep in a huge bowl.

'Have fun?' he said not stopping what he was doing.

'I don't know whether it was fun but it was definitely something,' said Mary smiling. 'I've been assured it gets easier and that everyone was like how I was on their first session, but I'm not so sure.'

'She did well,' said Millie. 'So, I'll see you Sunday? Out on the river?'

Mary grimaced. 'I'm not sure that's going to be a good idea.'

'Mum, you'll be fine. It's really beautiful once you get beyond the bridge. You have to see it.'

'Are you sure you and Bertie don't want to be on your own for a bit? You haven't seen him all week. You don't need your old mum...'

'I'm seeing him on Friday and Saturday. It's only for a few hours and he wants to get to know you.'

'But the river?' said Mary. Mary wasn't the strongest swimmer. What if she fell in?

'Oh, I haven't done that in ages,' said Jim. 'You've got to experience that at least once while you're living here. It's fun.'

'You must come along,' said Millie. 'That's if you're free.'

'I am, actually. I'm making sure I have Sundays off from now on. And I've just managed to find someone who'll fill in for me. I'd love to come, if that's ok with you?'

'Yes, that would be lovely. Are you a good swimmer?' said Mary.

Jim's eyes twinkled. 'The best.'

Mary's stomach did an involuntary flutter and her heart missed a beat. Was she getting anxious about boating on the river or was it that she was enjoying being with Jim more and more. The last time her stomach had reacted like that was when a boy in her class at school, whom she'd had a long standing crush on, had asked her to partner up in science. Mary looked over at him while he was chatting to Millie. He was so at ease with everyone and he was also rather attractive. How hadn't she noticed? She had noticed his beautiful and kind hazel eyes and the way his body moved as he worked the dough. They'd even flirted a few times, she was sure of it now, but she had passed it off, as Gerard had made her feel so unattractive.

Millie had lent her some leggings and little t-shirt for the exercise class and although she hadn't looked as elegant as the other women, she did have the same nice curves and shiny hair. Millie had also told her that Mary had the longest eyelashes that enhanced her huge round eyes and that she didn't need make up. Millie was upset that she hadn't inherited them from her mother.

Mary had been in a loveless marriage for so many years. With this fresh start, it would be so nice if she could meet a kind man who wasn't controlling and who she could have some fun with. She looked at Jim and her stomach fluttered again. Millie had found someone so why couldn't she?

Chapter Ten

♥

Saturday 25th June 2016

'You like nice,' said Jim as Mary came into the kitchen.

Mary had been procrastinating upstairs about what to wear and had taken a lot longer than usual to decide on the appropriate outfit. For one thing, she was meeting Millie's boyfriend and wanted to make a good impression and also she wanted to look nice for Jim. Eventually she'd decided upon some leggings, a blue and white floral floaty shirt, and some flat pumps. Practical yet cool.

Jim looked gorgeous in a pair of light chinos and a short sleeved shirt which matched his eyes. It was strange to see him in something other than his chef whites. Mary could feel her heart racing that bit faster when she looked at him.

'All set?' he asked before reaching out to pick up a rucksack from off the counter.

Mary raised her eyes at him wondering what he'd thought of that she hadn't.

'Just some refreshments,' he said in answer to her look. 'Shall we go then?'

'Yes?' said Mary with some apprehension. She had not been looking forward to this. She'd have much preferred just a picnic on dry land but Millie had been adamant.

'You'll love it,' said Jim ushering Mary out the door. He locked it then turned, gave Mary a grin and they set off down the street towards the river.

'Have you always lived around here? asked Mary.

'No, I actually moved here from London about... wow... it's been nearly two years. My girlfriend at the time had this dream of setting up a coffee shop in the Cotswolds. I would cook and she would be front of house. So I sold my flat and bought these premises. She did the décor while I was happy creating in my kitchen and being my own boss.'

'And your girlfriend?' asked Mary tentatively wondering if she was around or something bad had happened to her.

'My ex-girlfriend met a far more suave and sophisticated chef than me at our favourite Italian restaurant that we used to go to.'

'Oh,' said Mary. 'I'm sorry.'

'I'm not,' said Jim cheerily. 'They are much more suited to each other than we ever were.'

Mary gulped. He was single then. It also got her thinking back to what Mo had said a few weeks ago in the café, about them being a good match. Mary's stomach fluttered at the thought of finding love, something that she'd given up hope of ever having. But first she needed to deal with Gerard before she could even contemplate having a relationship with someone else. She was still married after all. How was she going to convince Gerard to divorce her, God only knew?

'There they are,' said Mary waving her arm at her daughter in the distance.

Millie ran up to Mary and gave her a big hug.

'You made it,' Millie said smiling.

'I had to drag her here kicking and screaming,' said Jim winking at Millie.

'Mum! Did he, really? Were you having second thoughts?' said Millie.

'And thirds, and fourths,' said Mary.

'Morning,' said Bertie to Jim and Mary, appearing from around a small wooden boat house. 'They're just bringing the boats round now.'

'Boats?' said Mary.

'Er… yes, if that's alright. The four seaters have been booked up and seeing as Jim is here I thought he wouldn't mind doing the punting?'

'Oh yes,' said Jim rubbing his hands together. 'I might even get Mary to have a go too.'

Mary blanched. 'Me?' she squeaked. 'No way. I need two hands on the boat and my bottom is going to be literally stuck like glue to the seat.'

'Who's going first?' said a young man pulling up a boat alongside the jetty next to where they were all standing.

'You are,' said Mary quickly wanting to see how Millie got into the boat. She didn't want to embarrass herself too much.

Once Millie and Bertie had pushed away and were drifting up the river, it was Mary's turn.

'It's going to tip over,' said Mary carefully putting her foot down then feeling the boat begin to lean she brought her foot back quickly so it was on solid ground once more.

'Look, if I get in first then I'll steady it as you get in, ok?' said Jim almost gliding onto the boat so that it barely rocked. He stood with his feet wide apart and seemed to be doing a very good job of balancing. He then held his hand out for her to take.

Mary reached out and as she touched his hand, a wave of electricity passed between them and she stumbled forward into the boat screaming as she went.

'It's ok,' said Jim. 'I've got you.'

And he really had. Mary found herself face pushed up against his chest and his arms were wrapped around her in a large embrace.

'Thank you,' Mary said her voice muffled within his shirt. Mary didn't want the moment to stop. She'd never felt so comfortable, so protected and certainly had never felt her stomach flutter for someone this much before. She briefly glanced up and his eyes looked down at her concerned.

'Are you ok to sit down now, just where you are?' asked Jim.

Mary lowered herself to the seat all the while Jim's hand never left their grip on her.

'Thank you,' Mary murmured slightly embarrassed that she was making such a scene.

'It's fine,' said Jim leaning over to get the pole from the young man.

'You know what to do?'

'Yes I've done this before,' replied Jim.

The young man nodded then wandered off to greet more customers.

Mary looked in surprise as Jim was indeed very proficient in the art of punting. Was there nothing this man couldn't do? He made it seem effortless, and she watched him in awe. Soon however her attention began to waiver as she looked less at his punting skills and more in the way his body was moving. The muscles in his arms sprang up as he planted the pole in the water and brought it up again.

'Mum! What do you think?' shouted Millie as they caught up with them.

He's very good looking, and he's kind and he's definitely turning me inside out, thought Mary answering her daughter's question. Oh, she meant the scenery. Mary pulled her eyes away from Jim and looked around her properly for the first time. Reeds lined the water's edge, a mother duck and her ducklings swam by, a little boat floated next to a wooden jetty which led up to a grand and very beautiful house partially hidden by trees. Willow trees draped their fronds over the river and shoals of fish broke the stillness of the water.

'It's amazing,' said Mary.

'See? I told you so,' beamed Millie settling into her seat and looked up at Bertie with such a look of complete adoration.

Mary still hadn't found out how Millie and Bertie had got together but from the looks of things they were smitten. Oh my God, thought Mary. That's how I was looking at Jim. Millie and I had exactly the same looks on our faces. Mary glanced up at Jim who was concentrating on the work at hand. Mary blushed wondering whether he'd noticed how she'd acted towards him. She'd made it blatantly obvious that she liked him, she only hoped that he liked her back in the same way too. But she hadn't caught him looking at her in a different way for a few days now, not since she'd left Gerard. So maybe there wasn't anything there after all and she'd just been imagining it those weeks before. Mary's heart sunk, she would have to step back a bit, it would be very embarrassing if she made a fool of herself.

'Do you want to have a go?' asked Jim.

Mary gulped. 'Who me?'

'There's no-one else here on this boat I'm talking to. Yes. You,' said Jim. 'I'll show you what to do.'

'Go on mum!' shouted Millie.

'Well, you have to do it too then,' retorted Mary thinking if Millie didn't do it then she wouldn't have to either.

'Ok. I will,' said Millie. Millie stood up and Bertie and Millie swapped places their boat only rocking a little bit. Millie was soon at the back of the boat and doing a very good job of punting. 'This is only my second try but I think I've got the hang of it,' Millie said sticking her tongue out in concentration.

Mary sighed. Bother. This was not going to end well. Millie's balance seemed to be a lot better than hers. Mary gingerly stood up. Jim took her hand and he held onto her waist as they passed each other. His hands were so big and reassuring. Mary delighted in his touch. This was worth it just to feel his hands on her again, she thought.

'Stand sideways on,' said Jim. 'And use the pole to steady yourself. That's it. Bring the pole up. Mary, you need to bring the pole up.'

'I can't,' squeaked Mary tugging at the pole then she did one tug too many, the boat rocked to the left and she felt herself falling but somehow Jim brought her back into the boat with one hand and she fell down in a crumpled heap while he tried to grab the pole with his other hand before the pole slid away into the water. He managed to grasp it with his fingertips and held on to it for dear life but then he totally lost his balance and went careening into the water with a huge splash.

'Jim!' screamed Mary as he disappeared from view.

'Jim!' shouted out Millie and Bertie as they tried to make their way over to Mary as quick as possible.

'I'm alright,' said Jim spluttering as his head and shoulders arose out of the water. 'I can stand. Here, take this.' And he handed the pole over to Mary. 'It got stuck in some weeds.'

'I'm so sorry,' said Mary looking at a very wet Jim.

Jim grabbed hold of the boat before it drifted away then launched himself in.

'Arghh…' screamed Mary again as the boat tilted precariously and she could feel herself falling.

'Mum! It's alright. Just hold on!' said Millie beginning to laugh.

'I am,' screeched Mary.

Jim stood up and Mary momentarily got distracted again as Jim's wet clothes clung to his body. And what a lovely body it was.

Jim shrugged, 'Nice day for a swim. And at least my clothes will dry quickly in this heat.'

'Really?' said Mary. 'You don't mind? I'm very sorry.'

'No, I'm fine and it wasn't your fault.'

'Are you alright mate?' said Bertie coming up alongside them trying not to laugh with Millie.

'My head is swimming,' replied Jim.

'Wat-er you want to do next?' asked Bertie

'Oh I'm happy just to go with the flow,' said Jim winking at Mary who still couldn't believe that they were now joking between them.

'You're all in-seine,' said Mary laughing as she joined her daughter.

'Nice one Mum!' said Millie.

'At least I'm not in de Nile,' said Bertie quickly.

'Dam it!' said Jim shaking his head trying to get some water out of his ear. 'Hey, joking apart, shall we go to that river bank and moor up? I've brought some snacks. I think I need some energy I don't know about you lot.'

'Oh mate. That's brilliant. Millie and I forgot about food.'

A few minutes later, their boats side by side, they were all tucking into home-made blueberry muffins and drinking elderflower wine.

'Oh, that was delicious,' moaned Bertie as he'd finished his and was eyeing up Millie's.

'Here, do you want the rest of mine?' said Mary. 'I'm full.'

'Oh yeah thanks.' Bertie swallowed it whole. 'Um... What are you two doing Saturday night?'

Jim and Mary looked at each other. 'Er...' said Mary. 'Nothing?'

'Yeah, I haven't got anything planned,' said Jim.

'Well, you see Anthony, my step dad has just finished decorating and setting up a cinema in the basement of mum's house and we're going to watch a film in 3D with proper surround sound. He's really excited so we're making a night of it. Millie's coming. Do you want to join us?'

'What's 3D?' asked Mary.

Millie laughed. 'Come and find out! You'll love it!'

Chapter Eleven

♥

Saturday 2nd July 2016

'Thanks for driving,' said Mary as she got out of the car.

'It's no problem. You couldn't exactly have driven anyway, seeing as though Millie's got your car now,' said Jim coming round to her side.

'She does need it more than me. But I think she's looking at cars with Bertie so I'm sure I'll get it back soon, then I can drive you instead.'

'Where are you going to take me? Anywhere nice?'

'Oh, well... I didn't mean... I just meant I could pay you back,' said Mary. She averted her eyes away from his, she didn't know where to look because it really had sounded like she was taking him on a date. Is that what he meant? Oh God, she couldn't stop putting her foot in it. 'This is a lovely house,' Mary said looking up at the roses covering the entrance. And big, she thought looking at the three tall double windows looking out on to the drive.

'Mary! Jim! You're here,' said Cecilia, Bertie's mum opening the front door. 'Come in, come in. I'm so glad Bertie invited you both. Mary, it's so nice to put a face to a name.' And she leaned forward and gave Mary a hug. 'Considering our girls have been such good friends over the years, I'm surprised we didn't meet sooner... Well, I'm just glad it's happened now.'

'Me too,' said Mary bowled over by how friendly Cecilia was.

'And Jim,' said Cecilia giving him a hand shake. 'Bertie hasn't stopped going on about the delicious food you make. As it's a movie night, I'm afraid I haven't gone all out, it's just some hot dogs, nachos and popcorn.'

'That sounds amazing,' said Jim.

'Hi darling,' said Cecilia as a tall handsome man with longish red brown hair came up and put an arm around her waist.

'This is Millie's mum, Mary. And Jim,' said Cecilia.

'Nice to meet you. I must say, I can see where Millie gets her looks from,' said Anthony.

'I hope that's a good thing,' said Mary feeling somewhat taken a back.

'It is,' whispered Jim close to her ear and laughed.

'I've got some low alcohol beers if you want to partake in one with food?' asked Anthony.

'Thanks, that'll be brilliant.' And Jim wandered off with Anthony.

'Um... I just wanted to say thank you,' said Mary catching Cecilia before she followed them into the kitchen.

'Whatever for?'

'For taking in Millie... when...' said Mary feeling exceedingly embarrassed. Mary knew she would have to face Cecilia tonight, mother to mother and she knew that she'd been a bad one by not sticking by her daughter.

Cecilia gently took Mary's hands into her own and looked deep into Mary's eyes. 'Of course I would have looked after Millie. I owed her one. When Richard died, your daughter was there for mine and if it hadn't been for Millie, I don't know whether Clarissa would have made it through as well as she did. You have nothing to be thankful for. And, I don't mean to pry, but Millie did tell us about the situation and it doesn't seem that you've had it easy either.'

Tears sprang to Mary's eyes at how kind Cecilia was being to her, she'd expected judgement, not that Cecilia would have done that, but it was her own negative self judgement that had spilled over and the lines had got blurry.

'Hey,' said Cecilia. 'I'm here if you need me too. For anything. Even if it's for just a cup of tea and a chat. Ok?'

'Thank you,' said Mary. 'I might actually take you up on that.'

'Good, I hope you will,' said Cecilia. 'Right, are you hungry? Let's get some food and then Anthony will do the grand unveiling.'

'Are you ready?' said Anthony holding on to the door handle.

'Yes!' they all shouted.

'Mary, Jim as you two haven't see any of it before, you go first,' said Anthony holding open the door.

'Go on, ladies first,' said Jim.

Mary looked at the concrete steps that led into utter darkness.

'There are lights at the bottom of the steps which will come on as you go down. They're motion detector ones,' said Anthony.

Mary held on to the wooden bannister and gingerly made her way down. As she went blue led lights lit up her way. When she reached the bottom, she looked around in amazement as all the lights switched on. There were two rows of eight comfortable looking leather chairs, the back row being slightly higher than the front. The walls looked like they'd been upholstered in a dark grey velvety material that looked spongy to touch and they matched the springy grey, black and white striped carpet. It was very sumptuous. Mary couldn't see a screen as it looked like it was hidden by some heavy burgundy curtains.

'Wow!' said Jim coming up behind her. 'A proper cinema.'

'I can't wait to watch this film,' said Millie following Bertie into the back row.

'No hanky panky at the back there,' said Anthony. 'I know what you two are like.'

'Young love,' said Cecilia.

'A bit like us really,' said Anthony planting a loving kiss on Cecilia's head. 'Mary, go on, sit in the middle. You'll have the best view.

'Oh no I couldn't,' said Mary.

'Millie mentioned you haven't seen a 3D film before?'

'No I haven't.'

'Go on then, first time, sit there. We'll have loads of time to sit where we want. Please?' said Anthony.

'Ok,' said Mary sitting down. The chair was as comfortable as they'd looked. She was going to have to be careful not to fall asleep.

Jim sat down next to her and their elbows touched. It felt nice, feeling him there.

'Put these on,' said Anthony passing some glasses around.

Jim must have noticed Mary's look of puzzlement at the glasses and whispered, 'They're so that you can see in 3D, they're special glasses.'

'Oh,' said Mary feeling her heart quicken at his voice and warm breath near her ear.

The curtains were drawn back to reveal a huge TV screen.

'That's big,' muttered Mary.

'No hanky panky in the front either,' laughed Millie.

'What?' said Mary. She could hear her daughter and Bertie sniggering. What had she said now?

'That's what all the ladies say,' said Jim struggling to contain himself, his shoulders jigged against her. 'Sorry,' he said leaning towards Mary again. 'Your daughter started it.'

Mary realised what they were implying just as the movie began to play, she shrunk into her seat further wishing she could be swallowed up right then and there. Foot... mouth... again.

Mary wasn't sure whether she could the see difference between 3D or not at first but the story was interesting enough. A nice action one. It wasn't until the film got to the Hoover Dam when everything seemed to kick off at once. It was the simultaneous sound of explosions and people screaming and the screen seeming to come out at her that set her pulses racing. Her senses were on overload.

'Arghh...' Mary screamed.

Jim grabbed her hand. 'It's cool right?'

'Oh my God, yes! It's all so... It feels like you're actually there.'

Jim didn't let go of her hand after that. And it felt nice. He must like me, thought Mary. Cause you don't hold hands with just anyone.

The rest of the film was non-stop action and Mary did jump with fright maybe once or twice but then she got a reassuring squeeze from Jim and a smile. It felt like they were on a first date to the cinema and she didn't want it to end.

'Well, I must say, darling, all your hard work paid off because I really enjoyed that,' said Cecilia giving Anthony a peck on the lips.

'It was good wasn't it?' beamed Anthony.

'That was amazing,' said Millie. 'I can't wait to have more movie nights with you. So, mum, what did you think of it? I heard you scream.'

'I never imagined you could watch a film and feel it all so much. The vibrations went through me and after watching that, I think it would be rather boring watching a film without all those extras again.'

'My job is done,' said Anthony. 'We have a converted. 3D and surround sound is it.'

'Well, you've certainly converted me too,' smiled Cecilia. 'I'll arrange another movie night so that you can experience it again, Mary.'

'Thank you,' said Mary. 'I'd love that.'

'Do you want me to walk you in?' said Jim hovering by his car.

'No it's alright, I'll be fine.'

Mary dropped her bag as she fumbled through it for the keys to the café. Jim was making her nervous. At the end of the film, he'd taken his hand away and Mary had felt it. She didn't feel so safe and secure without him there. It was a new experience for her and she wasn't sure she liked it as it made her feel vulnerable too. What she really wanted was for him to come in, take her upstairs then go back down and lock everything up for her. But she just didn't want to be like that. She needed to stand on her own two feet.

Jim quickly crouched to the ground trying to pick up the keys for her, struggling in the semi-darkness, just as she also bent down to look for them.

'Ow,' said Mary as they banged heads.

'Oh no, are you alright? I'm sorry,' said Jim.

He leaned in closer to her and their lips met. His lips were so soft and he smelt wonderful. God, what was she doing? Just as she was about to break away, he backed off before she could.

'I'm sorry,' he said. 'I didn't mean that to happen.'

'No, I'm sorry,' Mary said searching for her keys so that she could run away and hide. He hadn't wanted to kiss her. He'd said so.

'Got my keys!' she squeaked. 'Thank you for driving tonight. Hope you have a good day off.' And with that she scootered into the safety of the café and let out a huge sigh once she'd shut the door and heard him drive away. On Monday, she would have to act as if nothing had happened and she really hoped that he would too.

Chapter Twelve

♥

Monday 4th July 2016

Act normal, act totally normal, Mary thought, as she paused at the door hearing Jim clattering away in the kitchen. He'd arrived earlier than usual that morning but she hadn't wanted to go down until now. She just didn't know what to say to him or how to act. One... two... three... Mary pushed open the door and nearly collided with Jim.

'Morning!' said Jim. 'I've just poured myself a cup of coffee, do you want one?'

'Um... yes please,' said Mary following him through the kitchen. 'Did you have a good day off yesterday?'

'Yes thanks, I went to the driving range. I haven't played golf in ages and I was quite rusty. My mate, Eddy, came along then we went for a pub lunch down by the river. Rowing the other week, it made me remember a nice little place that I hadn't been to in a long time. You can dine outside overlooking the river, it's so nice. You'll have to go sometime.'

So it was a 'you' not a 'we', Mary thought. She'd really got his signals wrong. He definitely wasn't interested in her then. Mary's heart sank. It was probably just as well; it would have only complicated matters. Strictly friendship from now on.

'Oh yes, Millie and I could go. I doubt she'd have been there either.'

Jim's face changed and Mary detected a fleeting sadness. What was that about?

Jim glanced at the clock in the café. 'I've got to nip out, are you alright making a start on the salads and holding the fort till I come back? I'll be an hour tops.'

Mary nodded. She could easily cope on her own in the café at this time of the morning. She knew pretty much all the regulars and what they had, there were only a few who deviated from their usual. Who'd have thought she'd pick it all up so quickly. Gerard had been wrong, she wasn't useless. He might have been right about her not being able to find another man who'd love her but she would take that. She'd prefer to be on her own and be independent than be in that type of relationship ever again.

Half an hour later, Jim was still not back and the café was beginning to fill up. Any more people and she might just panic.

'What can I get you?' she asked looking up at the next customer in front of her.

'Mary? What are you doing here? I can't believe it,' said Rosemary, the vicar's wife from her church that she hadn't actually attended since she ran out on Gerard.

'Hi,' said Mary as brightly as she could, feeling the ground beneath her slip away.

'Gerard said you were ill.'

'Ill? Oh yes, ill. But I'm fine now!'

'You do look well,' said Rosemary. 'You seem to have changed. You look brighter. Have you been working here for long?'

'Um... no. I'm um... Look I don't mean to be rude, but I'm on my own here and there's a queue of people behind you and...'

'Oh right, sorry,' said Rosemary glancing around the café.

'What can I get you?'

'A takeaway peppermint tea please and a slice of that marble cake. I'm having a treat.'

Mary got on with her order, quickly. The sooner Rosemary was out that door the better then she might be able to think more clearly. Rosemary was bound to say something to Gerard which meant that Gerard would inevitably come and find her. Mary was going to have to face him and she wasn't looking forward to the showdown.

A few minutes after Rosemary left, Jim came running in.

'Sorry, it took longer than I thought. Everything ok?' said Jim.

'Everything's fine,' said Mary thinking actually it's far from it.

'For a Monday, it seems awfully busy, maybe people are taking advantage of the nice weather and getting out and about before schools break up for the summer. You've done really well,' smiled Jim going off to take some orders.

Mary went off in the other direction to go and make a full English breakfast, she nearly burnt the bacon as her mind kept on wandering off visualising all the different outcomes of when Gerard would eventually turn up. None of them were good but the thought of going back to her old house and facing him was a complete no no. At least here, she had the advantage of witnesses, during the day anyway, so that he couldn't physically do anything rash.

Ten o'clock on the dot, Mo and Bill, Mary's favourite regulars came in. Mo fussed over Mary and even more so since she'd started living above the café. She was always offering her advice and asking after her well-being. It made Mary think about her own mum and how she'd died so young and wondered how her life would have turned out if she'd survived. She was sure there would have been no Gerard, but there would have been no Millie either. No more dwelling on what could have been. Mary would face Gerard and be strong. Her new found courage still didn't stop her from looking anxiously every time the doorbell jangled though.

What Mary didn't expect to see coming through the door was a distraught young lady. She was dressed in a sleeveless pink floral dress which came to a stop a few inches above her knees. Her sleek brown hair had been pulled back into a pony tail and her makeup still seemed to be immaculate despite the tears.

'Oh great,' muttered Mo. 'Look who's just walked in Bill? Her ladyship.

'What?' said Bill twisting around in his chair.

Mary wandered who had got them in a twist. Mary went to go and see the young woman but Mo put a hand out.

'I wouldn't. Let Jim deal with her. If he has any sense, he'll send her packing,' said Mo with a steel in her eyes, a side to her Mary hadn't seen before.

'Who is she?' asked Mary just as Jim came out of the kitchen carrying some food. The woman practically launched herself at him and nearly sent the food flying. He motioned frantically to Mary to come and take the food.

'Jim. Oh, Jim!' heard Mary. 'I've missed you so much. I didn't realise it, but you're the one for me. You've always been the one for me.'

Mary placed the food down in front of the customers and turned to see the woman draped all over him then she planted the biggest kiss right on Jim's lips. Mary felt sick. It must be his ex but maybe she's not so ex now. Mary could see Jim was trying to calm her down and they both disappeared through the back.

'Excuse me?' said a voice to her right. Mary came out of her trance and looked around the café. Mo's and Bill's eyes were on her and so was the person the voice belonged to. Pull yourself together, she thought. Nothing had happened between her and Jim, nothing had been said and she was sure of one thing, she didn't want to lose her job.

'Yes, how may I help you?' she asked turning her attention away from what was going on at the back of the café.

It was barely a minute later when Mary had to go into the kitchen and make an order. She listened for a few seconds, couldn't hear anything then ventured in. It wasn't until she was stood in the kitchen quietly making the food when she heard some raised voices coming from out in the store room and then some uncontrollable sobbing. It was none of her business. Just get on with the work. Concentrate on the work. Food plated, she went back out to the front of the café. Made some coffees, made some teas, dished out some cake, made some more coffees. By the time, Mary entered the kitchen again Jim was on his own looking harassed.

'Oh hi,' he said. 'Is that an order? I can do it.'

Mary handed it over then left.

Jim stayed in the kitchen after that. He cooked and cleaned all the while deep in thought with a sad look on his face.

Chapter Thirteen

💙

Saturday 9th July 2016

Mary had been waiting in anticipation for Gerard to turn up and if he was going to turn up, today would be the likeliest one. It was a Saturday and even though he played golf on a Saturday, he still might just postpone it and venture over.

Mary was as nervous as a mum walking around a china shop with a toddler. And that was scary. She knew because she'd been there and the same feelings were coursing through her now. Will he? Won't he? She hadn't told Jim about Rosemary coming in because that had happened on the same day his ex had turned up and since then he'd been distant and mono syllabic. He'd tried to smile at her but it just didn't feel real. It was only for appearances sake. And Mary didn't want to pry, he hadn't asked her difficult questions about her relationship with her husband so she wasn't going to either. She just missed their cheery chats and it wasn't until they'd gone that she'd realised just how much she missed them.

His flirtatious nature had also disappeared and Mary had felt that too. Even though she knew he didn't mean anything by it, it had somehow brought her out of her shell, got her wearing some makeup, got her thinking about what to wear. She'd liked that side of her, believing it had gone for good. Well, after she'd sorted things out with Gerard, maybe someone else could do that for her too. Her heart faltered as she still really wanted that someone to be Jim.

Mary's heart skipped a beat as she looked up out of habit and saw Gerard enter the café. She nearly ducked down behind the counter as she'd done when she'd seen her daughter but she needed to face him. Her heart raced and she felt sick with nerves. His beady eyes spotted her from across the room and she saw his lips narrow, a look she wished she'd never had to see again. He walked slowly towards her, Mary took a step back but there was nowhere to go.

He got to the counter then pointed his finger at her. 'You! How dare you just go off like that?' he whispered under his breath. 'I thought something had happened to you. I've rung around all the hospitals in case you'd had an accident. I nearly put in a missing person's report but the fact that you'd stripped your wardrobe bare made me think you'd left on purpose. You left your phone, you left no forwarding address. How dare you?' Gerard said beginning to raise his voice. 'After all I've done for you. Looked after you, kept a roof over your head when there was no-one else! I took you on! You owe me!' he shouted.

Mary flinched as she saw him make his way round to her side of the counter and went to grab her. But a hand got in his way.

'I don't think so,' said Jim coming out of the kitchen. 'This is my café and she is a member of my staff. You will stay over on that side. And she owes you nothing! I saw what you did to her, how she turned up for work with those bruises and cuts.'

Gerard blanched. All eyes in the café were now on him, even his daughter's, who'd just come through the doorway.

'You're a bully!' screamed Millie. 'And I hate you! For how you've treated me and mum! You don't deserve her, you never did!'

'You're not a man,' said Mary. 'You're a vile specimen that has just come crawling out of a rock. I'm never going to let you treat me like that again.'

'And I will never let you come near her again,' said Jim making sure he was now standing between Mary and Millie and Gerard. 'If you come making a scene like that in my café again or even think of touching Mary again, I will call the police. Do you hear me?'

Gerard nodded. Then as if he was trying to get the last word, to get some form of control back, he said, 'That's fine with me.' And just before he made his final exit he turned and shouted back over his shoulder. 'Oh and look out for the divorce papers my solicitor will be sending over in due course.'

'Mum, are you ok?' asked Millie giving Mary a hug once her dad had left.

'I'm fine now, are you? You were great!' said Mary feeling rather shaky.

'So were you! Mum! You stood up against him. I knew you could do it.'

Mary felt Jim pat her shoulder. 'You did good.'

'Thank you,' whispered Mary.

'You don't need to thank me. I would do anything for you? Don't you know how I feel?' said Jim looking into Mary's eyes.

Millie took a step back.

'What? No?' said Mary shaking more from what Jim was insinuating rather than the aftermath of Gerard.

'But we kissed? And I'd wanted to do that since the first moment I met you.'

Millie stood open mouthed looking from Jim to her mother in disbelief.

'But... but you never said anything... and your ex...'

'Is my ex. And that's all she'll ever be,' said Jim leaning down and brushing his lips against Mary's. 'It's you I want to be with. I just didn't want to come on too strong when you were coming out of a bad relationship.'

'Oh, I thought it was because you didn't like me.'

'Oh I really do,' said Jim and leaned in to give Mary a proper kiss.

'I told you,' muttered Mo from the other side of the room. 'I'm never wrong.'

The End

Pasture Prime

♥

Chapter One

Monday 31st October 2016

Kat surreptitiously hid a yawn just as her two flatmates came back from the bar.

'I saw that!' said Stella deliberately placing a drink and a shot in front of her. 'You are not disappearing on us like you did on Saturday.'

'You promised!' whined Phoebe pushing a lock of her blond hair aside.

'I'm here aren't I?' snapped Kat.

'Yes and you're staying here, unless of course a gorgeous man sweeps you off your feet,' said Phoebe.

'Phoebe, we were here on Friday night too. It's the same people. It's boring!' muttered Kat taking a swig of her drink then grimacing at the far too sugary liquid. 'And this is disgusting, what the hell is in this?'

'It's called vampire's kiss. I think it's champagne mixed with vodka and raspberry liquor. I like it!' Stella said taking a sip. 'The red sugar on the rim is yummy!'

'Do we have to try every Halloween cocktail tonight? I really would prefer just a plain G&T if I have to be here.'

Kat looked around the nightclub at the grinding ghosts, the leery zombies and the strutting vampires. Tonight was no different than all the other nights that they came to this club or one of their other popular haunts Kat's flatmates liked to go to. And she didn't know how they managed to drink for so many nights in a row and keep their complexion spotless and their energy levels high. Kat felt like she was twenty-two going on forty-five. After four years of bumping into the same people doing the same thing, for Kat it had become just plain tedious.

Four years ago, fresh from finishing A-levels, she'd been spotted shopping in Oxford Street. A talent agent had given her their card and told them to get in touch. Kat was taking a gap year in which she was supposed to be deciding what she wanted to do career-wise and needed something to fill her time. At first, she thought it was a joke but her twin sister, Bella, had told her to give them a ring. She'd ended up moving into a flat with Stella and Phoebe who were also with the model agency and basically had never looked back...until now.

It had been fun at first, the travelling, the beautiful locations and she'd got used to earning some good money on top of it. She'd also gained quite a few clients over the years which meant she was now much in demand. This also meant that her wage had increased exponentially and it was still climbing. She knew that there'd be a point where it would come to a halt. Modelling was a short term thing, her parents had warned her of that when she'd turned down going to university. Kat knew she had a few years yet but didn't know whether she actually wanted to continue for that long and what else could she do? The only other thing she liked doing was knitting and coming up with her own patterns, she couldn't exactly make a living out of doing that and if she did, she certainly wouldn't be able to earn as much as she was making now.

At eighteen she'd been naïve and had got caught up with being able to wear the latest trend, and be the actual trend setter and had loved being put on the VIP lists of all the popular and trendy pubs, clubs and restaurants. It was all about the trend. But then she realised that she was getting bored of it, of looking a certain way, dressing a certain way. She wanted to shake everyone and say stop caring about what other people think. Wear what you want, behave how you want, be with who you want without the constant feeling of being in a goldfish bowl. Because that's what it boiled down to. Everyone was going around in circles gaping at each other and trying to better the other person. The only problem was Kat didn't know what to do other than what she was doing now and she didn't know how to get away from it.

Kat hadn't wanted to go to university unlike her sister Bella. Even though they were twins, they were opposite in every way, looks and personality. While she was tall and slim, Bella was short and curvy, while she struggled at times socially, Bella could talk to anyone and everyone. Bella was unique and had never followed what was acceptable and Kat had secretly envied her, believing she could never be like her.

'Kat! Stop being a bah humbug! It's Halloween, have some fun!' said Stella flicking long red hair over her shoulder.

'I swear you only wanted me to come tonight to make up the third witch. You could have roped in someone else. What about Jade? She's got brown hair,' said Kat.

'Jade's been planning to be Cruella for ages. She would've said no. Anyway, it wasn't just about us coming as the Witches of Eastwick tonight, we actually wanted you here with us. So lighten up and put that down you,' said Phoebe handing her a shot of what looked like an eyeball. 'Down it in one.'

Kat acquiesced and she almost choked as the jelly like substance slid down her throat.

Phoebe shrieked beside her and jumped up. 'Yes! It's the Monster Mash! Come on, we've got to dance to this. Please! Come on, get up!' she said holding both hands out to Kat, Stella was already making her way over to the dance floor.

Kat danced alongside Phoebe and Stella copying their moves as everyone on the dance floor moved together. All they needed now was a sheep dog to round them all up. Kat sighed, and here was the wolf, a six foot four, very good looking zombie who seemed to have put her on his tracking beacon and was making his way across the dance floor heading straight for her.

'Kat!' he said whispering in her ear synchronising his dance movements to fit with the rest of the crowd around them. 'I've finally hunted you down, you're a hard woman to find.'

'Only from you,' she said smiling sweetly not wanting to be the latest notch on his bedpost, that and the fact that her flatmate was besotted with him. Goodness knows why!

'Giles!' said Phoebe blushing. She had had a very big crush on Giles since they'd spent one night together a few months ago but unfortunately for Phoebe it had been only the one night. Giles was a notorious womaniser but Phoebe hoped that she'd be that one woman he'd change his ways for.

Giles, realising that Kat wasn't going to reciprocate his feelings that night, ignored Phoebe and wandered off to find a different poor unsuspecting girl.

'Pheebs, you need to see him for what he is. Seriously, he's a sleaze bag. I don't know why you don't just say yes to going out on a date with Clive's assistant. He's cute and kind and he always bends over backwards to get you whatever you need on the shoots. What's his name?' said Kat.

'Dylan?' said Phoebe. 'No way! He's shorter than me!'

'Only when you're wearing heels,' said Stella. 'And most men are shorter than us unless we get lucky. I mean, I would go out with him if he acknowledged my existence.'

'But I like wearing heels,' Phoebe said to Kat. 'Why don't you ask him out then?'

'Because he's only got eyes for you,' said Stella twerking her bum towards her.

'He's just not my type ok?' said Phoebe clearly getting irritated.

'What and Giles the serial philanderer is?' said Kat walking back to their seats.

'He's simply misunderstood...' said Phoebe staring sadly into her drink.

Kat didn't bother replying. Phoebe had her blinkers on and there was nothing she could do about it. Kat glanced at her watch. 1:00 am. It was the fourth night she'd been up this late drinking and bed was seriously calling her.

'I'm sorry Pheebs, I've got to hit the sack. Do you want to grab a taxi with me or stay with Stella?'

Phoebe's eyes scanned the room and found Giles. It looked like he was going in for the kill, a cat purred beneath him loving every second.

'I'll come with you,' said Phoebe. 'Just let me go and tell Stella we're leaving. I'll meet you outside.'

Kat nodded and weaved her way towards the exit.

Chapter Two

♥

Thursday 3rd November 2016

'Up a bit...and look to the right. That's it...lovely.'

Kat wanted to look right up at the ceiling and it was hard not to. She was supposed to be concentrating on her pose. The rain was pounding against the reinforced stained glass window above her head. As the rain dropped, it dispersed creating pretty patterns and the pitter patter sounded like a lullaby making it hard to focus.

'Kat, darling! Let Karl put his arm around you, yes there, on the hip. Perfect. Now I want you looking towards that palm tree. The one next to Philippe. Brilliant!'

Kat wanted to wrinkle her nose in disgust but had to refrain from doing it as she didn't want to ruin the photos, the less time she had to spend with Karl the better. He'd had garlic for lunch and he reeked, she was sure he'd done it on purpose. Kat not being the social butterfly had put her foot in it with Karl and offended him the first shoot they'd been on. It had been stupid really, a misunderstanding and she'd apologised but he'd been po-faced around her ever since, he obviously wasn't going to let it slide.

Modelling wasn't glamourous, no matter what anyone thought. She was wearing a gorgeous dress with killer heels and her face was beautifully made-up but she ached, her feet were sore and she was blooming freezing. They were in a red bricked basement with no heating whatsoever in November and she was wearing a silk dress which skimmed over her and did little to keep her warm.

'Ok. Great. Thank you for your time. We'll call it a day. You've both been brilliant,' said the photographer.

Kat relaxed and mumbled a, 'see you around,' to Karl but he'd already marched off to get changed. One mistake. Just one. Or maybe he was like that with everyone. She leant down and took off her heels and rubbed the balls of her feet.

'I'll take those off you,' said a woman walking past.

'Thanks,' said Kat trying to smile but she was absolutely knackered. Thank goodness she didn't have work for the next few days. She was going home to her parent's house to celebrate their thirtieth wedding anniversary. There was going to be a big party. They'd even gotten a marquee erected on their lawn and outside caterers in. Her mum, who loved parties, had probably invited every single person she'd ever met in her life or tried to at least. Her dad was easy going and laid back so wouldn't mind, he'd just go and play golf with his mates and stay out of the way of the preparations.

Her mum was Bajan, brought up in Barbados the whole of her life and had fallen instantly head over heels in love, at a drinks' party, with the newly appointed English ambassador. It was a whirl wind romance and when her father's contract finished, he relocated taking a pregnant wife with him.

Kat's phone was ringing from within her bag by the time she got back to her little corner where she could change.

'Hello?' she said putting the phone up to her ear before she managed to look at who was calling.

'Sweetie, um... I've heard they've got some great shots the last few days, you must be tired but I've got one last job for you to do. It's tomorrow. It's only a short one and it's near your parent's neck of the woods so you won't be too far away to head on to them afterwards.'

'A short one?' sighed Kat. Christmas was coming up and she wouldn't mind the extra money.

'Yes, very short. A couple of hours. And you get to wear knitted jumpers so you won't even get cold darling. What do you say?'

'Where is it exactly?'

'Well if you say yes, I'll message you the post code. It'll be an easy drive. They've promised me. You just need to put it in your sat nav.'

'Ok. Go on then,' said Kat pulling up her jeans. 'Send me the details.'

'Fantastic! They asked for you specifically!'

'Yeah ok. I've already said yes, you don't need to convince me anymore,' said Kat.

'Byee!' said the voice on the other end of the phone hanging up.

'Bye.'

Kat's phone rang again and she let it ring while she pulled a hoodie over her head.

'Kat!' screeched her sister down the phone.

'What? What's happened?' said Kat.

'Nothing! Why? Has something happened?' asked Bella.

'No, you were screaming down the phone at me.'

'Oh sorry some fire engines went by at the same time you picked up the phone. I was worried you wouldn't hear me.'

'So there's no fire near you?' asked Kat.

'No.'

'Good. So what's up?'

'I've just picked up mum and dad's present, it looks amazing. I think they'll love it. Are you still good to go halves with me?'

'Yes definitely, I wouldn't know what to give them and you can't afford it all by yourself on your teacher's wage.'

'Oi! I do alright!' said Bella. 'And you're picking me up tomorrow at four?'

'Ah about that...' said Kat. 'I was actually going to ring you later, I'm still at work. I've been asked to do a shoot tomorrow, just a little job but it's near mum and dad's as in it's not in London, so you'll have to make your own way.'

'Oh ok. I'll get the train,' said Bella. 'At least I don't have to put up with your riveting conversation. I'd get more chat out of a doorstop.'

'Well you could do with one of those in your mouth, you never shut up!'

'I love you too and don't be late... we're having a pre family dinner on Friday evening.'

'I won't!' said Kat shoving the phone in her bag and pulling on her leather boots.

Another couple of beeps came through on her phone. She wasn't going to look at them now, she just wanted to get back to the flat, have a bath and curl up in front of the TV in her pyjamas.

Kat towel dried her hair and listened. Bliss. The flat was silent. Stella and Phoebe had gone off to the cinema and this time no amount of persuasion had made Kat change her mind on her evening's plans. Her phone dinged again and this time she went to look at her messages. A few from Bella reminding her to bring some smart clothes for the weekend and two from her agency with the details of her job.

She clicked on the link and it sent her straight to a map. Bloody Tessa! It was nowhere near her parent's home. It was possibly twenty minutes less than the usual route but still. It was pretty much in Wales and then she'd have to drive up the M5. She hated that motorway, there was always way too much traffic or silly buggers doing stupid things. So M4 across to Swindon, over the bridge, do the shoot then take the more scenic route back up to her parents in the Cotswolds. Sorted.

Chapter Three

♥

Friday 4th November 2016

The biting wind blew straight through the holes in the jumper dress she was wearing. It was a lovely chunky one with bright colours that zig zagged down the length of it. Ordinarily, Kat would have loved this shoot set against the backdrop of an old castle and in her favourite knitwear to boot. However, it was so cold that she was struggling to keep her jaws from chattering. The fake snow machine was sat there, off to one side left idle because the real McCoy was floating down around her. If they didn't get a wriggle on, someone would have to stand nearby with an umbrella above her head. A short one, Tessa had said, four hours in Kat swore she would never believe what came out of her mouth again.

'Ok Kat. We need just one more change and this time you can stand underneath the arch, at least it will shelter you a bit from the elements. I can't believe we've been so lucky with the weather,' said the lady with the clipboard.

Kat didn't reply. She knew she would say something inappropriate and didn't want to lose this client because they actually were a lovely company.

Kat's phone rang again. It was bound to be Bella checking up on her while she was happily reading on the train. One more change, she thought, shivering as she peeled off the dress being careful not to touch her hair and make-up otherwise she'd be there for even longer.

She stepped towards the arch and put her hand up against the rough-hewn rock and looked out. It was a beautiful part of the country; it was just a shame it was so friggin cold. She hoped her parents had hired some decent heaters for the marquee otherwise it was going to take a large amount of alcohol to forget about the icy temperatures.

'That's a wrap. Thank you so much Kat for doing this at the last minute. We really appreciate it,' said the lady coming over to her. 'It looks like the snow's coming in fast. Drive carefully won't you?'

Kat thought of her little mx-5 and wondered if she was going to even manage to make it to her parents. She shook her head. No, positive thoughts only. It would be fine. She'd never hear the end of it if she didn't arrive there on time, Bella would chew her ears off let alone her mum, it really wasn't worth thinking about it.

A record fifteen minutes later, Kat was setting off for the Cotswolds. The local travel news cut in interrupting a song to inform her that there were now delays in both directions on the M5 due to heavy snow so it was just as well she wasn't going that way. She smiled to herself then as her car crawled along the road parallel to the River Severn. But her smiles soon faded as she saw a man waving the cars down by the side of the road. She wound down her window and stuck her head out to try and hear what he was saying. The words 'accident' and 'diversion' were transmitted on the wind. And then he was pointing up the hill. How many more minutes would be added to her journey now?

From what she could make out, a few cars were at a standstill further ahead. One car was doing a six point turn in the middle of the road, obviously going back the way they'd just been while the 4x4 in front of her bumped across the grass verge on the left-hand side and took a single track up the hill. That must be the diversion, Kat thought. This was when she'd wished she hadn't gone for the little whooshy whooshy convertible with front wheel drive. But at the time she'd never believed that she'd be going off-roading in it.

Thinking herself very smart and quick thinking she followed the 4x4 which had just disappeared from sight. The front wheels turned in the mud and for a moment Kat thought her journey was coming to an end already but she put the accelerator down and the little car set off again at speed narrowly missing the ditch bordering the hedge.

Her phone rang again as she tried to avoid the potholes that looked like huge craters in the road. Some diversion. With the trees overhead at least it was stopping the majority of the snow from falling therefore making it slightly easier to navigate. The car hit another hole and she winced. The last thing she needed was to knacker her tyre. Trying to change a wheel with her work nails on was unimaginable.

The car ahead vanished from view so she put her foot down just as her phone began to ring. Even though it looked like she was off the main road, she didn't want to look at it. She was still driving. Whoever it was could blooming well wait. The caller was very persistent though and rang quite a few times then the ring cut off half way through. She glanced at it in relief, her car still hurtling along but in that split second she looked away her car crested the hill.

Kat let out a huge scream as the track shot downwards. It was very nearly a steep drop and exceedingly stony. And it was most definitely not road worthy, well not for her type of car anyway. Kat went to put her foot down on the brake but was far too late and her car careered down the hill, slipping and sliding as it went. Kat had no control whatsoever. It didn't help that the road was covered in snow as well, the woods having melted away before her, and the car that she'd been following at a distance was now barely metres away. She was going to crash.

'Help!' she shrieked at the top of her voice hoping that the person in front had seen her. They hadn't.

Kat pulled the wheel to the right and the car veered off and crashed into the one and only tree that stood on the hill. The car's airbags blew up in her face and she was jolted back and forwards.

A knocking on her window brought her out of her stupor and she screamed at the noise. Her car door flung open and a man gingerly took her out of the driver seat then planted her down on the ground.

'Are you alright?' he asked with concern.

'Yes, I think so,' she said looking up at a grubby older man's stubbly face that looked like he'd just walked out of a cesspit. She wrinkled her nose at the smell which was coming off him.

'Good,' he said. 'Good.' He paused for a moment. 'Then what the hell do you think you're doing driving this car on my land?' he shouted at her waving his arm towards her car and the field around them. A cow mooed nearby showing their disgruntlement too.

'I...I thought this was the diversion. I heard there was an accident,' she said really not liking the idea of being alone with this man seemingly in the middle of nowhere.

'Yes, on the M5, that's why the roads were chokka. All you had to do was wait a bit longer.'

Kat grimaced as he put his dirty fingers through his hair in frustration.

'Alright well you'd best come with me, and we'll ring for someone and see if they can come and get you.'

'Um...I can do it thank you.'

Kat didn't like the look of this grumpy and rude man and she didn't know him from Adam. He could be a psycho serial killer for all she knew or going by his behaviour he might want to lock her up in a cupboard and keep her as his pet. Yeah no. She'd be fine out here. She had her own phone, she didn't need his.

'There's not much reception here, you'll be lucky if you manage to get many bars,' he said standing there with his hand on his hip, a determined expression on his face.

He just wanted to kidnap her, thought Kat. He wanted to lure her away and...

'Suit yourself,' he said walking back to his car. 'But if you change your mind, follow the path down the hill, take the right and my house is at the end.'

Kat nodded smiling now that he was leaving her.

'And,' he said sticking his head out the window, 'make sure you stick to the path and shut the gates properly behind you. I don't want the bulls getting out.'

Kat gulped. Bulls? There was no way she was going down there then.

Kat watched the car until she could no longer see the red of his tail lights in the greying light. She grabbed her phone from the passenger seat footwell and shone it at the front of the car to see the damage. She winced and sucked in a breath.

'Oh God, that is bad! Really bad!' She would need to get someone to tow it away, by the looks of it it was probably going to be destined for the scrap yard. Her dad would know what to do, he'd help.

She went to make a phone call. No blooming reception. The man had been right. She shivered in her not so winter coat. She'd brought it because it'd look nice for the weekend, not out of practicality. She stamped her feet to get warm and her beautiful Italian leather boots disappeared beneath some muddy snowy slush. She screamed inside her head and a slew of swear words came forth. Could this get any worse?

Kat walked away from the car waving her arm up in the air to and fro in the hope of getting some signal. Nothing. She was stuck here. The snow was beginning to soak through her coat and she could feel the cold and wet seeping on to her jumper. The crack of a branch made her jump and look behind her. She thought she saw some movement in the trees.

'Hello?' she whispered.

Oh she really didn't like this one bit. Her heart quickened as she heard a whistling sound and then a thud. Ok so maybe the guy wasn't a serial killer and maybe there was one now lurking in the trees, hiding and waiting until dark came and then they'd pounce on her... a poor defenceless woman. That was not going to happen. She didn't want to be the top headline in the newspapers the next day. 'Body found in woods, mutilated beyond recognition.'

Hell no! I'm out of here. I'd prefer to take my chances with the stinky man. Plus, he mentioned a phone, she thought pulling her suitcase out of the back of her car. The suitcase landed with a thump onto the stony ground. It was heavier than she remembered but then she hadn't packed it thinking that she would have to lug it over a couple of fields in her high heeled boots.

What did she have in there that she could actually use in the countryside anyway? A slinky dress for a black tie do? Nope. Some lovely elegant high heels? Nope. A pair of black satin trousers? Nope. Basically the only thing worth taking was some clean underwear, her toiletries (which actually didn't amount to much because she'd thought of borrowing some of her sisters, she had way more skin toning and cleansing products than she did) and her pyjamas.

Having put her suitcase back in the boot without the afore mentioned items, Kat set off down the hill. She really was hoping that she wouldn't have to use them and that she'd be able to get out of there that night but the snow was falling thick and heavy and she didn't want her parents to come in case they had an accident too. Maybe the guy might be able to take her to a B&B nearby.

The mud and snow squelched beneath her feet and she knew without a doubt that one of her favourite pairs of shoes were ruined. Kat shone the torch on her phone in front of her sidestepping most of the worse bits. A wall loomed out of the mist that had now come down and she saw a wooden gate with a sign on it. She squinted through the mud splattered on it to read, 'Beware Bull!' Kat looked to the right and saw some yellow lights in the distance shining through the snow.

So was this the only way to reach the house...with a bull or bulls out there somewhere? Was he having a laugh? So he did want to do her an injury... There is no way that she was stepping foot in that field with those deadly and fierce beasts waiting for her, ready to gore her in the stomach and stampede over her with their hooves. Nah uh!

Kat looked to the right of the wall and followed it along until she got to a barbed wire fence that surrounded the field. She couldn't go any further. She could see the house and it actually looked quite inviting with smoke coming out of its chimney and the lights casting a warm glow into the gloom around it.

A cow mooing just behind her made her jump. What the...? Kat turned around and saw silhouettes of at least five hulking beasts coming towards her. She let out a shriek, grabbed hold of the rock on the wall and vaulted over the entire thing. Her boots came down hard, with an enormous thwack and her ankle rolled over.

Her scream echoed into the night as she fell to the ground, stones jutting into her at every angle and then she smelt it, through the pain, the most disgusting smell imaginable. Cow poo. Fresh steaming runny cow poo. Her scream was soon replaced by a sob. Kat never cried, not really, she saw it as a sign of weakness but there was no-one here now and she'd had enough. Her car was a right-off, her leather boots were for the bin and she was covered in animal excrement and the only person around to come to her rescue was a stranger with anger issues.

Kat was crying so hard that she didn't hear the footsteps approaching.

'What are you doing down there?' shouted an irritable male voice.

'I'm sun bathing, what does it look like I'm doing?' retorted Kat through her sobs at the ridiculous question. 'I fell alright? I couldn't get my phone to work...'

'I did tell you...' muttered the man under his breath.

'Yes thank you...' she said sarcastically. 'And so I came here to ask if I may use your phone, like you kindly mentioned before.'

'Can you stand?' said the guy crouching down to look at her.

In the fading light, Kat thought that she saw a flicker of pity but she must've been mistaken. Kat made to stand up.

'Ow!' she said sitting herself back down. 'I think I've hurt my ankle.'

'I'm going to carry you into my house, is that alright with you? You're not going to spit at me are you?'

'Spit? Why on earth would I spit, who do you take me for? I'm not one of your geese, you know,' hissed Kat.

'I don't have any geese, but if I did, they'd probably behave nicer than you, and they're a mean bunch of...'

'I don't know how you're insulting me when you're the one...'

Kat stopped mid-flow as she was lifted up off the ground. She looked up at the man in surprise. He was stronger than he appeared as he carried her without catching his breath. As if she was as light as a feather...

They were only a few metres away from the house when she quickly studied his face. He had a strong jawline, bushy eyebrows that needed a seeing to, and a rather bulbous nose from which a noticeable bump protruded. Was there a wife or someone inside that was going to go for her because he had his arms around her? Kat squinted and leant out, trying to peer in through windows of the house as they passed.

'Stay still,' he said. 'You're worse than the sheep. Do you want me to drop you?'

'No,' said Kat going like a statue. She was just going to have to face whatever was coming her way.

The man ducked beneath the doorway. He was either taller than she realised or he lived in a house meant for snow white and the seven dwarves.

'Fly! Get off there now!' he cried out.

Fly? He had a fly as a pet? Kat was ceremoniously dumped on a chair as she saw the white tip of a what looked a tail go out of her line of sight. Was that a dog? Please tell me it was a dog. She liked dogs, dogs she could do.

'I've already rung my mate,' the man said going to the sink to wash his hands. 'He's busy tonight, the snow has brought some casualties. You're lucky you weren't one of them.'

Kat didn't look round to answer because she was too busy taking in everything around her. There was a comfortable three-seater sofa and two chairs surrounding a wood burner that was letting out enough heat that it felt like she was back in Barbados. Blankets covered the seats and were filled with three sheep dogs. One paid no attention to the additional human, the other was clearly passed out, while the third one sat looking at her intently. Maybe that was Fly, Kat sensed a feeling of displeasure being aimed at her, and it was her seat that she was in.

Kat's eyes wandered over to the little TV which stood on a round stool in the corner of the room as if it had been placed there as an afterthought and at the amateurish paintings. One she recognised as having been painted from where she'd crashed her car. It was pretty good, whoever was the creator had a good eye.

'Well?' said the man.

'Uh?' said Kat having zoned out entirely.

'Do I have to repeat myself?'

Kat pulled a face.

A growl escaped him, 'I said that he might be able to come out tomorrow, weather permitting but in the meantime is there anyone who can pick you up or take you home?'

'Er...well... Can I use your phone to ring my dad and tell them what's happened? It's just that they're expecting me.'

'The phone's there,' he said pointing at it.

'And I don't live near here. I live in London...' said Kat.

'Well that explains it,' he muttered. 'Typical city...'

'And my parents live in the Cotswolds, about an hour and twenty from here, so not far,' she said quickly before he went into a full rant.

'It's far enough in this weather,' he said and seeing Kat struggle to get up, he handed her the phone instead.

'Dad?' Kat said breathing out a huge sigh.

'Are you alright? Are you on hands free?' he said.

'I've had a crash! I'm fine, just a hurt ankle but the car's a right off.'

'Oh god sweetheart! Where are you? What happened? Was anybody else hurt?'

'Just a tree. I'm in the forest near the Wales border and... hold on... Where are we?' she asked the man.

'Let me speak to your dad, it'll be easier.'

'Oh right, well, if you're sure... you'll arrange everything then?'

'Yes,' said the man sighing stroking one of the dog's heads before taking the phone off her again.

'Hello? Mr...? Right, Mr Fletcher-Jones, your daughter was trespassing on my land and...'

Wait a minute, I wasn't trespassing, there was no trespassing, I was following a car that... for heaven's sake... I was trespassing, thought Kat. What was her dad going to say to that?

'It's alright, I don't think she meant to...' Pause. 'Yup. Oh right, she does does she?' And the man smirked in her direction.

I do what? What do I do? Kat was getting rather irritated that she couldn't hear both sides of the conversation.

'Uh huh!' he said smiling.

Kat frowned. He was smiling. She didn't know he had it in him. He actually looked quite handsome and his eyes had a mischievous glint in them that she didn't wholly trust, sexy and steely at the same time. Oh God, she must have banged her head more than she thought. He must be at least twenty years older than her and... no...just no... What was she thinking? The problem was that she clearly wasn't.

'Yup, I'm ok with that, there's plenty of room.' Pause. 'Uh huh! Really? I wouldn't have thought that, she's barely skin and bone...oh right.' Pause. 'Whenever you want... My name's Ben. Ben Jones. And my address is...'

What did he mean by whenever you want? She wasn't staying here. Kat looked down at her jeans and hoodie. She was a mess and she smelt just as bad as him, Mr Ben Jones over there.

'Ok... do you want to speak to her? Alright, well I'll see you when I see you... No problem. Bye.'

'Didn't he want to speak to me?' Kat asked. She didn't normally have lengthy phone conversations with her father. She hated the phone and spent as little time on it as possible but just then she actually wanted to hear her dad's voice. She was feeling rather vulnerable. It wasn't the fact that she was in a strange house with a strange person, she was used to that in her job. It was... she didn't know... and tears came unbidden, a drop escaped rolling down her cheeks. She didn't cry either but here she was...again.

'Hey!' Ben said patting her on the shoulder. 'Your dad's going to sort it all out as soon as he can. And I've even got a spare room for you to stay in.'

At that, Kat began to sob uncontrollably while Ben hovered nearby.

'Is it your ankle?' he asked once her crying had subsided.

Kat shook her head. 'No... Is he coming to pick me up tomorrow?'

'He said he'll try but it's all dependent on the weather, there's a big storm coming. Right, well if you're sure you ok, I've got to get the cows down from off the hills.'

'You're leaving me here? Like this?' she said pointing at her clothes. 'I need a hot shower.'

'I don't have a shower but there's a bath. You'll have to wait though, while the water heats up, I wasn't expecting a visitor.'

'Fly! Mist! Jet! Out!' he said opening the door.

A gust of cold wind blew in and brushed past Kat and she sunk lower into the chair glad that she wasn't out there still.

'Make yourself some tea if you want, there's milk in the fridge.'

The door banged shut and Kat was alone but she didn't feel lonely. The room was cosy and had a nice feeling about it. Oddly enough, it felt like she'd come home. At the small windows were thick heavy curtains and they were tied back with some gold rope. Snow was falling thick and fast; it should have been darker than it was but the heavy white clouds somehow brightened up the sky. She didn't know whether there was another person living in the house or not besides him. He hadn't mentioned anyone else but Kat stayed alert. Well tried to... but watching the flames flickering in the burner made her eyes heavy and her mind drowsy.

Kat wrinkled her nose as a delicious smell wafted her way. She heard a clattering of a pan and she sat up, yawning.

'Oh good you're awake. Here...' he said handing her a plate of shepherd's pie and a good helping of peas and broccoli. 'Eat this, it'll warm you up.'

Kat couldn't help it but instead of looking at the plate of steaming food, her eyes roamed over his fingers and hands. They were clean. Thank goodness.

'Take it then!' he said. 'There's nothing else for tonight so if you're vegan or...'

'No, no, it looks delicious,' she said smelling it. 'Thank you.'

Ben looked at her in surprise then sat down opposite her and begun tucking in.

Why was he surprised? That she ate meat or... oh... the thank you. She had been a bit rude considering he'd done nothing but help her out. Kat had the decency to blush and glanced across at her knight in shining armour.

'So... are you married? Is there a girlfriend around?' she asked.

'Why? Are you offering?' he said with a seriousness in his tone.

'What? God no!' said Kat.

Ben looked affronted and frowned at her. 'There was no need to say it like that. I know I'm past my prime but I am a man of means. I have land, I own my own house, I'm also regarded as a valuable member of the community... and I'd only beat my wife if she did something really wrong...'

'Beat your... Are you for real?' asked Kat.

'No I'm being facetious. Now eat your food up while it's warm and mind your own business.'

'No...um I just meant...' said Kat at a loss for words for once in her life. It seemed she'd met her match. 'I just wanted to know if there was someone that was going to be angry with me being here.'

'Yes there is,' he said scraping his plate clean.

'What? Who?' said Kat.

'Fly, you've taken her seat.'

Fly was indeed looking particularly miffed and was staring at Kat almost willing her to get out of the chair.

'You could have put me in the other one over there,' sniffed Kat.

'That one over there is the furthest away from the front door. You may look like a skeleton but you still weigh a fair amount,' Ben said putting his plate in the sink.

Kat gave him a withering look. 'I am not a skeleton and I eat a lot. I've just got a fast metabolism!

'Yeah so your father said.'

'What else did he say?' asked Kat with her mouth full.

Ben was silent.

Oh now he's choosing not to speak.

Kat finished her food and got up to put her plate in the sink too. She pressed down on her ankle but it seemed ok, it had just needed a bit of rest.

'Do you want a cuppa?' Ben said not realising Kat was beside him and nearly sent her falling again but he caught hold of her waist and pulled her into him.

She could feel the warmth of his breath on her neck, and his big hands sent shocks through her body. Kat gazed up into his eyes to see warm and kind brown hazel eyes gazing back at her. For a moment they didn't move, they both seemed to be in the same trance. Ben broke away first.

'I didn't see you there, you're more like Tinkerbell, but a much larger version...'

'You sure know how to compliment a woman don't you?' said Kat getting used to his ways.

'Oh you want compliments now, first you offer me marriage and then you expect niceties in return... I'll get you a cuppa and seeing as though you're on your feet, I cooked so you can wash up.'

'That's fine with me!'

'Good, well... yes... fine,' Ben said.

Kat smiled as he noticed his skin turning a shade of red at the back of his neck.

'So, Ben, seriously, why no girlfriend, no wife? And no I'm not offering before you say anything. But you're... well... not bad looking and as you say so yourself you're a man of means...'

Ben leant against the counter. 'I had a girlfriend, we were at school together but she didn't like the farm life. There's only a certain type of girl that can put up with a farmer and his hours and his animals. And I suppose I've been too busy to find one and I wouldn't know where to begin.' He shrugged and poured the hot water into two cups.

Kat didn't say anything. She had plenty of opportunities to meet a boyfriend, in the clubs she frequented and through work but none had caught her eye so what chance did he have?

'Thanks for doing that,' he said pointing at all the clean pans and plates drying on the rack. 'I gave you one sugar, I don't know whether you take it or not but you've had a bit of a shock today.'

'Thank you,' said Kat at his kindness. 'I don't normally no but in this instance...'

'So,' Ben said sitting down next to the dogs. 'Am I going to have a jealous boyfriend beating down my door?'

Kat laughed. 'No. Your door will be fine.'

'Thank goodness for that,' he mumbled blowing into his tea, the corners of his mouth showing the beginnings of a smile.

'Do you think I could take a bath now?' Kat asked. 'And is there any way I can wash these?' she said pointing to her clothes.

'Yup, there's hot water now. I'll get the tub filled up, do you want it in here or the barn?'

'The... what?' asked Kat thinking no wonder he had no-one else living with him.

'And of course the sink's free now you've done the washing up so you can wash your clothes there...'

Kat didn't know whether he was teasing her or not. His face was deadly serious. The house did look quite basic. After all there weren't even any radiators, just one main burner.

'I... um...'

Ben chuckled. 'The bathroom's upstairs. And my sister sometimes stays in the spare room so there'll be some of her clothes in the cupboard. She's the same height as you. They might be a bit big but you'll find all you need. Just save me a bit of water. It's not an endless tank.'

Kat looked at him with a semi-bemused smirk on her face. No-one had teased her this mercilessly before, people tended to pussy foot around her and pander to her tantrums and moods but Ben... he didn't take any of her crap and she actually felt comfortable around him, she could be herself.

She opened the latch door and tiptoed up a steep stair case as it creaked beneath every step she took. Bookshelves reaching the ceiling lined the walls on either side. He loved to read then. She peered at the titles and recognised a few of the more well-known authors, a couple of Stephen King, Dean Koontz, Agatha Christie and quite a few she didn't know but the covers looked interesting. If she was bored...

Stepping on to the landing, she was stood in a long hallway with doors going off to the left.

'Second door on the left is your bedroom,' shouted Ben from below.

The first door Kat peered into, as it was open, was the bathroom and it was surprisingly modern and had a shower hose above the bath. There was a shower. Kat scowled and sent hidden daggers to Ben downstairs. She then opened the second door and switched on the light. It had been tastefully decorated in neutral colours. Two single beds took up the space, one wardrobe, a chest of drawers and what looked like an easel. A few boxes splashed with paint leant up against the wall to the side of it. Was this where Ben painted or his sister?

Chapter Four

♥

Kat had slept like the dead. After the shower she'd laid down on the bed nearest the window and passed out. It was comfier if not more so than sleeping in her bed at her parent's home. No traffic, the sound of the wind whistling through the trees and around the house and the odd animal noise. Her parent's house was at the far end of a little village surrounded by fields so she was used to the countryside but hadn't spent any amount of time in a place so rural – not like a farm.

It was still dark outside but she heard someone huffing and puffing in the vicinity. Kat quickly rooted through the drawers and found a pair of jeans, they were a bit big but nothing a belt couldn't solve and then spotted a long sleeved top and a knitted jumper. She bounded down the stairs and a warning growl came from the chair.

'It's alright Fly, I'm not going to turf you out of your seat.'

Kat peered out the window and gasped. Everything was white. It literally looked like a blanket had covered everything in the night. A grunt made her glance to her right. Ben was busy shovelling snow making a path from the front door to the barn. She knocked on the window and he looked up. She made the sign of drinking and he nodded.

'You won't be going anywhere today, I'm afraid,' said Ben taking his boots off several minutes later. 'The phone line's down and the snow is quite deep in places.'

Kat would miss her parent's party but she doubted it would go ahead anyway. At least she was safe and they knew where she was so they wouldn't worry. A part of her felt a bit of relief. She could hide away from everyone for a bit. And not do anything she didn't want to do.

'I need your help, if you're up for it,' said Ben sipping his tea.

Or maybe she would have to do something she didn't want to do. She looked at him questioningly.

'I need to clear some of the snow away.'

Kat's face dropped and he must have seen it, she didn't work out much and so had no muscles to speak of. Shovelling snow would pretty much break her.

'No, you don't have to do that. The tractor's going to do all the hard work, I just had to get to the tractor first. I need some help feeding the animals. George from up the road comes to help part-time but he won't be able to get here.'

'Um... I'll try, if you're sure you want my help?' Kat was hoping he'd change his mind. The thought of bulls charging after her was not filling her with any lovely warm feelings and her body shivered involuntarily.

'I'll get you kitted out so you won't feel the cold, don't worry.'

'Okaaay,' she said her eyes darting to the kitchen. 'Shall we have a bite to eat first?'

'No, feed the animals first, I'll cook us up something afterwards.'

'I can barely move,' said Kat walking around like a Michelin Man, she had that many layers on.

'I don't want you moaning of cold when we're on the top fields with the sheep,' Ben said rifling through a drawer.

'Top fields?'

'Yup. Here,' he said handing her a pair of well-worn gloves. 'And you put the two pairs of socks on like I said?'

'Yes!' she said.

'Good! Come on then, follow me!'

Kat stepped out of the house. 'Oh my God! That wind is...chilly!'

But Ben was already out of earshot striding away from her towards the huge barn. Mist gave a little whine then she ran after her master.

'I'm coming...' she muttered thinking of the nice warm bed she'd just left behind.

'Right, over there are bales of hay, you need to put some along this trough for the cows.'

At the mention of cows, a nose sniffed and made its way out between the bars, clouds of mist coming out of the nostrils. Two gorgeous doleful eyes gazed into hers and her heart melted. Up close, they were so cute. Before she knew what she was doing, she approached it and began to stroke the little tuft of hair sticking out of the forehead. Another cow came alongside the other one and soon she had both of her hands out giving them some attention.

'I didn't think you liked cows,' Ben said picking up the water hose.

Kat shrugged. 'Neither did I but they are safe behind these,' she said indicating the barrier.

'Give them some food then,' he said moving further along with the pipe.

Kat looked to where the rectangular bales of hay had been stacked up, walked over to them and pulled away a couple of handfuls then plonked them into the trough. The two cows devoured it in seconds.

'The hay's there,' said Ben glancing back at Kat.

'I know. I've already given them some,' said Kat indignantly.

Ben looked towards the bales with a funny expression on his face. 'The bales are all still there.'

'I know they're all still there... oh,' she said looking at the row of expectant faces. 'Not just a few handfuls then?'

Ben sighed. 'I don't know what I've done wrong to deserve this,' he said looking up to the barn roof. 'But I hope you've got a good plan.' And he walked over to the bales, picked up one whole one then brought it over to the trough, grabbed a knife from the side pocket of his trousers, cut the string then made light work of breaking it up and letting it fall along the length of the trough.

The cows' moos sounded like their demands had been finally met.

'It would have helped if you'd explained exactly what was expected of me,' Kat said pouting trying to pick up one of the bales. It was very cumbersome and he'd made it look so easy.

'Forget it, I'll do that! Fill up these two buckets with the grain from that metal bin over there. If you go through that door, you'll find the chickens. You'll need to go inside and then just spread it around the ground. Make sure none escape. Ok?'

Kat nodded. Chickens. The only time she'd been near a chicken was when it had been cooked and served on a plate. Their little sharp beaks looked lethal, they could peck her eyes out, make huge gouges in her legs. Kat turned to look back at Ben to see if she could get out of it but he was busy carrying the bales back and forth.

She wandered out to the chicken coop and upon seeing her the chickens squawked loudly and began to run around and around in circles. The huge tree hanging over the shed had done a great job of stopping the majority of snow from falling into their space but it was getting pretty muddy in places. Kat pulled the latch back and one of them made a move towards her.

'Shoo,' she screamed. 'Go away!'

But the chickens paid no heed and strutted towards her, their crazed beady eyes darting in all directions while their lizard like claws moved steadily forward. The Jaws theme song began to sound in her head. 'dunnnn dun, dunnnnn dun, dun dun dun dun dun....'

The deadliest chicken out of all of them, with an almost reddy tinge to its eye made a sudden move and shot forward its head diving into the bucket. Kat let out a scream as the rest of them followed suit and the bucket was pulled out of her hand by the sheer force of the feathered monsters. Grain spread everywhere and the chickens clucked and screeched even louder.

I've got to get out of here, she thought quickly tipping the rest of the bucket out. Because once they'd eaten that lot, they could come after me. It was karma. 'You eat us,' she could imagine them saying 'so we'll eat you.'

Kat flung the door open, remembering to duck her head and shut it behind her fumbling to close the latch in her haste.

'Well done!' said a voice behind her. 'That wasn't too hard now was it?'

'They're vicious evil things. And that one,' she said pointing to the leader, 'is the worst. It came at me, tried to attack me.'

Ben laughed. 'You had food... Look they're almost like pets,' and he crouched down by the mesh wire, picked up some grain in his hand and held it out. 'Marge? Come here girl! Show Kat, you're a little lady!'

The evil leader put her head up and cocked her head to one side at the sound of her name then strutted towards them at a sedate pace.

'There you go...a lady...aren't you Marge? What's she saying about you?'

Kat spluttered next to him. 'She was certainly not acting like that a moment ago.'

Ben chuckled as Marge pecked daintily at the grain on his hand. 'Maybe now they've met you, you won't scare them so much next time and...'

'Next time?'

'Yes, they get fed twice a day,' he said getting back up. 'Right now it's the pigs turn.'

'Pigs?' said Kat turning her nose up following Ben round the back of the barn where she saw a few corrugated sheds. As she got closer, Kat could hear the loud snorts and sniffing coming from out of them. The door to one of the sties was shuddering.

'Alright Hermione, you've got an itch have you?' And he dropped his hand over the other side of the door.

Kat peered over the edge. 'That is huge! And you're itching it?'

'I need to get her away from the door because we have to go in.'

'We?' she asked looking into the darkness. 'Are they dangerous?'

'No!' said Ben.

To the side of the shed, Ben opened another little gate and inside were more metal bins. 'Their food is in here. Pellets. Fill another couple of buckets...'

Kat waddled over. She was trying to get used to the multitude of layers that he'd made her wear. It wasn't that cold.

With the buckets full, Ben said, 'You do that one and I'll do these sheds over here.' And he began to walk off.

Kat opened the door and quickly shut it behind her. Immediately the pigs, obviously smelling the food began to butt her legs. Kat screamed flung the food up in the air and climbed over the gate...and got stuck. She was now sat astride it one leg over each side neither one reaching the ground and it wasn't particularly comfortable on her...

'What are you doing?' said Ben returning with empty buckets. 'You can open the gate you know.'

'Yes, thank you. But again your animals seem to have a habit of charging at me so I had to make a rather rushed escape. Now instead of laughing at me. Yes, I can see you trying to hide it. Please could you be so kind as to help me?'

Ben went to take her hand but then saw the pellets in a huge pile. 'You were supposed to spread it all out so all the pigs could get to it.'

'Well I didn't have a chance. If you hadn't left me... Please?' Kat said holding her hand out for him to take.

'This seems to becoming rather a habit doesn't it, me saving you from precarious positions...' he said and instead of taking her hand he put his whole arm around her waist and hoisted her off the gate. Kat lurched towards him as he put her down and their lips met. They both stood still. Kat's heart was beating like the clappers and a warm feeling was beginning to spread through her stomach. His lips were...were... manly and... just...felt nice. They felt right. How many people had she kissed and yet it was Ben that made her feel like this? Who'd have thought?

'Sorry,' said Ben blushing and stepping away from her quickly and looking into the shed.

'It was nice,' muttered Kat not believing that she'd actually said that out loud.

'It was?' said Ben slowly turning around to face her.

Kat nodded and ran her eyes up and down the gorgeous rugged older man in front of her. That's where she'd been going wrong. She'd been looking at the wrong people and in the wrong places. And her heart gave an extra couple of thumps against her rib cage in agreement.

Ben blushed. 'Oh well that's good then,' he said walking off back to the barn.

Kat stayed there for a second or two. Was that all he was going to say? Or do? Did he not like her? I mean she was used to having plenty of admirers, she was a model for heaven's sake... a stunningly beautiful woman, that's what she'd been told and she even admitted that she liked him, well, liked his kiss and he goes off? Seriously? Kat frowned and pursed her lips then hurried off after him.

By the time she'd reached him, he was sat atop a quad bike revving it up.

'Cool!' said Kat. 'I've always wanted to go on one of these. Can I drive?'

'No you can't, it's treacherous out there, it's going to be hard enough to navigate the terrain as an experienced driver.'

'Oh,' said Kat her face falling.

'I'd teach you if there'd been no snow,' he said quickly. 'Maybe if...' And he looked away from her again seeming to be embarrassed.

Kat went to sit behind him and as her foot swung round, she felt herself falling off. Ben put out his hand and steadied her.

'Sorry,' she said. 'I seem to be a bit clumsier than usual. It's all these layers, I'm losing my balance....'

Ben's lips pressed down on hers. She moaned as his arms wrapped around her in a warm embrace. After what felt like an age, he pulled away and grinned seeing Kat's stunned expression.

They then made their way slowly out of the barn pulling the small trailer of hay bales behind them. Ben put on a bit of speed and the quad bike lurched beneath them. So as not to fall off she quickly put her arm around Ben. Again he felt so good next to her...and cuddly. And she rested her head against his back.

Halfway up the hill, Ben shouted, 'How are you holding up? It's going to be even colder when we get to the top. Not long now.'

'I'm fine,' said Kat glad that she was snuggled up against him. It was absolutely freezing and the wind was having a good go at cutting through her clothes. Thank goodness Ben had told her to layer up.

By the time they reached the top, the snow was heavy and they could barely see a metre in front of them. Ben got off the bike and got to work cutting the string.

'We just need to spread it out, to make sure every sheep gets some,' said Ben moving away from her.

Kat pulled the hay apart and tossed it away from her. But seconds later, it came flying back at her and into her mouth. She spat it out in disgust. Her tongue glided over her teeth as she tried to get the grit out. Kat grabbed some more hay and threw it in a different direction, this time the wind took it further across the field.

The sounds of sheep bleating came from her right and before she could turn around to see them, something butted against the backs of her knees nearly sending her flying. But yet again Ben came to her rescue as Kat felt his hands grab hold of her.

'How did you manage to get so much hay on you? You're supposed to be putting it on the ground. And you wonder why the animals come at you? You're a moving hay bale at the moment,' he said laughing.

'It was the wind...' she said. 'I forgot about the way it was blowing.'

'Yeah, as a male, you tend to learn about that at a very young age,' he said pulling off the last of the bales.

Kat grimaced imagining what he was implying.

'I think I'm more of a hindrance than a help,' said Kat getting back on the quad bike.

'Nonsense!' shouted Ben as they made their way back down the hill, the sheep content. 'It was your first time at feeding the animals, it does get easier. Plus, it's nice having you with me and... you're a lot better looking than George.'

Kat smiled against his back. Ben wasn't too bad either, she thought noticing her heart race more now that she was cuddled up to him.

Once they were back in the warmth of the house and were peeling off their layers of clothing, Ben struggled to look at her. Whenever Kat glanced over at him, she would catch him quickly looking away as if he didn't want to be seen gazing in her direction. Now that they were enclosed in such a small space, and it was just the two of them, no distractions, their easy banter between them vanished and in its place was just an awkward silence.

For whatever reason, she was being pulled towards him and she liked it and after their physical connection, she'd been looking forward to getting to know him more on an emotional level. Kat caught his eye hoping to see the mischievous glint that had been there the last hour or two but his eyes had dulled again. At least they weren't angry like when she'd first met him.

'Full English alright with you?' he asked heading into the kitchen.

Kat's stomach rumbled loudly in response. 'Yes please, anything you want me to do?'

Ben shook his head. 'Nope, I'm fine.'

Kat looked at him as he bustled about in the little kitchen. He was the first man in such a long time that had made her heart quicken. She needed to find out if they had anything in common whether it could last if they did decide to get to know each other more.

'So...' said Kat leaning against the wall at the end of the counter, not wanting to get in his way. 'Are you the painter?'

'Ugh?'

'The paintings...' she said gesturing to the ones at the far end of the sitting room.

Ben's neck reddened again. 'It's nothing. Just a hobby. I started it when...'

And then he stopped. Kat waited for him to start up again but the silence between them continued.

'When...' she said looking at him expectantly.

Ben bent down and got some mushrooms and tomatoes out of the fridge underneath the counter.

'When my parents died...'

'Oh,' gasped Kat.

'It was a lorry, unavoidable. They'd been returning home from a weekend away. I'd told them to book one, I pretty much ordered it. They spent all hours here looking after the farm, me and my sister... I thought I was being nice...'

'You were,' muttered Kat.

'But if they hadn't have gone, they'd still be here now,' said Ben shaking his head.

'You can't think that. You can't take responsibility for their death. It wasn't your fault. How old were you?'

'I was nineteen, my sister just seventeen.'

Kat thought back to when Clarissa, her best friend's dad had died in a car accident. Clarissa had had her mum to lean on and she'd struggled. Ben had had no-one.

'So the farm and your sister...' said Kat.

'I grew up pretty fast and so did she. We managed and we've good neighbours. My parent's friends helped out too.'

Kat didn't know what else to say. There seemed to be no point in trying to lighten the atmosphere now, she'd already dug a deep enough hole to put herself in. Kat went to turn and walk away when she felt Ben grab hold of her around the waist. Her stomach dropped and she looked up in time to see his face lean towards hers and then he kissed her with such passion and heat that she felt her legs begin to give way.

'Sorry,' said Ben breaking away first going to pick up the knife and continue chopping the mushrooms. 'I... you... I don't know what I'm doing.'

Kat was speechless. She had no idea what she was doing either and she certainly wasn't fobbing him off.

'You're like an alien...' he said.

'That's slightly harsh...' she said interrupting him with a smile on her lips.

'No, not like that. I just meant that... it feels like you've crashed landed into my world and it's all turned upside down...' said Ben hacking at the mushrooms rather than chopping them.

'I'm sorry about the tree and the...'

'It's not that...' said Ben slamming the knife down.

Kat took a step back.

'I've been on my own for so long, I'd given up hope of meeting anyone or feeling anything of what I'm now feeling for you...' he said walking gently towards her again. 'And it's happened... out of the blue. And I can't control it.'

Kat's heart began to race, not from worrying what he was going to do but that she felt the same way. She'd been feeling the strong connection between them, it'd felt like a magnet and he was obviously feeling it too and it was getting stronger and stronger. They'd had that fleeting kiss, and she'd wanted more. She'd cuddled up against his back and felt his hands on her, and she'd wanted more. She enjoyed being in his company, she enjoyed chatting to him, laughing with him and berating him and she didn't want it to stop.

'I know...' whispered Kat thinking they must look like the last couple on earth that were suited to each other.

'You know I've been on my own for so long?' asked Ben uncertainty in his voice, his eyes searching her face for an answer.

'I...' said Kat then she uncharacteristically went on tiptoe and kissed him.

It was only the smell of burning minutes later emanating from the grill that made them separate.

'Fiddlesticks!' said Ben bringing a tray of some very crispy bacon from out of the oven.

Kat laughed. 'Please tell me you didn't just say that. Who says fiddlesticks?'

Ben smirked. 'I do,' and plated up the rest of the food and then sat down opposite each other. 'I stopped swearing when I began painting,' he said smiling at her just before he brought a mouthful of sausage and beans up to his mouth.

'That was so good,' said Kat patting her tummy.

'I don't know where you put it,' Ben said looking at Kat slouched on the sofa, Mist's head was on her lap. 'You eat more than me!'

'I told you I have fast metabolism and it's being outside. I eat more at home too.'

'So your parents live in the country?'

'Yes but my welly boots barely get dirty. I think I had more mud caked on my lovely Italian shoes than I've seen in a life time.'

'I still can't believe you followed me up that track,' said Ben budging Mist along and sitting down next to Kat.

'What do you want to do now? Read? I've got some books you can borrow...'

'I saw; you have a nice collection.'

'Thank you. Or do you want to watch a film. I've also got a few DVDs.'

'Have you?' asked Kat looking around the open plan room.

'Yes, in my bedroom, do you want to come and see?' asked Ben.

Kat let out a pretend horrified gasp. 'In your bedroom huh? I see your ploy, trying to seduce a poor young innocent girl and have your wicked way with her.'

All blood leaked out of Ben's face. 'No, I didn't mean it that way.'

'I know you didn't, I jest!' smiled Kat.

'Oh God, don't do that to me,' said Ben and then must have seen the strange look on Kat's face. 'Well, I am older than you, and I've just met you, and I wouldn't want you to think I was taking advantage you.'

'Hey! I am an adult you know, and you can't be that much older than me. And even if you were?' said Kat shrugging. 'How old are you anyway?'

'Forty-six...' said Ben almost choking it out.

Kat looked at him. She'd actually thought he was younger than that. He'd aged well. She'd put him five years younger. Forty-six. What would her parents say? Actually nothing, coming to think of it. As long as she was happy. Her dad was older than her mum by at least fifteen years so they weren't going to say anything. The only question was, could she be happy with him? Kat looked around the house. It felt like home. But an uneasy feeling streaked its way down through her originating from her brain. Fear. What was she fearful of? Of getting it wrong. She looked up into his eyes. They were pulling her towards him. She didn't want to hurt him, to lead him on to give him hope only to leave him.

'Kat?'

'I... um... I'm sorry...' she said getting up from the sofa missing the warmth of his body already. 'I... don't think it'd work. You're right. I am from another world and...' she said flinging her arms around, 'your animals really don't like me...'

Kat didn't dare look at Ben's face in that moment and she headed straight for the stairs, grabbed the first book off the shelf and ran to her bedroom. This whole thing was surreal. It was like she was in a bubble and she'd floated away from her life momentarily but she had to go back to it in the next day or so. And that blackness she was feeling that uneasy feeling was stopping her from doing anything but. Kat shut her eyes and a vision of her and Ben came to her mind. She was older, he was older but they were laughing and walking hand in hand across the field. She could see the cows in the distance. She wasn't afraid of them and she was happy.

Things were moving too quickly. Her thoughts and her feelings. She was getting overwhelmed. She wished she could talk to Bella or Clarissa right now. She'd never not been able to contact them before but with the phone line down and no reception. She'd also never felt so cut off. She'd never be able to live here.

A soft knock brought her attention swiftly back to reality. 'Kat? Are you alright?'

Kat got up off the bed and opened the door. Ben was standing there looking extremely uncomfortable holding a cup of tea in one hand and a plate of home-made biscuits in the other. The biscuits looked delicious.

'Did you make them?'

'Yes, they're my sister's and niece's favourite.'

Kat took one and tried it. 'Thank you,' she mumbled. 'They're scrummy!'

Ben grinned. 'Look...I... Clean slate? Friends?'

'Friends,' said Kat thinking her body and mind should be happy with that outcome but the sick feeling that was coming over her begun to make her think otherwise.

Chapter Five

♥

Monday 7th November 2016

'To new friends and new experiences,' said Kat clinking glasses with Ben. 'And thank you,' she said almost coughing as the burning liquid slipped down her throat, 'for opening this very expensive bottle of brandy. You really should've kept it for another occasion.'

'Oh no, saying goodbye to your car which has been wrapped around my tree and making my pleasant view look more like a scrap heap for the last few days was definitely a reason to open this bottle,' he said pouring himself an extra finger in his glass. 'I was also very thankful for the extra help...'

Kat's face lit up.

'...once you'd stopped scaring my animals,' Ben said finishing off his sentence.

'I scared them? Those chickens are evil, they still are and I wasn't too bad in the beginning,' said Kat pretending to pout. 'The animals got fed didn't they?'

Kat had actually loved the last few days being outside and helping Ben with the cows, sheep and even the chickens and pigs. Once they'd decided to remain friends, their easy banter had reappeared, the pressure gone. But Kat couldn't count the number of times that she'd wanted Ben's lips on hers again and the warmth of him around her. Her heart fluttered at the thought and then dipped as she heard the blast of a horn outside.

'Your dad's found us then,' said Ben getting up.

Kat got up at the same time and their bodies were mere centimetres away from each other. Ben's eyes glazed over as he looked at Kat's eyes, her nose and then her lips. Kat returned the stare trying to remember every detail of his face.

'I know we said just friends, but if ever you change your mind and you think you might possibly want to be with an old man like me then... I'm here,' he said.

'You're not old,' whispered Kat. 'It's that we're worlds apart, my life and yours.'

'Ok,' Ben said sadly walking towards the front door.

'Ben? Ben Jones?' said Kat's father.

'You've got the right place,' said Ben opening the door wider so Kat could go past.

'Dad!' screamed Kat launching herself at her father. She wasn't normally one for doing that, that was more Bella's thing but she'd hated being so cut off from her family.

'Are you alright darling?' he said looking her up and down. 'You seem to suit this country life; I've never seen you look so healthy. Thank you for taking her in,' Kat's father said directing the last bit to Ben.

'I'll make a farmer out of her yet,' said Ben.

'Kat? A Farmer?' said Bella, Kat's smaller and curvier twin sister, appearing from around the edge of the door. 'Hi, I'm Bella,' she said holding out her hand to Ben.

'I've heard a lot about you,' said Ben.

'All good I expect, I'm the nicer twin, the less acidic one,' Bella said laughing. 'Did she give you a hard time?'

'Well...,' said Ben scratching his head. 'It wasn't easy and she frightened my poor animals half to death.'

'I am here you know,' said Kat playfully punching Ben in the arm, 'and they scared me more, particularly your chickens.'

'Are you sure I can't give you some money or payment for any damage my daughter's caused?' asked Kat's father, Richard.

'Just a life time of therapy...' said Ben smiling at Kat.

The cheek of him, thought Kat but while they were all being nicey nicey her heart was sinking rapidly and a sadness was washing over her at the thought of leaving Ben and the dogs. Mist butted her head into Kat's hand for another stroke. I'll miss you too, she thought, maybe she'd come back and visit, but what would be the point? She'd struggled to remain only friends and visiting would just make it harder to leave again. And what if Ben met someone else? Ben couldn't live with her in London any more than she could live here in the middle of nowhere with him. London was also easy for her work at the moment. No. This was it. Kat looked at Ben properly for one last time then tried to put a smile on her face which didn't want to come.

'Thank you Ben,' she said giving him a hug and then she walked over to her dad's car leaving the two men to say their farewells.

'Here, let me help you,' said Bella lifting Kat's suitcase into the boot.

'Thanks,' mumbled Kat.

Once they were both sat in the car, Bella turned round to Kat in the back seat with a worried expression on her face, 'What happened Kat? Are you alright? Are you ok after the accident? Dad says you've got to get a new car.'

'Yeah I know,' said Kat trying not to meet her sister's eyes. She wasn't ready to speak to her sister yet about the last few days. She needed to get back to reality and process it. 'I'm just a bit tired.'

'Ok,' said Bella turning back round to face the front. 'It's seriously beautiful here.'

'It is,' whispered Kat her breath steaming up the window.

'Right, that's all sorted,' said Kat's dad getting into the car. 'You were lucky to meet him. He's a really nice guy.'

'Yes, he is,' said Kat.

Chapter Six

❤

Thursday 10th November 2016

'You're back,' said Stella, 'and you look amazing!'

'Yes well, I managed to catch up on some sleep didn't I without you two trying to get me out every night of the week,' said Kat smiling as Phoebe gave her a big hug.

'We were so worried,' said Phoebe, 'when Tessa filled us in on what happened. You didn't hurt yourself?'

'No, well yes, I didn't hurt myself when I crashed the car, I hurt my ankle when I was trying to get away from what I thought were fierce beasts.'

Phoebe gasped. 'What fierce beast? In the forest?'

'They were just cows,' said Kat remembering at how silly she'd been and how angry Ben had been but then... No, she mustn't think about the rest. She had to forget those bits.

'So was this farmer guy hot?' asked Stella.

Kat inwardly rolled her eyes, trust Stella.

'He was an old farmer,' said Kat trying to put off Stella from asking any more questions.

'Old? Shame. Like how old? I mean David Beckham's getting on a bit now but if he and Posh ever split up and he propositioned me... I wouldn't say no,' said Stella with a dreamy look.

Kat didn't want to talk about Ben because the age difference didn't matter to her, it was... just everything else. She looked out the window of their flat at the birds sitting upon the chimneys and rooftops. And from where she was standing she could just about see Vauxhall bridge and the river. When Kat had been away on her modelling trips, she was always happy to come home to this flat. It was her safe place, her happy place and she had her friends. Phoebe came to stand next to her.

'I can never get enough of this view,' said Phoebe sighing.

But Phoebe was a born and bred Londoner, Kat wasn't and whilst London and the flat and modelling had meant stability for her at a time when Kat hadn't known what she was doing in her life, looking at the view now and being back in London, something had shifted within her.

'I'm so excited that we're doing the same shoot today. The three of us together and on a boat,' said Phoebe whirling around.

'And Clive's there,' said Stella.

'And Dylan...' said Kat winking at Phoebe.

'I told you, he's too short for me,' Phoebe retorted.

'Come on, we'd best go otherwise Tessa'll be on to us,' said Stella hoisting up her huge bag onto her shoulder.

'Tessa wouldn't dare,' said Kat narrowing her eyes. 'Not after what she persuaded me to do. And I don't know why you're so excited about us going on a boat, you do realise that we're modelling bikinis don't you? We're going to absolutely freeze!'

'It's not just a boat, it's a super yacht and I'm sure they won't keep us hanging around out in the cold for too long,' said Phoebe who was still very much in-love with her job and she was a Brit, she didn't seem to feel the cold as much as Kat did.

I was half brought up in Barbados for heaven's sake thought Kat. I don't do the cold unless I'm cuddled up against Ben and... Why did her mind have to go back to him? She'd only been with him a few days, not even a week but he seemed to have left an annoying lasting impression on her. No-one had ever made her feel this way and it was becoming rather disconcerting. She'd hoped that by going back to her normal life and going back to routine, she'd forget about him or at least he would fade away into the background. Give it a week, in a week's time... he'd be forgotten.

Chapter Seven

♥

Thursday 17th November 2016

Kat laughed as the cute and very handsome guy regaled her with yet another story.

'I can't believe we've never bumped into each other until now,' he said leaning towards her again so that he could be heard above the music.

'I know,' she said sipping her drink.

Jerry was a really nice man; he was actually one of the nicest guys she'd met in a long time. He was a couple of years older than her, had a good job in the city, he seemed kind and he was also Dylan's older brother. The previous Thursday, Phoebe had finally given in and asked Dylan out on a date. It had been a hit and they'd been smitten with each other since. But with things still being rather new between them, Phoebe had cajoled Kat into a double date with Dylan's older brother.

'So,' Jerry said. 'I don't suppose you'd like to go on a date with me sometime, without my younger brother chaperoning us, would you?'

Kat glanced at Phoebe who mouthed a 'go on'.

'Yeah ok, that would be nice,' said Kat.

From what she'd seen from him so far, he was funny and charming and terribly good looking. What Kat couldn't understand was why she wasn't getting the tummy flutters. He was everything she wanted. He was pretty much perfect for her but... an image of Ben feeding the cows and stroking their heads came to her mind. He wasn't Ben. It had only been a week. She'd hoped Ben would be out of her head by now but hopefully Jerry would change that.

'Excellent,' said Jerry grinning from ear to ear. 'Are you free next Friday as one of my mate's is DJing at this new club that's just opened up in Camden?'

Phoebe gave her a thumbs up.

Chapter Eight

♥

Saturday 26th November 2016

Kat pulled the duvet over her head at the sound of Dylan and Phoebe mucking around in the sitting room. How could she face them? Face Dylan? Kat groaned and shut her eyes and cringed, visions of the night before flashed in front of her. Admittedly they were a bit of blur and she was sure some scenes were missing. That's what comes from drinking way too much alcohol and having eaten little in the way of food. Not a great combo! But what little she did remember wasn't great and was rather humiliating. She felt like a right cow for how it played out so much so that the thought of seeing Dylan made her sink further down into her little pit.

It had started off well, the evening. She'd made an effort to look nice, Jerry had commented on the fact. To begin with, he'd taken her to a lovely little Italian restaurant and usually Kat would have polished off a starter, main course and desert but it was too romantic for her. She didn't do romance at the best of times, it wasn't in her nature. And the small table for two tucked away in a little corner with a posy of flowers in a vase and the flickering light from the candles was overkill for a first date. Or any date in fact. Maybe not for some people but for Kat, it was a big no no.

Kat had become overwhelmed and when she got overwhelmed, her body would overheat. Her skin would become clammy then her stomach would begin to hiss and spit with the extra influx of acid. The first delicious meatball that made its way down sunk like a stone into the acrid pool causing pain to disperse throughout her body. So of course the only solution that Kat had thought of to dull the pain was to drink copious amounts of alcohol.

She'd noticed Jerry's concerned looks as he'd seen her chug down the wine and toy with the food on her plate. He'd even asked if everything was ok once the waitress had cleared away the main course. Jerry had carried their conversation along and Kat had thought he looked relieved when he was paying for the bill on their way out.

The cold fresh air had been a life saviour when they'd stepped out of the restaurant. And Kat had felt infinitely happier, feeling better. Jerry and Kat had chatted amicably and she'd realised they had a lot in common, tastes in films, books, they liked the same holidays but Kat had felt like she talking to a paper board cut out. It wasn't him, he was lovely. It was all her. There was something terribly wrong with her. Who'd think that about someone?

And it wasn't until she'd downed a few more shots with Phoebe, having met them there, that she'd realised that the only multidimensional person who was coming to her mind was Ben. And then she thought she began to see glimpses of him in the crowd. Kat had done quite a few double takes thinking that perhaps he was there but when

Kat had gone up to the person, it obviously hadn't been him.

'I've got to go outside for some fresh air,' she'd shouted to Phoebe, Jerry and Dylan.

Once outside, she'd rung her sister then, Bella. She couldn't remember everything she'd said to her but there had been a lot of crying, snivelling, snot and more crying amongst some garbled speech of not being able to get Ben out of her mind and that he was The One. Upon which Kat had turned round and seen two or three unhappy Jerry's standing there. Kat couldn't remember whether she'd seen him after that but did remember voices, a car of some sort and then being manhandled into her bedroom.

So that was where she was now, still with last night's clothes on and her duvet completely covering her. Kat pulled off the duvet and grabbed her phone. There were a few unread messages from Bella asking if she was ok and to follow her heart no matter what. None from Jerry. Maybe that was a good thing at least she didn't have to think of what to say to him.

Kat texted back Bella. 'ru sho I shd folo my hrt?'

'yes!' came the reply.

'wha if it goes rong?' texted Kat.

'wha if it goes ryt?' 'u'v evrytin to lose if u dnt n evrytin to win if u do!' 'folo yr hrt!' 'luv u! xxxxx'

'luv u too xxxxx'

Her sister had always been Kat's sage. Bella had a gift of making Kat see things that others couldn't. When Kat had been little, at times her mother would try and get Kat to do something and it wasn't until Bella stepped in that Kat could see clearly. And that's exactly what she was finally doing, seeing clearly. Why Kat hadn't spoken to Bella before about what happened with Ben, God only knew...

The only thing left to do was to find out if Ben had changed his mind.

Kat leapt out of bed, opened the door, mumbled a quick hello to Phoebe and Dylan who were sprawled out on the sitting room sofa and rushed into the bathroom glad that Stella hadn't been occupying it. The hot water pelted over her skin reviving her, as she washed she began to make a plan.

Kat stood by the farm house door squinting at the sun trying to see where Ben was. She'd spotted his quad bike at the top of the fields where they'd fed the sheep and she just hoped he was going to make his way down soon. She was so nervous that she thought her heart was going to burst.

After half an hour, there was still no sign of him and she was getting rather cold.

'Oh for heaven's sake,' she said out loud. 'If the mountain will not come to Muhammad, then Muhammad must go to the mountain.'

At least it's not an actual bloody mountain she had to walk up but a little hill, she thought minutes later, but even the little hill had her huffing and puffing. Kat was so intent, with her head down, on trying to avoid stumbling on the stony track that she hadn't noticed she'd been walking straight towards a bull until it was too late.

Kat looked at the bull. She hadn't come across it when she'd been staying there. Cows yes but the bull no. She paused not moving one digit while the bull cast his eyes over her. He was enormous. His head was almost three times the size of a cow's head and the muscles on him...

The bull let out a huge moo. Kat wanted to scream but held it in not wanting to draw attention however her legs had other ideas. Before she realised what she was doing she was running back down the way she'd come at full speed her heart now in her mouth.

'This was a bad idea, this was a bad idea,' she said over and over again.

'Kat?' said a voice next to her.

Kat glimpsed sideways to see Ben on his quad bike next to her with a huge grin on his face.

'Stop!' he said. 'Hercules won't hurt you! He's a softy!'

Kat slowed down as Ben pulled to a stop and got off the quad.

'What are you doing here?' he asked.

'I...um...' said Kat.

'Well at least you're dressed the part,' he said eyeing up her welly boots and the rest of her attire.

'So is the offer still open?' asked Kat finally finding her voice.

Ben's face lit up and he stepped forward.

'It sure is,' he said taking her in his arms and planting a huge kiss on her lips.

The End

Spoilt for Choice

♥

Chapter One

♥

Saturday 16th December 2017

'Oh my God! Would you get in there, you worthless piece of...' said Bella ready to explode. What was she doing? It was silly o'clock in the morning, it was the first day of her Christmas holidays and she was outside in the freezing cold... and dark...putting up a blooming trestle table. Because of her nature, she hadn't been able to say no. Kat, her sister would have done but she had this innate highly annoying moral thingamajig inside of her that couldn't help but come to people's rescue. She felt like the old guy, Jim, in the Vicar of Dibley who had a habit of saying 'no, no, no, no, yes!' That was her. Her heart would hammer against her chest and her stomach would toss around until she finally lamented. That's how she'd ended up here at this ungodly hour in the middle of a quaint little town in the middle of the Cotswolds. Fortunately, it was local to her parent's home so at least she didn't have to familiarise herself with the surroundings and one of her friends, Millie, worked at the library just a stone's throw away.

Melanie, whose stall this was, was going in for an operation. When Melanie had asked around, everyone had either work or were busy with kids. Bella, having no work and no children, naturally had been the only one available. It's easy, Melanie had said. Just lay it out nicely, I've already done the hard work. Hopefully putting up the table would be the hardest bit, Bella hadn't even got started on the little gazebo yet.

'Oh for heaven's sake!' she cried out as the table collapsed again.

Bella looked around hoping to see some of the other stall holders arriving. There was no-one, not a jot, save a few cats having a spat in the church graveyard nearby. A light mist hugged the pavements and cobbled streets. Pretty Christmas lights from the shop windows twinkled through the haze and one of the street lamps flickered on and off next to her. Melanie had said she should get there early before the shops open but maybe she'd taken it too literally. But she'd been awake half the night and what was the point in staying in bed worrying and not sleeping. Also Bella hadn't wanted to get stuck in any traffic coming out of London. People had a tendency to drive like nutters when there were barely any cars on the roads and accidents happened, particularly along the road that she'd had to take. Bella yawned. She could do with a coffee and her mind wandered back to the thermos flask full of hot liquid caffeine that she'd thought to make but not thought about taking with her.

Bella shook her head at her stupidity and rubbed her hands together trying to get the blood back into the fingertips. No, no, no, no! That was all she had to say. Melanie's daughter, April, could have done it, ok, so she was a tad unreliable but still... Bella had really needed this break. Her brain was frazzled and her body was a tight ball of string that needed some serious unwinding.

The last week of term had been really hectic, for some reason even more so than usual. The kids were always wired with the lead up to the festive holidays with their energy levels reaching boiling point and their focus levels, well, nil. Trying to come up with ingenious ways to capture their attention was getting harder and harder each year.

For you see the head teacher, the miserable old bat with eyes of steel, should have retired a gazillion years ago and her expectations were, at times, unrealistic and outdated. I mean who wouldn't appreciate a bunch of kids singing at the top of their lungs to 'C'est dommage' by Bigflo and Oli? They were having fun at the same time as learning the conditional tense but could she see that? No, of course not. What Bella hadn't needed at the end of a difficult term was a dressing down in the bat's office about what was expected of her. A thanks and a pat on the back would've been nice after all her hard work.

So no sooner had Bella got home from work, she'd eaten, watched some Christmas movie that was on then had passed out while attempting to watch said movie. But then she'd woken up in the night, fully clothed and remembered that she'd got to get up early for the Christmas fair...and panicked. Sleep had not come to her after that.

Bella's eyes drifted back to the slab of wood that now lay at her feet. It wasn't rocket science and she'd actually put some up at school just recently for their Christmas fête, albeit with the help of Mr Davis the exceedingly hot and buff PE teacher. Ok so maybe he'd put them up and she'd just ogled his muscles butting up against his rather tight shirt. Maybe if she'd spent less time on looking at him she might have learnt how to put the pernickety tables up and she wouldn't be in the predicament she was in right now.

'Oh God!' she said tempted to kick the thing.

'Can I help you?' said a softly spoken voice behind her.

Bella screamed. What the...? She swung around to see a man bundled up in a coat, and all she could see were the whites of his eyes as he looked out from underneath.

'Christ!' she said clutching her heart. 'You scared the bejesus out of me!'

'Sorry,' he said pushing his hood back so Bella could see the man's face and she immediately spotted the dog collar at his neck.

'I literally thought God was talking back to me then,' she said smiling. 'I thought no-one was around, you were so quiet and I had no idea how He was going to help me with this particular matter.'

'I didn't mean to startle you,' said the vicar leaning down to pat the dog that was being extremely obedient by his side. 'I was just taking Zebedee here out for a walk.'

At the mention of his name, Zebedee wagged his tail and stepped forward as if introducing himself.

'He's gorgeous,' said Bella stroking him. 'What breed is he?'

The vicar chuckled. 'I have no idea. He's a rescue dog and the vet thinks he's a mix of quite a few different breeds. Anyway,' he said, 'I'm not Christ but hopefully I'm the next best thing in your hour of need.'

'Ah,' said Bella feeling herself blush. That hadn't been her finest moment. 'I don't seem to be able to put this table up.'

'Here,' he said holding out Zebedee's lead, 'I'll see what I can do.'

Bella felt her heart pound unexpectedly as she watched the vicar lift the table up. He must be new to the church in the town because she hadn't seen him around before, she would have definitely remembered him if she had. He looked awfully young and hot for a vicar. He couldn't be more than a few years older than her, weren't vicars supposed to be old?

'There you go!' he said taking the lead back from her.

Bella pressed down on the table making sure it wasn't going to collapse again as soon as the vicar had gone.

'Thank you,' she said. 'You're my life saviour.'

'Well thank goodness someone thinks so,' he replied looking at his watch. 'Right I'd best be off. Maybe see you later?'

'Yes you probably will as I'm going to be at this stall for the next week.'

The vicar smiled and then wandered off slowly down the pavement, Zebedee happily trotting beside him.

Car lights shone in Bella's eyes as it swung round the corner heading in her direction. She squinted trying to see who was inside. A big white van following the car parked up right behind it.

Yes, thought Bella, some more stall holders. I'm not alone.

A woman with brightly covered fingerless gloves heaved herself out of the car and waved in her direction.

'Are you Bella?' she asked coming over.

'Yes.'

'Melanie called me to let me know she wasn't coming to the fair this year and that she was sending you instead. She asked me to help you out and show you the ropes,' the lady said offering her hand. 'I'm Ruth. I've got the stall next to you.'

Bella felt her body relax. 'Oh that would be great, thank you! I was a bit worried as I've never done this before.'

'You'll be fine, as long as you've got your card machine, plenty of cash and a calculator on hand, the products will sell on their own merit. I always do well in this town and so does Melanie.'

'Alright Ruth?' said a man coming towards them. He was skinny as a rake and tall, he could give her sister a run for her money. He tugged on his beanie which read 'Tim the Timber man' and flexed his fingers. 'It's a mighty cold one this morning, isn't it?'

'It sure is,' replied Ruth. 'And yeah I haven't been doing so bad thanks. My arthritis is still playing up mind so this weather doesn't help.'

'Oh don't talk about ailments,' he moaned. 'I've got a list as long as my arm and my arms are long!'

'Tell me about it,' said Ruth. 'Enjoy being young, Bella! Anyways I'm going to stop moaning and get set up. Violet'll be here soon with her tasty delights. I've been hankering after one of her Eccles cakes.'

Bella picked up some poles and looked at them, listening to Ruth was making her feel hungry and want a coffee even more. As she tried to figure out which way the poles went, Bella noticed the town getting busier around her. The street lights turned off as the sun began to brighten the grey clouds hovering overhead. Doors slammed, a Christmas song blared out of a window in one of the flats above the shops and some shouts could be heard as the stall holders and shop keepers got ready for business.

'Do you need help with that love?' asked Ruth.

Bella looked up and gasped because while she'd been trying to lay out the poles and sheet thing that was supposed to go over the top in a proper order on the floor, Ruth had put up her gazebo and the rails, which were crammed with lots of knitted items of clothing. She'd also erected a table which now had an assortment of hats and scarfs laid out on it. Bella rolled her eyes. Tim had all his stuff out and ready too. A wooden figure of a monkey laughing stood by the side of his stall and was pointing in Bella's direction. The monkey pretty much summed her up right now, she was a laughing stock.

'Yes please,' Bella said, 'as long as you don't mind.'

'Not at all,' said Ruth. 'I've been doing this for years and I've seen Melanie set hers up for nearly as long.'

Barely twenty minutes later, Bella was clasping a steaming cup of coffee in her hand, thanks to Tim, and was now standing in front of her stall table trying to memorise where the different fudges were. There were so many of them, she was going to have to get the customer to point out which one they wanted. Her mouth began to water as she scrutinised them. Salted caramel, mint chocolate, double chocolate, white chocolate with cookie dough, rum and raisin, salted dark chocolate toffee and it went on and on. Bella didn't know how Melanie managed to make so many.

'Bella,' said Ruth from her stall. 'You've got your first customer.'

Bella looked up and her eyes widened. It was sexy Stuart. Her heart began to pound and she automatically went to make sure her hair was in place and she licked her lips.

'Bella?' he said looking from Bella to the stall. 'What are you doing here? Is this your stall? Don't you teach now or something?'

Bella couldn't stop staring at him. Sexy Stu had been at the boys' school when she'd attended the girls' one. He was a couple of years older and was also the talk of her school. He had been exceedingly good looking and had dated the most popular girl in the year above her. Stu and Flo had been the golden couple. Bella hadn't had much to do with him except for spotting him from a distance when the schools did events together. It wasn't until later did she admit that one of her reasons for joining the choir might have been to do with the fact that he was also in the choir and that it had enabled her to spend more time in his company than she would have otherwise been able to do. Kat had scoffed at her when she'd joined. But Kat was stunning and tall and was a successful model, she wasn't a model then of course but she could have the pick of the boys. Bella was not any of those things. She was short, curvy and had also inherited really bad skin. Kat moaned about Bella having the brains and Bella moaned about Kat having the looks.

'Bella? Are you ok?' Stu asked leaning towards her.

'Yes, um yes, um I'm... I am a teacher, yes, I'm just here helping a friend out,' she stuttered tucking her hair behind her ears, then it just felt weird and so she untucked it. Stop it Bella. He's not interested so what does it matter what you look like.

'Oh right,' he said inspecting the fudge. 'I'm just over there, the corner shop with the green awning. I opened up an antique's shop with my father. I've been there for a couple of years now.'

Bella glanced to where he was pointing. It looked very smart and she didn't think she'd be buying anything from there in a hurry not on her wages anyway.

'Is Kat still modelling?' he asked. 'Is she around too?'

Typical, of course he was bothering to talk to her, he was after Kat's whereabouts.

'Yes she is,' Bella returned not wanting to give him any more details. 'And no she's not.'

'Oh right,' he said. 'Well I'd better be off. Father'll be waiting for his morning coffee and croissant.'

'Yeah alright, bye,' Bella said turning her back on him.

'Bella?'

'Yeah? I'll pop back and see you at lunchtime. I wouldn't mind tasting a bit of your fudge,' Stu said winking at her.

Bella frowned. Please tell me he didn't just wink at me? It was kind of a sexy wink too. Really? Was that aimed at me? Bella looked behind her. An old man with a contorted expression on his face slowly ambled past pulling a trolley contraption that was overflowing with newspapers. Well it couldn't have been at him. So Stu must have winked at her. Interesting. What was on his agenda? A discount perhaps?

Two hours later, Bella was desperate for a wee. She'd kept on looking over at Ruth to find the right time to ask if she could possibly look after her stall while she made a quick dash to the public toilets but Ruth had had a regular stream of customers. It never seemed to be the right time.

The cold didn't help either. Bella was sure she'd read somewhere that the cold made you need to go more often. Fortunately, it wasn't as cold as it had been when she'd first arrived but a white cloud still blasted from her mouth every time she opened it to breathe or cough. She hoped she wasn't coming down with something. That was the last thing she needed.

'Hold my hand!' Bella heard coming from a lady crossing the road. 'If you don't do as I say, there'll be no sweets and what'll Father Christmas think of your behaviour?'

Bella smothered a laugh and wondered whether that old chestnut was actually going to work on the snotty little boy whose face was now ever so close to her fudge. Don't sneeze, please do not sneeze she thought. That's why she taught older children but at times they still regressed.

'I like the way you've stacked them,' said the boy eloquently wiping the snot across his sleeve and ignoring his mum.

'Thank you?' said Bella.

'I'd like one pound of the honeycomb, one pound of the Christmas pudding and finally....one pound of the vanilla.'

Bella looked up at the mum to check but she'd wandered off to the side on a phone call.

'She'll pay for it, don't worry,' said the boy and then whispered out of the side of his mouth. 'And I know Father Christmas isn't real.'

Bella let out a startled cry. 'What? He isn't real?'

The boy looked at her his eyes wide.

'What do you mean he isn't real? Of course he is! If he isn't...' said Bella. 'Then who is leaving me presents under my tree? Are you sure? I mean no-one else can get into my flat apart from me...'

The boy stood there open mouthed obviously not sure what to say. The mother finishing her conversation came over.

'Jeremy, I hope you haven't been rude to this lady. Has he?' she asked anxiously.

The boy was now standing like a statue and unmoving waiting for Bella's reply.

'Was it three pounds of fudge you wanted?' Bella said.

The boy nodded.

'Yes that's fine,' the mother said trying to grab her phone as it started ringing again and handed her son a couple of notes.

'How old are you? said Bella.

'Six,' said Jeremy.

'Mmm... I see...' said Bella.

'What do you see?' he asked.

But Bella didn't answer only handing him the bag and taking the money off him. 'How do you know he isn't real?'

'I saw mummy come into my bedroom with the stocking?'

'How do you know she didn't bring them to you because Santa didn't have time to put them where she wanted to put them?' said Bella.

'Huh? But...' the boy said.

'Shhh...' said Bella putting her fingers to her lips and quickly looked up into the sky. 'Merry Christmas!'

The boy shot off after his mum, a totally different one to the boy who first came to her stall. It was sad not to believe in Father Christmas at such a young age...

'You're good with children!' said the vicar appearing from Bella's right.

'Er...thanks, look, I know I've only just met you but... would you mind looking after the stall for five minutes. I mean you're a vicar so I can trust you, I can't I? It's just that um, I need a break?'

'A break?' he asked wearily eyeing up the stall. 'I can get you some drink or food if you need anything...'

'I need to go to the ladies...' said Bella now hopping from one foot to another, she really shouldn't have left it so late.

'Sure um... is there...?' he said slowly going round to the back of the stall.

'Thanks!' said Bella rushing off not looking back to see if he was ok.

'Watch out!' said a gruff voice as she ran round the corner to the entrance to the toilets.

'Sorry!' puffed Bella and then she groaned as she saw a row of people waiting to use the one and only toilet. A huge sign was plastered across the ladies stating they were out of order. But the gents wasn't, so why was this man waiting? Bella waited a few more precious moments while a mother with a baby went in, then an older lady, then a mother with her young daughter and... whoa? The old man was going in. It was her turn and she was in pain now. Dire pain. 'That's the ladies, the gents is there,' she said pointing to the perfectly adequate and working men's toilets. And they were fine because she'd jealously been looking at all the men coming out of there with smiles on their faces while she'd stood there squirming.

'That there, is for everyone to use. And I've been having my daily wash for the last seven years in that toilet, so you can shove off and take your hoity toity self out of here!' said the man narrowing his eyes at Bella.

Bella held up her hands as if surrendering. 'I'm sorry, you're right. It is for everyone so...' she said, 'I don't suppose you'd let me go first would you?' she asked putting on her prettiest of smiles.

'No!' he said and went into the toilet slamming the door behind him.

Bella felt bad obviously, that the guy had to have a wash there in the first place, was he homeless? Poor man. Must be awful in this cold. She hadn't meant to offend him it's just that she was desperate... And then she thought of Stu and his shop over in the corner. He'd have a loo surely? And without another thought she did a funny walk across the road and entered his shop.

A little bell twinkled above her head and Stu's head appeared from behind the counter.

'Miss Fletcher-Jones! What a lovely surprise! Are you looking to buy something?'

'Er... sorry but... er no... Is there any chance I could use your toilet?' said Bella her legs pressed firmly together and her body bent at an awkward angle.

'The public ones are...?' he said his eyes glancing to the building across the road.

'Yeah, they're busy... oh purleeese can I just use your loo? I mean... unless you want a puddle on your floor?'

A deep chuckle came from the back room. 'Stuart, put the lady out of her misery and let her use ours. Is that the Miss Fletcher-Jones, the one you used to fancy?'

Stuart turned a deep shade of red as a shocked Bella scooted passed him. Fancy? He used to fancy me? He must have meant Kat, her sister. Huh, so Stuart had liked Kat.

Bella burst into the back room to come face to face with her old art teacher, Mr Sewell. Mr Sewell was sexy Stu's father? She'd never known.

'Lovely to see you Bella,' smiled Mr Sewell opening the door to the toilet.

'Thank you Mr Sewell, um... nice to see you too,' dashing past him.

Oh my God. Her old art teacher was sexy Stu's dad? She wondered if Kat knew. And Flo had certainly never mentioned it not that she'd spoken much around Bella in the first place, Bella was way too beneath her. But for all Flo's snobbery, Mr Sewell and Stu weren't exactly upper class. The way Stu and Flo used to gallivant around with each other anyone would think they were something special, royalty even. They'd had the looks, that was certain but character? Flo was a stuck up cow and Stu? Stu had been charming. She couldn't believe he hadn't offered up his toilet, he knew her for heaven's sake. Maybe he wasn't so nice either, but his dad was. Bella loved her art classes with him. If only it wasn't just a wee she needed, it would have served Stuart right for not being chivalrous. Speaking of chivalrous, the poor vicar, it must be more than five minutes now. Bella pulled the chain, washed her hands then darted out of the loo.

'Thanks Mr Sewell,' she shouted not seeing anyone nearby.

As Bella darted through the shop, Stuart called out to her but she didn't hear what he said as her thank you rode over his words and she was out the door and hurrying towards the stall.

'Blimey!' she said nearing the stall. There was a queue of people waiting to be served but no vicar. Where had he gone? Was he alright? Now that she felt better in her body, her head also felt better. Maybe she shouldn't have just left the poor guy like that.

The vicar's cheery face then popped up over the boxes of fudge and he was smiling.

'There you go Mrs Potter and I'll see you tomorrow at the eleven o'clock service? Excellent. See you then.'

'Sorry about that,' said Bella sidling up next to him.

'I think I've mistaken my calling,' he said with a mischievous glint in his eyes. 'This has been fun! I met quite a few of my parishioners and introduced myself to a couple of locals too. Would you like me to stay and help, I've actually got a bit of time on my hands?'

'Wow! Yes, please, that would be great,' she said eyeing up the ever growing queue.

The vicar smiled at her and Bella's heart quickened. Bella no, what are you thinking? He's a man of God and he... could he have a relationship with someone? A monk had to abstain but did he? Bella glanced at him quickly as he chatted to a customer. Oh what a waste if he couldn't. Ok mind out of the gutter Bella. Stop thinking ungodly thoughts about the local vicar. Bella looked at his nose, his lips, his ears and the tuft of hair curling over his collar. Stop Bella! Concentrate on the customers.

'Hello,' she said, 'what would you like?'

'I must get home now, I've got a lunchtime meeting,' said the vicar about an hour later. 'Are you going to be alright?'

Bella's heart sank at the thought of him going. It felt nice him being next to her. Everybody seemed to love talking to him and some people even went out of their way to come over to speak to him. He was easy going and good natured and out of bounds. It was probably a good thing that he was going then.

'Yes I'll be fine. I'll be packing up soon. We're only here until one. Thanks for your help,' said Bella smiling.

'No problem,' he said then disappeared off into the throng of Christmas shoppers.

'You did well for your first time,' said Ruth. 'And he was a nice chap helping you out like that, good looking too. Are you single? Is he your type?'

Bella didn't say anything. She was single but she didn't know what she thought about him and anyway he was only being friendly, even if he could have a relationship with someone, she doubted he'd be interested in her. Kat maybe but not her. He was definitely out of her league.

Packing everything up and returning it to Melanie's van had taken a lot less time than Bella had spent putting it all out but now she knew what to do, it would hopefully be a doddle tomorrow. Oh God, she'd done it again, she'd been ogling the vicar instead of looking at how to erect the table. It's just that it had been so long since she'd had a boyfriend and even when she did have one they'd had an ulterior motive... date her to get closer to Kat. She'd never told Kat this of course, Kat would have been devastated and all hell would have broken lose if she'd found out because in spite of Kat's sometimes frosty demeanour, she would do anything for Bella. They were twins after all. Just thinking about her, Bella's phone rang. It was Kat.

'How did it go?' Kat asked.

'It was cold,' said Bella.

'Now you know how I felt and I usually had far less clothes on than you do right now.'

Bella looked down at her jeans, long sleeved shirt and jumper beneath her big snow jacket and felt the softness of her thermals next to her skin. She was quite snug. It was her fingers and toes... and nose for that matter that were freezing. But she daren't complain.

'I managed to sell quite a bit of fudge, I don't know whether I'll be here the whole week unless Melanie's daughter tops me up.'

'Ow,' said Kat down the phone.

'What? What's happened? Are you going into labour?' asked Bella.

'No, they were just moving. It's alright, I'm fine. Don't stress Bella, you're worse than Ben. He's driving me up the wall. You would've thought with the amount of pregnant animals he's had on his farm; he'd chill out a bit when it came to me. Seriously Bella, I don't need you being a worry wart too. So seeing as though I can barely walk around at the moment or get out and about have you any gos?

'Did mum ring you to say they've arrived in Barbados?'

'Yes,' said Kat irritably. 'She's ringing me every day at the moment.'

'Well they were worried about leaving you seeing as you're so close to your due date,' said Bella thinking it would have actually been nice to have her mum and dad at home now. She was going back to their empty house.

'It's two weeks away!' said Kat.

'Unless they decide to come early. Oh by the way! You'll never guess who I bumped into, who lives around here now?'

'Who?' asked Kat her voice perking up.

'Sexy Stu!' said Bella.

'Bella only you called him that,' muttered Kat.

'No I didn't, the other girls did too,' said Bella.

'More like sleazy Stu,' said Kat. 'Is he still with Florence?'

'I don't know, I only used his toilet and I was in a rush!'

Bella heard a snort and a laugh escape Kat. 'What do you mean you used his toilet?'

'The public ones were busy and he's opened up a shop with his dad. Did you know Mr Sewell was Stu's dad?'

'Yes,' said Kat. 'Bella, we did go to the same school didn't we? I don't know how you missed the gossip the way you used to fly around chatting to everyone. A missed opportunity. Anyway have you seen Millie yet or Clarissa? Actually you won't see Clarissa, I've heard she's off to Paris with her new beau. She's being very quiet about him. Won't let on who he is. No idea why.'

'Millie's up in London this weekend with Bertie, she said she'd be around on Monday and she'd catch up with me then.' Bella let out a sigh that she hadn't meant to let out.

'Are you alright Bels?' asked Kat.

'I'm knackered, that's all, it's been a long term. I'll be fine after a hot bath and some food.'

'Ok. If you're sure. Um… hold on… Ben's calling me, I've got to go, love you,' said Kat.

'Love you too,' replied Bella ringing off.

'Have you sold all that fudge already? Was I too late?'

Bella whipped her head around. It was Stu. Why was he asking if he was too late? He was a local, he should know the market's hours. It was way past trading time. What did he really want?

'There's loads left, but the market's closed now. I'll be back tomorrow same time if you still want some then,' said Bella irritably picking up the last of the boxes from off the floor.

'I'm not around tomorrow. Ok, I'll come on Monday then,' he said looking slightly dejected.

'Look I'm sorry if I was a bit abrupt. I'm just really tired and I'm famished. It's felt like a long day already,' said Bella wishing she'd stop moaning to everyone about how tired she was. At least she could go home now.

'Well… um… I don't suppose you'd like to grab a bite to eat with me, my treat?' said Stu.

No, no, no, no… 'Yes, why not?' said Bella plastering a smile on her face. Why not? Because she wanted a bath, she wanted food sat on a sofa that's why not. However, it wasn't often that a hot stud offered to spend any amount of time with her. Hang on, was this a date? His treat? He was paying. Could be. She searched his face looking for any ulterior motive but she couldn't see any. There were no warning signs from her stomach telling her something bad was about to happen, only grumbling noises, probably due to the fact that it had been rather neglected of late.

'Violet's bakery does great food and you can normally find a place upstairs to eat,' he said looking keen.

'Sounds great,' said Bella still unsure why he wanted to eat with her. 'Just let me park the van up properly I don't want to come back to a parking ticket.'

'We've got spaces,' he said quickly. 'Round the back of the shop. Father won't mind if you use one of them.'

So it was alright for her to use a prized parking space, but not the toilet? He was either blowing hot and cold with her or had some weird sense of judgement going on. If only Kat hadn't mentioned that she thought Stu was sleazy then she wouldn't be overthinking every single little thing right now.

'Thanks for that,' said Bella trying not to sound too sarcastic. His prized parking space was big enough to fit a Smart car in not a big van. And did he attempt, just one little bit, to help her when she was trying to back into the space? Nope, not even a little beckon of his hand to tell her whether to straighten up or how much space there was until... she hit the wall. Melanie was going to kill her! No, he was too busy wincing and covering his mouth that was hiding a nice choice of swear words no doubt.

'You're welcome,' he said trying not to glance at his dad's car to see if she'd scraped it or not then he placed his hand at the bottom of her back gently guiding her forward through the tiny alley way. At his touch, Bella felt a weird feeling pass over her and her heart stumbled slightly. She didn't know what to think of it and without thinking began to compare him to the vicar and how her body had reacted around him. Her body was excited with Stuart, while she felt at peace and comfortable with the vicar which is probably what you're supposed to feel around a man of the cloth.

They walked over to the bakery in silence. Bella for once had no energy to fill it with her usual chatter.

'Have anything you want,' said Stu as Bella looked at the menu boards in front of her. There was every filling for a sandwich you could think of, there was even peanut butter and egg. God that sounded disgusting, but each to their own. Bacon and marmalade… Nutella and brie… Did they actually sell many of those?

'Just one BLT baguette and a latte please,' she said her mouth watering.

The lady behind the counter nodded, gave them a wooden spoon with the number thirty-one on it and Bella followed Stu up a winding stair case hoping that that wasn't the amount of people in front of her, otherwise it would be a really long wait.

Stu found a table right next to the window. He took his coat off and hung it over the back of the chair and Bella did the same.

'So,' he said looking at Bella intently. Bella's heart began to pound again as she realised that she was actually sat opposite her childhood crush and alone. Not totally alone, there were obviously people sat barely a metre away from them, but it was just them nevertheless. She couldn't remember how many times she'd lain awake dreaming of this very scenario, willing it to happen. And five years on, she'd made it but now she had absolutely no idea how to act or what to talk about.

'So,' said Bella.

'How come you ended up looking after a fudge stall?' he asked his hands clasped together in front of him.

This wasn't awkward at all she thought sarcastically. He looked like he was there to interview her, she could've sworn he wasn't this uptight at school.

'I'm helping out a friend,' she said.

'Oh yes, sorry you mentioned that... And um where do you currently live?' he asked.

'London,' said Bella.

'And you teach?' he asked raising his eyebrows.

'Yes I do.'

'What do you teach?'

'French.'

'Oh right, I was never particularly good at French,' he said then looked out the window wistfully. 'I wish I lived in London.'

'What's stopping you?' asked Bella.

'It doesn't agree with me or rather I don't agree with it. I...um...got mixed up with the wrong crowd when I worked in the city. Their motto was work hard, play hard which also meant taking drugs to keep that life style going and I suppose I'd felt a bit of peer pressure too, they were taking it, offering me some and I didn't want to feel the odd one out. It was school all over again.' Stuart turned to face Bella and his face crumpled. 'I'm sorry too much information, I don't normally overload on people like that. But things are good now,' he said brightly. 'My father came up with the idea of going into business together and the hours and pace are a lot slower than in London. He's the art expert and I do the numbers.'

'It must be nice working with your dad,' Bella said and nearly clapped her hands in delight when she spotted their food wending their way towards them.

'Tuna mayo? BLT?' said the waitress smiling at Stu trying to make eye contact but he wasn't paying attention for he was looking at Bella instead. So the waitress ceremoniously dumped the BLT in front of Bella and gave her daggers as she walked away. Chill, she thought, I'm not his girlfriend. Yet another girl who had the hots for Stuart.

The conversation petered out once they began to eat. Bella let out an inappropriate groan as she bit into her sandwich that made Stu look her way.

'It's so good,' said Bella quickly wiping away some juices that were running down her chin. Wow! Way to go, Bella. He must think you're so attractive, not! She inwardly winced. You really know how to look sexy when you're eating. Although... the way he was looking at her right now suggested otherwise. He was actually looking genuinely interested in her. Seriously? Bella reddened and quickly shoved a cherry tomato into her mouth. Coming over all hot and bothered by his sudden attention, she forgot to chew and swallowed it whole. Oh my God, it was stuck... Bella began to panic. As she tried to take a breath she realised that she couldn't. Her body tightened, her chest tightened. She was going to die. She couldn't breathe. She leapt up from the table and started waving her arms around. Pat my back Stu! Pat my back! Help! she screamed in her head. But Stu just sat there looking around them at the people staring at her getting more embarrassed by the moment. I'm going to die in any second, Bella thought grabbing his arm and trying to point at her back to get him to do something. Suddenly arms wrapped around her and she felt a tight squeeze and the cherry tomato came flying out. Relieved, Bella sucked in a huge breath. That was close, she'd nearly felt herself passing out as stars had begun to appear before her.

'Oh my God, Oh, my God!' Bella said bending over trying to catch her breath. That had been scary. She literally hadn't been able to breathe. And Stu had not done a thing!

'You're alright now,' said a gruff voice she semi recognised beside her. Bella looked up to see the old man from outside the toilets earlier on.

'Thank you,' she said and the man nodded, grunted and walked off.

Bella finally sat down and looked at Stu with utter disdain. Conversations around them started up again and Stuart at least had the grace to appear slightly mortified at his less than hero like actions.

'I didn't know what to do,' he mumbled. 'You're alright now though?

Bella nodded and pushed away her plate. She wasn't hungry now, funnily enough.

'I'd best get back to the shop,' Stuart said making a move to get up out of his chair.

As they walked back across the road, Stu looked as though he wanted to say something so Bella waited. Even though he'd been a complete plonker and not come to her rescue, she still couldn't believe that she was spending time with sexy Stu, the boy who'd appeared in all of her childhood dreams. But now that her dreams had become a reality, they hadn't turned out the way she'd imagined it would. The problem was they never did.

'Thank you for lunch,' said Bella getting into the van. At least getting out of this parking spot was going to be a darn sight easier than it had been getting in. She was about to pull the door shut when Stu called her name. She paused and looked at him. He was still very good looking. And now her stomach was full and she'd got over the trauma of the stuck tomato, it actually did a flutter, in an excited way.

'Would you like to go out with me another time?' he asked. 'As on a date?'

'Me?' said Bella.

'Yes, you.'

Bella's heart quickened. Why would he want to do that? He could have any girl he wanted, they all threw themselves at him she thought, thinking back to the pretty waitress.

'On a date?' she confirmed.

'Yes, that is if you want to?'

'Um, ok,' said Bella shocked that he wanted to go on an actual date with her.

'Is that yes ok or ok I'll think about it?' he said and Bella saw the twinkle that she remembered come back into his eyes.

'Yes ok,' said Bella.

'Stuart?' hollered a voice from inside of the building.

'I'll see you Monday? We can arrange to go out then,' said Stuart.

Bella nodded and upon seeing her reaction he darted inside.

Chapter Two

♥

Sunday 17th December 2017

'Oh my God! Seriously? What is going on with this table?' said Bella letting out a quiet shriek and then proceeded to jump up and down on the spot like a crazed woman. She couldn't ask Ruth or Tim for help setting up again, it was too embarrassing.

'This is a bit déjà vu.'

'Oh, hi!' said Bella feeling very happy indeed that he was the person to come along then. Zebedee darted forward for a stroke and Bella was happy to oblige.

'Alright, you give Zebby here some fuss and I'll put this up.'

'Thank you!' gushed Bella. 'If you're sure you don't mind.'

'No,' he said crouching down. 'I don't mind.'

Bella attempted to see what the vicar was doing but Zebedee had begun to pull on his lead having caught some scent on the wind.

Once the table was up, the vicar took the lead off her and smiled. 'How long are you here for?'

'Until Saturday or the fudge runs out, whichever comes first.'

'As we seem to keep meeting like this, I don't suppose you'd be interested in me putting up the table while you give Zebedee some attention for me? I think he rather misses some female company.'

Bella's mouth gaped open. Did he just call her a bitch?

'I mean that he likes you, not that you... um...'

Zebedee's head butted against her legs then he sat down and put his paw up.

Bella laughed and the vicar joined in.

'I think that's agreed then,' said the vicar. 'And seeing as we're becoming more acquainted; I don't suppose I can ask you for your name.'

'I'm Bella.'

'Bella by name, Bella by nature,' said the vicar.

Was that just a bit cringe worthy, thought Bella? Did that mean he thought she was beautiful on the outside or just on the inside?

'Sorry,' he mumbled. 'I couldn't help myself, you...er... I just think you're beautiful... But that's not why I'm helping you with the table,' he said quickly. 'I mean it is, but it isn't. Oh God, please come to me in my hour of need.'

Bella laughed.

'Don't!' he said. 'I'm normally really good at articulating what I need to say but I get near you and I become a gibbering wreck. It's the effect you have on me.'

'Is that a good thing?' smiled Bella liking the fact that this charming, kind and actually quite hot man was making a pass at her.

'Oh it's good, that I like you, but not, in that my filter goes a bit skewed and whatever I'm thinking comes straight out of my mouth.'

'Ooo really? Like a truth serum?' asked Bella.

The vicar put his hand up to his mouth and pretended he was zipping it up.

'No, you can't do that. You haven't told me your name,' said Bella.

'It's Tom.'

Bella and Tom, that had a nice ring to it. Hold on, if he was admitting to liking her, then that meant he could have an intimate relationship. He didn't have to live life like a monk.

'Can you marry?' she asked.

'What?' said Tom. 'Yes, if I want to. Can you?'

Bella looked at him strangely. 'Of course I can!'

'Well you asked me the question... Oh, you thought that because I was a vicar I couldn't marry?'

Bella nodded.

'So if you were thinking about it, does that mean you might like to go out on a date with me one time?'

Bella gulped. Her stomach was getting some serious butterflies at the thought of getting to know him better. But what about Stu? I mean, he was her childhood dream. Stu had also asked her out. Bella and Tom. Bella and Stuart. Bella and Tom rang off her tongue better but she'd already agreed to going on a date with Stu. Could she go on a date with Tom too, at the same time? Well, not exactly the same time, that would be weird... a day apart, or two days apart. Unbidden, the lyrics to the song 'It's Raining Men,' came to her mind. Typical! it had literally been a drought over the years with barely a man in sight and then two had come along at once.

'Um... yes?' said Bella because she did really like Tom.

Tom's shoulders sagged almost in relief. 'Brilliant, I haven't got my diary on me at the moment and presumably neither do you?'

What was the point of having a diary if you had nothing to put down? During term time, her diary was maxed out with parent's evenings, marking books, lesson planning but the holidays? The most exciting thing happening in her evenings at the moment was indulging in some Ben and Jerry's and watching whatever BBC or ITV had decided to put on their channels for Christmas. And then on Christmas Eve she was heading over to be with Kat and her husband. She was looking forward to that. So no, her diary was pretty free at the moment. Ah, and then she remembered that Stuart was popping over tomorrow to arrange their date, she just hoped the two men didn't pick the same night.

'I'm actually free most evenings,' Bella said stressing the word most.

'Excellent,' said Tom cheerfully. 'I'll come by before you pack up later on.'

'Ok,' said Bella not quite believing that she was going on not just one date but two. She had to ring Kat. Bella went to grab her phone then noticed the time. Kat would not be too happy if she rung her now, although since she'd moved to the farm, she'd had to change her waking hours to help Ben feed the animals. Bella still chuckled at the fact that her model sister, who used to be worried about what everyone thought, and used to wear the latest fashion, was now pregnant with twins and knee deep in muck every day. And she was happy. Kat had never ever been truly happy and now she was and Bella couldn't be happier for her but now it was her turn to find happiness with someone. She wanted to find that love and connection that would last forever like it had for her parents.

Bella sank down into the bath, the bubbles going over her. It had been a particularly cold day and standing around had gradually made her body turn into one big ice popsicle. And it was only now that she was finally thawing out and relaxing. In one hand she had a glass of wine and the other Sarah Morgan's latest Christmas book. Her books were full of just what Bella needed... romance and a happily ever after. Stu's face came to her mind then but it was his face when he was much younger and at school. Why wasn't the older, adult face of Stuart appearing? Maybe it was because she'd dreamed so much of him when she was younger that that image came up automatically. Her mind then wandered over to Tom who was ever so kind and amiable and bent over backwards to help her.

Her phone rang beside her and she quickly put down her drink and book. It was her sister.

'Are you alright? You've not gone into labour have you?' said Bella.

'No!' replied her sister. 'Although those Braxton Hicks sure make you feel like you're going to. They are strong!'

'So does that mean you could go into labour at any minute?'

'Bels it's fine. It's usual at the later stages of pregnancy.'

'Oh ok,' said Bella. She was more nervous about Kat giving birth than Kat was. It was nerve-wracking to think that two babies were going to come out of her tiny frame, but then their mother had done it and survived. Kat would be fine.

'So how's it going at the stall? I know you did your friend a favour but I wish you were here,' said Kat admitting vulnerability that she normally wouldn't dare show.

'I'm sorry,' said Bella. 'I felt bad for her and it's only a few more days. I'm missing you too.'

'What with sexy Stu to ogle at?' said Kat. 'Have you seen him again?'

'He's asked me out,' said Bella.

'What? How? When?' asked Kat.

Bella told her everything that had happened but left out the stuck tomato bit, she didn't want Kat to get upset.

'Bels you know I want you to be happy but just watch out for yourself. I know how much you liked him at school and he could've changed. Just don't go in with blinkers.'

'I won't,' said Bella. 'Anyway the vicar has also asked me out on a date!'

'A vicar? Bels, I know I've gone for a bloke who's older than me, but a vicar? They're ancient!'

'He's not actually, I think he's only a couple of years older than me and he's kind... and good looking!'

'Go for him!' said Kat. 'The way you're talking it sounds like you really fancy him. What's that saying? You wait ages for a bus, then two come along at once.'

'I know,' said Bella smiling. 'I'm rather spoilt for choice.'

'So when are you going on these dates?'

'Um that's the problem, they're both supposed to be coming to see me at the stall tomorrow to arrange them. I just hope they don't come at the same time.'

'Sod's law,' said Kat chuckling.

'Don't,' said Bella. 'You've probably jinxed it now.'

'You'll be fine! Well keep me up to date with what's going on. Love you,' said Kat.

'Love you too.'

Chapter Three

♥

Monday 18th December 2017

Bella glanced at her watch for the hundredth time. She hadn't seen hide nor hair of Tom despite him saying that he'd help put up the table in the mornings. Maybe he'd changed his mind about the date and her. Hopefully something had come up, not to him, or to anyone else but just that something had come up where he was unable to walk his dog. But he would have had to walk his dog. I mean you can't just say to a dog, no walk today so you can't do your business. So maybe he walked Zebedee earlier so as to avoid her on purpose. Bella could count on her hands the amount of times she'd been stood up. Not that she'd been stood up this time exactly, it wasn't a date, but it still felt like she was being stood up, before even possibly being stood up on her date. She needed to stop overthinking, Bella thought as a stabbing pain shot into her temples and she put her head in between her legs hoping that by putting more blood into it, the discomfort would ease.

'Have you lost something?' Bella heard from above her head.

Just the plot, she thought recognising Stuart's voice. Disappointment spread through her as she realised she'd wanted it to be Tom.

'Are you free to go out tomorrow night? 7pm? It's just that I've already booked a table, the place gets terribly busy and if I cancel I'll have to pay a fee,' said Stuart.

So he'd asked her out but he wasn't giving her a choice of when or where or even giving her a chance to back out. Not that she wanted to not go on the date but still... it just felt like he was being a tad domineering. There was no fluffy, nice romantic aura around the proposition. And Bella felt quite deflated.

No, no, no, no... 'Yes!' said Bella. 'I'm free. Seven... great!'

Stuart visibly relaxed, his shoulders dropped from being up by his ears. 'I'll pick...'

Bella didn't want to drink in case she had to rush to see Kat. The sound of those strong Braxton things, she'd looked it up on the internet, it meant the babies could come at any second. Also a part of her wanted to be involved in planning one part of their date.

'I'll meet you there. Where is it?' said Bella wondering why she was being so abrupt with Stuart.

'Oh, are you sure? I can pick you up at yours?'

'No really. I'd prefer to drive myself.'

Stuart nodded and Bella swore she saw a steely look come into his eyes. Her stomach began to turn and in a not so nice way. It was her warning sign. She usually had to pay attention when her body reacted in that manner. Maybe she should back out. No she couldn't he would have to pay a cancellation fee. Or maybe her body was just getting nervous about going on a date and she was getting it wrong, it wasn't a warning sign but nerves.

Stuart told her what restaurant they were going to but she was barely listening to him because out of the corner of her eye she saw Tom approaching.

'Ok great! Restaurant 101, got it!' Bella said her heart pounding at the thought of the two men standing side by side in front of her. She had to get rid of Stu without being rude. 'Right, well see you then. I'm looking forward to it. I've just got to take this,' Bella said putting her phone up to her ear then turned her back on him, yes that was kind of rude but needs must. 'Hi,' she said loudly hoping Stuart would leave. Bella kept her phone up to her ear for a few more seconds, nodded a bit, said ok, then added a goodbye to the pretend person.

'Hello,' said a voice from behind her. It was Tom. But had Stuart left? Bella shut her eyes tight, wishing she could be abducted by aliens and teleported to another world. She opened her eyes a smidgen and slowly turned around going anticlockwise, that way she'd see if Stuart was there before she'd see Tom so she could hopefully think of something to say as to why she was going on a date with the both of them. One pole came into her view then the end of the table, then a bit more and a bit more and... Tom's coat. Stuart was no longer there. Bella let out a whole load of air that she hadn't realised she'd been holding. That... had been seriously close. Squeaky bum time close.

'That was a big sigh,' said Tom. 'Were you ok this morning putting up this table? Sorry I couldn't make it. I would've texted you if I'd had your number.'

'Oh don't worry I was fine. Yes, I managed to put it up,' said Bella breezily. He did want to see me, something did come up, thought Bella. He didn't stand me up. 'It was actually easier than expected. God knows why I was having a problem before.'

'Well I'm glad you had a problem...' Tom's face contorted and reddened. 'I didn't mean it that way. I just meant that I wouldn't have spoken to you if you hadn't. Once again, I seem to be struggling to say the right thing.'

Bella smiled glad that she had that effect on him.

'So,' he said. 'Could we possibly exchange numbers then if something comes up again, which I'm sure it won't, I can get hold of you and vice versa.'

'Yes sure,' said Bella reeling off her mobile number.

'Right, now, what do you like to eat? And do you want smart or casual or super casual?'

Tom was the complete opposite of Stuart, almost over caring. Could someone be over caring? And then an old boyfriend of Kat's came to her mind, Todd, he had been over caring and ended up making Kat feel so smothered she'd dumped him. She really hoped Tom wasn't like that. Why was Bella being so negative? She hadn't even found out anything about the poor man yet and already she was getting cold feet. What if she liked him and then he dropped her like the other guys she'd dated? But Tom wasn't Todd, he was just being nice. That was all there was to it. So why did the funny feeling start up again in her stomach? It must be nerves. Don't be silly Bella. Don't muck this up. Positive thinking.

'Casual?' she said. 'And I like most food. Lasagne or pie and chips?

Tom rubbed his hands together. 'I know this fantastic little pub in Little Thirston, the next village along from here, I don't know whether you've been before.'

'I've heard of it, but never been. That sounds wonderful.'

'I'm free Thursday or Friday night if that's any good?' said Tom.

'Thursday'd be perfect! And my parent's house is actually on the way.'

'Do you want me to pick you up then?'

'Yes please!' said Bella wondering why it was ok for Tom, a complete stranger to pick her up but not Stuart who she'd known for quite a few years.

As Tom walked away with Zebedee, Ruth sauntered over.

'Two dates with two hot young men,' she said smiling. 'Not bad going if you ask me. Personally, if I was in your shoes I would go for the vicar.'

'Why?' asked Bella.

'I just don't think the charming one is as nice as he comes across. Wolf in a sheep's clothing comes to mind but I could be wrong. I've seen him on occasion around the place. Anyway I don't want to gossip, wouldn't be good to speak ill of others and I dare say you'll make up your own mind. You've a good head on your shoulders.'

'Yes, well, it's just a date,' laughed Bella. 'I'm not going to marry the guy!' And Bella could feel herself blushing as she'd already imagined what it would be like to be his bride many a time.

Chapter Four

♥

Bella squinted through the fog as she drove slowly down the road, she could barely see a metre in front of her and it didn't help that a car was right up her backside. But she could do nothing about that, her satnav said the restaurant was here or rather back there. Because when it had said 'here' it blatantly hadn't been and Bella had nearly driven through some farm gates into a muddy field.

'Back off!' she shouted looking in her rear view mirror. 'There is no need to tail gate. I'm not going that blooming slowly. It's foggy! What do you expect?'

A black sign with elegant gold writing came into view and Bella only just managed to glimpse a '101'. That was it and so she slammed on the brakes and swung left through a pair of very grand black wrought iron gates that could have belonged to a stately home. The car behind her beeped angrily and much to Bella's chagrin, it continued to follow her.

Restaurant 101 stood before her, its honey coloured Cotswold stone lit up by floor spotlights. Thousands of fairy lights twinkled in every tree up the drive. Bella swore under her breath. It was a stately home. There was even a doorman stood outside the main entrance ushering people in. And he didn't look like your usual doorman either. There was a certain air of regality about him. Bella parked up and looked down at her jeans in dismay. These weren't going to cut it. What was she going to do? She'd looked up the postcode but not the dress code.

Bella gingerly got out of her car at the same time as the person driving the car that had been so rude behind her. Whoever it was had better not give her a hard time. Her heart began pounding at the thought of a possible confrontation.

'It was you? Behind me? Beeping at me?' cried out Bella looking at an astonished Stuart as he turned to face her.

'Ah yes, well you did break awfully hard, I nearly went into you,' he said looking affronted.

'You were stuck up my backside for the past ten minutes!' said Bella. 'You do know that when driving in fog, you're supposed to leave more of a gap between cars? It was like soup out there tonight; you could barely see a metre ahead. What were you thinking?'

Stuart pouted like he was a little child being told off. Bella could feel herself getting angrier by the second. Say sorry, she thought, say sorry and then I'll see if I actually want to go in with you there tonight. She glanced at the building that seemed to beckon her over. It was so beautiful and festive that she really wanted to venture inside and see what else it had to offer.

'I'm sorry I braked,' conceded Bella. Maybe she shouldn't have braked like that. Maybe she could've over shot the entrance and then turned back on herself. Ok, so it was partly her fault. She glared at him but it was partly his as well and he wasn't offering an apology.

'Shall we go inside?' he said holding out his arm for her to take.

Bella nodded and the way he was looking at her then made her heart melt. His attention was on her and he was smiling, his eyes boring into her, what she wouldn't have done to have this back in school.

As they walked up the steps, his hand grazed the back of her coat sending electricity through her. His hand felt warm and comforting.

'Mr Grantley-Sewell,' said the doorman nodding at Stuart.

Grantley-Sewell? That would've been why she hadn't put her art teacher and Stuart as father and son. He was known as Stuart GS. Sometimes Bella astounded herself with her intellect.

Bella was expecting high ceilings, intricate embellishments around the rooms, gorgeous antiques and chandeliers and it didn't disappoint. She eyed up the tinsel hanging from the antlers of a stuffed stag taking pride of place among the gigantic gold picture frames depicting scenes from years ago. They'd walked straight into a banqueting hall that was, well, very long. Tables were lined up along each side of the walls and small candelabras on each table let off a lovely warm glow.

'Do you like it?' asked Stuart.

'It's magical,' said Bella secretly glad that Stuart had surprised her. She'd also had a quick look at what the other customers were wearing and she was fine. It was a smart place but you didn't need to dress up, some had but some hadn't.

Bella smiled at Stuart. She'd got him wrong; she'd been over thinking things again. And she could see why it was hard to get a table, it was clearly a popular venue.

They were led to a table and the gentleman pulled out her chair for her. Bella smiled up at him and sat down and her eyes widened at the amount of cutlery on the table.

'How many courses are there?' she asked picking up a tiny little fork furthest to her left. 'This is diddy.'

'It's a set menu and there are seven courses,' said Stuart picking up the wine menu. 'And you work your way in,' he said glancing at the cutlery.

Bella hid a gasp behind her hand as she looked around. Stuart was going to have to roll her out the door. How could someone eat that much in one sitting?

'Seven?' she muttered.

Stuart dropped the menu slightly, his eyes peering over the top of it at Bella. 'Just wait...' he said then his head disappeared from view.

Bella gazed to her right at the couple next to them, but they were in between courses or had just arrived like them.

'We all get served at the same time,' Stuart said then went to speak to the waiter who'd approached to take their drinks order.

'Just a coke for me,' said Bella quickly then noticed Stuart's disgruntlement. 'I'm driving. And I've got work tomorrow.'

'Just one little drink, I've chosen a lovely little wine which will go excellently with the meal.'

No, no, no, no. 'No!' Bella said almost shouting at him. She was not going to say yes.

'Fine,' Stuart said through gritted teeth, his charming persona vanishing. Bella looked at him, he was still good looking but she didn't like what she saw and her stomach began to do loops again. It was really disconcerting. She needed to remember how she was feeling now because one smile, one kind word and Bella had a tendency to forget about the other stuff. No blinkers, she'd promised Kat.

Stuart still got the wine. God knows how he was going to get home; he'd best not ask her to be his taxi. Although to be fair, he had offered to drive her so she shouldn't be complaining. It was up to him. Somehow he was getting under her skin and making her into a person that she wasn't normally like and didn't want to be. She was feeling irritable and moody and she wasn't enjoying it. Stuart didn't seem to be trying to have a conversation with her and was still looking morose so she scanned the room stopping at certain parts of it to look at the details. One mural took up one whole wall, she didn't know much about history but people were wearing togas and the pillars looked grand.

'Louis Laguerre painted them,' said Stuart. 'He was a French painter who mainly worked in England. His paintings are found in Blenheim Palace, Chatsworth House and Frogmore House where some of the Royals reside. That painting there is one of his lesser known paintings and not many people know it's here. My father was involved in the restoration project about five years ago and these were uncovered.'

Bella stole a quick glance as he was speaking. His eyes lit up as he talked about the painter and then she saw his father in him. How could she not have realised? If only she could see him like this more often and she'd be able to fall in love all over again. The penny dropped. She wasn't in love with him and she never had been. He'd been nothing but a childhood crush and it had been all about the idea of being in love with him. The playing field had just levelled out between Tom and Stuart and Stuart was no longer way in the lead, in fact, he had some work to do. Tom was inching ahead of him.

'They're beautiful,' said Bella craning her neck.

'Mademoiselle, your hors d'oeuvres,' said the waiter gently placing a plate on the table in front of her.

It was a little plate and Bella could see why she might be able to eat all seven courses. The portion was tiny. It was going to take maybe four bites to demolish the food. Her stomach grumbled. Now she hoped that there would indeed be enough food to curb her appetite.

The crunchy Bruschetta topped with garlic sautéed mushrooms went down a treat.

'What do you think?' said Stuart. 'Wasn't that divine?'

Divine might be a bit strong, thought Bella. They were just mushrooms on a bit of bread. Cordon Bleu food was definitely wasted on her. She enjoyed fried mushrooms with some buttered toast and baked beans more than she enjoyed that and at probably more than half the cost. Bella stilled. Who was paying? Oh yes, he was. Thank goodness. She dreaded to think how much this meal would've set her back.

The plates were taken away and Stu carried on talking about the French painter. Once started, he was obviously unable to stop. Bella didn't mind, it was actually rather interesting but what she didn't like was that he was coming across a bit too arrogant for her liking. Being a teacher herself, there was a fine line between extending knowledge for people to learn so that they felt comfortable asking questions, and being talked at, which is what Stuart was doing now. He made her feel stupid and naïve.

Bella's eyes lit up as the waiter came over with the next course. She looked down in anticipation only to find something which resembled the contents of her washing up bowl, once she'd cleaned the dishes. She gingerly picked up a spoon.

'Not that one,' said Stuart holding a more rounded and deeper spoon.

Bella nearly rolled her eyes and was thinking about using the spoon that she'd picked up but didn't want to aggravate him needlessly.

With the proper spoon in her hand she scooped up a few fine noodles and a leaf with some of the murky brown water. She blew on it and the leaf flew across the table.

Oops.

Stuart glared at her, then looked around quickly as to make sure no-one had seen. She hadn't meant to do it, and it wasn't that big of a deal. What was his problem? He was so worried about what other people thought.

The broth, which is what Stuart called it, was actually rather tasty but again there wasn't a lot of it.

Those bowls were then cleared away and after sitting in silence for a minute or so, Stuart dragged her attention to the painting on the ceiling and began to give her a detailed monologue about it.

The next course consisted of a small, (of course) fillet of fish with some lemon laid on top and was garnished with some more edible greenery. Bella glanced around the room expectantly. Were there any potatoes or rice coming, maybe a few vegetables? But then Stuart began to eat.

Mmm, delicious,' he said. 'Such flavour. Are you going to start?'

So obviously this was it.

Another four mouthfuls and a few more minutes of being subjected to a lecture on art. It wasn't that she minded him talking about paintings and painters but it was terribly one sided. He hadn't bothered asking much about her life and when she'd tried to ask him about his, he'd brushed the questions over and went silent. On the plus side, the food was nice if not a little thin on the ground and the setting was magical. It was just a shame about the company.

Stuart poured himself another glass of wine.

'Are you not driving back?' asked Bella.

Stuart chose to use the interruption of the waiter placing down the fourth course as an excuse not to answer.

'This looks delicious,' he said softly prodding the small round medallions of beef with his fork. 'Perfection.'

At least this time there were some potatoes and carrots accompanying the meat.

Silence ensued while Stuart polished off the entire contents of his glass, wiped his mouth to take away his red moustache then proceeded to tell her about... Ok so she'd switched off now. She couldn't listen to him talking at her any more. She'd reached her saturation point. Not once had she laughed. And she usually did with her friends. It was important to her and something that she was looking for in a relationship. Bella looked at Stuart blurring his face. The younger Stu had smiled regularly and laughed a lot. He just wasn't the same person anymore and neither was she.

She had two men vying for her attention but she'd prefer to be on her own than be with someone who turned her into someone she wasn't and who brought her down. Stuart was now no longer in the running for her attentions. The blinkers were off. Kat would be relieved.

Four courses down three more to go. She would be polite and then that would be the last she would see of him, well in this context anyway.

Bella gradually tuned in to what he was saying. She didn't think she'd missed anything, and anyway he didn't ask her questions.

Bother, she thought looking at his face, he'd asked a question and he was expecting a reply. Did she say yes or no or mumble a 'mmm'? She would play him at his own game.

The waiter came and placed the fifth course down. Desert already? thought Bella eying up the little yellow ball of ice. So what were they eating for the next two courses?

'Ah, a nice lemon sorbet to cleanse the palate,' said Stuart. 'How refreshing after the beef.'

Bella nodded pretending to be as enraptured as he was. 'Delightful,' she said.

'So?' Stuart said. 'Would that be ok?'

Oh God what was ok? What did she have to agree to? Ok that he never wanted to see her again. Well yes that would be fine. Or ok that... was he asking for her to give him a lift back to his?

'Would what be ok?' she said averting her eyes trying to find some focal point down on the table that wasn't just her empty dish.

Stuart didn't say anything and the seconds ticked by or they could have been minutes but enough time passed that Bella began to feel so uncomfortable she had to look up at his face.

One is not amused, thought Bella. Stuart looked exceedingly disgruntled.

'Were you actually listening to a word I've been saying?' he whispered leaning forward in his seat almost hissing at her like some aggrieved swan.

Something inside Bella exploded, it was pretty much like one of those squidgy bath balls that once you'd manhandled them too often, they burst all over you. That was how she felt now. She'd had enough of the way he talked to her, the way he behaved around her and blow it if she was going to spend another minute in his company.

Bella shot up out of her chair, it making an almighty screech before it tipped over backwards on to the floor behind her causing an even louder crash and drawing the attention of everyone in the restaurant. There was silence. That saying where you could hear a pin drop? Well you could've heard one, it was that quiet.

A number of emotions seemed to pass over Stuart's face in quick succession, shock, embarrassment, anger and then rage.

'What are you doing?' he said through gritted teeth. 'Sit. Back. Down. Now!'

'No!' cried out Bella. 'You've made me feel this small,' she said putting her thumb and finger close together and waving it at him. 'Everything is about you! You! You! You! You like you own company so much, you can have it. I'm out of here.'

Bella's heart was pounding, she couldn't believe the words coming out of her mouth, she was usually so good natured and pleasant and friendly. Kat felt Bella's support behind her, her sister wouldn't have put up with him either. The silence after she'd finished soon brought her to her senses and she looked around at the hushed diners.

'Sorry,' she said loudly. 'Not at what I had to say but for disrupting your evening.'

Bella breathed in and walked through the middle of the tables keeping her head held high. So this was how Kat felt when she was on the catwalk, all eyes on her. It was uncomfortable and absolutely terrifying. But she refused to scuttle out of the restaurant like a crab about to be eaten.

'Mademoiselle,' said a prim voice to her right. Her coat was being handed to her. 'I do hope you enjoyed your meal and you will return to us soon.'

Was he being sarcastic? Why would he want her back again? She'd just caused a ruckus in the restaurant. She was surprised she wasn't being escorted out. Oh she was. It was just a polite way of doing it.

'Thanks,' she muttered as he closed the door behind her.

The cold air of the night hit her and she began to shake as she fumbled around in her bag looking for her car keys. Thank God she'd decided to drive. No sooner had she found them, she jumped into her car, put her car into reverse then put her foot down. The wheels skidded in the now not so impeccable drive kicking out little stones in every direction. She saw the front door to the restaurant open behind her in the rear view mirror as she drove out. In case it was Stuart chasing her down, she doubted it was, he would've been far too embarrassed to go after her, she turned the mirror in a different direction so she couldn't look into it on her way down the drive. She never wanted to see his face again.

Bella arrived at her parent's home flustered and tired. What could have been a joyous occasion had turned out to be a complete and utter nightmare. The drive home had been more than awful, visibility being virtually non-existent and she hadn't been able to stop trembling from the shock of confronting Stuart in a very public place and then realising she'd probably made a huge spectacle of herself and so was now wondering how quickly word of what happened would spread on the local grapevine. And of course she'd be at the stall in the market square on show for all to see tomorrow, just so long as nobody put her in any stocks and hurled rotten food at her.

Bella poured herself a huge glass of wine then sat down to ring her sister.

Chapter Five

♥

Wednesday 20th December 2017

Bella spent most of the morning hiding behind piles of fudge. Any time she thought someone was looking her way in a particular manner, she'd duck, count to five then peer over the top of the table making sure that they'd carried on by. She didn't have to worry about the customers because they barely looked at her, the array of goodies on display took all their attention.

The night before, Kat had had a good laugh at her expense. Bella knew she would when she'd decided to ring her but Kat always gave Bella what she needed to hear, the confidence to move forward in her life again. At the beginning of the phone call, she was adamant she was never going on another date ever again after her undeniably dismal success rate on the dating scene but by the time she'd said good night to her sister, Bella was looking forward to going out with Tom. Very excited in fact.

'Bella!'

'Millie?' said Bella clapping eyes on one of her best friends. 'Oh my God! It's so good to see you!'

And she looked so well, thought Bella. It was amazing to see the change in her. Millie had had quite a strict and secluded upbringing no thanks to her unbearable dad but since her father decided to have nothing more to do with her, Millie had grown into a confident and self-assured woman, it probably also helped that she had the love of a gorgeous man who happened to be their best friend's brother. Millie of all people had found love and she'd been practically a hermit so there was definitely hope for her.

'Sorry I haven't been to see you sooner, I forgot how busy it gets in the holidays,' said Millie giving her a hug. 'How's it going?' she said looking at the fudge display. 'I might have to get some.'

'It's actually going well,' said Bella. 'I had a few difficulties but Ruth and Tim over there, they've been great. And the vicar...'

'Vicar?' said Millie. 'I didn't know you'd started going to church.'

'I haven't. He was walking his dog and offered to lend a hand putting up the table.'

Millie frowned. 'Are you talking about the local vicar to this town? I mean I didn't attend the church here but are you sure?

Bella groaned. What was wrong with Tom?

'Why?' Bella asked tentatively.

'Well, he's so old...'

'Nope, that's not him,' said Bella. 'This one is young, our age and rather cute.'

'Our age? Well that would make a change... hold on... you said he was cute,' said Millie.

'He is,' said Bella. 'And I've got a date with him tomorrow night.'

Bella heard an 'ahem' behind them. 'Sorry, I'll get to you right...' Oh crapola, she was in doo doo. A lot of doo doo. Bella's stomach dropped.

'Hello Stuart,' said Millie smiling at him.

'Hi Millie,' returned a not so happy Stuart.

He was no longer sexy Stu more like stroppy Stu. Bella was so glad she could see the real him now rather than the childhood version of him.

'Hello Bella,' he said. 'I do hope you got home safely last night as you never returned my messages or calls.'

Millie looked at Bella and raised her eyebrows, her mouth doing an O shape.

'I crashed out,' said Bella. 'I was so tired and then obviously this morning... I had to get up early to be here, and... well, it's been really busy.'

Bella and Millie stared at Stuart waiting for a reply.

Thank God Millie was here; this was where strength in numbers was really helping her situation. He wasn't going to have a scene, it wasn't his thing and there were also far too many people around to witness it. So he'd heard she was going on a date. She hadn't intended for him to find out but they hadn't been exclusive. It was one meal.

'Well as long as you're ok,' he said. 'And... um... I might see you around?'

See me around? What did that mean? That they were friends? Acquaintances? Or that he still wanted to continue seeing her?

As soon as Stu was far enough away from them Millie asked, 'What was that about?'

'I might've gone on a date with him last night and walked out halfway through?' said Bella cringing at the last bit.

Now in the light of day, she was thinking that she might have over reacted, just a tad, and now she was feeling a bit sorry for him. Any other girl would've loved to be in her shoes last night, the waitress in the coffee shop for one, but his character just didn't go with hers and she'd put him on a pedestal so when he wasn't that person she wanted him to be, she'd reacted badly.

Millie mouthed another silent 'O'.

'It didn't go well, no,' said Bella.

'At least you know,' said Millie.

Bella was thankful that Millie was so tactful, unlike her sister, and didn't bring up how much Bella had gone on about wanting a date with Stu when they'd been at school.

'Yup! And hopefully the next date will turn out better,' said Bella. Well it couldn't be any worse... could it?

Chapter Six

♥

Thursday 21ˢᵗ December 2017

'You look lovely,' said Tom when Bella opened the door.

'Thanks,' said Bella thinking how nice he looked. Should she say that to him, what she thought? Or was that not the done thing.

'These are for you,' he said holding out a bunch of flowers.

Bella almost sighed out loud. This was the first time anyone had given her flowers. She felt so special. Yes, this was what a date was supposed to be like. One that made her feel all warm and fuzzy.

'Thank you,' she said then once she'd got them, she had no idea what to do with them. Do you take them with you? Nah, they'd be all droopy by the time she got home. 'Wait there, I'll just put them in water.' Oh God it was cold outside, she couldn't expect him to stay out in the cold. 'Actually, come in,' she said beckoning him in.

Bella rushed off leaving him by the front door. Her nerves were fried. Dating was like doing an obstacle course. There were bits which were easy, some was just down right messy and some needed a bit of teamwork. If you managed to complete it, in one piece and the both of you were still smiling by the end of it... success. Unless they fell for your sister afterwards... No she wasn't going to go there. Her sister was well and truly off the market and Tom wouldn't do that anyway. He must have a serious moral radar being a vicar so at least she was safe with him in that sense.

'Ready!' she said walking towards him.

'You've got a sister?' he said peering at the photograph of her and Kat on the table. 'Older or younger, it's hard to tell.'

'Younger... by four minutes.'

'Twins!' he said. 'Close?'

'Very,' said Bella. 'We had our moments when we were younger but we've always had each other's backs.'

'I wish I had that. I'm an only child. I think if you've never had siblings, you're always interested in those that do. Right,' he said, 'shall we go?'

Not only did Bella get flowers for the first time, but that was also the first time someone hadn't mentioned Kat's beauty or insinuated that she wasn't as good looking as her sister. But then again, he had already told her she was beautiful. Bella's heart swelled with happiness. This could be it. She might've found herself a prospective boyfriend. And she prayed that nothing was going to go wrong.

'I love eating at the pub we're going to tonight. I found it quite by chance. I was lost and took a wrong turn when I was new to the area. I'd stopped and asked for directions and had ended up staying for some food,' he said concentrating on the road. 'That's your parent's home, I take it?'

'Yes, it's where I grew up, well partly. My mother's originally from Barbados so I've spent a lot of time there too over the years with my grandparents, when they were alive. That's where my parents are now but only for a few weeks. My sister's about to have a baby or babies should I say...'

'How wonderful! You're going to be a very busy aunty then,' he said smiling. 'So where's your main residence?'

'London... at the moment,' said Bella. 'But now that my sister is local, well, about an hour away, and not living in London, I was thinking of moving back here to be nearer to her and my parents.'

That was news to her, thought Bella. Moving hadn't even crossed her mind until now, so why had she said it? But it did make sense. And if... Bella glanced at Tom, and if... by any chance things went well and progressed, she'd be nearer to him too.

'How about you? Where did you grow up?' asked Bella.

'Dorset. Not half so exciting as you, but I did have a beach on my doorstep.'

Bella's phone began to ring. It was Kat, maybe she was ringing her to give her some good luck. She couldn't take it now, he might overhear their conversation and tact was not Kat's forte.

'It was just my sister. I'll ring her later,' said Bella.

'You can talk to her, I don't mind,' he said smiling.

'Thanks but it's fine, I'm sure it's nothing that can't wait.'

Barely a minute later, Bella's phone rang again. It was Kat. Bella began to panic and her hands started to sweat. Kat never did a double ring, that would normally be her.

'Hello?' said Bella.

'M... m... my waters have broken,' shrieked Kat then yelled in agony. 'The babies are coming!'

'Oh my God!' yelled Bella. 'Kat, what do you want me to do?'

'Get to Gloucester hospital. I need you!' she screamed.

'Ok, I will. I'll be there. Is Ben with you?' asked Bella imagining Ben on top of the hill beyond her sister's reach feeding the sheep.

'He's pulling up outside now…. Holy mother of… it hurts!' Bella put her phone down, in shock.

'Your sister's gone into labour?' he said looking at Bella having pulled into a layby. 'Which hospital is she going to?

'Gloucester. I have to go. I'm sorry.'

'Don't say sorry. Why don't I drive you there?'

'You'd do that? You don't mind?'

'No of course not, you don't look in any state to drive.'

I'm going to be an aunty. I'm going to be an aunty thought Bella over and over.

Bella jumped out of the car and leant down, 'Thanks for dropping me off. I'll see you?' she said and rushed through the doors.

'Hi, I'm the sister of Katherine Fletcher-Jones?'

'Yes, she's through here, follow me?' said a nurse.

Two hours later Bella came out of the ward dazed. It had been the most terrifying experience of her life but the most amazing and wonderful too. Kat had done brilliantly, Bella was so proud of her… and Ben. And she now had a nephew and a niece whom she could spoil rotten. She'd offered to go get some food for Ben and her and also it'd been an excuse to let the new parents have some alone time.

'Tom?' she said her eyes drawn to a lone person sat on the chairs lined up outside the ward.

He got up awkwardly and he looked concerned. 'Did everything go alright?'

'Yes!' beamed Bella running up to give him a hug. 'Kat's got one of each and they are beautiful. I was so worried.'

'Oh that's fantastic news,' he said with arms around her. 'I'm so glad! But I had a feeling you would be anxious, that's why I stayed, to make sure you were ok too.'

Bella tilted her head up and before she realised what she was doing she planted her lips on his.

'Oh sorry,' she said pulling away.

'I've been wanting to do that since the first moment we met,' he said giving her another kiss.

Bella's heart pounded and she felt her legs turning to jelly as it dawned on her that this was the One. They fit like... a key in a lock? She was being soppy; she knew that but that's how she was feeling.

'There's one thing I need to talk to you about, before I ask you if you want to go out with me and possibly only me? I did hear about you and Stuart...'

Bella's heart almost stopped. Oh God, he did find out. 'I... um... yes... you both asked me out at once and...'

'It's ok,' he said leaning in to give her another hug reassuring her then he pulled back and looked deep into her eyes.

'Me... being a vicar, it tends to put people off wanting a proper relationship with me. I don't want to fall for you even more than I have done and then you... well... I'm sure you wouldn't. You're different from anyone I've ever come across... in a good way... I mean... oh God. So do you go to church? Not that it matters if you don't, or if you do...'

Bella smiled as she watched him tie himself into knots.

'I'm more of a hatches, matches and despatches girl...'

'A what?' said Tom looking perplexed.

'Hatches are christenings, matches are weddings and despatches are funerals. But in answer to your question I am totally happy dating a vicar... Actually I couldn't be happier.'

And then she went on tiptoes and gave him another kiss.

The End

Dear Reader,

First of all, thank you for reading this book and I hope you enjoyed it.

If you did, could you possibly leave a review on Amazon, I would be very grateful as it helps us Indie Authors a lot.

Many thanks

xx

If you would like to subscribe to my newsletter and find out about any new releases please go to www.csadamsbooks.com.

You can also find me on Facebook, Instagram and TikTok.

About the Author

My childhood was spent moving from one school to another and between various countries. I then worked in a variety of different jobs ranging from working as Mary Poppins at Disneyland Paris to trying to navigate the parts of a propeller at an airplane company. My journey led me to training as a psychotherapist and then I tried my hand at teaching languages at secondary school until my third child came along. It wasn't until I was a stay at home mum that I put effort into making my dreams a reality...to become an author.

I now live in a lovely part of England near a forest with my husband and three children. When I'm not writing, I love reading, watching tv/films and being out in nature.

I love to write all genres, mainly fantasy and romance, so keep checking in or subscribe to my newsletter at csadamsbooks.com.

Printed in Great Britain
by Amazon